D0696749

Dear Reader,

The editors at Harlequin and Silhouette are thrilled to be able to bring you a brand-new featured author program for 2005! Signature Select aims to single out outstanding stories, contemporary themes and oft-requested classics by some of your favorite series authors and present them to you in a variety of formats bound by truly striking covers.

We want to provide several different types of reading experiences in the new Signature Select program. The Spotlight books offer a single "big read" by a talented series author, the Collections present three novellas on a selected theme in one volume, the Sagas contain sprawling, sometimes multi-generational family tales (often related to a favorite family first introduced in series), and the Miniseries feature requested previously published books, with two or, occasionally, three complete stories in one volume. The Signature Select program offers one book in each of these categories per month, and fans of limited continuity series will also find these continuing stories under the Signature Select umbrella.

In addition, these volumes bring you bonus features...different in every single book! You may learn more about the author in an extended interview, more about the setting or inspiration for the book, more about subjects related to the theme and, often, a bonus short read will be included. Authors and editors have been outdoing themselves in originating creative material for our bonus features— we're sure you'll be surprised and pleased with the results!

The Signature Select program strives to bring you a variety of reading experiences by authors you've come to love, as well as by rising stars you'll be glad you've discovered. Watch for new stories from Janelle Denison, Donna Kauffman, Leslie Kelly, Marie Ferrarella, Suzanne Forster, Stephanie Bond, Christine Rimmer and scores more of the brightest talents in romance fiction!

The excitement continues!

Warm wishes for happy reading,

*Marsha Zinberg*

Marsha Zinberg
Executive Editor
The Signature Select Program

SPOTLIGHT

# JEANIE LONDON

In the Cold

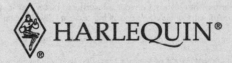

# HARLEQUIN®

TORONTO • NEW YORK • LONDON
AMSTERDAM • PARIS • SYDNEY • HAMBURG
STOCKHOLM • ATHENS • TOKYO • MILAN • MADRID
PRAGUE • WARSAW • BUDAPEST • AUCKLAND

ISBN 0-373-83676-7

IN THE COLD

To my beautiful daughter Eriene.
Since the day you were born, you've inspired me to reach beyond myself and push past my limits. You're amazing to watch as you explore life, test yourself and fly past each challenge and every goal. You're such a special person, and I love everything about who you're growing up to be ;-)

# PROLOGUE

*Prolonged silences*
*Like pointing fingers*

A FITTING SYMBOL FOR a shrine. The brass door knocker depicted a grinning angel with a halo of wings, a whimsical device so reflective of the woman who'd once lived here that Simon Brandauer almost smiled. Almost. He couldn't find any comfort in her memory, couldn't even remember when he'd turned this town house into a memorial for her, a woman with no grave to rest in, no headstone to mark her death.

After turning the key, he stood in the doorway, lost in the silence that smothered the empty rooms and sheet-draped furnishings. He looked around as if expecting to find Violet, as if he hadn't sacrificed her on the altar of covert government operations three years ago.

Hanging his coat on the rack above ice skates dangling from knotted laces, he moved through the interior and thrust open French doors to a courtyard overlooking Washington, D.C.

Time and the February cold had left the garden brittle and wasted but Simon still saw reminders of Violet in the wild symmetry of the bordered plots, in the delicate wrought-iron furnishings, in the fountain where a fairy held a sculpted flower—a violet, appropriately.

Drawing the shutters, he opened windows along the east wall. Sunlight flooded the living room, illuminating dust that swirled to life in a collision of stale air and winter wind. If he could purge the grief left behind in Excelsior Command by Violet's loss as easily, the day ahead might not look so grim.

She would have been thirty today.

Simon could almost hear her explaining how this would be a great year, how zeroes always brought good luck. Something about the start of a new decade, he recalled her saying on her twentieth birthday. That year her zeroes had delivered a bump in operative status, a pay raise and, from what her teammates had said, a new love interest.

That year she'd also brought the first birthday cake into Command. Not for her birthday, though, but his. He'd turned thirty, another zero phenomenon, and she'd surprised him with a cake and a chorus of "Happy Birthday."

He recalled feeling uncomfortable with the attention.

There hadn't been a party since she'd been lost. No one at the black operations national security agency he directed had ever discussed why, but with that bond born of tragedy, they'd all agreed the tradition couldn't continue without Violet.

Not a problem until her birthday rolled around. Then those unlucky enough to be in from the field pretended not to notice she wasn't there. Time hadn't healed this wound yet, and he knew her presence would be everywhere in the secured maze of tactical and surveillance sectors that made up Command today, underlying every word, every glance, every gesture.

Thirty. This should have been a great year.

Another blast of wind swept through the open windows, drawing Simon from his thoughts. He glanced around at the candles dotting the various surfaces. Fat ones on round plates. Tapered ones in cut-crystal holders. Small ones in jewel-colored votive cups.

Each time he visited this town house, Simon glimpsed some new facet of the woman Violet had been, a woman who'd been special to everyone who'd known her. He'd seen the candles before, but hadn't paid much attention. Today he noticed every one. They seemed to symbolize how well he'd known the operative, but not the woman.

Retrieving a cardboard box from his jacket pocket, he removed a roll of bubble wrap, unwrapped a fragile figurine.

"Happy birthday, Violet."

Sentiment wasn't his style. Neither was obsession, yet here he was again, ignoring the incontrovertible evidence that Violet would never come home. Why?

Simon only knew he wasn't ready to let her go. He kept his guilt alive with these visits to her town house, pieced together the puzzle of the woman he hadn't taken the chance to know, to hope against hope that someday he'd finally bring her home.

Carefully, he set the figurine on a buffet beside last year's gift, an amethyst brooch shaped like a violet. While the sculpture had been inexpensive by comparison, he was pleased with his choice. The ceramic had been painted and glazed to match the incredible color of Violet's eyes.

"Eyes like violets by a river of pure water," Oscar Wilde had once said. And that was how Simon tried to imagine her, at rest on the slope of some deep-running river. A place where sun shone through a lattice of leaves, warming the banks. At peace.

A thick layer of dust covered every surface in the town house, accentuating the figurine's newness, so he made a mental note to send in a cleaning crew. Not that anyone else cared if the place took on the look of a long-ignored attic. Violet had no living family. But shrines were meant to be tended, and Simon would see that hers was.

# CHAPTER ONE

*8:57 a.m. EST*
*Washington, D.C., 21°F*

EXCELSIOR COMMAND pulsed with energy around the clock. Highly trained operatives monitored the elaborate overhead network of U.S. reconnaissance satellites 24-7. With spot photography, sound surveillance and scanning devices that grew more sophisticated almost daily, Systems Ops was the hub of Command, overseeing every military, scientific and technological development throughout the world that might impact the United States and its allies.

Simon wound his way through the maze of secured corridors toward his office, meeting forced smiles and sensing the gazes that rested on him long after he'd passed. The emptiness of Violet's memory felt pumped in with the climate-controlled air.

Or maybe his mood only made it feel that way.

"Good morning, Simon." Frances Raffa stood behind her desk when he walked into the reception area.

At some point in his life, Simon had formed the idea that older Italian women should be shorter than five feet and sport tufts of white hair. He was completely off the mark where Frances was concerned, a fact that still occasionally surprised him.

Tall and regal, his assistant must be close to seventy, although he'd have had to pull her hire record to be sure, since she routinely lied on her evaluations. Employee prerogative, she said. He didn't argue. She'd reigned over the preceding acting director's administration for over forty years before Simon had taken over the agency. She knew every trick in the book.

"Status?" He walked into his office and set his briefcase on the desk.

She took his coat to the closet. "Major's profiling the South American mission. He'll be tied up all day but said to call if you need him. Quinn's questioning our Islamic friend. She's in Containment, cell three."

Simon glanced at his watch. He'd give Quinn more time before checking on her progress with the man they believed to be a direct link to a terrorist cell. "Have we heard from Niky?"

"He wrapped things up in Palestine. Maxim is debriefing him and his team en route."

"ETA?"

"Nine hours."

"Good." Simon snapped open his briefcase, pleased Niky's transport wouldn't arrive back in the States until tonight. His presence in Command on Violet's birthday would only make a tough day even tougher.

As team leader in the ill-fated mission that had claimed the lives of Violet and another four of Excelsior's most skilled operatives, Nikos Camerisi, known as Niky to his friends, had been the only one to return alive. But not unaffected.

"I'm drafting a communiqué for the White House

about last week's NATO summit." Simon circled his desk and sat down.

"Do you have a minute before you start?" Frances asked.

"Of course."

"Let me get something." She stepped back into her office to retrieve a thick accordion file from her desk.

"What's up?"

Returning, she pulled the door closed behind her. "I may be imagining things, Simon, but I want your opinion."

Untying the string that bound the file, she withdrew a stack of magazines and trade-size paperbacks marked with Post-it notes. "I happened across an intriguing story in my leisure reading and found more of the author's works. I've marked the stories. I want you to read them."

"All of them?"

"Please. They're all short stories with the exception of two novellas. They won't take long."

"Done."

She smiled a smile that suggested his response hadn't disappointed her. "I'll let you know when Quinn takes a break with the interrogation. Otherwise, I'll hold your calls."

Frances left, and he leafed through the material, written by an author named Claire de Beaupré. Mysteries, action-adventure stories, an anthology of romances and another of political thrillers.

Setting the anthologies aside, he chose a short story entitled "The Spy."

Compartmentalizing his thoughts about the awaiting communiqué and the questions he had about six active

Excelsior missions and the dozens of operatives he had scattered around the globe, Simon tuned out the steady hum of Command and began to read.

The protagonist in the story reminded him of the hero in a recent blockbuster film—a larger-than-life spy romanticized by the movie industry. The prose was concise, the plot tense, a fast read as Frances had promised. But as the story unfolded, the lead character took on new depth. His actions grew less entertaining and more familiar.

The second story was a gritty mystery about a cryptanalyst in the former Yugoslav Republic, who secretly defected from his homeland to act as an agent provocateur for the United States. In a surprise plot twist, the defector had been manipulated as a double agent instead, striking a blow to a black ops agency. The terminology was dead accurate, the plot twist real. *Too* real.

The third story involved operatives on opposing sides of a Valentine operation in Northern Europe. This story wound up with characters living happily ever after, but the similarity to a real-life drama that had played out tragically confirmed Frances's decision to bring these stories to his attention.

For the next two hours Simon read about characters and scenarios that were all impossibly familiar.

Fiction based on real missions was by no means unique—Leon Uris had detailed the Sapphire case in his novel *Topaz*. What Simon found significant was that these stories appeared to be based on highly classified missions perpetrated by Excelsior—a black operations agency no one but the president and an oversight committee knew existed.

Frances would have recognized the similarities. As a key figure in their agency, she sidestepped the intricate hierarchy of levels and clearances in the same way he had—by an oath to the president.

The clearance levels were signature devices unique to each operative, and the only one with authorization for this particular combination of missions would be the operative who'd participated in each one—Violet.

But Violet had been lost during a mission into northern Bosnia during the civil war that had reigned in the Balkans for the better part of a decade. Mission objective had been to extract a defecting military commander from number twelve detention camp. Simon had needed the man's testimony about the atrocities being committed inside his camp to convince NATO to take action against the invading army.

He'd gotten *Code 13* instead.

*Sever all ties to protect Excelsior.*

The sound of Violet's voice as she shouted that grim command over the comm still haunted him.

*"Code 13."*

Shots had rung out. Harsh commands in Serbo-Croat. A scream.

Then static, and nothing.

Simon had carried out the safety protocol he and his Command staff knew by rote, but had never implemented during his tenure. He'd had no choice but to turn his back on his compromised operatives as he shipped out control units to handle active missions from remote locations around the globe. He'd locked down Command.

Only Niky had returned alive from that mission. The rest of his team had been executed. Simon had eventually recovered all their remains—except Violet's. She was still out there somewhere, in the cold.

The author of these stories knew something about her.

By the time Simon reached Systems Ops, he'd narrowed his racing thoughts and formulated a plan. Putting all surprise firmly behind him, he initiated action to locate this author and learn what she knew about Violet.

His eyesight quickly adjusted to the electronic glow of the wall-size display monitors making up the core of Systems Ops. Tavares Jenkins, a communications operative known as TJ, nodded, but didn't glance up from his computer.

Simon scanned the monitor, where simulated images marked his operatives en route from Palestine. "I'm downgrading your mission priority."

"What about comm? Maxim's debriefing Niky."

"Turn him over to one of your people."

That brought TJ's head up. His eyes flashed white against his dark skin, and he thrust his chair back and said, "Ash, take over monitoring Casanova. Stay on A channel."

The fair-haired operative looked Simon's way as TJ tapped out a rapid-fire combination of keys to turn over Niky's handling. The computer monitor went blank.

"So what's on the menu, your highness?" TJ asked.

"Find Claire de Beaupré."

TJ entered a series of pass codes and the name. Screens flashed open and closed. "Nothing's coming up on the usual channels. I need a different route. What else do you have?"

"She publishes short fiction."

Simon named her publishers then reined in his impatience as TJ took various national and intergovernmental databases through their paces with a salvo of blips and bleeps.

"This is damn strange," TJ said. "I've got twenty-four possibilities but none traceable to the checks cut by the corporations holding these publishing interests."

"Is the author writing under a pseudonym?"

"She could be copyrighting under a pseudonym, and I could track her with our systems."

"Who cashed the checks?"

TJ tapped a few keys. "Whoa! If this is your target, she's got as much smoke around her as we do."

No federal, state, county or city sources possessed any physical record of the woman who'd written these stories, not in the United States or any international databases. This author seemed only to exist as the payee on checks that had been cashed through an account belonging to the administrator of Safe Harbor, a social services facility in Sault Ste. Marie, Ontario, a branch of the well-known Global Coalition.

A not-for-profit organization of more than a million members from over one hundred and sixty countries and regions around the world, Global Coalition supported human rights through various charitable campaigns and projects. They provided assistance to countries torn by war or catastrophe.

*People helping people*—the catchphrase of a humanitarian giant.

"I'll check this out myself," Simon said. "Download everything you can find on Safe Harbor onto my system in the jet. Research the Global Coalition's involvement in the Balkan recovery efforts then take what you get and run a simulation on how they might have gotten information about a prisoner in a detention camp."

"You're not talking about—"

"Don't speculate. Just run the sim." He pressed the transmitter on TJ's intercom. "Frances, make arrangements for the jet to transport me to Sault Ste. Marie within the hour."

"U.S. or Canadian side of the border?" Her voice shot back over the speaker.

Simon gave her the details. "Arrange for a rental car and call the administrator of Safe Harbor to set up a meeting. I'll be traveling under my official cover."

Ending the communication, Simon watched the display monitors as window after window opened to document Global Coalition's movements during the breakdown of Yugoslavia.

"Keep this to yourself," he told TJ, when Quinn entered Systems Ops and headed toward them. "How's the questioning?"

"I believe he's our man," she said.

"What faction?"

"Military intelligence."

Simon digested the information, satisfied. "Condition?"

"I'll give him a few hours in the infirmary, then go back to work on him. What's happening here?"

"I'm leaving for the rest of the day. Call me on my cell if you learn anything relevant."

Quinn Davenport eyed him as if his evasion was of no more than mild interest. Simon knew better. As team one's psychology and interrogation's expert, she was uniquely qualified to see through him. But Quinn wouldn't ask questions. They'd worked together too long for her to expect even her deftest manipulations to yield results.

"I will." The cool undercurrent in her voice confirmed that she knew something was up.

Simon wouldn't brief her until he investigated this lead. He wouldn't let those who'd been closest to Violet share in the emotional upheaval that any news about her would bring.

He'd earned that privilege.

*8:32 p.m. GMT*
*Off the western coast of Africa*

"CASANOVA?"

Reluctance edged the deep-throated voice, and even with his brain layered in sleep, Niky Camerisi understood why. He'd finished his tactical debrief not an hour before and had announced plans to spend the rest of this flight dreaming. The grind of powerful engines hurling the bulky transport through high Atlantic winds let him know the flight wasn't over yet.

Rolling on the narrow bunk, he fixed a sandpaper gaze on his team second. The poor guy looked as reluctant as he'd sounded, which came as no shock given Niky's self-acknowledged crankiness when he exceeded his exhaustion threshold.

He'd exceeded it about sixty hours ago.

"It's Counselor." Team second held up a mobile telephone unit.

Every muscle in Niky's body shrieked as he forced himself upright. After fifteen days with virtually no sleep, he wasn't about to trust himself to take this call with his head on a pillow. He reached for the phone.

"Hey, Counselor." Niky followed protocol by using Quinn's code name. Satellite transmissions could be monitored and although team second had retreated to a discreet distance, he was still within earshot. "This had better be good."

"King Arthur is checking out a lead on Wolfgang."

He heard the concern in Quinn's crisp tone, the matter-of-fact words, but it was the sound of *her* code name that diffused the clouds in his head.

*Wolfgang...Violet.* He stared at the phone, surprised to find it still in his hand.

"What lead?" If Simon investigated, this intel must be hotter than any that had surfaced in years.

"He hasn't briefed us yet, but we've been chasing Delinquent through the system. Looks like we've got a fiction author who's publishing stories that read like Wolfgang's mission briefs. King Arthur flew out a while ago to find the author and question her."

"Who is she?"

"No idea, but you're still hours out. Maybe I'll know more when you get in."

"You'll be there?"

"I'll be here." A promise.

Niky found no comfort in her reassurance, felt nothing beyond muscles that screamed with exhaustion.

Quinn couldn't provide anything more than a name. Then she said goodbye, leaving him to prepare himself to deal with this bombshell before he returned to Command.

The line disconnected, and Niky stared at the receiver, wanting to laugh at the irony of new intel now, while he was trapped inside this transport over an ocean. He couldn't do a damn thing to protect himself.

A movement in his periphery snapped him back. Team second waited to return the phone unit to the cabin, probably expecting him to go back to sleep. Another joke.

Dismissing the guy, Niky lay back, acid already burning a hole in his gut. He threw his arm over his eyes to block out the emergency light overhead, to block out the memory of Violet.

*Three years ago*
*Number Twelve Detention Camp, -22°C*

NIKY HAD BEEN LYING in that shallow pit, jammed tight with the rest of his team, hour after hour, as night turned into day then back again. The injuries he'd sustained in the avalanche throbbed dully with every heartbeat. His muscles screamed with the ruthless inactivity. He writhed on the frigid dirt floor.

But physical misery didn't count in this place. His wounds had started to heal. Blood clotted. Bone knitted. All without his permission. Given a choice, death would have been a reprieve from this gravelike pit, from the constant howl of mountain wind through stripped tree trunks that formed a lattice above his face. Death would have been easier than inhaling the stench of his team's fear. Only death could stop what was coming next.

They all knew what was coming.

So they lay in that hole waiting for boots to scrape over the frozen ground. They waited to hear the clink of metal locks on the grate and the arrival of guards to take the next prisoner to the red room for interrogation.

Standard procedure for POWs—interrogate, determine who was in charge then execute all but the team leader.

He was the team leader.

But they hadn't come for him yet. His injuries made him a weak link in the chain, so they tortured the others first to intimidate him. One by one they took his team away. They'd sent his first operative back a corpse.

Niky knew smart business in war meant keeping variables to a minimum. As captured Americans in a Serbian detention camp, they were serious variables. The military commanders suspected one of their comrades had intended to defect to the West. They would torture Niky's team until someone named that traitor.

But his team wouldn't give up the name of their target. Simon needed this defector to testify before NATO about the torture happening inside these detention camps, *death* camps as they were known locally.

His people would keep their mouths shut. If they failed to exfiltrate the defector, they'd leave him for Simon, who would send in another team. They'd keep silent, even if that silence cost their lives.

I swear my life to the Excelsior Agency. I forsake all ties to my former identity. I accept the charge of United States national security and the mission to protect the interests of our great nation at any cost.

A blood oath. Literally.

"She broke, man. Wolfgang gave us up, and they slit her throat." Fear finally had a go at Parella.

"She won't break." Blake barked a laugh. "But she might've pissed them off so bad they slit her throat."

"She's not dead," Niky said. Violet was just tough

enough, and stubborn enough, to endure whatever they did to her.

But she wasn't dead. Niky would have known in his gut.

"You really think she's still alive?" Reiger's hoarse rasp barely carried over the howling blackness. "It's been over three days since they took her. That's a long time."

The only other woman on their team, Reiger guessed what Violet was likely enduring right now, a blonde in a camp filled with soldiers who would want a break from the local entertainment.

"Yeah, I do."

His hourly pep talks to keep up team morale weren't doing the trick anymore. Not when Compton lay beside them with his throat gaping open, killing them all with the smell of death as it congealed around them.

Then the sound of boots…the makeshift gate above creaked open. Violet rolled into the pit. She landed unceremoniously on top of them, boneless. For a stunned instant, Niky thought Parella had been right after all. Carefully maneuvering his shattered leg, he levered himself up to gain access to a pulse point.

A flashlight sliced in from above, shining onto Violet's face, illuminating hair matted with dirt and blood, the once-beautiful features now swollen beyond recognition.

"Since you didn't like our hospitality, bitch," the guard said in a mixture of Serbo-Croat and fractured English. "You can spend another night freezing in this pit with your friends."

"Drop dead." Her voice came broken and raw.

And Niky had never heard a more welcome sound.

# CHAPTER TWO

*3:49 p.m. EST*
*Sault Ste. Marie, -9°C*

"THE ADMINISTRATOR WILL see you now, Mr. Brandauer."

Following the secretary through a door adjoining the reception area, Simon took in the spartan office, the frosted panes of the bare windows. The administrator rose from behind her desk, a sixtyish dynamo dressed neatly in gray wool.

She eyed him with an equally assessing gaze, and Simon knew his impression of Safe Harbor's administrator had been on target. Verna Joyce might not stand much more than five feet tall, but her no-nonsense stare made him feel every inch of his own considerable height.

She had run this facility since its inception over two decades before, sheltering political refugees and integrating them into their new environments.

He extended a hand over the orderly stacks of paperwork. "Thank you for agreeing to see me."

"I'm curious about what business warrants a visit from the Special Liaison to the United States Security Council." She accepted his identification, gave it a

sharp glance before returning it. "Most intergovernmental inquiries are routed to Global Coalition headquarters. Despite your credentials, I've never heard of
you."

No surprise. His official cover was nothing more
than smoke. "My inquiry is sensitive."

"Please have a seat. May I offer you something?
Coffee?"

"Thank you, no." Pocketing his ID, he sat down.

"What can I do for you?"

"I'm looking for a woman named Claire de Beaupré.
I understand she's connected to Safe Harbor."

"An employee or a resident?"

With one question, Verna Joyce dashed any hope
that this interview would quickly provide the answers
he needed. "I was hoping you would tell me."

Lowering herself into her chair, she swept a hand
around in a gesture that encompassed more than this
room. "Mr. Brandauer, you must understand that Safe
Harbor is a large complex. We staff a hospital, a school
and a residential facility. There are strict rules govern-
ing confidentiality."

"I'm not asking you to break rules. I'm trying to
learn Ms. de Beaupré's whereabouts. She's proving
difficult to locate."

"Perhaps you might tell me a little more about your
interest in her."

He'd anticipated this line of questioning and had
come prepared. His people still hadn't tracked down
anything concrete on Claire de Beaupré's existence,
which was understandable given the framework of the
Global Coalition. With a vast network of resources,
this organization safeguarded human rights, regardless

of political or religious affiliation. They were good at what they did.

So why did Claire de Beaupré need so much safe-guarding?

On an off chance something might turn up, Simon had arranged to send a team into the public facility that stored Safe Harbor's hard records, but it would be hours yet before his team was in place and that search yielded results. He had no intention of waiting for what he expected to be another dead end.

Opening his briefcase, he extracted an eight-by-ten glossy of Violet's most recent evaluation photo, taken only months before her capture. "I believe Ms. de Beaupré has information about this woman. She was one of my employees."

The administrator's steely gray brows rose a notch, just enough to make Simon question if she recognized the photo. "What happened to her?"

"She disappeared three years ago," he said. "I'm try-ing to confirm her death."

"She worked for the United States National Security Agency?" Passing the photo back, Ms. Joyce sat straighter in the chair. "Is there some sort of security risk I should be aware of?"

"That would depend on the information Ms. de Beaupré has about this woman."

While he appreciated the administrator's concern for her people, his own thoughts raced. Ms. Joyce couldn't recognize this photo, not unless she'd seen Vi-olet. But that wasn't likely. Nothing in the personnel records he'd reviewed on his flight into Sault Ste. Marie had indicated any connection to the Global Coalition resource office in the Balkans.

Was he misreading the administrator's reaction?

No, and they'd reached a deadlock. Ms. Joyce's frown suggested she fully understood the awkwardness of her position. She was harboring a woman off the public record. He was a high-ranking United States government official who'd skirted the usual channels to contact her. Not only did a border sit between their countries, but she couldn't anticipate the consequences of withholding her cooperation.

They were operating outside the rule book here, and he half expected Ms. Joyce to reach for the phone and put in a call to security. She surprised him by turning to stare out the icy window, clearly deep in thought.

Simon recognized the opportunity here. He didn't need Quinn's psychological expertise to know Violet's picture had troubled this woman. He needed to shake loose the reason why.

Reaching inside his briefcase, he retrieved a second photo and slid it across the desk. "This was submitted as evidence in the war crimes tribunal."

Glancing back almost absently, she dropped her gaze to the desk....

A firing squad executed civilians. Men, women and children collapsed into a mass grave. A woman in the background, emaciated and hanging from a noose, her white-blond hair the only splash of color besides the blood on that snowy mountain.

Violet.

A beat of stunned silence passed before Ms. Joyce closed her eyes. She trembled.

He'd expected the horror, but in her face he saw so much more than compassion for the grim reality of war. He saw pain for a woman who wasn't only an image on paper.

His gut told him that Ms. Joyce had known Violet, but he also knew that was impossible. Violet had been part of Excelsior since her parents' accidental deaths when she'd been sixteen years old. She'd lived in Command during her training, and after reaching the age of majority, she'd moved to D.C., close enough to be mission ready in minutes. She'd assumed an alias and interacted with no one outside of Excelsior. She'd had no involvement with Global Coalition, no ties to Sault Ste. Marie.

And now she was dead.

"She was a prisoner," Ms. Joyce whispered.

"In a detention camp during the war in Bosnia." Reaching for the photo, he returned it to his briefcase. "This photo was taken more than five months after I received word of her execution. Obviously my intel was flawed. I personally oversaw the teams that exhumed the mass graves in that camp. They're still trying to identify victims though DNA testing, but I haven't been able to locate this woman's remains. Claire de Beaupré is the only lead I've had in a long time."

"But how do you know—"

"I can't divulge that." He wouldn't tip his hand about the published stories or raise questions about the material contained therein. To the world, this author's work was simply fiction. To Simon those stories were a direct link to Excelsior.

A threat.

Instead, he changed tactics, taking a calculated risk on Ms. Joyce's character. He shared the truth, or as close to the truth as he could. "Let me explain the situation to you. This woman was part of a team sent into Bosnia to exfiltrate a defector who agreed to testify about what was happening inside those detention camps. My team and their target were executed instead. All except for this woman, who managed to stay alive long enough to convince another man to defect. As a direct result of his testimony, this photograph and others he brought back, my country and several allies were able to convince NATO to take action and shut down those camps."

But to secure that defector's escape, Violet had equipped him with her transponder. Her red blip had disappeared from the display in Systems Ops, and she'd become invisible to Simon.

"I lost five people during that mission," he said. "With the exception of this woman, I've brought them all home. Will you help me?"

Seconds ticked by, marked only by the whisper of their breathing, the hum of the heating system as it cycled on.

Finally, Ms. Joyce met his gaze. "I might be able to help, but I need some time."

Relief prompted Simon to reach for his business card. Verna Joyce would have her time and he would have her cooperation.

And with luck he might finally start unraveling the mystery of what had happened in number twelve detention camp.

"Here's where I can be reached. Thank you again for meeting with me." He snapped his briefcase shut then rose to leave. "And for helping me."

It was a start.

He turned to go, but she called to him before he'd reached the door. "Yes?"

"What was her name?"

He studied the face of this woman he sensed held all his answers behind troubled eyes. Violet's name would mean nothing to her. The young linguistic prodigy he'd met long ago at a Brussels symposium had dropped off the grid when she'd become an Excelsior operative. She'd taken a new name and identity that only existed within the walls of Command.

The price of covert operations.

But Simon recognized sincerity and strength in Verna Joyce's expression. And resignation. She would help him whether she wanted to or not. He believed it. He needed to.

"Violet Lierly."

*8:17 p.m. GMT*
*Over the mid-Atlantic*

SHOULD NIKY WAIT TO find out what this author knew about death camp number twelve? He'd been lying on this bunk ever since Quinn's call trying to answer that question, and kept coming back to the fact that the truth served no purpose now.

The truth wouldn't bring back his team, people courageous enough to die rather than betray mission objective and Excelsior. The truth wouldn't save the refugees, men who'd sacrificed themselves for the vain hope of sparing their families from killers; mothers who'd murdered their own children rather than let them be tortured.

The truth wouldn't help Violet, a vibrant, loving woman who'd suffered because Niky had abandoned her.

The truth would only take away his chance to do penance for his sins.

He'd been repenting every second of every day since his release. He'd debriefed, rehabilitated physically and psychologically, endured Simon's fanatical yearlong inquiry. Then he'd resumed Excelsior's cause with a new purpose.

The end doesn't always justify the means. Individuals should not become casualties to the greater good.

Sometimes Niky could carry out mission objective without sacrificing one for the other. So he did. Which pissed Simon off to no end. The big guy didn't like unnecessary risk. But it wasn't as if a little humanity around here would kill anyone.

Violet had understood that, and Niky had simply taken up her cause. He'd stopped chiseling people down to statistics, targets and mission objectives. People were human. He was human. *Flawed.*

His penance. His catharsis.

But now…what the hell had made him think he deserved a second chance?

No one who came out of that mountain hellhole alive deserved one. Most weren't getting them. The international war crimes tribunal hunted the commanders of the death camps like animals. They wanted blood for the thousands of rotting corpses and the screams that would haunt that region forever.

Only those under the devil's protection were safe.

Niky was safe. That thought spurred him to reach for his duffel bag in stowage beneath the bunk. Then he strode through the transport, no longer noticing the heaviness of his muscles. He locked himself inside the bathroom with a click of a metal lock.

Even using a frequency the pilot wouldn't detect without specific cause to look, making a phone call from this transport involved a risk he wouldn't normally have taken. He was too well trained to leave so much to chance.

But right now, when he stared into the warped mirror at the sickly green cast of his skin, Niky knew if he didn't make this call, he was looking at a dead man.

He made the sign of the cross and dialed.

*5:32 p.m. EST*
*Sault. Ste. Marie, -11°C*

OUTSIDE SAFE HARBOR'S main gate, Simon sat in his rental car, engine idling to run the defroster. He'd arranged to get a perimeter team en route to Sault Ste. Marie, but it would be hours before his operatives arrived and moved into place.

A stream of nine-to-fivers had been pouring through the main gate shortly after the close of the business day. He logged tag numbers into his laptop to learn who came and went on the property and what information might be had about them while waiting for TJ to hack into Safe Harbor's computer system.

He couldn't fathom what events could have brought Violet to Verna Joyce's attention. He wouldn't speculate, either. What he needed most right now was information.

If he were a savvy administrator harboring a woman with information on an employee of a high-level U.S. government agency, he would protect his charge at all costs.

Which meant Verna Joyce would backstop his cover.

Sure enough, the hits began soon after his departure from Safe Harbor. Calls and record searches were patched through to Command, where he'd assigned several operatives to field the inquiries. This administrator researched him every bit as thoroughly as he'd researched her, and Simon gained respect not only for Global Coalition's resources, but for Verna Joyce. The woman took the responsibility of her charge very seriously.

When the stream of traffic through the gate slowed, Simon pulled up the specs on Safe Harbor. This Global Coalition outpost was a high-acreage compound made up of four separate facilities—administrative, medical, educational and residential. The residential safe house sheltered refugees with a dedicated wing for orphaned children or those permanently separated from their families.

The educational building was a traditional elementary-secondary school, funded largely by private donations with programs designed to prepare multicultural students for integration into culturally diverse societies.

As was common with facilities dealing with children, a security wall enclosed the property. A security guard monitored the main gate, logging license tags of visitors. For all the good he did, which wasn't much apparently.

Simon had been parked adjacent to the main gate for nearly an hour, not openly within range, but nowhere near hidden. The guard had scarcely looked up at Simon, let alone inquired why he was sitting here. Had Excelsior been securing Safe Harbor's perimeter, Simon's operatives would have known what assembly line the car had rolled off and the names of the last five people to sit behind the wheel.

"Got you into the guard station, your majesty," TJ said through the audio device in Simon's ear.

"Good. Any luck with Safe Harbor's system?"

"This isn't like hacking into the local library, boss man. You got lucky on this one. Your babysitters are out-of-house, so their system is linked to a private security service, which *was* like hacking into the local library."

With a series of keystrokes, Simon accessed the monitoring program currently running inside the gatehouse. "Good job. I'm in. Keep working on Safe Harbor's system."

"You got it."

He maneuvered through the various programs used by Golden Hawk Security. The guard had logged many things during the past hour, but Simon's rental car tag number wasn't one of them.

Despite extensive Global Coalition resources, Verna Joyce wouldn't keep Claire de Beaupré's whereabouts a secret for long if Golden Hawk Security was the best protection she could offer.

The security company's program maintained visitor logs quarterly before system purge. Simon intended to review each and every entry to find what he was looking for.

He didn't have to look far.

Claire de Beaupré apparently visited Safe Harbor often. She had arrived at eight that morning and hadn't logged out until Simon had been visiting the administrator. Bad timing. While this author hadn't written anything but her name, arrival and departure times, a system scan provided her address on file—81C East Innis Avenue. No telephone number.

"I'm on the move," Simon said.

"Find what you were looking for?" TJ's voice shot back over the audio device.

"I'm paying the lady a visit."

His GPS targeted the location. Setting aside his laptop, Simon slipped the car into gear. The address was only a short drive. He would stake out the residence before making a move.

Snow swirled beyond the windshield, making it difficult to see into the shadows of the dark streets, but he was about two blocks south of his destination, when a pale flash of hair caught his attention.

A woman climbed onto a bike in the glow of light at a corner market. Pulling out onto the sidewalk, she waved back at a man in the shop window.

A glance at the dash showed Simon the temperature as minus eleven degrees Celsius, but this biker wore no more than a bomber jacket and jeans, a knit hat pulled low over a face he couldn't make out at this distance.

But there was something about her... He watched that pale hair lift on the wind when she wheeled away from the shop, and instinct urged him into action. Simon slowed to follow her and absently noticed a classic Mustang flip on its headlights and pull away from the curb behind him.

The biker was no more than a wraith in the darkness, neon reflectors winking. She slowed as the headlights of an old-model compact shot past on the cross street before vanishing into the night with a gleam of red taillights.

She turned. Onto East Innis Avenue.

This part of town might have once thrived with daytime activity, but now every third and fourth shop sat vacant. Hazy plate-glass windows displayed faded lease signs in the shards of light thrown by street lamps.

Simon followed, barely aware of his hands on the steering wheel or his foot on the gas pedal. He kept his distance as she rode off the sidewalk, crossing from the south side to the north, not altering her pace to suggest she'd noticed him.

He altered his, though, when high beams flashed in his rearview mirror, momentarily blinding him. Flipping the mirror up, he redirected the glare. The Mustang had turned onto the street behind him. The car rode his tail for a minute then gunned its engine and swung out to pass.

Fearing he would block the view of the cyclist, Simon decelerated to give the impatient driver a clear view.

The driver of the Mustang didn't slow down, but gunned the engine and swerved right toward the bike.

Jamming his wheel around, Simon collided with the Mustang hard enough to alter the car's trajectory.

But not soon enough.

The Mustang clipped the back tire. No match for the impact, the bike skidded sideways, sending its rider airborne for a suspended instant in a tangle of arms and legs. Then she compressed tightly and hit the ground in a skilled roll that hinted at extensive physical training. She came to a jarring stop against the curb while the Mustang fishtailed away, tires screaming for purchase on the snowy street.

Simon pulled the rental car to a stop, ground in the parking brake. Adrenaline propelled him across the street. He reached the biker as she struggled to sit up.

The knit hat had disappeared, revealing a sweep of straight blond hair that covered her face.

"Let me." Kneeling, he gripped her elbow to help.

She lifted her head and when she did, silky hair threaded over her shoulders to reveal the finely drawn lines of her profile. His heart pulsed a single hard beat.

*Violet.*

Over the past three years, Simon had cultivated scenarios about finding her, visions that had varied with his moods. Survivor guilt, Quinn had said. Normal. He'd sent the extraction team into number twelve detention camp. No matter how noble the cause, when people died the responsibility came back to him.

With Excelsior, everything came back to him.

According to Quinn, fantasizing about best-case scenarios was typical, too. Sometimes he'd be in Systems Ops and see Violet's signal miraculously appear on radar, hear her voice suddenly ringing out over the comm, *"Bring me in."*

He had dreamed about the Bosnian boneyards, the mass graves where he'd conducted oversight through long weeks of exhumation to begin DNA testing for identification. Testing that was still taking place as forensics specialists tried to attach names to remains and return victims of a brutal civil war to grieving family members.

In another dream, Simon had stood inside one of these graves, digging to find Violet, unable to reach her. She'd died a violent death to provide him with a second defector. She'd given him the evidence he'd needed to close the detention camps.

But nothing could have prepared him for the reality of staring into those wide, incredible eyes.

She appeared to be fighting off dizziness, yet there was a calmness about her at total odds with the situation. She took a deep breath then forced a smile, as if three years hadn't passed since he'd last seen her, as if kneeling together on this snowy street was the most ordinary thing in the world.

"I'm okay." Her voice echoed through the hushed night, a jarring, familiar sound from the past.

He held on to her as she scooted back against the curb, for a stunned, impossible moment, not knowing what else to do except hang on tight so she didn't vanish.

"Really." She glanced down at where he held her, then around the dark street. She frowned. "I'm okay."

He followed her gaze to the buckled fender of his rental car then to her mangled bike nearby.

"You hit that car?" she asked.

An eternity passed before her question registered, longer still to comprehend her question. He noticed the slow rise of color in her face and realized he was making her uncomfortable.

Violet had no idea who he was.

A hot wash of adrenaline urged him to say something, *do* something. This was *Violet*. She was team one. Simon might move operatives around a global chessboard according to their specialized skills and his mission objective, but team one was *his* team.

Of course she knew him. She had to.

Simon could only stare, his mind racing with questions. He found himself reaching out to touch her instead, curling his fingers around her chin to prove she was real.

Her shallow breaths burst as faint white clouds against his hand. She trembled when he tilted her chin upward until the street lamp cast her face in bright relief. Faint scars threaded beneath the curve of her jaw, disappeared behind her ear.

Ligature marks from a noose.

"Please." The alarm that flared in those incredible violet eyes finally broke through his shock.

"Are you hurt?" He forced the words out, though the question sounded absurd because she was alive. Impossibly alive. "Let's get you to a hospital and have you checked out."

"I'm fine."

Simon didn't think so. He glanced down to where the concrete had shredded the worn leather sleeve of her jacket, noticed the torn jeans growing damp with snow.

"You went down hard."

"No, really. I can't." She shook off his help and stood.

Backing away to give her some room, he rescued her bike. The collision had buckled the tire and twisted the handlebars.

"Not too bad," he said.

"I should be able to get it fixed."

She didn't say she needed to get it fixed, but Simon suspected he was holding her only transportation. Yet despite her obvious worry as she inspected the bike, he recognized Violet, her strength and the pride he was all too familiar with.

"How about a ride? This won't make it."

"I only live a few blocks away. I'll walk it home." Retrieving her hat from the sidewalk, she brushed dirty slush from the rim. She'd started to shiver.

"You're wet, and it's cold."

She glanced up and considered him somberly. "Why should I trust you?"

"I want to help." Forcing a smile, he extended his hand. "Simon Brandauer. I'll be happy to see you home…"

"Claire. Claire de Beaupré."

# CHAPTER THREE

IVAN ZUBAC PLACED the call on hold and motioned his assistant to leave, a clever young man whose willingness to please had recommended him to the post upon Ivan's arrival in the capitol two years ago.

"You must go home now, Ciril," Ivan said. "And why do you not take a few hours in the morning to sleep in? I have kept you working far too long this night."

"But it was a productive night, was it not, General? We drafted the new defense proposal for the high representative."

Ivan smiled, entertained by his young assistant's flush of success. "Indeed, it is a job well-done. Now go and find your bed. Security will see me out after I take my call."

With a nod, Ciril headed toward the door.

"I do not want to see you again before noon, Ciril."

"Thank you, General."

While Ciril's trustworthiness had far surpassed even Ivan's expectations, the young man could not overhear this conversation.

As defense minister of Strpski Grad Republika's

military cell, Ivan worked under the prime minister to oversee defense during the construction of two separate states beneath the Federation of Bosnia-Herzegovina flag—one Bosnian Serb, one Muslim. He also liaised with the international court prosecuting war crimes committed during former Yugoslavia's collapse.

He wielded much power as a result of his appointment to this post—power he intended to enjoy for a long while.

Ivan lived by the rule, "Always safe, never sorry." It had served him well. When his office door shut, he reached for the phone, a secure line with a new number only one man possessed.

"We had a problem," said a gravelly voice.

The man on the other end, an international death dealer known as the bootlegger, was the only man in his profession who based operations out of North America. Brokering assassins from a place as unlikely as St. Louis, Missouri, the bootlegger snubbed his nose at the security of a country that arrogantly boasted its superiority and strength to the world. Ivan thought that spoke highly of the man's abilities.

The bootlegger had been very capable in their past dealings, so capable that Ivan hadn't considered anyone else to deal with the bomb his Western contact had dropped earlier.

A woman with a connection to number twelve camp.

Ivan did not know who this woman was yet. Her identity did not matter. Anyone with a connection to the officers running the long-closed number twelve camp must be under his control. Or eliminated. He would not risk his affiliation being exposed. He had already survived one such disclosure when a traitorous deputy commander had defected to the West and betrayed his country to the war crimes tribunal.

By the sheer grace of God, Ivan's face had not been one of the images captured on a photographic device that had been submitted as evidence. He had no desire to be declared a war criminal at this late date. A fall from grace now would ruin all his careful plans for Strpski Grad's reconstruction.

Yet Ivan understood that loose ends happened in wars where new nations formed out of the wreckage.

Loose ends were tied up fast and tight.

"What problem?" he asked the man on the phone.

"The courier couldn't deliver your package." *The assassin could not make the hit.*

"Why?"

"Your recipient lives in a gated community. We didn't have the codes to get past security." *The target is under protection.* "I assume you didn't know?"

"No."

His Western contact hadn't told Ivan this woman was protected. This surprised him. His contact in the American government had bought his freedom because Ivan had foreseen his usefulness. In the years since the Dayton Peace Agreement had ended the slaughter against his people, the man had proved meticulous in his transfer of information. Ivan would have to find out what had happened today. A mistake? Or a setup?

"Do you want me to attempt another delivery?" the bootlegger asked.

"No. Research the address and tell me what you learn." *Find out who is protecting the target.* "I'll tell you when to attempt redelivery. Understood?"

"Yes."

Ivan disconnected. He had not thought the woman had to be alive for him to uncover her connection to number twelve camp, thought it best she was not.

Now the situation had changed. Ivan must understand who she was and who protected her before he could decide his next move. He must question his Western contact.

Always safe, never sorry.

*6:54 p.m. EST*
*Sault. Ste. Marie, -12°C*

CLAIRE HESITATED ONLY briefly before getting into Simon Brandauer's car. She could have walked home but couldn't resist the promise of heat inside his car. Snow had seeped through her clothes and the fall had aggravated a not-so-old sternoclavicular injury. She'd be hard-pressed to get her bike up the stairs to her efficiency with this stiff shoulder.

*If* she made it home. This stranger was a solid, powerfully built man, not muscle-bound like the bodybuilder wannabes who ran Safe Harbor's gym–physical therapy facility, but athletic and tall. He could easily hurt her with those strong hands.

This man clearly wasn't a degenerate. A businessman, she guessed by his expensive suit and car. Not someone used to dealing with hit-and-runs, because he hadn't suggested they call the police. Not that she wanted to, of course. The car that had hit her was long gone by now. Any report would only wind up on Ms. Verna's desk and get her started again on how Claire shouldn't have moved out of Safe Harbor's residential facility.

She did *not* need another lecture.

Yet something about Simon Brandauer… The way he'd looked at her. His clear gray eyes had seen right inside. There'd been an instant when she'd held her breath, thinking, *hoping,* he'd recognized her. No such luck.

What was it about him?

Wedging his broad shoulders through the driver's door, he turned over the engine, flipped the heat switch to high.

He had this totally chiseled, sharp-lined face with a jaw clenched so tight she kept expecting to hear crunching bone. But Claire didn't think any bone in this man's body would make such an undignified sound. He reeked with authority. As if to emphasize the point, he leaned inside, draped a heavy coat over her and solicitously tucked it beneath her chin.

He was so close she could see silver glinting in his jet-black hair, dark stubble that shadowed his mouth beneath the knifepoint flare of his nostrils.

"Thanks." Nestling inside the warmth, she smelled him in the thick lining, fresh and wintry with some underlying male ambrosia that was neither sweet nor spicy, yet somehow both.

"I'll get your bike."

The door shut, sealed her in a warm cocoon. She rested her head against the plush seat, let her eyes drift closed to the muffled thumps from the trunk.

She really shouldn't be here, but the hot air blasting from the vents convinced her to go with her gut on this one. She hadn't had anything else to go by in the two-and-a-half years since she'd awakened from a coma to an unfamiliar world.

Most people outside Safe Harbor gave her the willies. But not Simon Brandauer. There was something about him. Claire just wasn't sure what.

Cold air rushed in when he opened the door again. He sank into the driver's seat, and she was struck once more by how big he was, not bulky or awkward, just *big*.

"All set. Feeling any better?"

His concern seemed genuine enough. He was being considerate when he didn't have to be. He hadn't been the one to take out her bike. "Warmer. But this is silly. We're only a few blocks from my place."

"It's cold outside."

Gazing out the window, she saw the snow had started to fall again. "It is."

He slipped the car into gear and with her direction, headed down the street. She noticed his back seat filled with computer equipment, and expensive stuff from the looks of it.

"Do you work from your car, Simon?"

"When I'm on the road."

"What kind of work do you do?"

When he didn't answer right away, she glanced at him, curious why he hesitated to share something so simple. Here's hoping she hadn't made a mistake by getting inside this car.

"I'm a journalist."

"Really? I write, too. Nothing earthshaking like the news, though. Fiction."

"I'm hoping to break into that market. Any pointers?"

She trailed her gaze over his clear-cut profile, the hard geometry of his jaw, the no-nonsense curve of his mouth, and gave a soft laugh. As if someone this dignified and capable needed advice from her. Her bike should have clued him in that she hadn't exactly made the *New York Times* bestseller list yet.

But he'd been polite enough to ask, so she would be polite enough to answer. "Your journalism credentials will work in your favor. Get a decent agent."

"Good advice. I just signed with one. At least I think he's good."

"You're a step ahead of me, then."

He only nodded, and she was glad when they neared her building, "the tenement" as she referred to it. Not a joke.

"Pull up there." She pointed to the brick stoop.

Simon wheeled the car against the curb, where a plow had piled snow earlier in the day, and Claire hopped out before he cut the engine. Simon had lived up to his end of the bargain. She was home safe and sound.

Circling the car, she waited while he lifted her bike out of the trunk.

"Here, I'll take it," she said. "I've got to drag it upstairs or someone will steal it. Stellar neighborhood."

He didn't let go, but slammed the trunk shut one-handed. "What floor do you live on?"

"Third."

He fixed his gaze on her building, his jaw working a mile a minute. "The penthouse?"

"Yeah."

"Allow me."

One glance convinced her an argument would be a waste. But Claire had limits, and she hit one when they reached her efficiency. She wasn't about to let this man, whose car probably cost more than this entire building, inside.

Two months ago moving into her own place seemed to be a monumental accomplishment. Now all she noticed were the smoke-stained walls and cracked plaster moldings.

"I really appreciate your help." Inserting her key in the lock, she pushed the door open a crack and hoped he'd take his cue to leave. "I'll look for your byline."

He hesitated for a moment, and she thought he might object. Then he smiled, a smile that melted the sternness from his face, made his clear eyes sparkle. "The pleasure was mine, Claire."

He handed over her bike and headed back down the stairs.

She stood there, gaze clinging to him until the darkness swallowed up her view of his broad shoulders and dark hair. Then she wheeled her bike inside the efficiency and smiled at the irony of fate. Figured she'd meet a man whose kindness touched her in all sorts of crazy places when she had scrambled eggs for brains and lived stuck in survival mode.

SIMON CIRCLED THE BLOCK, suppressing a chill that had nothing to do with the cold. That Violet would get into the car of a man she believed to be a total stranger shed new understanding on Verna Joyce's efforts to protect her charge.

Violet needed protection. Simon had witnessed the hit-and-run and still couldn't decide if the Mustang had deliberately struck her. Logic told him the accident was what it appeared to be.

What were the chances of him showing up during an attempt on Violet's life?

Then again, Simon knew nothing about the events that had led her from number twelve detention camp to 81C East Innis Avenue. And something about the way the situation had played out had his instincts on red alert.

The first payment for Violet's published work had run through Verna Joyce's account over a year and a half ago, which meant she'd been affiliated with Safe Harbor for at least that long. The facility was hardly what Simon would consider secure. Yet Verna Joyce had kept Violet off the official record.

Was it possible Violet was a target on someone's hit list? If so, whose? And was the person after his operative or an author named Claire de Beaupré? Who else might have seen her stories and recognized their significance?

Simon didn't like his answer. *Anyone* could have read her stories. Had she buried clues between the lines to what had happened inside the detention camp? Or were her stories just a way of reaching out to him?

He considered all the possibilities because now that he'd finally found Violet, he would not let her go.

Her windows faced east, so after making another turn around the block he slipped the rental car into an empty space across the street, where he could watch the entrance of her building. He would put a perimeter team in place here as well, but his tactical operatives were still an hour away. He would brief them when they were closer to landing.

Meanwhile, he would try to make sense of this situation.

Flipping open his laptop, he patched into Command via satellite signal, then punched in the Mustang's tag number for a trace. His search yielded results quickly, along with a police report. The car had been reported stolen while he had sat in Verna Joyce's office. It hadn't been recovered yet.

Simon stared at the information on his display, troubled. Both the sequence of events and the timing marked this incident as impossibly coincidental.

Professional.

Unless someone had targeted Claire de Beaupré, the assassin had followed him here to take out Violet.

But not even *he* had known Claire was Violet.

TJ had speculated, but only Frances had known of the potential link to Violet before Simon had left Command. He'd since briefed Maxim, his second-in-command, who was coordinating the teams currently en route. The operatives on those teams knew only their functions and mission objective. They hadn't been told specifics about their target.

But he'd encountered Quinn in Systems Ops, too.

"Delinquent, I want a confirm on who knew I was making this trip today."

"Son of a bitch." The curse hissed through Simon's audio device on a sharp breath. "I hate your team, just so you know."

"Team one?"

"Who else?"

Who else indeed? He'd handpicked each operative for his or her highly specialized skills. But along with those skills came an attitude that made each one resent being left out of the loop—especially about one of their own.

Violet had been team one.

"Who questioned you?"

"They tracked me through the system. By the time I shut them down, they already knew enough to piece together the rest. I told Ma'am, and she's pissed."

Frances would be. "What did she say?"

"To tell you that I didn't say a damn thing to any of them. She told them to talk to you. They took her to mean literally, so they're on the way. ETA forty-two minutes. They'll be waiting at your hotel."

"Did Casanova get in?" he asked.

"Just as Counselor and Cowboy were hopping on a transport. He's with them."

Now Simon would add team one to his list of people who'd known why he'd come to Sault Ste. Marie.

Now all suspects for a leak.

Unfortunately, the only one with an obvious connection to the detention camp was Niky. Simon had to examine the unpleasant scenario that Violet had some information buried in her memory that Niky wouldn't want her to remember.

Simon had been here before. He'd conducted a long and difficult investigation into Niky's involvement in highly questionable circumstances, probing how Violet could have possibly survived...*again*.

The snow stopped, and Simon felt the heavy silence of the darkness beyond the windshield. Gazing up at her window, at the sickly wash of light, a television or computer, he imagined her up there, impossibly alive, *alone*.

Being run down hadn't fazed her. Why would it when she'd suffered so much more? Physical torture evidenced by the scars on her throat. Psychological torture buried beneath an apparent memory loss.

She lived in a dilapidated building and wore clothes that didn't protect her from the cold, unaware of who she was and what she'd sacrificed to close the detention camps and protect Excelsior.

He flipped a switch on the dash, the heat in the car suddenly choking him.

*Two-and-a-half years ago.*
*Excelsior Command*

FOR MORE THAN FIVE MONTHS, Simon watched the display in Systems Ops where four red blips signified his dead operatives halfway across the world. He hadn't achieved mission objective and the atrocities taking place in the Balkans raged unchecked. He was forced to stand by and wait for the improbable—another defector to surface and a window to open so he could recover his operatives without international incident.

In the interim, people continued to die.

He'd placed Niky on medical leave indefinitely. Meanwhile Simon conducted an investigation into the failure of the extraction mission and the happenings in number twelve detention camp. He wanted answers.

So did the president's oversight committee, who conducted their own inquiry into Simon's handling of the affair.

When one of those red blips on the display went mobile, Simon, the president and Oversight got their wish—answers.

Simon stood at that display watching Violet's blip move west beyond the hot zone. He sent a recovery team in. He ran sims on why an operative's remains might be moved from a detention camp.

And he waited, fighting an absurd, impossible hope that somehow that vibrant, incredibly gifted woman might have found a way to survive and come back.

Simon got part of that wish—Violet had indeed survived, long enough to convince someone else to defect.

More than five months after he'd sent an extraction team into number twelve detention camp, she'd accomplished mission objective. Violet had sent back a shift commander willing to testify about the atrocities he'd witnessed as price for asylum.

Now Simon must try to piece together the startling actions of the operative he'd believed to be dead. And for the first time since assuming the role of acting director, he tried to balance successful mission outcome against its cost.

The defector hadn't yet turned twenty. A young, sallow-skinned man who'd been serving his mandatory two years of active service in the Citizen's Army. He jumped when the door opened, relaxed only slightly when Simon stepped inside.

"I'm sure you want to get through this quickly, and with your cooperation, we can," Simon said. "So tell me about the woman you say gave you the transponder and imaging device."

"I never know her name," the man said in unpracticed English. "She is tall and fair. She come before I am assigned to number twelve camp. I know only she is American prisoner, one of a team captured on the mountain."

"Were you told what happened to the rest of the team?"

"Another guard say they are dead. He shows me the pit where they are buried."

"Do you know why this woman was kept alive?"

He shook his head. "I think the commandant wants her information, but she never gives it to him."

"Did she tell you who she was?"

"She say she work for the American government and a man who will stop the murders. She say he will close down the detention camps if I bring him proof of ugliness there."

"You believed her?"

That earned a smile. "No. I do not. Not at first."

"What changed your mind?"

The man exhaled hard, lifted his shadowed gaze to Simon, reconciled. "My government order the paramilitaries to attack a Muslim village. They kill many people but bring back many. Number twelve camp has almost five hundred detainees. Men, women, children cramped inside airplane hangar like many cattle in a pen.

"'There is too many,' we say. 'We need to open another hangar to make place for the others.' But the commandant say to fit them all, so we do. It is impossible. The snow on the roof breaks the wall, and we move the detainees to a new hangar to repair the wall. All the guards must work, but I am stationed in the security hut. I am happy to be warm.

"On the monitors, I see two mothers with young children. They wait when the farm truck brings chickens and eggs and milk. One mother calls the guard, and as I watch, I see she offers him sex to give other mother a chance to smuggle the children into the truck.

"I will be blamed if detainees escape, but the guard

outranks me. He pulls the mother off of camera to take her offer. I do not know if I should sound the alarm.

"I feel shame," the commander said with passion. "I am oldest of my mother's sons. She has sons still young. My superior make this mother whore to free her children.

"The American woman sees them, too, and she block the opening so others not see the children go through. Then she disappears and when she comes back, she drags the guard under the camera so I am sure to see her. She breaks his neck. That is when I know she will let those mothers go free. I sound the alarm."

"What happened after you sounded the alarm?"

"More guards come. But they do not take away the American woman until the truck is gone through the gate. She say the guard try to rape her. The commandant have much anger. The guard's weapon is missing and he thinks the American woman take it. She will not tell him where it was."

"Did the commandant learn of the mothers' escape?"

"Yes."

"Were you implicated?"

The man shook his head, still didn't meet Simon's gaze. "I erase the tape so my superiors not know I wait to sound the alarm. They think this all happen out of my camera."

"Do you know what happened to the mothers and their children?"

"I ask questions in town when I go off duty. I hear they make it down the mountain. After that, I not know. Their fate belongs to God."

As this young man's future had belonged to Violet. Because hearing this story of her courageous and kind actions confirmed their collaboration as surely as the transponder that had turned this deputy commander into a red blip on Simon's display.

Brave, idealistic and caring to a fault…*Violet*.

"So seeing the American woman help the mothers and their children changed your mind about her?" Simon asked.

"No, but after that I watch her. The commandant chain her hands to keep her from causing trouble, but that does not matter to her. She already know the camp and the men better than I think the commandant does."

"Why did you think that?"

"She know the routines. The guards. She know how to avoid the ones with a taste for the women. She know I feel shame. It is not my place to question my superiors. They tell us the detainees are murderers who bomb our children, but these people are not militia. I see one mother smother her little one to save him from the red room. These are scared people."

"The red room?"

"The warehouse where the commandant question detainees. Most not come out alive. And the screams… the blood…"

His voice trailed off, and Simon watched as he scrubbed a hand over his face trying to rein in his emotion.

"But not the American woman," the man finally said. "She come out alive. She is strong that one, tough to kill. She say she take pictures, like I do in monitoring station. She say if I bring them to her superior, we stop this bloodshed."

"And you believed her?"

"No." Not a hint of a smile this time. "She tell me when I see enough death she can prove what she say."

Another truth to corroborate the man's story. In addition to a tracking device, his operatives carried two nontraceable imaging devices. Standard procedure to provide evidence in the event of an operative's death.

"When did you see enough death?" Simon asked.

"After I see a young man cut to pieces. They bury him in different graves to torment his mother."

"The American woman showed you pictures?"

He shook his head. "She gives me piece of plastic and say how to connect to a disk for my computer. I never see such a thing. But I see the pictures and know she speaks the truth."

Two imaging devices. Standard procedure. Violet could have turned over one device to this deputy commander to prove her claims and still retain the backup in case the man failed.

The man hadn't failed. She had chosen well.

"So you took the imaging device and the transponder to signal us when you left your shift?" Simon asked.

"She tell me travel thirty kilometers before you will see me. I wait until I have leave to see my family. Then I take her devices and go."

Simon braced his hand on the wall beside the intercom, the need for some tactile connection suddenly overwhelming, as he forced himself to ask, "Where was the woman when you left?"

"Dead," the man said apologetically. "There is much medicine missing from the infirmary. Medicine for the guards and the officers. The commandant think the American woman take it for the sick children."

"Did she?"

He nodded.

"How did she die?"

"Hanged. I take a picture with her device before I go on leave. I know not if it take but I try. I think you might want proof that I know your woman."

Hanged? But Violet had been beaten to death. She'd been thrown into that pit on top of Niky, the last of his team, before he'd been dragged out for interrogation. Team leader.

The pieces had fit.

Even more importantly, Simon knew in his gut that Niky would have never taken advantage of an opportunity to escape if it had meant leaving Violet behind alive.

He tapped the intercom, connected to TJ. "You've read the imaging device?"

"Downloaded the files to your system. Piece of cake. The memory was almost full. Wouldn't have been room for many more."

Simon moved to the comm station, logged on and opened the folder. He scrolled through files, blindly processing images of people herded inside the detention camp in extreme conditions, didn't allow himself to feel, only to assess…until he saw the final shot, saw the woman in the background, hanging from a noose, over five months after she'd been reported dead.

# CHAPTER FOUR

*1:16 a.m. EST*
*Sault. Ste. Marie, -17°C*

NIKY BOLTED UPRIGHT in the recliner and gazed around the Sault Ste. Marie hotel suite where he and the other team one operatives had been burning the midnight oil waiting for Simon.

"TJ says Simon's on his way," Major Hickman, team one's strategist, drawled in a pronounced Midwestern twang that hadn't faded in all the years Niky had known him.

Niky had been dozing on and off for the past few hours, while Major and Quinn had been reading Claire de Beaupré's stories. They'd curtailed their speculation about this mysterious author for his benefit, and he was glad he could claim mission exhaustion to divert Quinn from psychoanalyzing him all night.

She wanted to prepare him for news about Violet. He wanted to prepare himself for more shit on his conscience. He'd passed this author's name along to Ivan Zubac and expected Simon to walk through that door with news of her sudden death.

It wouldn't be the first time Zubac had taken care of a problem expediently.

Niky had learned a few things about Zubac in the years since death camp number twelve. The man wielded the sort of power through his sphere of influence that Simon did, only without half the conscience.

He also rivaled Simon in persistence. The situation with Violet was classic. Simon wouldn't close the case on the Balkan extraction mission until he brought her home. Didn't matter that they were pushing three years.

Zubac was no different. Niky's deal with the man should have been one shot. Niky had traded the defecting target's name for his life. Obligation ended.

Not quite.

No one ever really left death camp number twelve.

When the hotel suite door finally opened, Niky forced his hands onto the chair arms, all remnants of weariness evaporating on a rush of adrenaline that made his palms sweat. Simon filled the doorway, looking cold and resolute.

This was a look Niky had seen often enough to recognize it, but there was something else tonight, some sort of intensity that manifested itself in a physical way.

That surprised Niky. Simon Brandauer didn't let his guard down. No one ever knew what the man was thinking. It was a constant source of speculation among everyone in Excelsior. King Arthur. The code name depicted the man. Noble. Incorruptible. Willing to do whatever it took to accomplish mission objective. Every operative in the place strove to emulate him, to live up to his expectations.

Simon had devoted his life to Excelsior. That was that. Just like the rest of them. He never struggled with the side effects of that isolation, the sometimes heavy stress of facing life-and-death situations. He never let emotion leak through. Niky had decided long ago that Simon didn't have any to leak.

Simon was leaking tonight.

He stopped when he saw them but didn't pull his nine-millimeter SIG. He didn't point it at Niky and call him a traitor. Simon only gave a disgusted snort.

"I didn't invite you," he said.

"That's why we crashed, my friend." Major spread out over half the sofa, legs before him, ridiculous blue Western boots glowing in the light of the muted television's glare.

Niky's heart slowed, one cautious beat at a time.

"Frances wouldn't crack," Quinn said. "But you should have known better than to think TJ could handle us."

No doubt there. TJ was a kid who, despite his genius at tactical control and his smart-ass mouth, didn't stand a chance against three level one operatives with their minds set on extracting information. Team one had wanted information tonight.

Simon set his briefcase down and hung up his coat.

Running a hand through his hair, Niky summoned every ounce of skill he possessed to keep panic at bay. He was part of the most elite special ops team in the world. He could handle this. Since Simon hadn't pulled a gun yet, things were looking up.

"Shouldn't you be in Command sleeping off the past week?" Simon slanted a cool gaze Niky's way.

He shrugged. "Didn't want to miss the party."

"You're compromised. You need time to recover."

"I've been sleeping all night. On the transport. On the flight here." He motioned to the recliner. "While we've been waiting on you."

Simon frowned, but Major drew all their attention when he clicked off the television and asked, "Do we have a lead on Violet or what?"

"We tracked TJ through the system, so don't yell at him," Quinn said. "So how does this author know all these details about Violet's missions?"

Simon snapped open his briefcase and withdrew his laptop but didn't answer their questions.

"Couldn't be coincidence, could it?" Niky asked. Oh, please, God, don't let him have jumped the gun in calling Zubac.

Major frowned. "You didn't read the stories. There's nothing coincidental. Maybe this author met Violet somewhere."

Niky sprang to his feet, cursing the rush of adrenaline that suddenly made sitting impossible. "If Violet had gotten close enough to anyone to breach protocol, we'd have known."

Excelsior was a lifelong gig. Fellow operatives and Command staff became friends and family united in a common goal—to protect their country at any cost. Secrets were tough to keep. Niky knew that firsthand.

"What if they met in the detention camp before she died?" Quinn said, and Niky suddenly found everyone staring at him.

He saw the concern in their faces, had been on the receiving end of their worry so often these past few years he could recognize it with his eyes closed. They pitied him, damn them. His closest friends in the world, and they pitied him.

Before death camp number twelve he'd had their respect.

Some barely functioning part of his brain argued

that they didn't blame him for losing a team. Or for Violet. He'd seen her dumped into that grave. They all knew the price of their work for Excelsior. Missions went awry. Sometimes people died.

"Did you speak to the administrator of this Global Coalition facility?" Major broke the silence.

Simon booted his system. "I met with her earlier. She agreed to call me."

Major exchanged puzzled glances with Quinn. "That's it?"

"She wanted to check out my credentials. Frances and TJ have been fielding inquiries all night."

"We're...*waiting?*"

Niky heard Quinn's surprise and squelched a similar response. *Waiting* wasn't exactly Simon's usual MO.

"Since you've followed TJ, I assume you know that everything Safe Harbor has on Claire de Beaupré isn't accessible through the usual channels," Simon said dryly. "I've sent in a team to infiltrate their hard copy storage, but they hadn't found anything the last time I checked. They won't."

"You're sure?"

Simon nodded. "Safe Harbor's administrator intends to protect Claire de Beaupré to the limits of her resources."

Niky spun back from the window, struggled to maintain calm. "Who is this woman?"

"I wanted to know the same thing, so I found Claire de Beaupré to ask her myself." Simon typed in keystrokes.

"Good," Major said. "What does she know about Violet?"

"Claire de Beaupré *is* Violet."

Niky heard Simon's words, struggled to understand when blood throbbed so hard in his ears his head might explode.

*Violet.*

In his peripheral vision, Niky saw Quinn talking, but all he could hear was the sound of *her* name.

*Violet.*

"That's crazy," he heard himself say as if from a distance. He was halfway across the suite before realizing he'd moved. He didn't get any farther before Major and Quinn each had one of his arms and shoved him back into the recliner.

"Take it easy," Major warned.

But the lash marks on Niky's back—one of the more physical souvenirs he'd brought back from the Balkans—ignited into flames. Phantom pain that felt so damn real.

"She's dead, Simon." Niky's voice broke. *"Dead."*

How much more freaking proof did these people need?

"Apparently not." Simon lifted the laptop toward them.

They all fell silent. Violet's face stared at him from the monitor, gaunt, her finely sculpted face and hollow cheeks making her eyes seem too big.

She'd always worn her hair sleek, a blunt cut at the shoulders that covered one eye whenever it slipped from behind her ear. Now long bangs brushed her jaw, and the ends trailed untrimmed around her shoulders. With those too-big eyes and ragged hair, she looked young…haunted.

"Shit." Major sounded stunned. "What did she say?"

Niky braced himself for the next salvo, forced his

brain to shift into gear to understand what was happening.

"She had no idea who I was," Simon said. "Or who she is. She's apparently lost her memory."

"Amnesia," Quinn said. "Biological or psychological?"

"I don't have that information. I hope Safe Harbor's administrator will save me the trouble of finding out for myself. I do know Violet's been affiliated with Safe Harbor for at least a year and a half. Given the facility's resources, they should be able to shed some light on her medical condition."

"I want to see whatever medical records you can get a hold of. Memory loss would be a common result for someone as brutalized as Violet was. But there could be any number of causes. Unfortunately, many are permanent conditions."

Simon nodded. Then he placed the laptop back on the desk, where Violet's image presided over the room, and dragged a chair around to face them.

Niky dropped his face into his hands, tried to take in a decent breath, to manage the phantom fire searing his back, while Simon explained the sequence of events since his arrival in Sault Ste. Marie.

An administrator who recognized Violet's photo.

A familiar woman on a bike.

A hit-and-run.

*Jesus.*

"I can't say if the incident was an accident or an attempt on her life," Simon explained. "Until I understand what has happened to her since the photo at the death camp was taken, I simply don't have the intel to evaluate."

"How could it have been an assassination attempt?" Major looked doubtful. "You said she's been here for a while. Why would someone try to take her out right in front of you? That's too much coincidence to be taken seriously."

"Agreed. What if someone followed me in?"

A beat of stunned silence while the implication of *that* registered.

A leak in Command.

"But, Simon, *you* didn't even know she was Violet," Major pointed out. "The thought never crossed my mind when I was reading those stories."

"Look at what we have here—a car that was stolen and abandoned within hours. Make and model unusual enough to be noticed. These are the marks of a professional."

"But who'd order a hit? Someone from the detention camp?"

Simon shrugged. "Perhaps. I had TJ assign an information retrieval team to compile the files on the detention camp commanders. We have substantial information in our sublevels, and my NATO connections will give me some access to war crimes tribunal archives. But I keep coming back to Violet's stories. Did she write them to contact me?"

"Maybe on some level, she knows she needs to be brought in." Quinn agreed. "Especially if her life is in danger."

"Why *now?*" Niky tried to sound reasonable, when hysteria still hammered at his calm like fists.

Only he knew the answer to that question.

He'd put Zubac on *Violet's* tail.

Quinn crossed to the minibar. Pouring water, she offered him a glass. He almost choked on the first swallow but forced himself to drink, needed to clear his head. He couldn't get away from the phone call he'd placed while flying over the Atlantic.

"I don't have enough information to evaluate," Simon said. "What if there are clues in her stories, clues that we don't recognize but someone else might?"

"Then someone could have followed us to those stories, then here." Major frowned. "That doesn't leave too many people, Simon. Four of them are sitting in this room."

"We assume that's all who knew. I wish that were the case. It would narrow the suspect list considerably."

Quinn frowned. "Are you thinking Oversight?"

Simon nodded. "You tracked TJ through the system. Oversight has even better access."

*Oversight.*

Niky took a deep breath. While he'd been suffering through Simon's yearlong inquiry after his return from the death camp, Simon had been suffering through an inquiry from a presidential oversight committee that had lasted even longer. Only the president knew who'd been on that committee, and they damn sure would have known each and every detail about Simon and the extraction mission.

If Simon suspected Oversight, there were a few more suspects between him and the truth—he was as guilty as hell and Violet had suffered *again*.

"We also can't discount Safe Harbor or Global Coalition," Simon said. "They're in the business of transitioning political refugees, yet they handled Violet differently. Until the administrator decides to talk, I won't know why."

"This all presupposes the hit-and-run wasn't exactly what it appeared to be—a freak accident." Major exhaled heavily. "I'm with you. I don't like this one bit."

"You've got to bring her in." Niky forced the words out. "Get her into Command."

Where Zubac couldn't touch her.

Simon's steely gaze swung his way, dashed all hope with one level stare. "She might not be safe inside Command, and, judging by her condition tonight, I'm not convinced bringing her in is our best option anyway."

"What are you thinking?" Quinn asked.

"I can't assess the situation until the administrator briefs me on Violet's condition and the logistics of her life at Safe Harbor. She lives off property, but from what I saw in the security company's records, she spends most of her time there. If we can gain the administrator's cooperation, infiltration might be an option."

"Infiltration?" Major sounded surprised.

"Violet has the information I need to find out what happened in that detention camp. Keeping her safe until she can tell me is mission priority."

Cold bastard. It was always about mission objective.

"What if she can never tell you?" Quinn asked.

"Like I said. Until I have more information, I can't evaluate. I've laid the foundation for a cover."

Major frowned. "*Your* cover?"

With one nod, Simon stepped down from his ivory tower and shocked the hell out of them all. "I'll take point. We have to protect Violet until we have some idea about who might want her dead. The only way we're going to find out is by understanding what's been happening in her life."

Simon had worked in the field long before becoming acting director, but nowadays he stood on the pulse of world politics. He made split-second decisions that influenced governments. He left the dirty work to others.

Protecting Violet obviously wasn't dirty work.

"But infiltration, Simon?" Major shook his head as if to clear it. "That'll be a logistical nightmare. Are you sure you want to direct that sort of manpower here. We've got active missions on four continents right now."

"Violet struck me as being entrenched in her lifestyle. I don't want to jeopardize her psychological well being by taking her out of her environment. It doesn't feel right."

No one said anything. No one ever questioned Simon's feelings. Not only was the man intimidating with his noble ideals and ruthless managerial style, but he was *that* good.

His instincts were dead-on again. Zubac was no coincidence, nor would he call off a hit after one failed attempt.

"You can't leave Violet here." Niky shoved his voice past the knot in his throat. "Not after what she's been through. She needs to be with people who can help her and care about her."

"I'll reassess when I have more information."

Niky knew better than to argue, but, oh God, he just couldn't keep his mouth shut. They were talking about *Violet.* "If you're right and she's in danger, why would you leave her exposed? You can't honestly think someone inside Command will hurt her."

Quinn suddenly came up behind him, rested her

hands on his shoulders. Her touch cautioned him to pay attention to what he already knew—Simon wasn't in the negotiating mood tonight.

Niky forced himself to feel the strength of her hands, to breathe deep, to calm down, to shut up.

"Trust that my decision will be based on what's best for Violet," Simon said simply. "I will not risk her safety, either physically or psychologically."

*"You are risking her,"* Niky wanted to shout, but then Simon and team one would ask why.

Niky's time had come. His golden opportunity to admit what had happened in death camp number twelve.

He'd known with every instinct he possessed that Violet had been dead. She'd tumbled into that grave on top of him that last time, and while he hadn't gotten a chance to check her pulse or capture her on his imaging device before being dragged out for his trip to the red room, Niky had seen her, lifeless like the rest of them. She didn't tell the guards to drop dead.

Niky had no clue how she'd survived long enough to send the young deputy commander back to Simon. He didn't know now how she'd wound up at Safe Harbor with no memory. But he could guess. Zubac had played him for a fool.

*"American, all I need is the name of your target. Tell me who wants to defect and I will stop your pain."*

But Zubac had needed more than a name. Once Niky had given him the name in exchange for his freedom, Zubac had needed someone to hand over to the death camp's officers.

Violet had been the only one left alive.

Some desperate part inside of Niky felt redeemed he hadn't been the only one to screw up.

Violet was still alive.

Simon hadn't known. Neither had Zubac, obviously.

But when Niky stared at Simon—the man whose cause Niky had given his life to—when he looked at the operatives whose backs he'd protected in the field, his friends, Niky's time came and went.

He couldn't open his mouth.

Not when only he and Zubac knew the truth.

*12:52 p.m. EST*
*Sault Ste. Marie, -4°C*

"ARE YOU THERE, Claire?" a voice said over the intercom.

Claire recognized the administrative assistant's voice and wheeled the chair from the desk. She tapped a button on the phone and said, "I'm here. What's up?"

"Ms. Verna needs you to translate some things. Don't come to the office. She's in the observation room."

Claire would have told just about anyone but Ms. Verna to take the proverbial hike. Safe Harbor's school served as a jumping-off point for students from cultures all over the globe to mainstream into Western society.

Many programs were in place to facilitate this transition. Speech classes that taught English as a second language and stronger communication skills. Her publishing center was designed to encourage enthusiasm for reading through writing, a literacy program that offered students the chance to publish their own books.

Whether a story consisted of four sentences in a first grader's careful print or twenty pages of teenage melodrama, students let their imaginations run when they visited Claire.

Committing a story to paper and seeing it become a hardbound book fostered pride in these kids. And their excitement at seeing their name on the cover fed Claire's soul.

She had considerable skill with languages and used that skill to communicate with people who'd been forced from their homes by wars or disasters, people who often felt isolated and alone. She didn't know where she'd developed her skill or how she'd used it before, but she was so grateful she possessed a way to give back to those who'd done so much for her. Helping gave her a sense of accomplishment when she often felt needy.

Today her schedule involved kindergartners' stories. And since these students weren't old enough to commit even a sentence to paper, Claire had designed a template to help them create a personalized "All About Me" story they could illustrate.

The downside of this template meant she had to input each student's individual data. There were *three* kindergarten classes. "Tell Ms. Verna I'm on my way."

The publishing center was an old maintenance room located inside the school. Claire locked her room and strolled down the halls to the front school entrance by the main office.

She crossed the grounds to the administration building. Waving to the switchboard operator in the lobby, she headed down the hall where the observation room was located. Knocking, she pushed open the door and smiled.

A table had been pushed against the wall, and Ms. Verna sat on an elementary-size chair, surrounded by file folders.

"Hey, hey, Ms. Verna. What are you doing here today?"

"I needed a place to spread out these files. Would you mind giving me a hand, dear?"

Claire tossed her jacket onto the table and resisted the urge to look into the tinted observation glass that ran the length of the wall. She hated these rooms. Since arriving at Safe Harbor, she'd been in enough of them during psych evaluations to hope never to see one again.

Skirting the edges of the folders, she kissed Ms. Verna's cheek. "What do you need done?"

"I'm gearing up for the annual audit, and I've got paperwork on some residents that I can't read, which is making it difficult to file properly."

"I'll bet." Pleased to help out in every way she could, Claire lowered herself to the floor, schooling her expression as every muscle from her shoulder down shrieked in protest.

"What's wrong, dear?"

"Nothing, why?"

"I'm not buying it. I saw your coat."

She'd never lie to Ms. Verna, but she wasn't above fudging. "Wiped out on my bike last night. No biggie."

"Were you hurt?"

"Toasted my shoulder. I'm okay."

"Michelle will want to check you out."

"Without an appointment?" Claire grabbed a stack, glanced at the top paper and recognized the Cyrillic letters. Russian. "It's almost noon. She's already running an hour behind."

"She'll work you in."

That much was a given, but Claire couldn't face a round of physical therapy today. Meeting Ms. Verna's worried gaze, Claire admonished gently, "You promised not to worry about me."

"No. You demanded I stop. I never agreed."

"Then agree, will you please? You've got plenty of other people to worry about. I'm okay. Have some faith in me."

"I do." Ms. Verna's expression softened as she reached inside a tote propped against her chair. "I have something else for you, too—a birthday gift."

"Thought today was as good a day as any, hmm?"

"Yes, in fact."

Claire scooted closer, eager to open the small, foil-wrapped package. Easing the tape from the wrap, she flipped open a velvet box to find a beautifully detailed gold crucifix. "Why are you giving me a gift? You do so much for me already."

"I thought it would help protect you." She gave a wistful laugh. "Well, it makes me feel better to think it will."

Ms. Verna might have devoted her life to the Global Coalition and the ongoing war against human suffering, but personally, she was a very spiritual woman with a strong faith.

Directing Claire to lift her hair, Ms. Verna fastened the chain around her neck and drew back to view the result. "It's lovely."

"*You're* lovely. I'm so blessed to have you." Blinking back tears, Claire touched the crucifix. It felt solid beneath her fingers, a lot of strength in a small package. Like Ms. Verna.

"Don't cry yet, dear. I haven't asked you for my favor."

"This is a bribe?"

"It's about helping out where you're needed, which I know you like to do. We've got the annual fund-raiser coming up."

Everyone within screaming distance knew the annual fund-raiser was coming up. Global Coalition ran a lot of facilities. Safe Harbor ran one of the largest medical centers in the area. Claire knew personally how its continued existence depended on donations.

Reaching for another paper, she had to work a little harder for this one—African that resembled Swahili but a dialect that didn't look familiar. "You know I'll do what I can to help."

"Good because a national newsmagazine wants to feature us. This is a marvelous opportunity and the timing couldn't be better. The feature will run right before the fund-raiser and should boost donations considerably."

"Great. What do you want me to do?"

"Be our poster child."

It took a moment for *that* to register. "Excuse me?"

"A journalist from this magazine will spend some time with you and write an article that'll show the world what wonderful work we do here at Safe Harbor."

Claire blinked, still not sure she'd heard Ms. Verna right. "I thought the cafeteria must be serving decaf this morning. No wonder I've been struggling to nail this dialect."

"The coffee's fine. And so are you. You're our best-case scenario for the interview."

"I'm a basket case and you know it."

"Claire, you awoke two-and-a-half years ago from a coma with debilitating physical injuries. Now you have a career, your own home. You'll make a great story."

"In the time I've been here, I've figured out exactly three things." She ticked them off one by one. "I have a tremendous command of languages, I possess an active imagination and I can ice-skate. Makes for a real short story."

"The executive director is pushing hard for this. He wants tangible proof that his funding is serving our residents."

"I'm not a resident anymore."

"Others won't be either unless Safe Harbor attracts generous contributors."

"I suppose I've beggared the place with my care."

"Something like that, dear."

Why did Ms. Verna have to do guilt? Claire could never repay these people no matter how many papers she translated or books she published. "You know why I don't want to rehash my angst. It's not as if you've been encouraging me to put my face on milk cartons, so why are you asking me to do this?"

"You've given up trying to find out who you are," Ms. Verna said simply. "You seem content not knowing, and I think you need a push. This sort of exposure could lead to some clues."

Claire tried to toss off the surprise and the headache that had started pounding in her temples. "Where did *that* come from?"

"The same place it came from the last time I brought up the subject. And the time before that. You're ignoring me."

"I'm not ignoring you. I just don't agree."

"You're shutting out the past."

"I'm moving on with my life."

"You're hiding."

"I already have a psychiatrist, thank you."

"Not from what I hear. Rachel told me you canceled your last three appointments. Martin said he hasn't refilled your prescription in over five months."

"A conspiracy. Great." Shoving to her feet, Claire couldn't sit anymore and prowled the perimeter of the room, ignoring the dark glass that symbolized everything she wanted to put behind her. "Getting off the medication is a good thing."

"I think that's for your doctor to decide, don't you?"

"No, I don't. I'm tired of taking drugs to control symptoms and regulate my moods. I'm tired of remembering things that give me horrible nightmares and anxiety attacks. If my memory doesn't come back, well, then…it doesn't. I'm through trying to put together puzzles without all the pieces."

"You're being impatient."

"I'm being *practical*." Taking a deep breath, Claire steadied her voice and admitted the worst truth of all. "Has it occurred to you if nobody has missed me that I might not have had anyone to miss? I have people I care about now. I don't want to sacrifice them to remember something not worth remembering."

"Claire, you can't know that's the situation."

"It feels that way, and that's really all I have to go by."

The look on Ms. Verna's face revealed everything she felt. All the hurt, the disappointment, the worry. She cared so much. "Come here, dear."

Taking a steadying breath, Claire knelt beside her, met her gaze, faced the woman who'd become so dear to her. A lifeline.

"You know I'd never do anything to hurt you, don't you?"

"Of course."

"Then you'll have to trust me on this. I would never ask you to hash through your experiences with a reporter unless I believed it was the right thing to do."

Right for *whom?*

Claire wanted to ask. Oh, man, did she want to ask. She didn't remember a thing about the mountaintop in Bosnia where a Global Coalition envoy had found her. She didn't remember the flight to an Austrian safe house or the emergency surgeries necessary to prepare her for transport to the North American facility capable of handling her physical rehabilitation.

Claire's first real memory was of Ms. Verna's voice. Every day after work, before she crossed the grounds to the bungalow on a wooded corner of the property where she lived, Ms. Verna would swing by the hospital, sit beside Claire's bed and read.

Claire remembered the clean cadence of her voice, the shift of her accent to the beginning of words. Before ever opening her eyes, she'd known the voice's owner had come from New England. She couldn't be sure how she knew, but she'd known all the same.

It was that memory, a woman who cared enough not to leave Claire alone inside her head before her body had healed, that squelched her reservations now. Was what Ms. Verna wanted really so much to ask?

"I don't suppose you'll take the necklace back?" she asked.

"No, dear. I won't."

"You're sure you want a basket case representing us?"

"You're not a basket case."

"A matter of opinion."

"Nice try, but my mind's made up. This will be best for all concerned. You'll see."

Claire felt manipulated and ungrateful for feeling that way. Ms. Verna had done so much and here was a small way to repay the debt. Claire should have agreed without hesitation.

"All right." That was the best she could do. "But have your secretary send me a reminder. I have a history of forgetting things I don't want to remember. *This* I'll forget. Guaranteed."

Ms. Verna smiled. "Have faith, dear."

*Right.*

## CHAPTER FIVE

A FEW HOURS SPENT in the publishing center churning out kindergartners' stories while nursing a headache that wouldn't relent, and Claire forgot all about her earlier conversation with Ms. Verna. A reprieve she wished would have lasted a lot longer. No such luck.

A knock sounded, and Ms. Verna popped her head through the open door. "The journalist is here."

"Wow, so soon."

"You know the old adage. The sooner you get started, the sooner you'll be finished."

"True enough." Claire managed to sound enthusiastic. She couldn't take back her earlier reaction, but she could conduct herself in a manner that would reflect well on Safe Harbor.

It was the only thing to do.

"I want you to meet the reporter. I don't think I mentioned the magazine he's from. *National News Weekly.*"

*National News Weekly?*

No wonder she thought this interview might shake loose a few clues to Claire's past. Was there anyone on the planet who *didn't* read that magazine?

She braced herself as Ms. Verna stepped inside to make room for the person with whom Claire would share her whole sorry story, and did a double take.

"Simon?"

He filled the doorway of the publishing center, broad shoulders blocking out the hall behind him. He looked larger-than-life, as he had the night before, just as stoic, just as big, just as...*wrong*.

Last night he'd been her knight in the expensive suit, shrouded by snow-lit darkness, a man crossing her path for an instant. Now he wore a black wool duster and jeans. He looked imposing with his chisel-cut features and sleek hair touched with gray. A man out of place.

"Last night wasn't a coincidence?" she asked.

"No."

That husky rich voice struck her with the same velvet force, and she mentally gave him points for his honesty. He didn't seem to care that he'd been caught.

"You met Simon last night?" This was news to Ms. Verna.

"I ran into Claire after she left Safe Harbor."

*Ran into* might have been funny, except Ms. Verna didn't need to know the gory details of that meeting. With a desperate glance, she entreated him not to say more and quickly offered, "Simon came to my rescue after I wiped out on my bike. I damaged the wheel so he helped me get home."

"I see."

No doubt Ms. Verna did. She took his stock with a glance, and while Simon might tower over her by more than a foot, she drilled holes in him with her stare. The guy didn't even blink.

"Simon will be yours for the next few days, Claire," she finally said. "I trust you'll assist him however you can. Please tour him around the grounds. I've sent out a memo so the staff from all our facilities will expect your visits."

"The next few *days?*"

"We'll start there." Simon sounded as if crashing her life without an invitation was no big deal. "I'm comfortable with my deadline so I can take time to familiarize myself with Safe Harbor. I want to understand this world and how you fit in."

She screwed a smile on.

"Then I'll leave you two to get further acquainted." Ms. Verna moved closer, slipped a hand over Claire's shoulder and gave a reassuring squeeze. She acknowledged Simon with a nod before heading out the door.

"You really don't want to get on her bad side," Claire cautioned once they were alone. "She might look all warm and fuzzy but she's tough as nails."

"You didn't want her to know about the accident. Why?"

"You've got to understand Ms. Verna. She'll do nothing but worry, and she's got quite enough on her plate already."

"She thinks you're worth worrying about." Pulling a chair from the worktable, he spun it around and sat down.

"Ms. Verna thinks everyone is worth worrying about. Hang around long enough, and she'll worry about you, too."

"You seem fond of her."

"She's easy to be fond of." Claire headed back to her computer. "Do you need my undivided attention?"

"No. I just want to share your day. You can talk to me while you work. I'm generally easy to talk to."

She couldn't argue. She'd been comfortable with him last night. She felt comfortable now. And this crazy urge to…well, *look* at him, as though she'd been waiting to see him. It was a crazy, fluttery feeling, but a feeling she recognized from a time and place gone from her memory. Claire didn't remember details, but she somehow knew this feeling.

"Looks like you'll get your wish, Simon."

"How's that?"

"You wanted to write fiction. Here's your chance. You're going to have to fictionalize me big-time to make Safe Harbor look good. You do want to make us look good, don't you?"

"From what your administrator has told me, you're the one who'll make Safe Harbor look good."

"Let me tell you something. Ms. Verna might have one foot on the highway to heaven with all her caring and devotion for those in need, but her other size five is on terra firma. The woman knows the meaning of public relations. Trust me."

He didn't reply, and she glanced over her shoulder to find him watching her with that look again, a look that made her breath catch in her throat. Claire wasn't sure what her deal was, why she felt this strange awareness around this man, but one thing was certain—she'd never last *days* of this interview if she didn't get a grip on her reaction to him.

"I'll talk while I work, Simon, if that's what you want. But if I have to *share my day*, I'd appreciate some help. Unless you'd rather just sit there."

He smiled, a smile that eased the *stern* from his face. She had the odd thought that he should spend more time smiling.

"What can I do?"

"Assemble books." She might as well get something out of this deal, and watching this man perform manual labor seemed like something she might enjoy.

Circling the table, she demonstrated how to insert the pages inside the covers. His fingers brushed hers as they worked, and the contact of skin against skin made her aware of his hands, strong hands with nails squared uniformly short.

And his hands weren't the only things she noticed. They stood so close that she realized the top of her head reached his chin, and Claire wasn't exactly short.

She was all caught up in this crazy need to look at him, so caught up that when his arm brushed her shoulder as he went for another cover, she backed away so fast a stack of books went with her, tumbling to the floor in a scatter of bright designs.

Simon glanced her way, had the decency not to laugh. "I'm making you nervous."

Since it wasn't a question, she didn't bother answering, just sank to her knees to retrieve the covers.

He earned a few more points for not offering to help. "So what is this place? Will you tell me what you're doing in here?"

"You're in the publishing center where I run a literacy program to help students practice their English. Every student gets to publish a book. The program was set up when I got here, but there wasn't enough manpower to run it. So I took over."

"You seem to enjoy your work."

Enjoy? This place had been her lifeline during the first painful months of her rehabilitation, when she'd been confined to a wheelchair and unable to talk, but had desperately needed some task to occupy her mind and make her feel useful.

"Yeah."

Returning the stack of covers to the worktable, she

went back to her computer. A refuge. She won an unexpected reprieve from Simon's questions when an explosion of footsteps echoed through the hall outside the open door. Leaning back in her chair, Claire waited, amused by the way Simon narrowed his gaze and stepped out from behind the table.

The only threat was a winded young boy who skidded to a stop in her doorway, all urgency and breathless energy. *"Pomagash mi, gospojo Klair?"* he shot out in Bulgarian. *"You help me out, Miss Claire?"*

"Depends on what it'll cost, Dmitar. Let's start with what it'll cost you. How about an attempt at English? And since it's the middle of the period, I'll need a pass, too."

He waved a scrap of blue paper.

"Where to?"

When he caught sight of Simon a grin slowly split his features, and he said in halting, but wonderfully clear English, "You got a boyfriend?"

"No boyfriends today. This gentleman is helping me catch up with the kindergartners' books. Now what about that pass?"

"The office."

"And what you want help with is worth what Dr. Wells will do to you if he catches you clear across the building?"

Dmitar exploded into his native tongue. *"Napisah oshte edna prikaska. Iskam da ia napravia na kniga za Baba."*

In response to a visual prompt from Claire, he took a deep breath and began again. "I wrote another story. I want to make it into a book for Grandma. They won't let her leave the hospital, and she hates it there. Evil

Edelson told me no because I published one this year. But that was for language arts class. Not my grandma."

A big difference, Claire agreed. Especially when Dmitar's grin vanished from his face as if it had never been there. "Get your story on disk. I'll talk to *Mrs.* Edelson."

White teeth flashed. "You rock, Miss Claire."

"And you're about one step from in-school suspension. I can't help you with that, so get to the office."

"I'm gone." Spinning on his high-tops, he left her staring thoughtfully after him.

Such a small effort on her part seemed so out of balance with his smile. Dmitar wanted to span the distance between his room in Safe Harbor's residential facility and the hospital where declining health had forced his grandmother to live. He clung to the hope that age and a hard life wouldn't defeat her, that she wouldn't die and leave him alone in the place where they were supposed to make a better life together.

He'd channeled that hope into a story, and Claire knew how precious hope was, how with one tiny kindness she could breathe life into it for a while longer.

"Not above favoritism, are you?"

Simon's voice brought her back to the moment. She'd withdrawn inside her head and forgotten all about him. She'd have to remember to thank Dmitar.

"A perk to the volunteer thing," she said. "If I don't get paid, I can't get fired."

But as she looked at Simon, she knew that wasn't entirely true. Sometimes there were debts of honor, and they had to be paid, like it or not.

SIMON REALIZED as the day progressed that while Violet might have agreed to this interview, she intended to make him work for any real information. And not only by assembling books. He asked the questions, but she wasn't yielding up much more than surface responses.

He thought of the eastern European boy who'd stopped by earlier and knew Violet's idealism had survived the loss of her memory. Simon had always blamed that idealism on her upbringing as the only child of two linguistic anthropologists. Violet had grown up studying dialects in remote locales that had made the world her playground.

She'd been a natural in the field and one of his most skilled operatives. From reigning monarchies or shifting political regimes to terrorist cells or drug-running street thugs, she could walk onto any scene and belong.

It had been more than her linguistic skill—although fluency with languages and her ability to pick up dialects had made her invaluable to Excelsior. But combined with that gift for adaptability, she'd been a chameleon.

He wasn't surprised that she'd slipped into life here at Safe Harbor and embraced the people and place with both hands.

"Claire, how did you end up at Safe Harbor?"

"Dumb luck." She made a few impatient keystrokes then rolled her chair to the printer cycling out a stream of paper.

"Ms. Joyce wouldn't tell me much. She said this was your story to tell."

"No mystery. A Global Coalition envoy picked me up on a mountaintop in Bosnia. I'd been injured, so they transported me to an emergency safe house in Austria. I needed rehab, and Safe Harbor had the medical facilities to accommodate my needs."

"What kind of injuries?"

"Nearest we can figure is that I was in some sort of accident. Broken bones, mountain sickness. The Global Coalition branch running relief efforts out of Zagreb put out an official inquiry with all the NGOs, but there were over three hundred in the province at the time. No one claimed me, so they shipped me back to North America."

Of course, Global Coalition would have targeted the nongovernmental organizations. There were no governments with military forces in the area at the time.

Except for his, and he hadn't been able to claim her.

*Code 13—sever ties to protect Excelsior.*

"Why do you think you were over there?" he asked.

"Haven't a clue, but I must have had some reason for being in the middle of a civil war. I'm obviously not a native."

"You know that for sure?"

She turned just enough so he could see her wry expression in profile. "Simon, I don't know anything for sure except what I live and what I've been told. The envoy that picked me up said I was talking to King Arthur in French. Go figure."

Years in black ops helped him contain his reaction, but no amount of training could wipe away the emotion that knifed through him with that name.

She'd been asking for *him.*

"Any guesses?"

She pushed away from the computer and stood. "Maybe I was researching local legends to write a book."

"In the middle of a civil war. There's a thought." He tried to sound amused. "What have you been doing to find out?"

"Global Coalition made routine inquiries, but there are a couple of factors at play here. The political situation is a nightmare over there." Shaking her head, she moved to the sewing machine to sit down and slip a thin stack of papers onto the tray. "I told you there were a lot of NGOs providing relief when I was found. Some were big names like Global Coalition and Feed the Kids, but others were nothing more than well-meaning university students who pooled their resources to rent a truck and make a grocery run."

"What else?"

"I haven't exactly been in a position to travel. To be honest, whatever I was there for feels frightening and ugly."

"So you're content not knowing who you are?"

She gazed over her shoulder at him, bright eyes sparkling, a familiar expression from long ago. "But I do know. I'm someone who deals with not knowing the truth. I cope. Not always well, I admit, but I've been given a new life. I'm trying to live it like it means something."

He'd never understood Violet's determination to believe that everything would work out okay. Perhaps he'd seen too much ugliness. Life wasn't always fair. Good didn't always conquer evil. He lived that reality daily at Excelsior.

He'd seen that reality in number twelve detention camp, in Violet's sacrifice to protect Excelsior. She'd suffered to provide the evidence he needed to force NATO's hand, to carry out mission objective, but had lost herself in the process.

Yet still she believed life would work out in the end.

"You can close up that glue, Simon," she said. "We

need to discuss logistics. I've got to get some writing done so I'm heading home. I won't be back here until tomorrow morning."

"Not a problem. I'd like to see you work."

"You're a writer. You know as well as I do there's nothing to *see*."

"I'd like to see *where* you work then." Tightening the lid on the rubber cement, he replaced the jar on the shelf.

"Are you planning to *share my days* 24-7 until this interview is over?"

If Simon hadn't have known her so well, he might have missed the sarcasm. But he knew this woman, and recognized one of the first big differences between the Violet he'd known and this woman named Claire.

When Violet had been irritated with him, she'd never bothered to hide it.

"Not 24-7," he said mildly. "My powers of observation suffer if I don't sleep."

She didn't dignify that with a reply, just located a book with whales on the cover and grabbed her jacket. "Let's go. I don't want to keep you from your beauty rest, and I've still got to make a pit stop."

They headed out of the school into the bitter wind. Slipping the book inside her jacket, Violet flipped up her collar and jammed her hands deep into the pockets. She bristled with pride while leading him across the grounds, grim in her determination to freeze rather than admit her torn coat didn't protect her from the weather.

Glancing around the property, he assessed their surroundings. His perimeter team was in place, hidden eyes that swept the property wall in four-minute intervals, constantly scanning anomalies and potential threats. Safeguarding Violet.

Yet she walked by his side, still in the cold.

When they finally arrived at the residential facility, the sight of the three-story house only lent weight to Simon's mood. The place might have boasted a certain charm with its mansard roof and covered porch, but winter had bleached the life out, leaving worn shingles and faded wood. Two plastic Christmas cactuses flanked the front steps, a homey touch that only broadcast the transience of the residents who lived there.

Taking his cue from Violet, he stomped the snow from his boots before following her inside. She didn't remove her jacket but called out, "Hey, Christine, you around?"

A dark-haired woman appeared in a nearby doorway, balancing an industrial-size container of popcorn. "Getting ready for movie night. What's up?"

"Will she be going back to school tomorrow?"

The woman glanced his way before nodding. "If you don't get her worked up and coughing again."

"Promise." Violet turned to him. "I'll just be a few minutes. You can wait here."

She took to the steps and disappeared around the upper landing. He followed.

"Claire!" a child squealed.

"Hey, kiddo. How are you feeling today?"

Another squeal drew Simon to a door where he found a curly-haired girl sitting in the middle of a throw rug with a coloring book and crayons scattered around her.

Violet knelt and presented the whale book. "I thought you'd want to read it during circle time tomorrow."

"Everyone will think I'm special 'cuz you made mine first."

"That's because you are special, *les grands yeux verts.*"

"What's that mean?"

Violet brushed an eyelash and made the child blink. "Green eyes. Or do you like *grote groene ogen* better? That's Flemish."

The child dropped the book and threw her arms around Violet's neck with enough force to knock her off balance. They pitched backward in a tangle of arms and legs.

"Gabrielle, your elbow's digging in my ribs." Violet laughed. "And you can't start coughing. I promised."

The child—Gabrielle—only clung like a monkey while Violet maneuvered them into a better position. Then she stroked the dark blond hair from the child's face. Simon eased back into the shadows to watch, and they still hadn't noticed him when a coughing fit finally broke them apart.

Violet reached for the book. "Why don't you read to me? Practice for tomorrow."

With another cough, Gabrielle scrambled into her lap, and Violet cradled her close, resting her chin on top of her head.

Another favorite, he guessed.

Simon couldn't count the number of times Violet had dumped strays on him after missions. Orphaned children fleeing war-torn cities. The wife and infant of a mortally wounded soldier. The sister of a deposed dictator who would have been murdered. Refugees who'd been forced to flee their homeland.

She'd been young, idealistic. She'd believed the aftermath of mission objective was as important as mission objective itself, and she'd held him to that standard, never understanding that sometimes he couldn't serve both purposes. Sometimes he had no choice but to view the big picture and make hard choices.

He watched her kiss the child's head. Picking up strays was a part of her repertoire that had transcended memory. She and Gabrielle were a pair. Even their well-worn clothing connected them, bound them in circumstance, both beholden to Safe Harbor for their care, yet still proud, still believers.

He wanted to follow Violet's example and believe all would turn out right because he faced another hard choice now. To fulfill his obligations to Excelsior, and to her, he'd have to disturb this peaceful world she'd created for herself. He would force her to trade security for fear, to sacrifice love for the brutality she'd suffered for Excelsior.

He had the resources to give Violet time to remember, and he would. But he didn't have the power to grant her forever. He had to unravel what had happened in number twelve detention camp, or he couldn't guarantee her safety.

# CHAPTER SIX

CLAIRE CLIMBED OUT of Simon's rental car. This car wasn't the same car as last night's though, just as expensive, but a different model and color.

She didn't comment but led him inside her building, steeling herself to share her natural habitat. On the plus side, she'd have electricity. She'd paid the bill only a few days ago, with the payment from a magazine story that had finally run in last month's issue. She was good to go for thirty days. Now, if the furnace worked…

Claire fit the key in the lock and held her breath… It was warm inside. "Come on in."

Simon strode in, all six feet, however many inches of him, and seemed to suck up all the air in her efficiency. Those clear eyes raked over her possessions. His jaw worked double time.

Tension bubbled inside her, burst out as a stream of chatter. "I only moved in two months ago. It's taking a while to pull it all together. You've got to use your imagination."

Grabbing a fistful of his sleeve, she led him toward the window. "I hung the shade last week. Think Victorian. Floral and pinstriped valance. Lace draped over the futon. Doilies on the end table. Can you see it?"

For some inexplicable reason, she cared what this

man thought, needed him to understand that her place wasn't only a small efficiency in a run-down neighborhood, but an enormous step she'd made toward taking control of her life.

His stern features softened around the edges. "It'll look good. Thanks for inviting me."

Claire sensed no mockery and eased her grip. "Let me take your coat."

He slid his arms free, and she pulled it away. A coatrack hadn't made the top of her amenity list yet so she hung it inside her closet, beside her own.

"Want a drink? I'm making espresso."

He nodded, his gaze following her to the kitchenette. There was no missing the espresso machine that sat in a position of honor on the counter.

"My housewarming gift from Ms. Verna and the staff." She didn't mention she only brewed the El Cheap-O grind from the corner bodega. He'd find that out all too soon.

"Speaking of Ms. Joyce." Simon settled at the bar separating the kitchenette from the rest of her place. "She mentioned you'd moved from Safe Harbor recently. Why?"

"It was time. The cost of housing there is astronomical. And forget about medical treatment, counseling and job placement. There are others a lot needier than I am."

"Was this your assessment or Ms. Joyce's?"

"Mine," she admitted, hating the way that sounded. As if the basket case had diagnosed herself. "Ms. Verna wasn't crazy about the idea. She understands, though."

"Understands what?"

"That I need to take control of my life again."

"Isn't that what she wants for you?"

"Of course. But she thinks I'm impatient."

"Are you?"

She shrugged then reached into the cabinet for a mug. "I don't have real milk but I keep powdered creamer for Ms. Verna."

"Black is fine. So how is being impatient bad?"

"It's not—in my opinion."

Simon smiled, and Claire couldn't get over how one simple smile melted away so much sternness from his face. He was really very handsome when he smiled. She wondered if he knew.

"That's what I'm interested in. Your opinion."

The espresso machine sputtered, a welcome distraction from a moment that suddenly carried too much weight. Glancing at the machine, she watched ribbons of steam curl upward from the pot, unable to deny that her kitchenette had never felt as tiny as it did with this man on the opposite side of the counter.

That feeling was creeping in again, the same feeling that had prompted her to climb into his car last night. He felt familiar, although she couldn't say why. There was just something about this breathlessness, this ridiculous awareness that came so easily.

It was a crazy feeling, one that drew her gaze back to him, made her notice little things. The way the dark turtleneck spanned the width of his broad shoulders and chest, hinted at the flex of firm muscles below when he rested an elbow on the counter. The granite cut of his jaw when he glanced at the old computer system and her other secondhand furniture.

Despite the *stern* he wore like armor, Simon Brandauer was a very attractive man. Entirely out of her league, but then she hadn't always been in this situation. Before a Bosnian mountaintop and Global Coalition, she'd had a life.

Claire poured the rich black espresso into the mug, set it on the bar in front of him.

"Aren't you having any?" he asked.

"I'll make more." She withdrew her thermal mug from the drain board in the sink. "I drink industrial quantities."

He sipped, nodded his approval. "Just what I needed."

He didn't seem to mind the bitter stuff—or was too polite to comment. Emptying the filter basket, she scooped in more coffee. "Simon, would you mind letting me proof your article before you go to print?"

"Worried?"

"You're not using a recorder or taking notes. I just want to make sure you get it right."

"I'm not using a recorder or taking notes because I don't intend to use the details. I want to understand who you are and why you're here, so I can write about what Safe Harbor has done for you and what you do for the people who live there."

When he explained the situation like that, baring her soul didn't sound nearly as intrusive as it felt. "Then you won't mind letting me read your draft."

"I won't mind." His gaze caught and held hers, those clear eyes cutting as if he could see straight through her, as if he understood more about her than she did herself.

Claire had stopped speculating on what or whom she might have left behind in her life before Safe Harbor, but right now with Simon's gaze on her and that curious fluttering feeling making it hard to breathe, she couldn't help but wonder if she'd once had someone who'd made her feel this way.

SIMON PAUSED on the second-floor landing and waited for Violet to close her door before heading down the hall to the apartment he'd had his team set up as a hub in Sault Ste. Marie.

"I'm here," he said to TJ via his audio device.

Sure enough, the door to apartment 81B swung wide as he approached. He found Quinn waiting.

She took his briefcase, set it on the dining room table, and gestured around the room. "Is this what you had in mind?"

He glanced around. Generic rental furniture. Low-key electronic equipment. White blinds. No curtains. "Good."

"What did Violet have to say about you renting an apartment in her building?"

"I haven't told her yet."

Quinn arched a brow. "What are you waiting for?"

"Until she asks." Shrugging out of his coat, he hung it in the closet. "She seems willing to accept whatever I tell her."

"That's very good news."

"Status?"

"Everything's in place. The perimeter team is rotating in four-hour shifts and technical secured her apartment while you were at Safe Harbor. Delinquent," she said, talking to TJ through her own audio device, "switch King Arthur's frequency to Wolfgang's channel."

Simon heard a crack of static in the tiny device wedged in his ear and then what sounded like the steady tapping of keystrokes on a computer keyboard.

"Are you receiving?" Quinn asked.

He nodded. The crucifix around Violet's neck was transmitting loud and clear. She was exactly where he'd left her—hard at work on her latest story. "How's Niky holding up?"

"This is hard for him."

"This is hard for us all. Can I depend on him?"

"What assignment?"

"Protection." He intended to keep Niky under his thumb so he could keep an eye on him while keeping an eye on Violet.

"I think that's a good call. Niky's up to protection. I think Major will be much more use tracking down a threat."

Simon nodded, pleased she didn't question him further. He didn't want to draw any more attention to the fact that until he knew whether or not a threat had followed him to Violet, he had to treat Command as if there was a leak. Niky's connection to the detention camp made him even more suspect.

"You stocked food, didn't you?" he asked.

"I can make you a sandwich while you check in with Maxim. He has a few questions."

"Please."

Simon retreated into the bedroom, pulled off his boots, set them in the closet. He made contact with the operative he'd left in charge of Command in his stead, and by the time he completed his conversation, Quinn had a sandwich ready.

"Thanks." He carried the plate into the dining room and sat at the table.

"How are you?"

"Hungry. Violet doesn't stop long enough to eat a meal."

"This shouldn't be coming as news."

"It's not." Although that wasn't entirely true. While Simon had overseen Violet's training, he'd never worked in the field with her. As he was learning today, *watching* Violet work was different than *working* with Violet. Even without her memory, she was a woman who approached everything she did with passion and intensity.

"We can talk while you eat," Quinn said.

"I'm maintaining."

"Of course. But how do you feel about all this? Violet is in a frightening place right now. How does that affect you?"

He envisioned her sitting upstairs at her computer, writing about a world she didn't consciously recognize as her own. Was she also writing clues that put her life in danger? "I want to know Command is secure so I can bring her in. I want her safe and getting the help she needs."

"Do you believe that's the best course of action?"

He reached for the sandwich and took a bite while considering his answer. Then he said, "You heard her earlier. She feels that if anyone from her past cared, they would have found her by now."

"That's how Claire feels, Simon. Not Violet. Be clear on the difference."

"I should have found her."

"Guilt is a normal response. Your commitment to Excelsior requires you to make choices. They're never without consequences."

"I know."

"We're all having trouble detaching."

"I brought her into Command."

"She was old enough to make her own choices."

"I started recruiting her the minute I met her. I just didn't invite her to join us until she had no place else to go. She was vulnerable."

"She was," Quinn agreed. "Most girls her age would be. She'd just lost her parents in a tragic accident, and you were a family friend. Violet lacked direction. You offered her something to believe in."

"Not because it was best for her."

"Because it was best for Excelsior. You needed a linguist. Violet was the best choice for the job."

He took another bite of the sandwich, but the food lodged in his throat. He'd only become involved with Violet's family so he wouldn't lose his chance to woo Violet into the agency as she matured. The fact that he'd wound up genuinely liking her parents had been nothing more than an unexpected bonus.

"You're the absolute power in Excelsior. You decide what constitutes a threat to national security. Several hundred highly skilled employees answer solely to you. Periodic reports to the president and Oversight committee aren't the same thing as sharing the responsibility, Simon. The burden of power is bound to weigh heavily at times. You know that."

A mental image of Violet's kitchenette sprang to mind, scrubbed so clean that every surface shone despite the stove's cracked enamel surface and the scarred linoleum floor.

*"I've been given a new life. I'm trying to live it like it means something."* Her words echoed in his memory, so heartfelt.

He pushed the plate away. "You spent the day reviewing her medical records. What's her prognosis?"

Quinn glanced at his uneaten meal, and he regretted asking her to prepare it. "Not as bad as it could be. Her amnesia doesn't appear to be biological. But understand that Violet's a survivor of political imprisonment. She witnessed indiscriminate killing. She suffered interrogation and torture. These are man-made traumas, the most difficult to rationalize. She'll have to learn to integrate what happened into who she is now."

"Do you think she can?"

"Even knowing Violet isn't helping me with that assessment. Her strength of will gives me hope, but the bottom line is—I can't evaluate with any certainty until I talk to her."

Quinn gave a smile meant to reassure, but the gesture only drew attention to how none of them had any objectivity. Seeing glimmers of his operative in the woman who called herself Claire only made him regret how he hadn't known she'd liked candles.

"Keep the faith, Simon. Five months in that detention camp didn't kill her. Neither did her injuries. Once you see her medical files, you'll realize what a miracle that is. The fact she's survived this long tips the odds in our favor."

"What can we do to help her remember?"

"That's the tricky part. Technically, she's suffering post-traumatic stress disorder. There are no absolutes. Each victim is an individual case."

"What if I pull in team one and keep throwing familiar faces at her? Do you think she'll recognize one of us?"

"She already recognizes one of us." Quinn met his gaze and this time her smile reached her eyes. "According to what Ms. Verna said this morning, Violet steers clear of anyone outside Safe Harbor. The fact that she's so willing to accept you into her life suggests she recognizes you on some level. At least she knows you're not a threat."

Simon digested this information. "What's your opinion? Should I bring her in?"

"Her safety is at issue anywhere until you pinpoint the threat. But I think your instincts are on target. She feels safe here. She's progressing through the healing process and taking control of her life. I think she'll be much better off remembering on her own than by us forcing her."

He glanced at the file folders stacked neatly on the coffee table in the living room. Violet's life since number twelve detention camp. "All right. Give me some time to review her files. Then I'll decide."

Quinn disappeared, taking his plate back to the kitchen, which told him she didn't think he'd have much appetite left after he saw what was inside.

Simon sat on the couch, opened the first folder and scanned through doctor's reports dating back to Bosnia.

Undepressed skull fracture.
Sterno-clavicular separation.
Fractured clavicle. Dislocated pelvis.
Contusions on seventy percent of body.
Paralytic phase of hypothermia.
Acute mountain sickness: cyanosis of the lips and fingernails, retinal hemorrhage.

But for the Global Coalition envoy, Violet would have died on a mountaintop, and Simon would never have found her. And as he scanned page after page of dry facts, his head echoed with the voices of witnesses who had testified before the war crimes tribunal. Starvation, beatings, executions committed in the name of ethnic cleansing.

He'd sent a team into that detention camp, never thinking about worst-case scenario. He'd considered mission failure only in global terms. If his team didn't extract the defector, NATO couldn't move. Tens of thousands more lives would be forfeit.

Violet's life and the lives of her teammates had been forfeit instead. He'd sacrificed them, had rationalized his actions in the name of national security. She'd sent back another defector, and that man's testimony had accomplished mission objective.

But every time he'd stood inside her town house, every time he'd caught her watching him with that curious expression today, Simon had to ask himself if the sacrifice could be balanced against the cost. His rationale seemed to crumble with each page he scanned of carefully detailed medical evaluations.

*The first words she'd spoken after ten weeks spent with her mouth wired shut to set her broken jaw.*

*Her first trip down a hall in a wheelchair when she'd recovered enough to sit upright.*

*Her first steps with a walker to rehabilitate her pelvis.*

*The date when the header on her files had changed from Anonymous Female Origin Bosnia to Claire de Beaupré.*

Simon wondered if she'd chosen the name or if someone had chosen it for her. She'd created her alias for Excelsior, too, a beautiful name for a beautiful operative that he'd never let himself know on any level except professional, a woman who'd haunted him since the day he'd lost her.

And as Simon sat there, considering Violet and his obsession with her, his obligation to her and his opportunity for a second chance, he knew what he had to do.

Glancing up from the folders, he found Quinn still in the kitchen. "Team one goes into place. I'll keep point. We'll find Niky a position in the school where he can back me up. You'll go in as a new psychiatrist, and we'll ask Ms. Joyce to assign Violet as your patient. Maybe you can get her to talk.

"Major will be my literary agent. He'll offer to represent Violet so she'll send her work to him. That'll stop any more stories from circulating in the public sector. I'll place Frances in charge of analyzing her work. If there are any clues that are leaving a trail of bread crumbs, she'll find them."

"Agreed," Quinn said. "You do realize there are no guidelines to dictate Violet's recovery, though. How long are you prepared to stay?"

Simon closed the last folder. "As long as I possibly can. She's been waiting three years for me to find her."

*5:45 p.m. CET*
*Strpski Grad Republika, -2°C*

THE TELEPHONE CALL CAME as Ivan Zubac's driver drove through the main gates of his villa. Cradling the receiver against his ear, he spoke to his assistant.

"Put him on hold then transfer the call to my house phone."

His Western contact could wait. Not only did Ivan prefer to take the call in his office where all lines were secure rather than on his cellular, but the man on the other end obviously needed a show of power. A reminder.

Ivan expected his people to serve him with competency and respect. Providing misinformation was neither. Misinformation could place his identity in jeopardy, and that would not do.

Reputation was everything, for without it, he could not command, could effect no changes for his country. Because geography and man-made boundaries had not favored his people with an abundance of Adriatic coastlines to attract tourists did not mean they would be forced to serve others.

The years of oppression were over. He helped usher in this new era, would earn his country respect from the global community. After decades in the Citizen's Army within Yugoslavia, Ivan had the expertise and the connections to effect this change. Rising to the appointment of defense minister in the newly formed Strpski Grad Republika had been a big step.

But it was only a first. While the international stabilization and implementation forces—SFOR and IFOR respectively—kept peace within their borders, Ivan would lay the foundation for an army and continue his rise to the top.

The car stopped at the entrance. His butler appeared at the door, and Ivan stepped out, strode up the portico steps with a sense of contentment and pride. His villa was comfortable rather than large, a home befitting the post of a defense minister, yet not so conspicuous as to invite censure in a land struggling to recover from war.

His staff had assembled in the foyer to await his arrival. Six people he trusted in his home. Greeting his people with a nod, he handed his coat to his housekeeper, advised his chef of a guest for the meal. He handed his briefcase to his aide-de-camp then made his way into his office and closed the door, knowing his security chief would post himself outside.

Seating himself at his desk, Ivan reached for the telephone, satisfied the man on the other end would be impatient to get to business. A power play, true, but a necessary one.

"Explain yourself," he spoke into the receiver.

"My agency already had a lock on the target."

His contact sounded inconvenienced, perhaps even hurried to make this call in secret. Good. "You didn't know?"

A harsh laugh. "There are a lot of things I don't know."

"What is this woman's connection to number twelve camp?"

"Our investigation cleared her. She's under surveillance because her published works raised red flags. Turns out they're all fiction. No threat to us."

"You reported this woman to me without evidence?"

"I had evidence. My agency was investigating her. Would you rather I waited until we discovered a legitimate connection?"

The silence fell heavily, left Ivan debating whether he should accept such an explanation. His contact was with the United States National Security Agency, trained by a government boasting its superiority to the world. He was no paramilitary guerrilla who'd been handed an assault rifle and told to pretend he was a soldier.

An image flashed in Ivan's mind, a memory of his

Western contact pleading for his life inside number twelve camp.

*"I have the name, but you don't get it free."*

Even bloodied and on his knees this man had negotiated, which meant he was probably lying now.

"You have placed me in an awkward position," Ivan finally said. "A dangerous one."

"That's why I called. The threat has been eliminated, but my agency won't bring the woman in. They'll keep her under surveillance for ninety days. Standard procedure. I wanted you to know to cover your tracks. This won't happen again."

That much, at least, Ivan knew for truth.

He disconnected the line then dialed a number with a Russian country code by memory. A bright feminine voice answered on the third ring, "Yes."

"Nadia, my sweet. I need information...."

# CHAPTER SEVEN

*7:08 a.m. EST*
*Sault. Ste. Marie, 11°C*

"An agent, Simon? But why?" Claire took a fortifying sip of espresso, stared into the cup to avoid the freshly showered look of the man who'd arrived over an hour early this morning.

No good. There was nothing to rival the sight of his still-damp hair and cheeks that glowed faintly pink from a recent shave. She took another hot gulp.

"It's a matter of function," he explained. "You write. The agent sells."

"I understand the premise. I understand why you'd want one, and it speaks to your credentials that this agent is willing to leave his writing conference and cross the border to have breakfast with you. I don't understand why you want *me* there."

"You're an author, Claire. This is an opportunity for you to get a reputable agent to represent your work."

"You're joking, right? I don't have your credentials."

He arched a dark eyebrow, clamped his hands on the countertop and leaned over the bar. "You have your own credentials. You've published a lot more fiction than I have and have even won some industry awards."

"I don't know how it works in the journalism world, but in fiction land, industry awards are nothing more than promotional hype. I'm only as good as my last sell-through and until I break into mass market, I don't have sell-through."

"But you have the novel you're working on. You said it's almost finished."

"The first draft is done. As soon as I finish revising, I'll send it out."

"That's what an agent does. He gets editors to respond quicker."

That Simon had arranged this meeting didn't surprise her. He'd been tossed smack into the middle of her sorry situation, and he wanted to help.

Claire understood. What she didn't understand was why his offer prickled her pride. She'd been the recipient of enough charity since coming to Safe Harbor to know the drill. But for some reason accepting Simon's help made her raw and defensive. She wanted to shine in front of him and didn't understand why.

Why should she care what Simon Brandauer thought of her?

Taking a deep breath, Claire pushed aside all the emotional stuff and decided to accept his gesture at face value. "Thank you for including me, Simon. I'd like to meet your agent."

"Good. We're meeting for breakfast at a diner not far from here. We'll have plenty of time before you're due in the publishing center."

So before she'd indulged in a second cup of espresso, Claire found herself inside his car again, clutching a box that held the first draft of a full-length manuscript. She'd also brought along copies of a few short stories and a novella to represent the quality of her published work.

As she stared out into the city streets, paled with the groggy winter dawn, she rehearsed questions to ask during breakfast. She wanted to present herself professionally, so Simon wouldn't regret his kindness.

She kept her gaze fixed through the window, so aware of him beside her, filling the compact space with his presence, in command of the quiet. Even his silence gave the impression that big things were going on inside his head.

"Claire, I'm curious. Why did you start to write?" His rich silky voice had the power to convince her he'd been giving even this simple question a great deal of thought. "It seems like an unusual choice. The market's tight, the pay sporadic. I can think of so many easier ways to make a living."

"No doubt there, but I sort of fell into writing. I had some injuries that prevented me from talking. A wired jaw. Then some surgeries to put in implants and bridges, so I could smile." She flashed a wide one, so he could admire the marvel of modern dentistry. "I had to communicate somehow, so I wrote."

"How did communicating turn into stories to sell?"

"I was having dreams." She willed herself to stop obsessing over Simon's opinion. Her whole life had been a string of humiliations since she'd awakened with no memory. Why should now be any different? "My doctor suggested I write them down. It was an exercise to help me describe and control what I was feeling."

"Do you think those dreams were clues from your past?"

God, she hoped not. She'd given Simon the G version. Her *dreams* had been *nightmares*. And not the bogeyman variety.

Shrugging, she dragged her gaze from the sidewalk that swept past them, where sand and snow combined to make a muddy mess. "I think I just have an active imagination."

His frown suggested her answer had somehow disappointed him, and the silence fell heavily. She couldn't help wondering if he'd stopped asking questions because he thought she was too fragile to answer them.

"All right. You want to know what I *really* think?" she asked, not waiting for a reply. "I have an active imagination because I needed to make up wild stories for some excitement in a totally forgettable life."

Simon shifted his gaze from the road to look at her then, a flash of *something* in those translucent eyes that made her want to take her admission back.

She was saved from any further conversation when he wheeled into the diner's parking lot, parked the car then escorted her over the icy lot into the busy restaurant.

Claire had never met a literary agent, but somehow Major Hickman didn't fit the image she'd had in her head. When she thought of literary, she thought of New York, which she must have seen sometime because she had a clear picture of what it looked like in her head.

Major Hickman wasn't Manhattan. He wasn't any one of the boroughs. The man who strode across the diner toward them was chapped around the edges, a cowboy off the cover of a Western novel. He smiled lazily when he saw them and waved a large hand. He removed his hat and Claire saw that he had just enough curl in his brown hair to give him a serious case of hat hair.

"A pleasure to meet you, little lady."

Claire wanted to clap him on the back and say, "You, too, partner." But she resisted, extending her hand and muttering a greeting that wouldn't make Simon regret inviting her along.

"And here we are in real time." Major did clap Simon on the back, but her stoic companion didn't seem to mind.

They followed Major back to a booth, where he motioned for coffee and got straight to business. Claire listened with interest as he and Simon discussed positioning his work to the market. She was further impressed with this agent when he talked craft, complimenting Simon on his characterization and making a few recommendations about pacing that she found informative.

"Simon's quite a fan of yours," Major said after a server had left with their order. "He's got nothing but high praise for your work. Why don't you tell me what you've got going on?"

"I've been selling steadily for the past year and a half." Claire rattled off her sales history, amused by how successful she sounded. Success that hadn't exactly translated into cash.

"The market's flooded with police procedurals and sleuths right now," Major said. "So your espionage worlds could attract some interest. But you're writing across the board. Straight suspense. Mysteries. Romance. Have you thought about developing your name in one market?"

"The editors I sell to can't publish me often enough to keep me busy. I've had to diversify."

"Mass market will be different. Are you planning to cut back production with your short stories?"

"I'll have to."

Major nodded. "Why don't you send me everything you're working on right now?"

He sounded as if he'd already decided to represent her. "I heard most agents aren't interested in short fiction."

"Most aren't." He flashed a wide grin and reached out to pat her hand, an easy gesture that suggested all this touchy-feely stuff was an inherent part of the man. "Neither am I. Fifteen percent of your article pay won't make me rich."

He was a charmer this one. A hero from a Western who knew how to pave his way with his Midwest drawl and rugged allure.

"If we work together, Claire, it's in my best interest to help you sort out your schedule so you can make time to write things I can sell. Send me everything you've got. I'll take a look and then we can talk again."

She found Simon watching her with an encouraging expression and decided the man would have no hesitation whatsoever about strong-arming this agent into representing her.

"So you're willing to help me plan my career," she said. "I gathered from your conversation about Simon's book that you like a hand in editorial, too."

"I like my hands in it all, little lady. The editors prefer I only offer them a certain caliber of work. Makes their jobs easier, which makes my job easier. And it gives me clout. As far as career planning goes, that's good business, too. I need to know where you want to go, so I can help get you there. So, where do you want to be a year from now?"

"On the *New York Times* bestseller list. But I'll settle for contracting with a house that will give me a reasonable advance and a decent print run."

Major laughed. "Sound plan."

Claire met his gaze and smiled, feeling sure that her career had just taken a turn for the better.

NIKY SEARCHED FOR the woman he'd once known in the tall blonde who walked through the door to the administrator's office, all cool beauty and bristling pride.

"Thank you for coming, Claire." Ms. Joyce smiled. "You, too, Simon. It's reassignment time at Global Coalition, and we're fortunate enough to have several new staff members joining us. This gentleman is of particular interest to you, Claire. He's our new assistant principal and will be handling our volunteer programs. Niky Camerisi, meet Claire de Beaupré, the woman who single-handedly runs our school publishing center."

"A pleasure, Ms. de Beaupré." He extended his hand, felt his breath hitch as her cool fingers glided against his, his sense of unreality growing.

Violet might have no memory of her life before Safe Harbor, but the beautiful woman she once was still shone through the woman who looked at him now. She greeted him as a stranger, but he recognized her gaze— gorgeous violet eyes sweeping over him, summing up the man and his character in a glance.

He wished she would smile. Laughter had always been their special gift, the connection that bound them. But no recognition flickered in those amazing eyes. Violet only nodded politely and said, "Welcome to Safe Harbor."

She withdrew her hand, and the moment ended.

Moving to a seat before the desk, he sat beside Violet, another person who proved escaping the death camp was worse than dying inside it.

In Violet's skewed reality, she somehow missed how they all sat poised on the edge of her every word, waiting for her to suddenly wake up and remember the past. Simon wanted every grisly detail. Niky wanted the truth to stay buried forever. For her sake. He wondered what Ms. Joyce wanted.

The woman took control of the meeting, confidently explaining the cover they'd provided her. He interjected when necessary, offering background information from a made-up history with Global Coalition.

Simon hovered. He watched them all perform like monkeys, not from Systems Ops over a long chain of satellite signals, but from two feet away. Instead of issuing orders from a distance, he was able to mold and shape the course of events at his whim.

And Niky sensed his agitation. As acting director of Excelsior, Simon had carte blanche to move around the globe like a shadow. But even though he'd plunged himself into the thick of this mess, he couldn't do a damn thing to fix Violet.

Quinn had explained how Violet appeared to have accepted that Simon wasn't a threat. Niky hoped she might sense the trust they'd once shared, too, remember on some level the countless times they'd depended upon each other to survive.

He needed her to.

"Funding is a constant struggle," Violet told him. "With so much need at Safe Harbor, there usually isn't money left for extraneous programs, no matter how important they are."

Picking up the pencil, Niky forced himself to take notes, to play his role. "Where do we draw the funds now?"

She launched into an explanation of allocations for school improvement, and Niky met Simon's gaze above her head, a goddamned expressionless gaze as if listening to this brilliant, beautiful woman pitch some ridiculous kid program wasn't ripping his heart right out through his throat.

Maybe it wasn't. Simon's only concern was mission objective—prying the truth out of Violet's memory.

But not even Violet knew the truth about Zubac.


"WE DID IT." Claire held up a book covered in kittens to show Simon. "This is the very last one."

Of course they'd started yesterday and had worked until six o'clock last night in a marathon session of cardio-vascular book publishing. But after meeting the new assistant principal yesterday, she'd jetted between her computer, printer and sewing machine while Simon had glued pages into covers, cracking jokes about how they didn't notice the passing hours because they were high on rubber-cement fumes. No argument there. And they'd started frying brain cells even earlier this morning.

"Seventy-five kindergartners' books done with three days to spare till Winter Festival. This is a record. I'm usually gluing up until the last minute. I couldn't have done it without you."

He gifted her with a rare smile. "My pleasure. The least I could do since you've been such an accommodating interviewee."

No argument there, either. "The students will have

plenty of time to illustrate their books before they go on display." She glanced at the clock. "In fact, if I hurry, I can deliver these before lunch starts."

"What about Ms. Joyce? She asked you to stop by her office this morning."

"I'll drop these off on the way."

Simon clearly assumed he was invited because he moved to the door and grabbed their coats.

If he noticed she'd swapped her leather jacket for a gorgeous dark wool that Ms. Verna had given to her privately after meeting the new assistant principal, he didn't say anything. The coat had come with the donations, clearly a casualty of someone's whim because it looked brand-new.

After grabbing the books, they left the publishing center and wound through the hallways toward the kindergarten classrooms. The students saw them as soon as they opened the door, and excited chatter started at her familiar appearance.

The teacher, who apparently knew she didn't stand a chance at containing the chaos until she gave out the books, smiled indulgently while they deposited the stacks on her desk.

She clapped. "All right, clean up your centers. When that's done, I'll pass out your books. Now let's thank Miss Claire."

Twenty-four young voices raised dutifully in chorus. Claire introduced Simon and the students thanked him, too.

"You got them started when you sent Gabrielle's book for circle time yesterday," the teacher said as the students cleaned up their supplies. "They've been waiting for you ever since."

"My pleasure." And Claire was glad Simon could see her someplace where her skills mattered, where what she did counted.

As she worked her way toward Gabrielle, she strolled through the tables, greeting the young students in a game they liked to play. For each one who greeted her in English, she greeted them in their native tongue. Soon the classroom filled with enthusiastic voices calling out, "Hello, Miss Claire."

"*Selamat pagi,* Chandra."

"*Jambo,* Shani."

"*Kalimera,* Stavros."

"*Zdravstvuite,* Lena."

"*Ni hao,* Eumeh."

And on and on until she finally reached her target with a laughing, "*Bonjour,* Gabrielle. Feeling better?"

"Yep." She wrapped her arms around Claire's legs and gave a hearty squeeze to demonstrate her strength.

Claire stroked her wispy curls. "You have a great day."

"Will you come to lunch?"

Claire often slipped away from the publishing center to pop by the cafeteria and share a little together time, a bright spot in her days. "I've got to see Ms. Verna, so I can't promise. But I'll try, okay? If I can't today, I'll come tomorrow."

Another hearty squeeze assured her a promise was good enough. So dropping a kiss onto Gabrielle's head, Claire slipped away, motioning Simon out the door so the teacher could get the class under control.

"Another perk to the volunteer thing?" he asked as they left the school.

Claire flipped up her collar and blocked the wind

from pouring down her neck. "The students are great, aren't they?"

"Yes."

One word and she felt washed in his approval. In her peripheral vision she caught a smile playing around his mouth, a look that made her aware of how much she liked seeing him smile.

Claire didn't know why this man affected her this way. Yes, he was attractive. And yes, he kept going out of his way to make this interview less offensive. But something made smoothing away the stern from his expression an accomplishment.

She had absolutely no business feeling this way in light of her circumstances, and she came head to head with proof why when she stepped inside Ms. Verna's office.

"Put your happy face on," the administrative assistant said. "You get to meet our new assistant psychiatric director."

One look at Simon, and Claire knew he thought he'd been invited to this meeting, too.

*Wrong.*

"Why don't you have a seat?" She rushed to Ms. Verna's door without waiting to be announced. "I won't be long."

Claire saw his gaze narrow just as she caught the doorknob and turned. He'd realized what she was up to but couldn't cover the distance before she slipped inside and flipped the lock.

"Claire?" Ms. Verna glanced up in surprise. "Are you all right? Where's Simon?"

"A new assistant psychiatric director?"

"Dr. Davenport. She's reviewing our active cases."

"I'm off for good behavior since I'm already doing my bit for Safe Harbor this week."

Ms. Verna got that you've-got-absolutely-no-choice look about her. "I'll call and ask her to squeeze you in today so you can get this over with as quickly and painlessly as possible."

"A procedural overview can wait until *after* my interview. I'm sure there are plenty of other cases she can review."

"I don't want you to wait, dear. I bullied you into this interview and, frankly, I'd feel better if you touched base with Dr. Davenport. She comes highly recommended."

"I'm fine. Please let's not rock the boat."

"Nice try. Would you like an appointment today or shall I let you stew over this for a few days?"

For a woman with a heart of gold, Ms. Verna had a stubborn streak as intractable as steel. "*After* Simon leaves."

"Speaking of Simon, where is he?"

"Never far." Inclining her head toward the locked door, she gestured to the reception area beyond. "If I go quietly, will you cut me a break and take him on a tour or something? I can't get into questions about treatment."

Ms. Verna gave a resigned sigh, got up and circled her desk. Resting a hand on Claire's cheek, she asked, "What's wrong? Why are you so bothered by this?"

Now there was a loaded question. Claire couldn't explain why. Suddenly Simon was everywhere. At Safe Harbor during the day. In her apartment at night. He was helping her make books, and she was preoccupied with making him smile.

Claire didn't want to see his compassion when he learned she was an active psychiatric case. It was stupid. In her situation treatment would be a given. He knew. That's why he'd made his first rescue attempt by introducing her to an agent.

But everything about Simon Brandauer felt too personal. Who knew why? She only knew that she was being sucked into a vacuum of emotions, when something inside, some intuition or instinct, shrieked that she should be wary around this man, shouldn't let her feelings get away from her.

Leaning into Ms. Verna's touch, she drew strength from the familiar while the rest of her world was tilting sideways.

# CHAPTER EIGHT

EVERYTHING ABOUT Dr. Quinn Davenport was chic. Suede pumps complimented her tailored cocoa suit. Shiny black hair had been pulled back to reveal classically feminine features. Creamy skin glowed with the perfect combination of good health and an enviable sense of daytime makeup.

This new assistant psychiatric director was exactly the kind of woman Claire imagined might inhabit Simon's real world, the one he lived in when he wasn't interviewing amnesiac writers who wore hand-me-down clothes.

"Come to my office." Dr. Davenport motioned down a hall. "I'm so glad you could make the time to speak with me."

"No problem. My secretary just shuffled around a few appointments and here I am."

When Dr. Davenport chuckled, Claire decided she needed to ditch the sarcasm pronto. It wasn't the doctor's fault she'd been assigned to Safe Harbor at an inopportune time. Nor was it her fault that Ms. Verna insisted they meet before Claire had finished her interview with Simon. So she kept her mouth shut while following the doctor inside an office.

"Make yourself comfortable." The doctor pulled the

door closed then took a seat behind her desk. "Ms. Joyce has told me so much about you. I'm looking forward to chatting."

Chatting? She made it sound as if they were two old friends who hadn't seen each other in a while. Avoiding her gaze, Claire glanced around and tried to decide where to sit. The chair in front of the desk? The couch?

The office, unlike the doctor, was generic. Calming colors, stock wall art, a shelf of popular self-help titles and padded leather furniture that was supposed to look inviting. It didn't. She went to stand by the window.

With the sleeve of her sweater, Claire wiped the condensation from the glass. Though winter veiled the courtyard, she recognized the tiers of white blanketing the low hedge that edged the walkway where the groundskeeper would plant bright annuals once the snow melted.

"I'll bet it's lovely in the spring," Dr. Davenport said.

"Sometimes the crocuses come up in time for Easter. By May there are tulips and lilacs and the fountain attracts all kinds of birds. The children like to hang out and feed the squirrels."

"I'll remember to bring popcorn when it warms up."

Claire only nodded, and the doctor came to stand at the window beside her, so close their shoulders almost touched.

To her surprise, the doctor didn't try to make eye contact, just stared into the courtyard as if she could see it alive with dramatic colors after the bitter winter, lush with the full green of summer, bathed to drowsy grays by the rain.

"See that window there?" Touching a fingertip to the

glass, Claire tried to point out the specific one, but when the heat cycled on, the window fogged again. "Ground floor. The third from the left. That was my room when I first came here."

"You used to watch the children feed the squirrels."

"Mmm-hmm. Once I could get around, they'd push me outside in a wheelchair so I could feed them, too."

"I see a lot of caring happening at Safe Harbor. It seems like a special place."

"Ms. Verna makes it special."

Claire wasn't exactly sure why she was talking. Maybe she needed a distraction from the doctor's nearness. Or maybe the doctor herself inspired confidences. This did feel more like chatting than an official evaluation.

"I gathered from our conversations that Ms. Joyce cares a great deal about you. I see it works both ways."

Claire nodded, not sure what to say, but feeling guilty she'd come here so thoroughly prepared to dislike this doctor.

"I read in your file that you haven't been in therapy for a while, so we don't have to conduct a formal review." Dr. Davenport backed up and half sat on the edge of the desk. "Why don't you just tell me how you're doing?"

"I'm fine. I moved out of the residential facility two months ago and got an apartment. I write for a living and sell enough to pay the rent."

"Excellent. Ms. Joyce told me all about your volunteer work in the publishing center, too. Sounds like you're staying busy."

"Very."

"So how do you like living alone? Must be a big

change from the slumber party going on in the residential facility."

Claire smiled. "Slumber party describes it."

Dr. Davenport shuffled papers around on her desk, slipped one from the pile, made a notation with a pen, seemed in no particular rush to resume the conversation.

"Living alone is okay," Claire finally said. "There was really no reason for me to be taking up space in the residential facility when I'm perfectly capable of living on my own."

"Doesn't sound like you've been alone much lately, though. Ms. Joyce mentioned you have a shadow."

"Simon."

"He's the journalist?"

She nodded.

"So how's that going?"

Leaning against the windowsill, Claire braced herself on her hands and took a deep breath. God, what could she possibly say about Simon? That he'd segued into her life as though he belonged there? That he was so caring and patient that she was getting all caught up in spending time with him?

Dr. Davenport prompted by asking, "What's he like?"

"He's...*right*." The words popped out, not what Claire had meant to say but as good a description as any.

"Right? In what way?"

"I looked up one night, and there he was. I didn't realize anything had been missing until I saw him."

"Missing? Does he remind you of someone you knew?"

"Yes. No." Claire shook her head. "I don't know. I

look at him and he looks right but he's wrong, too. Like a picture in the wrong frame. Does that make sense?"

The doctor nodded. "Go on."

And to Claire's surprise she wanted to. Thoughts and feelings were suddenly bubbling inside, bursting to get out. "I test his patience. He never comes out and says anything, but he does this thing with his jaw when he's stressed. Sometimes I can't help but stare. I'm waiting for his face to crack."

Dr. Davenport laughed. "Do you think he's worried about getting his story?"

"No. I'm a captive audience and he knows it. I'm not really sure what his deal is. He's a nice guy. Although I'd bet money he doesn't think so. He's so disconnected from his feelings that I'm like an emotional roller coaster around him. He tries to hide it but I rattle him. That makes him uneasy."

"How does that make *you* feel?"

"I rattle the best of them." She turned back to the window. "I've been at Safe Harbor a long time. Everyone's dealing with baggage around here and we all accept it and help each other muddle through. Simon's trying, too."

"You said you're like an emotional roller coaster. How so?"

Simon could look at her with those clear eyes and spiral her from feeling pathetic to *right* in a glance. Claire didn't know why. She only knew that she'd felt this way before. It wasn't anything Simon said or did. She knew she rattled him sometimes, but he'd walked a fine line between treating her like a normal person and a basket case.

This was about wanting to prove herself. To him. To

herself. Maybe it was a natural response to prolonged amnesia. This doctor would know, but did Claire really want to go here?

"This isn't about Simon," she finally said. "It's about me and everything I've forgotten."

"You know that Ms. Joyce is concerned you've given up finding out who you are."

"I know. I'll remember when it's time."

"No urgency?"

"If I had something important to rush back to, I'm sure someone would have noticed me missing by now."

Dr. Davenport frowned. "I can think of any number of reasons why no one would look for you here. Can't you?"

Claire stared at the drapes, noticed how the muted tones reflected the way she felt inside. Colorless. "I know I'm not being fair. At least, I know it in my head, but I don't feel it." She ran her hand along the stiff fabric. Lifeless. "I feel as if someone just dropped me off here and never looked back. I feel…" She didn't know how to describe the sense of abandonment without sounding resentful and petty.

"How do you feel, Claire?"

Running her fingers along the drapery, she avoided Dr. Davenport's gaze and stared through the foggy window. An icicle hanging from the fascia board caught her eye, and she watched as the wind made a droplet of moisture that clung to the icy tip shiver. For a suspended moment that droplet struggled before breaking away. Claire watched it drip down the glass pane, was reminded of a tear.

*Abandoned. Betrayed.* "I feel like I died for something I believed in, but it all turned out to be a lie."

*3:14 a.m. CET*
*Strpski Grad Republika, -9°C*

IVAN HEARD THE COMMOTION *from outside his suite in the*
*Hotel Brijevek. Rough curses. A cry. Then terrified*
*sobs. He cracked his door to see into the hall without*
*being seen, recognized several soldiers of Edvard's En-*
*forcers, a paramilitary patrol touring this region to*
*tighten the stranglehold on all non-Serbs.*

*Although he was a high-ranking commander in the*
*Citizen's Army, Ivan had been ordered to ignore these*
*men's obscene actions. The current president of the*
*united provinces had elevated these pretend patriots*
*onto footing equal with the commanders, although most*
*had no true political convictions or military experi-*
*ence, only a zeal for violence and power.*

*Since the Citizen's Army had been ordered to turn a*
*blind eye to their behavior, Ivan could not intervene in*
*the scene unfolding outside his door. Still, it went*
*against his grain to stand by and watch this group of*
*women from the nearby detention camp, shepherded by*
*savage men who wore the same uniform he did.*

*The Yugoslavia he'd served had died a violent death.*

*Edvard had leased the suite beside Ivan's. He would*
*take his pick of the women then send the rest downstairs*
*to entertain his men. A reward for allegiance to the con-*
*quering army.*

*Stepping back to close his door, Ivan intended to shut*
*out the distasteful scene, but a girl stumbled, whim-*
*pering. She looked at him with desperation in her eyes*
*and triggered something in his memory....*

*He did not know her name, but he knew her face. A*
*Muslim girl who'd played the violin accompaniment to*

*his granddaughter's piano performance at the exclusive music academy in Sarajevo both girls had attended before the war.*

*They'd made exquisite music together, and he had taken great pride and pleasure from their skill. Ariana was sheer joy on the piano with her graceful hands caressing magic from the keys, and her accompanist had been equally talented.*

*Ariana had told him afterward that they'd devoted so much time to perfecting the fiendishly difficult duet that they'd become friends. To Ariana all Bosnians were Bosnians, no distinctions between Serbs and Muslims. At fourteen, she was too young to comprehend the political discontent that tore apart the fabric of Yugoslavia, too young to care beyond the fact that she'd made a new friend. And had she understood, she still wouldn't have cared. She had strength of will, this one, like his beloved wife.*

*But idealism had no place in the world. All hell had broken loose in Sarajevo, and today the music academy served as a detention camp to house refugees—prisoners of the army that had once protected them.*

*Yugoslavia had ceased to exist, a jumble of breakaway provinces and politicians fighting to retain remnants of power like dogs scrambling for fallen scraps from a table.*

*Ivan was no different, only smarter. He did not fight like a dog, rather he used his reputation to win allies in strategic positions. While others ripped at each other's throats in front of the world, he quietly built his power base.*

*This scene would never have happened among his regiment. Each and every one of his men knew he would*

*have been shot on the spot for abusing a prisoner. But
Ivan had no control over the paramilitary, which is
why he could do nothing to help this young violinist
without jeopardizing his own position.*

*But the girl screamed to him anyway. She glanced
back over her shoulder at him with terror in her face....*

*Only now she wore Ariana's face.*

Ivan awakened to the sight of his bedroom in blackness. He threw off sleep quickly, a habit well honed
from his years as a soldier, but he did not toss off the
shock of seeing his beautiful granddaughter so easily.
Terror had eclipsed her always-smiling face in his
dream, and the image haunted him as he pushed himself upright and reached for the bedside light.

Dreams had plagued him in the months after his
wife's death. Again after his son's. Ivan had conquered
his feelings of powerlessness with action. Working toward the day his people would toss off the yoke of the
West proved a balm for his soul.

But in light of his Western contact's deceit, he found
himself with new worries. Awaiting information from
Nadia so he could take action weighed on his mind. So
Ivan pulled back the blankets and left his bed, joints not
so eager to be hurried.

He would get no more rest this night.

*11:54 a.m. EST*
*Sault. Ste. Marie, -13°C*

CLAIRE CAUGHT UP with Gabrielle in the cafeteria, just as
she emerged from the lunch line, looking sweet with her
surprised eyes and pleased smile. "Want some company?"

"You came!"

"I did." Not only had she made lunch, but she'd come alone; an unexpected perk, a phone call had kept Simon in the medical center on his cell while she'd made her escape.

Gabrielle passed off her lunch tray, and Claire took it, following her and her four companions to a table where the group attacked their meals with youthful enthusiasm.

"You can have my potato dinosaurs," Gabrielle offered generously, grabbing her spoon to dig into the pudding.

"Dessert first, hmm?" Claire tucked a napkin into Gabrielle's collar in an attempt to preserve her white turtleneck. "Thanks, but you eat up. I'm not hungry."

Meeting with Dr. Davenport had effectively curtailed Claire's appetite for the time being.

"I've got a loose tooth, Miss Claire." A girl with long dark hair grinned broadly, used her tongue to push forward a central incisor and reveal the bloody pulp of her gum below.

"Wow, Chandra. Looks like you'll be getting a visit from the tooth fairy soon."

Not to be outdone, the rest of the children regaled her with their own tooth stories, and Claire covered her eyes when the table's only boy treated her to the sight of two gaping holes where his central incisors had once been—while he was still chewing.

"Ugh, Stavros. Swallow first, or that dinosaur is going to jump right out of your mouth."

"My tooth is loose, too, isn't it?" Gabrielle gave Claire a chocolaty smile, a victim of peer pressure.

She took a few hard swallows then opened wide.

"Let's see what we have here." Claire lightly ran her

finger along the tiny white teeth for any movement. Not a one budged. "Won't be long now."

She was about to suggest Gabrielle try a few bites of corn dog to jostle those teeth along, when the sound of raised voices drew her attention to the patio outside the back doors.

Scooting back in her chair, she glanced through the windows to see three teenage boys knotted together, testosterone clearly flying. One teen waved his hands and when another grabbed a handful of his collar and shoved him out of sight, Claire glanced around the cafeteria to see one harried lunchroom worker and no sign of Gabrielle's teacher, who'd likely disappeared into the teacher's lounge for her own lunch.

"Back in a minute, Gabrielle," Claire said. "You stay put and eat that corn dog."

"One bite?"

"Three. And make them big ones."

Making her way around the lunch tables to the patio doors, Claire saw Louis, a boy from Mexico who'd recently moved into the residential facility. She didn't know the other boys, but she recognized trouble.

Louis was on his knees, shielding his face with an arm, trying to break the grip of a tough-looking black boy who held him. She burst through the door to hear him yell, "Get off, man. I'll get it to you. I swear."

"Wrong answer." The other teen, a wiry boy with pale stubble for hair and a silver stud through his eyebrow took a swing at Louis's head. The blow connected with enough force to nearly knock Louis from the black boy's grip.

"Hey. Hey. Enough." Claire grabbed Silver Stud by his sleeve and pulled him away.

Her presence didn't do a thing to deter the teen, who shook her off with surprising strength. "Take off, lady."

"You don't belong here." Reaching for the black boy's collar, she twisted her fingers inside and applied enough pressure to force him to release Louis. "I'm not playing. Shove off or I call security."

"You gonna make us?"

Claire would not engage in a pissing contest with this hostile kid, but she hadn't yet loosened her grip on the black boy before Silver Stud lunged.

She hit the wall, and starbursts of white light exploded in her head. Suddenly Silver Stud was in her face, his bloodshot gaze revealing a hostility that was tragic in someone so young.

Claire didn't have to see the gun. She could feel it jab into her ribs.

"Don't mess with me, lady. I'll hurt you."

"What the hell, Reese," the black boy shouted, panicked. "Shit. Let's get out of here. This loser ain't worth nothing."

Claire stared into those bloodshot eyes as the threat stretched between them. She heard another shout, this one muted behind the cafeteria's windows. Louis called her name.

The black boy grabbed Silver Stud's arm hard enough to rock him back on his heels. "Come on."

Silver Stud shrugged him off.

With a roar in her ears that drowned out everything but her own heartbeat, Claire snapped her fingers in his face. He blinked, his gaze darting to her hand. She shoved the pistol aside, locked her hands around his wrist and twisted until the gun pointed upward.

Silver Stud didn't get a chance to react before she

hooked her leg behind his, yanked his arm back and brought them both crashing to the ground. He hit the icy concrete with a grunt, still clinging to the gun as if he might get a chance to use it.

A finger snapped in the trigger guard as she pulled it free. Levering her weight forward to contain Silver Stud, she aimed the pistol at his friend. But the black boy was no threat; he scrambled backward so fast, he stumbled over a frozen metal newspaper rack near the door.

"Stupid move," a hard voice said, and Claire glanced up as the new assistant principal plucked the gun from her hand.

He pointed it at the boy. "In the corner. Face the wall."

The boy did as he was told, clearly unwilling to test this man's patience. Claire understood why when she watched Mr. Camerisi plant a booted foot on Silver Stud's back, jam the gun into the waistband of his own pants and extend a hand to help her stand. "You all right?"

Then Claire noticed the wide-eyed students crowded inside the windows, staring out at the scene around her. *At* her.

Adrenaline rushed through her in a nauseating wave.

# CHAPTER NINE

SIMON BURST ONTO THE PATIO to find Niky pinning a cursing kid to the ground and a cell phone to his ear. A kitchen worker hung on to another unresisting boy by the scruff of the neck.

"Where is she?" he asked.

Niky cocked his head the way Simon had come. "Bathroom."

Heading inside, he passed a teacher directing students back to their tables and ignored the titter of juvenile laughter when he pushed open a door clearly marked Women.

The sour smell of vomit hit him instantly. Beneath a stall door, he spotted Violet huddled on the floor.

"How are you feeling?" He rolled out a length of paper towel, tore it from the dispenser. "Claire?"

She didn't reply and for a paused moment he wondered who he'd find inside—his operative or the woman she'd become. Had she consciously disarmed that student or had her training protected her from harm as it had after the hit-and-run?

Quinn had given him no guarantees about Violet's condition. Her memories could return in a rush, in pieces or not at all.

"Claire?"

"Do you have radar or what?" Her voice sounded raw and more than a little annoyed.

Simon had let Violet leave the medical center without him because he'd monitored her session with Quinn and had been impatient to discuss the prognosis. He'd put Niky on Violet and a perimeter operative on Niky then let them go to the cafeteria.

Now he had to wonder what his impatience would cost.

Wetting the paper towel with warm water, he circled the stall and tried the handle. Locked. Through the slit beside the hinges, he could see her head braced over her arm on the toilet.

"Open up."

"This is a *ladies'* restroom. Didn't you see the door?"

"I saw."

Slipping off his coat, he slung it over the towel dispenser. "I'm not leaving."

Finally, the lock slid free. He cracked the door inward, found her leaning back against the stall, eyes closed. She looked so completely drained that he wondered if she'd ever have the strength to face the past when she'd faced so much already.

"You okay?" Kneeling beside her, he held out the wet towel and resisted the impulse to press it to her face, to trace the curve of her cheek and touch her.

"I just… I—"

"Skillfully defused a dangerous situation."

She gave a broken laugh that echoed through the tiled quiet. Pain hollowed her eyes to jeweled spheres. "What kind of person points a gun at a kid?"

"Someone who cares enough to take action so others don't get hurt."

She appeared to consider that. Taking the towel from him, she bathed her face.

"Do you see these scars?" Tipping her head from side to side, she exposed the abraded skin below her jaw, only faintly illuminated by the weak overhead light. "They're from a rope. The way they curl behind my jaw means the rope wasn't used as a garrote, but like a noose."

She lifted her gaze to his, those brilliant violet eyes filled with questions, uncertainty. "What kind of person hangs, do you think?"

"Someone who's been hurt." His voice caught on the words.

She looked away, as though ashamed of the response she'd evoked in him.

Simon's chest constricted around a tight breath, laid his pride bare. He'd never been good at talking to Violet. Once, when her parents had been alive, maybe, but she'd been another person then, a brilliant girl who'd laughed easily, challenged him with her opinions and made him think. After her training had started, their relationship had changed. As acting director, he couldn't afford to get too close to his operatives.

But as Simon watched her turn away and hide beneath the fall of her hair, he recalled every meal he'd shared with Quinn, every beer he'd drunk with Maxim, Major or Niky.

Not Violet, *never* Violet.

He'd rationalized his behavior. He couldn't send his operatives into the action without detachment.

But an empty town house in D.C. branded him a liar.

The man he'd once been with her had been bleeding through the armor of his distance. He'd never handled her the way he handled his other operatives.

"I've got to get out of here," Violet said suddenly, tipping her chin defiantly and motioning him to back off.

And he did, needing the distance as much as she seemed to.

Steadying herself on the toilet, she stood then went to the sink. He waited while she washed her hands, rinsed her mouth. She didn't look in the mirror.

When they emerged from the bathroom, one table of teens cheered, several applauded. One yelled, "Lock and load, Claire."

She looked as if she might be sick again. Simon got her past two of his perimeter operatives who'd taken up posts at the cafeteria entrance, and outside. He wrapped her coat around her shoulders, but she'd already started shivering.

Slipping his arm around her shoulders, he held on to her when she tried to pull away. "I'll take you home."

She didn't say a word on the drive to their building. But Simon sensed she was deeply shaken. She'd survived number twelve detention camp and long months of painful convalescence, only to face this terrible journey back to herself.

With him pushing her hard to remember.

"Simon, I know you've gone through a lot of trouble to interview me," Violet said after they arrived back at her apartment. "You've been really nice and I appreciate it. But I can't handle this anymore. I hope you have enough material for your article." She slipped through the door, and when she went to close it, he blocked it with his hand.

"We're not through."

"Please."

"Tell me what the problem is. We'll resolve it."

"I didn't have any problems until you came. All of a sudden I'm coming apart. I can't let that happen. I won't."

Her pain mocked his efforts. He had no choice but to push her to remember—for her sake and Excelsior's—but he was hurting her. He didn't know how to make it any easier.

The acting director of Excelsior shouldn't care.

The man he was did care. A lot.

"We're not through, Claire."

"I am." She tried again to push the door shut.

Pitting his strength against hers, he held the door, facing the pain that sharpened her features. Her eyes brightened with a frustration that mirrored his own, made him face that he was no more in control of his emotions than she was.

He didn't want to push her too hard, didn't want to harm her. He needed to end the threat to Excelsior and get a lock on any threat against her. He wanted her to remember the tremendous sacrifices she'd made to accomplish mission objective. He wanted pride in her actions to fuel her recovery through the brutal memories of what she'd suffered. He wanted to know how she'd survived when witnesses had seen her die.

He wanted to pull her into his arms and hold her until she stopped shaking, lend her his strength until she found her own.

She only wanted to get away from him.

But as he stared down into her moist eyes, Simon was powerless. He could reveal her true identity, explain why she'd been in Bosnia, but he couldn't force her to understand.

And that realization, so staggering in its simplicity, made him back away from the door.

"I'll go now, Claire. You take whatever time you need, but understand we're not through. I'm not leaving Sault Ste. Marie until I get what I came for."

"Goodbye, Simon."

The door closed. The lock clicked.

SIMON MONITORED Violet on audio. She showered. Brewed espresso. Worked on her computer. Fell silent. Was she asleep?

The silence never lasted more than a few hours.

The wail of a marine horn marked the passing time, signaled fog on the lake. Simon worked from his apartment on the floor below, communicated with Command and reviewed profiles on two upcoming missions.

He skimmed through Violet's personnel file for a clue how to reach her. Years of evaluations, on her trainings, her missions, commentary on each newly acquired skill set that had made her so valuable to him in the field. But he found nothing personal inside this file. No mention of ice skates or candles.

He'd wasted so much time. And as the minutes turned to hours then days, he was still wasting time.

Once, he knocked on her door. She answered. Coolly polite and painfully remote, she assured him she was fine, thanked him for his concern. The next time he knocked, she didn't answer.

Unable to cope with inactivity any longer, Simon finally pulled his perimeter team into the building, sent two into her apartment under the guise of workmen then left late in the afternoon on the second day.

After making the short drive to Safe Harbor, he entered Quinn's office unannounced. She was alone. "Get Ms. Joyce and the rest of team one in here for a briefing stat."

Crossing to the window, he stared down at the courtyard. He counted the windows. Ground floor. The third from the left, where Violet had lived during her convalescence. He envisioned her by the fountain, unable to walk, talk, remember that she had a reason to live and people who cared for her.

"Should I bring her in?" he asked. "I can take her to a safe house somewhere. Just her and me. No outside threat."

"And tell her what? She's not going to leave Safe Harbor to go anywhere with you."

"I could tell her the truth."

Quinn inclined her head. "You could, but telling her isn't going to make her remember. The process of rediscovering her identity is bound to be painful no matter where she is, Simon. I still believe she's more comfortable here."

"Comfortable?" He bit out the word. "Violet hasn't been comfortable since she left Command on a transport to the Balkans three years ago. And I'm forcing her to remember."

"You're doing what's best for everyone. You know as well as I do that hiding from the past isn't what Violet would want. She reached out with her stories for a reason."

"She won't leave her apartment."

"Apparently she needs to be alone."

He spun on her, powerless to conceal his frustration. "For two days? She hasn't eaten. She drinks espresso constantly so she barely sleeps."

"Has it occurred to you she doesn't want to sleep? She's had a problem with nightmares." Quinn looked thoughtful. "What's the real issue here? Violet's behavior, or your inability to protect her?"

The answer should have come easily, but all he could remember was standing inside that bathroom at Safe Harbor, not knowing what to say to comfort her.

Yet dozens of conversations they'd had in the days before she'd joined Excelsior echoed in his memory, proving that he hadn't always been so speechless around her.

And Simon finally had his answer.

His relationship with Violet had changed because he'd needed it to change. He'd originally courted her for a spot on his Command staff. Her linguistic skills would have served him with the dozens of active missions he ran out of Systems Ops daily. She'd have spent her days with him inside Command. Safe.

It hadn't been until training that he'd recognized her potential for fieldwork, a potential he couldn't ignore.

But even though he'd known Excelsior would benefit most from directing Violet's skills into the field, Simon hadn't been prepared for the reality of sending her into the action, of watching her face danger from the wrong end of a bouncing satellite signal.

And that was the real problem, he realized.

He cared. Too much.

The proof was in the way he'd been unraveling a piece at a time ever since he'd lost her in the Balkans, in the way he'd been becoming a man who cared, a man he couldn't afford to be.

"I can't detach," he said simply.

Quinn appeared behind him, rested a hand on his

arm. "Be patient. This situation is difficult for all of us, but we don't share your burden. You've been living Violet's life since we got here. You're bound to experience survivor guilt."

"Is that what this is?"

"Only you can say for certain what else you're feeling."

This felt like so much more. "I can't detach enough to understand what I'm feeling."

"You rely very heavily upon your detachment sometimes."

"Detachment is the tool I use to keep me focused."

"But it's just a tool. You're not perfect. It's unrealistic to think you can always distance yourself from your feelings."

But emotions only clouded his vision, made it difficult to make hard choices. Had he dwelled on what might happen to the operatives he'd placed on the extraction team, he would never have sent them into number twelve detention camp.

"What can I do for Violet?" She had to be his focus now. He had no choice but to force his detachment. He needed to think clearly and objectively so he could discover what had happened to her and protect her until he could bring her safely home.

Then, and only then, could he tackle his feelings for her.

"You can't do more than she'll accept. Try to understand that PTSD victims can feel shamed by their symptoms. They can handle that by hiding what they're going through. I think that's what Violet's doing. She's emotionally invested in you, but she doesn't understand why. Think about that, Simon. That has to be frightening. If she needs to hide, you need to let her."

Quinn paused until he met her gaze. "You're doing everything right. You're keeping her safe and bridging the distance to her past. Violet's stuck in survival mode right now. She has to find her way back. All you can do is listen without judging and be there when she needs you."

"She won't let me."

"Not at the moment. But that's not to say she won't an hour from now, or tomorrow, or the next day. If you're committed to this plan, then we need to talk about how we can help you."

"I'm not the one who needs help."

"I disagree. What I'm most concerned about is you realizing you can't fix Violet. Trauma happens, Simon. It isn't your fault that you can't take it away. You have to accept that."

What was it Violet had said during her session with Quinn? *"I can say it, but I don't feel it."*

He understood, because he knew Quinn was right but it made no difference whatsoever when he thought of Violet locked in her apartment, isolating herself from life. From *him*.

A knock on the door ended their conversation, and Niky strode into the office.

"Has she come out yet?"

Quinn shook her head. "I'm trying to convince Simon if Violet needs to hide, we need to let her."

"Not a problem for me. Let's hope she stays hidden through Winter Festival. Talk about a logistical nightmare. I don't need to tell you I've been going through the agonies of the damned over what happened outside the cafeteria."

"You contained the situation," Quinn said.

"But Violet was scared and not because of those idiot kids."

That fear had prompted a violent physical reaction and retreat. Violet had been so vulnerable and so determined not to need Simon or anyone else.

Simon should never have let her leave the medical center without him. "Why weren't you there when she was being slammed against a wall by a kid with a gun?"

"I can't ride her too close," Niky protested.

"Looks like you weren't close enough. If my eyes aren't on Violet, I expect yours to be. Am I clear?"

"Yes." That one grudging word brought the events of three years ago to life and set them squarely inside the room.

Another knock on the door interrupted the moment and brought Major into the fold.

Simon was glad for the distraction. "Status."

Major leaned against the wall, folded his arms across his chest and a pack of Marlboro cigarettes in the pocket of his leather vest. "I've got a lock on Violet's stories. I was able to buy back every one that hadn't gone to print yet. There are still a few weeks before her next release date, so we don't have to tackle that problem just yet. From now on everything she writes goes straight to Frances."

"Good. Now let's discuss the potential threat against her."

"TJ and I have been running backgrounds on everyone affiliated with Safe Harbor. Unless someone else materializes, we've got nada." Major flipped up the front of his Stetson with a snap of his fingers, and drilled Simon with a stare. "I'm coming up with nothing to suggest the hit-and-run was an assassination attempt. Isn't it possible that it was exactly what it appeared to be—an accident?"

*I feel like I died for something I believed in but it all turned out to be a lie.*

"We're overlooking something," Simon said.

"Everything we've learned about Violet's life here doesn't suggest she's made any enemies as Claire de Beaupré."

"We're left with someone following us to her."

"Someone powerful and well funded enough to cover his tracks," Major said. "Because we're digging deep."

"Agreed," Simon said. "Is Ms. Joyce coming?"

Quinn nodded. "She'll be here as soon as she can get free."

The administrator arrived while they discussed security for the Winter Festival, when people would be coming and going on the property, turning his perimeter team into ornamentation.

"Forgive me for keeping you waiting," she said, breezing into the office and accepting the seat Niky vacated for her. "It's that young boy who was involved in the trouble with Claire. I had to plead a case to keep him here. Once these children get mixed up in drugs, the authorities find it easier to send them to juvenile facilities. I prefer rehabilitation."

"Thank you for coming." Simon took the chair behind the desk, leaving Quinn standing by the window.

"I assume Claire's still hibernating," Ms. Joyce said.

"Hibernating?"

"Her term. She's done this before."

"Often?"

"Only when she needs to regroup. I've found it best

to let her be. She always comes out, usually feeling ready to take on the world again."

"So you suggest we wait." Why wasn't he surprised at yet another person telling him to back off?

"Claire gets unsettled by change." Ms. Joyce swept her gaze around the room. "And she's had a lot of changes lately. Give her a chance to adjust."

"Frankly, I'm concerned. She doesn't have much by way of necessities in her apartment."

"I understand, Simon, but have faith, she'll manage."

"She's been through enough. I would like your suggestions and help."

Quinn came to stand behind him. He didn't miss the glance she exchanged with Major.

Ms. Joyce rose from her seat, drawing everyone's attention as she faced him across the desk. "I've done everything you've asked of me to ensure Claire's cooperation. *Despite* the fact that you've been less than candid."

She raised her hand to halt his explanation. "I know you're a public official, Simon. As I'm sure you're aware, I checked out your credentials. I'm willing to accept what you tell me without too many questions, but I'm not willing to act against what I feel are Claire's best interests. She trusts me, and I won't betray her trust."

Quinn gripped his shoulder tightly. He ignored her. "You won't even visit to bring her food?"

Ms. Joyce shook her head. "You're doing Claire an injustice with your unfavorable comparisons to the woman she once was. I never knew Violet. The woman I know came to us so damaged that it took weeks before we knew what she looked like. Since then she's endured physical rehabilitation and psychiatric treatment. She's created a new identity for herself, and a new life."

Disapproval sharpened every line on Ms. Joyce's face. "You all speak of Claire as some unstable remnant of this woman you knew, when before you stands a woman of incredible strength, who contributes so much to the people around her. Accept who Claire is now, and I feel certain you'll know how to help. Now if you'll excuse me."

Ms. Joyce accepted her coat from Major and headed back through the door with as little ceremony as she'd entered. In her wake she left the senior members of the most covert United States security agency and their acting director speechless.

NIKY WATCHED THE OFFICE door swing shut behind Simon and Major, found himself alone with Quinn.

"He blames me."

Taking a seat behind her desk, she eyed him thoughtfully. "Are you sure this is an issue you want to tackle now?"

"I don't want to tackle this issue ever. But that doesn't change how Simon blames me for leaving Violet in the Balkans. Now let's add getting roughed up by an idiot kid to the list."

Quinn didn't intend to deny his charges and until this moment, Niky hadn't realized how much he'd needed her to.

"Watching Violet struggle is difficult for all of us. Keep that in perspective, and don't hinge your emotions on Simon's reactions. Try to remember he shares your concerns about her."

"He blames me."

"He blames himself for what's happened to her, much in the same way you do."

"I was the one who left her in the death camp. I was the one who was supposed to be watching her."

"Simon assigned her to the extraction team. He left her yesterday to talk with me. We could argue blame in circles."

Quinn might be skilled at hiding her emotions, but Niky sensed her frustration. They'd debated blame too many times. As always, she wanted him to relinquish it; he was determined to hang on. He didn't know why he bothered opening his mouth today—except that now more than ever, he needed to get his emotions under control. He had an objective and needed to focus.

Throw Zubac off Violet's trail.

"Listen to me, Niky," Quinn said. "You're so determined to crucify yourself that you're missing the point. Like you, Simon has heavy guilt issues to face about Violet, but he's facing them. Consider following the example. Yes, it's hard and yes, it's painful, but if you face your guilt, you can move past it."

More than anything Niky wanted Quinn to stop holding Simon up as a shining example. Yet he clung to her words, hating how much he needed her to let him off the hook—even when he didn't believe her. If she knew the truth, she'd be pointing her finger just as the rest of them would.

"I failed her again."

Quinn shook her head. "You were a victim like she was."

There'd been victims in death camp number twelve, all right, but he hadn't been one of them.

# CHAPTER TEN

"PATCH ME INTO Wolfgang's channel." Simon powered down the laptop he'd been working on in his second-floor apartment when TJ informed him Ms. Joyce had arrived in the building.

There was a crack of static. He heard Violet say over audio, "If Gabrielle's asking for me then I'm on my way."

So ended the fortunate timing of her hibernation—just before the Winter Festival was to begin. He was still puzzling through the administrator's change of heart when TJ informed him they were on the move.

Simon and Major made the brief trip to Safe Harbor to find most of the residents and workers on the property crammed into the auditorium to kick off the start of the Winter Festival. A band played, and teens, staff members and even children mingled easily in the large auditorium.

Quinn and Niky moved in to surround Violet, leaving him to watch the exits. If a threat arose, they would respond. That was the best he could do with so many people strolling openly onto the grounds.

"These people are happy. Make an effort to fit in." Ms. Joyce handed Simon some blood-red concoction that clung to the waxed edges of a paper cup. "Claire's back and she's fine."

"What changed your mind?"

"Seeing her friends is good for her." She disappeared back into the crowd.

Simon would have to agree with the assessment. Violet appeared to be having a good time. She looked pale and thin but her eyes sparkled, and her smile came easily. She chatted with the Bulgarian boy who'd visited her in the publishing center as he attempted to teach her some dance steps to amusing results.

As the night progressed, she provided a haven for Gabrielle, who crawled into her lap with a thumb in her mouth to watch the fun before being carried off by a woman whom Simon recognized as a residential aide.

Violet never noticed him.

At PRECISELY TEN O'CLOCK, Claire kissed Gabrielle good-night before the children headed off to bed, leaving the teens to mingle with the adults. The band stepped up its tempo, and she was determined to enjoy tonight's celebration. She wasn't going to wonder if Simon had finally left town or if he thought her terminally rude for cutting short their interview. And she wasn't going to feel guilty because he'd been so nice. She'd already written a letter apologizing. She would eventually send it and hope he understood.

When the band struck up a strong beat, a sort of samba-salsa number that made her want to dance, she decided a distraction was in order. Glancing around, she immediately dismissed several of the teens she knew would rather die than try the intricate steps that would work with the music. Then she caught sight of the new assistant principal.

Mr. Camerisi might be a school administrator, but

that was about the only similarity he bore to the other assistant principals of Claire's acquaintance—and she'd met a good few during her time at Safe Harbor.

He looked hard-edged and physical in a way that suggested an aggressively active lifestyle. An attractive man, he had ethnic features and wavy hair. His dark eyes had seen too much and hadn't made peace with it all, and, for some reason the thought made her sad, a feeling very unexpected, and *real*. Restlessness shrouded him like an aura, and she didn't think he laughed much, or danced.

Yet there was something about him that made her imagine him dancing to the strong beat. Dismissing any hesitation because he was new to Safe Harbor, she made her way through the crowd.

The music was loud, and she had to tap his shoulder to get his attention. He turned those somber eyes on her, leaned down to ask, "Having a good time tonight, Claire?"

"Would you like to dance?" She gauged his reaction, wanted to give him a quick out if he looked uncomfortable. But he didn't look uneasy at all. In fact, after his initial surprise, he looked quite wistful, as if once, a long time ago, he'd been very fond of dancing.

"My pleasure." Taking her hand, he drew her into the steps of a salsa.

After so many days of inactivity inside her studio, Claire enjoyed getting her blood flowing. "I knew you liked to dance."

"How did you know that?"

His voice was throaty, low against the beat of the music, and she relaxed herself against his arm for a dip before answering. "I don't know. I just had this feeling."

HOW MANY TIMES had Simon deployed Niky and Violet together because they passed as such a convincing couple? How many times had he watched from Systems Ops as they'd danced their way through some diplomatic function, a reception at a royal residence or a white-tie political fund-raiser?

Why couldn't he ever recall being bothered by the sight of them together?

"I don't know about you but this is so much like old times it's got me by the throat." Quinn watched the dance floor over the rim of her cup.

"Violet likes to dance," he said to distract himself from the unsettled way he felt.

"You sound surprised," Quinn said.

"I've seen her dance with Niky before during missions, but I didn't realize she enjoyed it so much."

"You should have socialized with us more. Violet taught us all to dance, and Niky does a killer Elvis impersonation. You missed some great parties."

Simon fell silent, thinking about all the sailing excursions and dinners he'd declined to attend and wondering how he could know so much about Violet yet know nothing at all.

He liked watching her dance. Her every motion was contained grace, beautifully timed with Niky's. They moved together naturally, and watching that dreamy expression take over her expression, eyes half-closed, lips parted, he thought she looked caught up in a memory.

Violet wasn't the only one. Even from this distance, Simon could see the glint in Niky's eyes, the too-tight expression. And when Niky lifted his chin to avert his gaze, Simon understood that Violet's memory loss protected her tonight.

Niky had no such protection.

"We're losing him," Simon said.

Quinn nodded, took his cup without comment as he stepped into the crowd, maneuvering through the dancers and catching Niky's gaze. In that brief clash of eyes, Simon saw so much more than friendship for the woman in his arms.

"May I?" he asked.

Violet looked only slightly less distressed to see him, but she didn't resist when Niky backed away. Simon took her hand, wrapped his arm around her waist, and led her into the familiar steps of a waltz.

"I have no idea what you were doing," he admitted, surprised by how much he wished he could have continued the skilled dance moves.

She followed his lead and fortunate timing was his again because the music faded, then slowed to a ballad.

Their first dance.

Violet's fingers rested lightly in his. She arched into his embrace, so close, and the feel of her slim curves against him made his awareness fade. Suddenly it was just the two of them. She lifted her gaze, and the hope he saw there stripped away his defenses.

"I'm sorry," she said.

"You have nothing to be sorry for."

"I've been unkind. Please be gracious and accept my apology."

He nodded, unable to voice the words when he was the one who should apologize.

But Violet seemed satisfied. She sighed and rested her cheek against his shoulder, a move that made the past vanish and her body align smoothly with his, a move that turned her from an operative to a woman who fit neatly into his arms.

"I should have been straight with you before," she said. "Something about you feels familiar. It frightens me."

"I don't want to cause you more pain."

She shook her head, burrowing her face gently. "It's not you. I'm tough to handle on a good day. Even for me."

"No." And his need to reassure her overwhelmed him. He wanted to rest his cheek against her silky hair, breathe her familiar scent, press close enough to feel her heart beat.

Simon wanted, and cursed himself for feeling that way.

*8:10 a.m. CET*
*Strpski Grad Republika, -10°C*

"GENERAL, PLEASE FORGIVE my intrusion during your breakfast," Ivan's aide-de-camp said as he appeared in the dining room doorway.

Ivan set aside his newspaper. "Come, come. What do you have for me."

"You asked to be notified when the information from Moscow came through. Your message has arrived." He held up a handheld computer to reveal the blinking red light.

"Thank you." Ivan accepted the device and glanced at the lighted display. A URL. "I must go to my office."

"Now, General?" There was genuine concern in his man's voice. "What of your breakfast?"

"Come, you sit and enjoy our chef's fine feast. I must go."

Ivan left his aide-de-camp blinking in surprise and focused his thoughts on the message awaiting him. Even the most efficient information broker had needed the better part of two days to track down his request.

Nadia was one of the best information brokers in this part of the world. Not easy to deal with, of course. She had a vast network of global connections that kept her services constantly in demand. It had taken Ivan well over a year to get a referral, even more time to be checked out and now he wired ungodly sums of money into her maze of offshore accounts just to get her to take his phone calls.

Yes, Nadia was much trouble to deal with, but her information had always proved well worth the effort.

He sat at his desk and typed in the URL. A page loaded, he was very pleased to find that she had cleverly uploaded a plain-text document to a secured Web site that he could view anonymously through a satellite uplink.

*Double Operations*
A story of political intrigue
by Claire de Beaupré

He scanned the story about a cryptanalyst who had defected from Yugoslavia to act as an agent provocateur for the United States. But this defector had actually been working for a powerful provincial politician who had cunningly assigned him as a double agent to feed a covert U.S. government agency misinformation during the breakup of the Republic.

There were no references to any military general. There was no suggestion that this story was anything but fiction.

But one detail stopped him cold.

The real villain in this story was a man who moved like a wraith between the Republic politicians, the international organizations and the European Community while secretly allying himself to war criminals and known arms brokers, a man who had remained so stealthy that not even the double agent had known his true identity. He referred to his superior only by an unusual physical characteristic.

*Bone where his heart should have been.*

Ivan knew that exact turn of phrase.

As a very young man, he and the beautiful girl who'd eventually become his wife had been racing their horses through the mountain trails. He'd been unseated and fallen down a steep cliff, severely injuring his sternum. While the physicians had repaired the shattered bone, they'd left Ivan with a fist-size depression in his chest.

By the time he'd grown to manhood, he'd developed muscle and hair to camouflage the damage. But his wife knew of the intricate webbing of scar tissue and bone in his chest. Whenever she became frustrated about what she called his hard head, she accused him of having bone where his heart should have been.

It was their private joke.

He had never repeated those words, except once when he'd lost his control with a prisoner. He had risked so much to slip back inside number twelve camp to question the female compatriot of his Western contact.

Only two of the American team had been alive by the time Ivan had arranged safe passage into that camp. But he'd learned much from them. He'd interrogated the woman first, but the man had proved easier to manage. Ivan had sold the man his life for the name of the defecting traitor and a photographic device with incriminating photos taken inside the camp. He had bought himself a useful contact within the American government.

Ivan had intended to retrieve the photographic device from the woman, as well. He had her kept alive, believing she would eventually break after many long months of harsh conditions.

On his second visit to number twelve camp, he had not received the device but obstinacy and hostility instead. A pale shadow of the woman he had left months earlier, she had still had the strength to turn his questions back on him.

When he had finally reached the end of his patience, Ivan had grabbed her hand, placed it over his chest and warned, "I have bone where my heart should be."

She had not heeded his warning, and he had felt shame that she had provoked him into firing a loving jest like a bullet.

She had outlived her usefulness that night.

He had ordered her death and her corpse cremated to ensure the photographic device could not be recovered from her remains. He had been assured his order had been carried out.

But unbeknownst to the camp commander, the American woman had passed along the photographic device to a traitor deputy before her death, and that deputy had supplied the war crimes tribunal with visual evidence of the conditions inside the camp.

Fortunately, none of those images had implicated

Ivan. And as he scrolled beyond the story to a list Nadia had provided of this author's published credentials, he wondered how many more incriminating details were peppered inside these stories. How could this author know of an exchange that had taken place between him and a dead woman?

These were questions that needed answers. But he had one important answer tonight.

His Western contact had lied.

*11:37 a.m. EST*
*Sault. Ste. Marie, -5°C*

"I'VE JAMMED ALL AUDIO." Simon pulled the door to Quinn's office closed. "We need to talk."

"Violet?"

"She's skating with Niky and some students. Major is monitoring." He stood in front of her desk, unable to sit, yet not wanting to be lured to the window or the snow-covered courtyard below.

Determined to detach from the emotions colliding inside him, he took a deep breath. "Does Niky love Violet?"

The glow from the lamp reflected off Quinn's hands as she brought them together on the desk. Her expression suggested she'd expected this question but hadn't looked forward to it.

"Yes."

He let the word filter through him, his gut clenched tight enough to mock his attempt at detachment.

"That's it? Just yes?"

Quinn shrugged.

Pressing a hand to his brow, he massaged his temples to relieve the ache starting to pulse there. "How did I miss this?"

"It's fair to say you don't deal comfortably on those emotional levels. You keep them shut out of your life."

"I know about my people."

"You can't know everything unless you read minds, Simon. You trained them. They knew the rules and respected the boundaries. Had they been living another life Niky's feelings might have become more. Who can say? As it was he channeled them into a constructive relationship. That's why he was so tortured to learn he'd left her alive. He would never have left Violet had he known she'd been alive. I truly believe that."

Simon wanted to believe that, too, but he still didn't have answers to what had happened inside the detention camp. Until he did, this information was only another piece in the puzzle. Nothing more.

The lure of that window finally became too strong. He covered the distance and stared outside unseeing, remembering, oddly enough, the night his parents had told him about his grandfather's death. He'd sensed them holding back, sugarcoating the truth for his benefit. That had bothered him.

*"How?" he'd asked.*

*"Grandpa had a stroke."*

*"In the hospital?"*

*"At home."*

*"Who was with him?" Simon had persisted.*

His father had finally given him all the facts. His grandfather had suffered a series of small strokes during the night that had made it impossible for him to reach a phone and call for help. He'd died of a massive hemorrhage hours later, on the floor in his bedroom, alone, possibly confused and scared.

Simon had never lost that image of his grandfather or the knowledge that he could have saved himself pain by not knowing.

Confirmation of a truth he already suspected should make no difference. But he couldn't shake the memory of the look on Niky's face—or how Violet had zeroed in on him to dance. He didn't want to know more and despised himself for that weakness.

Forcing his gaze from the window, he asked, "Was Violet in love with Niky?"

The pain that drew Quinn's features into a knot wasn't what he expected. She let her eyes drift shut then inhaled a deep breath, as if the answer weighed heavily.

"Was she?"

"Simon, Violet was in love with you."

Her quiet declaration filtered through him slowly, an experience of lingering sound and stunning context, curiously similar to what he'd felt when leveling a gun at someone's head realizing he would have to pull the trigger.

The wind hissed past the window, rattled the panes. He could hear it, wanted to turn around and stare down into that winter-bare courtyard, imagine Violet down there when the flowers were in bloom. But he wouldn't give in to the impulse, not while Quinn watched, so unnaturally still that he wondered if she thought any sudden movement might detonate him.

"Is this a psychiatric confidence?" His voice sounded as if it came from far away, belonged to someone who knew how to respond, what to feel.

"The trust of a friend."

"For how long?"

"Since she first met you."

"Violet was a young girl when I met her."

"When better to form an attachment to an attractive and powerful older man?"

Had there been clues?

Finally giving in to the urge, he turned toward the window. He could still see Violet as she'd been the day they'd met at a Brussels symposium.

With shiny hair pulled back from her heart-shaped face, she'd looked like any other thirteen-year-old. Her eyes had been huge in a face not yet defined by maturity. She'd been too tall, too thin, as if she hadn't quite grown into her body yet.

But the similarities to a teenager had ended there. Violet had faced six hundred scholars, scientists and special interest people like himself, deaf to their gasps and surprised murmurs.

She'd stood at the podium until the audience quieted. Then, as silence stretched into painful anticipation, she'd informed them that her father had experienced a breakthrough in his work with the Machiguenga families in the Peruvian jungle. It had been impossible to get away so she was delivering his treatise. She'd started to speak and held her audience spellbound. Violet had lived and breathed the science of language.

His search for a linguist had ended that day.

He was more than willing to wait until she grew up. So were others. Violet had been inundated with offers to meet with university program directors and renowned scientists, all eager to lay claim to such a gifted young talent.

Violet had chosen to meet with him instead.

When he'd asked her why she'd blown off more conventional offers to stay in contact with him, she'd told him simply, "I like what you have to offer."

Simon had thought she'd been referring to a career with the United States government. He'd doubled the highest offer so the money would be attractive. But now, knowing the impatient, impulsive and thoroughly disarming woman she was, he suspected Violet had meant exactly what she'd said.

He remembered her as a vibrant young girl who astounded him with her abilities, remembered her blushes whenever he'd touched her elbow to assist her from a car or escort her into a meeting.

As a recruit new to Command, she'd always been eager to test her skills, to do whatever it took to please him.

As a woman lost from herself, she trusted a man she couldn't remember.

The clues were there. He'd refused to accept them, but on some level he'd always known, and had distanced himself.

Now distance was no longer possible.

## CHAPTER ELEVEN

THE MORNING DAWNED COLD and clear. Claire finally broke free from the many indoor game and food booths to pull duty on the skating pond.

The wind stung her cheeks as she glided over the ice, working off restlessness with activity, needing the cold air to clear her head of the lingering ache of the past few days.

She should have known Simon would simply wait her out. He'd told her he wouldn't leave until getting what he came for, and he didn't strike her as someone who gave up easily.

She'd ask him what else he needed. If she could accommodate him, so be it. If he wanted anything more than another day of her time, she'd turn him down.

Claire might owe Safe Harbor, but she wouldn't let an interview undo all her hard work to move on with her life.

Not even for Ms. Verna.

When a tiny figure appeared on shore bundled in bright pink, Claire put all thoughts of Simon from her mind and trotted up the slope. "Hey, Gabrielle. I wondered what happened to you this morning. I wanted to paint your face."

Her mouth tucked into a tight little frown. "I had to fold my clothes."

A monumental task, no doubt. Gabrielle was a mini tornado on the best of days. "Did you bring your skates?"

She pointed to the scuffed pair discarded beside a steel drum where a bonfire raged. Claire scooped them up, put a hand on Gabrielle's shoulder and directed her to a bench.

"These hardly fit anymore. We need to ask Christine to find you a bigger pair."

"Tyshia has a bigger pair."

"But they still fit her?"

Gabrielle nodded.

"Then we'll make do and hope someone donates another pair before your toes grow anymore." Claire smiled but felt sad. "All set. Leave your boots on the bench."

Gabrielle waved at Mr. Camerisi, and Claire turned around to find the new assistant principal coming toward them.

He hadn't taken his eyes off her since she'd come outside and Claire couldn't help but wonder how much she'd rattled him with the scene outside the cafeteria. He hadn't been around long enough to become acquainted with everyone's stories around here. She couldn't really blame him for hightailing it off the dance floor when Simon had shown up.

"Good morning, Claire," he said. "Enjoying the festival?"

She nodded then turned to Gabrielle. "Go warm up. I'll be right there."

"How about you?" She watched her skating buddy hop-skip down the slope and chuck across the ice.

"Looks like I arrived on scene in time for the fun. I

didn't think we'd get the students away from the game booths inside, but skating with Miss Claire seems to be an event."

Claire wasn't going to tell him that it was one of the few ways she made herself useful around Safe Harbor. The first time she'd gotten on this ice, skating terms had popped into her head like magic, and she'd learned something else about her forgotten self. She liked to skate. And given her ability, she must have taken lessons sometime.

"We have a good time," was all she said, spotting Gabrielle skating in the opposite direction of the crowd. Kids were dodging her to avoid a collision, and if she didn't stop, she'd wind up on the thin-ice end of the pond.

"She never remembers to stay with the traffic. Excuse me."

Making it to the ice, she snagged Gabrielle and guided her into the center of the pond, out of harm's way. "Come on, let's work on gliding."

Practicing the push and stroke of a glide lasted all of five minutes.

"I want to dance," Gabrielle said.

"Okay, let's dance."

Clasping hands, they twirled like fools, the cold air biting their cheeks, the wind snatching their hair from beneath knit hats. Gabrielle's squeals of delight chimed through the cold air and lightened Claire's mood.

Did it really matter how she'd learned to skate as long as she could share the experience with others?

Her answer lay in this sweet child who sank to the ice in a fit of giggles. It didn't matter why or where or when or how, only that she could use the knowledge to fill Gabrielle's heart with laughter, fill her own life with some purpose.

"Ugh, I'm going to be sick from all this spinning." Claire reached down and pulled Gabrielle to her feet. "Let's practice gliding before our next set."

As they moved around the pond, she noticed the man who'd joined Mr. Camerisi by the fire—a tall, familiar man who didn't attempt to hide the fact that he was watching her.

She was too far away to see his expression, see what mood touched those winter-gray eyes, but he remained on the bank as Mr. Camerisi skated onto the ice.

She wasn't going to think about how his strong arms had felt last night while they'd danced or the way his hard thighs had pressed against hers. She would forget how safe he'd made her feel with his heart beating against her cheek.

"Come on, Claire." Gabrielle took off again, and Violet went after her, arriving just as Mr. Camerisi caught a fistful of puffy pink jacket and brought Gabrielle to a sharp stop before she got too close to the thin-ice side of the pond.

"Not that way," he said.

She stared up at him, eyes wide, and Claire tugged on her hood to get her attention. "You little daredevil. You need to skate *away* from the orange cones, remember?"

She nodded gravely before taking off in the right direction this time.

But she'd dropped a mitten, Claire realized, and bent down to retrieve it. Suddenly, Mr. Camerisi lunged, plowing into her with such force that she went down just as the ice exploded, spewing razor-edged shards all around them.

She had no chance to react before he wrapped her in an iron grip, pulling her into a roll as more sharp blasts rent the air.

Gunshots.

Claire knew this sound.

Frantic to get Gabrielle and the kids off the ice, she scrambled to get away, but he didn't let go. He only jerked hard, grunted a curse as the ice shifted beneath them. She cried out, but the sound was lost beneath the grinding of thin ice.

The world tilted. Mr. Camerisi's grip tightened around her, and she clawed vainly at the air as they slid backward into the frigid water.

"GET DOWN," SIMON SHOUTED. "Take cover."

Mass confusion reigned as more shots were fired. By the time he issued hurried instructions to TJ and got the kids near him under the benches, those on the ice were fleeing in all directions. His heart hammered as he moved to cover beside a steel drum then made his way to a tree.

The shots finally faded to a whining silence, and no more rang out. A sniper, Simon guessed, likely making his way back to the safety of the festival crowds now, the sounds of his passage masked by the frightened cries of twenty plus kids scrambling off the ice.

"Pull in Safe Harbor security," he growled to TJ. "Get staff out here to handle these kids."

He raced toward Violet and Niky, hiking boots providing no traction on the ice, losing almost as much ground as he gained. He finally dived across the ice and rode the slide toward them, realizing as he neared that something was wrong.

Violet was impeding Niky's attempts to gain a solid handhold on the ice. Water churned, and a huge chunk shifted, pinning them as Simon dragged his hands and boots to stop himself on the last stretch of unbroken ice.

But he was too close to the edge and wound up pitching forward as it crumbled beneath him. He plunged into the water before managing to overcorrect his balance and stop from sliding in. He was close enough to see the pale gleam of Violet's hair and caught a fistful.

Water exploded as she surfaced and the ice gave way beneath their combined weights. But Niky got the respite he needed to break free. Simon clasped his hand and gave him leverage to propel himself up then pulled Violet away. The ice wouldn't support them all.

She arched wildly, but he held on tight, rolling toward safety until she reared back and slammed her head into his face, a deliberate attack that caught him off guard. She broke free.

Shaking his head to clear his vision, he watched her shove backward. Water sluiced in her eyes, down her cheeks, over bloodless lips.

"Claire."

She stared at him blindly, her face all stark and brittle lines, and Simon realized the woman he knew wasn't on this ice. She was trapped inside her memories.

He could have overtaken and contained her, but her terror stopped him cold. He'd heard the testimony, could see a mental image so brutally clear.

*Men holding her head underwater so she couldn't breathe, eyelids taped open so she'd be forced to see those who tortured her until she gave them what they wanted.*

*Wolfgang. Team one. 51693.*

*Name. Rank. Operative number.*

She'd never broken. She'd trapped herself in a lifetime of the present, moments strung together, day to day. No past and no future. And now she ran scared.

From him.

"Claire."

She shook violently while scrambling to her knees, her skates hindering her. Fear fractured her beautiful face until he didn't recognize her. Their gazes met, hers wild, his most certainly desperate.

Her chest heaved. Her mouth opened. Her scream was nothing more than a strangled gasp.

She couldn't breathe.

Terror had paralyzed her, but when he reached out to reassure her, she backed away.

He caught sight of Niky in his periphery, movements clumsy as he made his way toward them in the skates, his expression pained. He'd been shot.

Simon sensed Violet's intent even before she lunged toward Niky, who sank to his knees as she collapsed against him.

"Come on. Breathe." Niky said, instantly understanding. He smoothed his hands over her tangled hair, caught her face between his hands. "Breathe. With me." He simulated the motion, voice breaking when he said, "Come on. You can do this."

His ragged voice faded as Simon knelt there, powerless, helpless and unreasonably angry that Violet clung to Niky without reserve or fear.

"Get Ms. Joyce," he issued the direction to TJ just as Quinn appeared on the hill with Safe Harbor security.

*"She's on her way,"* he shot back.

Quinn watched him while TJ gave him a sitrep from his perimeter team leader.

*Secure.*

His people had caught the sniper fleeing the concession area. He relayed the message to Quinn, instructed her to help security contain the chaos. Within minutes they had kids limping back up the slope in their skates as Ms. Joyce came down.

She brushed past, never glancing at any of them as she went to kneel in the snow.

Niky backed away and Ms. Joyce gathered Violet in her arms. "Claire, it's all right now."

"They're just…babies. They…don't understand." She trembled, her choked whisper yielding to sobs.

"Let them go." Ms. Verna stroked the tangled hair back from her face, held her tight. "You can't save the children. Let them go. They're with God. He'll care for them now."

Simon stood there helpless, watching others comfort her.

SOMEONE HAD DRAPED a blanket over Simon's shoulders some time after their arrival at the medical center, but he couldn't remember who. He was nearly dry now and placed it over a chair.

Quinn had sedated Violet, and now she slept, her wet clothes replaced with warm blankets. This wasn't the room she'd occupied upon her arrival at Safe Harbor, but Simon guessed it was similar. Barren walls. Antiseptic floors. A biohazards container above the sink. He saw nothing to reflect Violet here. No pink shade on the window. No brass angel on the door.

"I'd say you got your proof that Violet's a target,"

Major said when he and Quinn returned. "Wish we could bottle those feelings of yours."

Quinn spotted an ice pack on the utility cart and pointed to it. "You were supposed to put that on your eye."

Simon could only stare, and turned his attention back to Violet. Even in a drugged sleep, she looked raw with grief, and no one commented on how fragile she seemed curled up on that bed, a blanket covering all but her head on the pillow.

*They're just babies. They don't understand.*

They'd all heard testimony of the atrocities committed in the detention camps, but testimony and pictures weren't real. Only Violet and Niky had endured the reality.

"How's Niky?" Simon asked.

"Feeling pretty lucky right about now," Major said.

"Surface shoulder injury," Quinn added. "The shot bypassed much internal damage."

"The sniper?"

Major didn't take his gaze from Violet. "Looks like he arrived on the property in the employ of a food vendor. Not only did he have license to move around, but a bunch of easy places to stash his gear inside the equipment."

Knowing the caliber of assassin who operated within North America, Simon had assigned a team in Command to check out the credentials of all personnel associated with the festival. They'd been working around the clock for two days. "The sniper's identification passed more than a routine inspection. I'd say that narrows our possibilities considerably."

"You got that right," Major agreed. "Who are you going to put on it?"

"TJ. He can pick his people."

"What about the interrogation?" Quinn wanted to know.

Normally Simon would have assigned her that honor. "Maxim. He'll get answers. What's the sniper's ETA."

Major glanced at his watch. "He should be airborne by now. He'll be in Command in little more than an hour."

Simon nodded. "Any problems on the crime scene?"

"The locals were pissed we snatched the shooter out from under their noses. You're knee-deep in jurisdictional bullshit."

Simon nodded. "I'll make a call."

"Call someone important. It's pretty ugly outside." He forced a smile. "The locals are proceeding with their investigation like they don't trust us."

Simon glanced down at Violet and watched her sleep, mouth bowed gently around each breath. No struggles now, her panic the victim of sedatives. He had no such buffer from his emotions, though, and no distance. He wanted to believe she hadn't recognized him out on that ice. He couldn't. Instinct told him that on some level she'd known him, and she'd been terrified.

Had she remembered he'd been the one to send her into that detention camp?

The silence echoed. Major and Quinn watched him, unspoken questions in their eyes. He wondered if they knew he was shaken.

This assassination attempt changed everything. If Violet didn't awake with some memory of the past, he had a problem. She was a target and couldn't remain at Safe Harbor to risk her safety and others, but he had no compelling explanation to give her about why she had to leave.

"She's restless." Quinn came to stand beside him. "I should be here when she wakes up."

He shook his head. "Let me handle her. I've got to talk with Canadian intelligence and try to smooth things over. You go stay with Niky. Major, see what you can do to get things moving along outside. This festival is a huge fund-raiser for Safe Harbor. The sooner we get the police out of here the better."

Quinn inclined her head, gave him a smile of reassurance that fell short of the mark.

Major followed her to the door. "I'll see what I can do. Call if you need me."

Simon nodded, and the door closed behind them, leaving him alone again with Violet. Moving into the bathroom, he pulled the door partially shut. He needed to make calls, but didn't want to chance Violet overhearing his conversations if she awakened.

Simon contacted the head of Canadian intelligence on his cell. "I know this is awkward. But you've got my word I'll send this sniper back over the border as soon as my people are done questioning him. My best man is attempting damage control with your local law as we speak…. Yes, I know I'll owe you big. You claim that favor whenever you want."

After the intelligence chief promised to smooth ruffled intergovernmental feathers, Simon disconnected the call, dropped the phone into his jacket pocket and said, "Delinquent."

"What do you need, your highness?" TJ shot back over the audio device.

"Pull the files on all known and suspected death brokers and assassins operating in this part of the world. Get a team together to dismantle the layers of the sniper's false identity. I want to know how far he goes into the system."

"Your wish and all that."

"Good. Now patch me into Soldier's channel."

Static crackled in his ear. "Hello, my friend. How are you holding up with all the fireworks?"

"I have more control inside Systems Ops."

"I wondered how long you'd survive out there. I honestly can't remember the last time you were gone this long—" Maxim gave a snort of laughter. "Wait a minute. You've *never* been gone this long. Anyone ever tell you that you need a life?"

"You, in fact. Often."

"Maybe you should take my advice."

The joke wasn't funny today. But Maxim had been around too long not to notice the situation with Violet had been weighing heavily on Simon's shoulders. They'd been compatriots, and friends, since marine amphibious training at Quantico, two young officers with more boldness and skill than smarts. How they'd both survived after spending so many years in extreme action remained a mystery to this day.

Maxim thought they were too tough to kill.

Simon thought they were just lucky.

"Cut to the chase," he said.

"I spent my morning buried inside the transcripts of Casanova's debriefing after we picked him up. You ran that investigation to the letter, buddy. That's the only reason why Oversight didn't hang your ass. You had five bodies. Well, four bodies and one MIA. You didn't miss a beat."

"Did Casanova?"

"You trained him, remember? If he didn't want to fess up about what really happened inside that camp, he wasn't about to let anything slip."

"That's the problem with surrounding myself with good people. I have to trust them."

"That a complaint?"

Simon could practically see Maxim sitting inside his office in Command, door open and boots propped on his desk just so Frances could walk by and scold him.

He claimed to like the attention. Maybe that was true. Maybe not. Simon only knew that his friend had a 170 IQ and a gift for ball breaking that translated into as many languages and dialects as Violet spoke. If not for an irreverent attitude, Maxim might be the one running Excelsior. His strengths lay in different directions than Simon's, which had earned them the name "dream team" during their stint as Marines, but his courage and commitment were unquestionable.

Maxim's skill at diplomacy was questionable, however. And the amusing thought of Maxim sitting in for a session with NATO was enough to take the edge off Simon's mood.

"Not a complaint," Simon said. "But all this skill is making my job difficult today."

"Doesn't saving a comrade's life earn a guy points around here? Casanova took a shot for her today."

That familiar weight came down on Simon's mood again, heavier for its temporary absence. "I've got two people with direct connections to that detention camp. One can't tell me what happened. The other has already told me, but now I've got a sniper appearing out of nowhere. What should I think?"

"Casanova would never put a hit on Wolfgang, so if that's where you're going with this put me on record as saying you're crazy. Losing his team totally screwed him up, but he channeled that whole shitty experience into a purpose, man. His service has been exemplary since you put him back in the field. He cares about Wolfgang. He'd never hurt her."

Simon *wanted* to believe that, and *wanting* wasn't something he usually factored into his decisions. Given Niky's feelings for Violet…would Niky have stepped in front of a bullet to protect her if he'd wanted her dead?

*No.*

"What does your gut tell you on this one, King Arthur?" Maxim broke the sudden silence.

*King Arthur.*

Maxim referred to Simon by a host of sobriquets— sometimes disrespectful and always casual—but he only used that code name when he was dead serious. He was the only person alive who knew why Simon had chosen that name.

To Simon the legend of King Arthur epitomized humanity—honor, justice, free will, strength and weakness. He'd intended Excelsior to be Camelot under his direction. He'd vowed to wield his power to protect his country yet never forget he was human.

But as Simon peered through the opening of the bathroom door at the woman asleep on the bed, he had to wonder if he'd only been a man before becoming acting director. Had he forgotten how to be human, after all?

"My gut is going wild on this," he finally said. "I don't think Casanova would ever hurt her, but things don't add up. On the surface they might appear to—"

"You investigated him as hard as Oversight investigated you."

"I needed to be satisfied, and every time I think I am, I'm reevaluating because of some new development. I haven't gotten to the bottom of what happened inside that camp or there wouldn't be any new developments. My instincts tell me there is a lot I still don't know."

A heavy sigh transmitted over the device. "Then you trust that, my friend. I've bet my life on those instincts of yours more times than I can count, and I'm still around to take orders. Obviously we've sprung an inside leak, and with Oversight's involvement on the original investigation, we have a lot of potential suspects. If you say Casanova stays on the list, he stays. Just tell me what angle you want me to work."

Had Oversight infiltrated his system and tracked TJ's movements the way team one had? TJ wouldn't have caught their shadow subroutines. Oversight was fail-safe, but to Simon they were now potential links to the outside.

Given the involvement of the United States with the former Yugoslavia's civil war, connections abounded among those who might have made up the Oversight committee. The president himself had hosted the summit in Dayton, Ohio, where the historic peace agreement that had withdrawn Serbian troops from Bosnia had been hashed through and signed by the presidents of those countries and Croatia.

Simon couldn't investigate without knowing who was on the committee, and the president would never reveal which of his power brokers had been involved unless Simon cleared Niky and built a damn credible case.

Which didn't look like it would be happening any time soon when the missing piece of this puzzle remained locked tight inside Violet's memory.

And that's when it hit him.

"I had another obvious connection to the detention camp besides Casanova and Wolfgang," Simon said.

There was a beat of silence. "Are you talking about the defecting deputy commander?"

"Yes"

"He's dead, remember? Can't question dead guys."

"No, we can't." He felt an unfamiliar rush of excitement as possibilities took substance in his head. "But you've got a sniper en route to you as we speak. Doesn't it strike you as odd we've got *two* hit-and-runs connected to this situation."

"Shit."

Not long after testifying at the war crimes tribunal, the deputy commander Violet had convinced to defect had been killed in an apparent hit-and-run while jogging. Simon and Oversight had investigated the circumstances surrounding the man's death and had found no question of foul play.

What about in light of these new developments?

"I'm all over it, buddy," Maxim said.

"Keep me informed."

Simon signed off and left the bathroom. He glanced at the neat stack of clothing on the bed that Ms. Joyce had sent. The administrator had cared for Violet in his stead, and he remembered her warning to look at the woman Violet had become.

He stood beside the bed and watched her, wondered who would awaken—his operative or the woman he'd come to know as Claire, a woman who in many ways had reverted to the woman he'd known before she'd become team one, an emotional woman who'd lived and loved intensely, who'd embodied everything *human*.

Trailing his gaze from her tangled blond hair to the lashes forming dark crescents on her cheeks, Simon thought of all he'd learned about her life since his arrival at Safe Harbor, about his operative and the woman called Claire.

And he knew what to do.

Crossing the room, he opened the door and directed one of his operatives to bring him a roll unit from the treatment room. Within minutes he was searching through drawers, gathering items on the adjustable table. Scalpel. Antiseptic. Plastic sutures.

Shoving his jeans below his hip, he felt for a bubble beneath his skin, a low-frequency signifier that linked him to Command. As acting director, he'd been outfitted with a special frequency backup in case of a kidnapping attempt. A bit of technology that had become as natural as his heartbeat.

A stroke of the scalpel and a physical bond to Command popped into his palm. He swabbed the area then applied a suture.

He could have authorized another transponder for Violet that would link her to Command, never let her be invisible to him again, but he wouldn't trust anyone with her safety right now, not his operatives, not Oversight, not the president.

After disinfecting the device and the scalpel, Simon drew the blanket away. Her skin gleamed pale in the dim light, and he swept his gaze along her body to the scar marking the site where her transponder had been before detention camp number twelve.

What had she used to make that twisted knot? A piece of broken glass? A stone? With one action, she'd changed the course of a war and had been lost to him.

Cleansing an area below her hip, Simon made the incision. She only sighed and shifted uncomfortably as he slipped the transponder beneath her skin, smoothed a suture in place.

No one would ever notice he wasn't wearing this device unless Violet moved beyond a certain range and sounded an alarm.

She would not be out of his sight again.

# CHAPTER TWELVE

CLAIRE WASN'T SURPRISED to find Simon sitting beside the bed when she awoke, so close she had only to stretch her fingers to touch him. He watched her with a steely, intense expression. A bruise swelled around his eye and cheek.

She willed herself not to wake up, to stay buried in sleep. This was a wish she'd made before, and she couldn't understand what was so damned hard about staying asleep.

"Claire?"

His voice tugged her further from her drugged sanctuary. She felt him touch her brow, warm fingertips that smoothed hair from her face. Squeezing her eyes tightly shut, she felt her face crumble against the effort, felt hot tears steal through her lids. She heard the ragged sound of his breathing, and willed herself to stop existing, right here, right now.

But the bed rocked, and he sat beside her, lifted her into his arms. "Everything's okay now, Claire."

Everything wasn't okay. He'd been understanding and kind, and she'd repaid his kindness by dragging him into this bottomless pit where she lived. She hadn't gone to pieces in so long, and now everything was coming apart.

Claire cried until she simply had nothing left, and still he held her, cradled her against his chest, stroked her face. He whispered soothing words to guide her through grief. She couldn't bear his gentleness that absolved her of accountability when she was to blame.

Touching his cheek, she molded her palm over the swelling, not touching, not wanting to cause more pain. "I'm sorry."

He threaded his strong fingers around hers. "Don't."

One word. One command. That stoic look on his face. The firm grip of his hand, and Claire knew.

No man would subject himself to this without caring.

And he shouldn't care. Not even a little. He was kind and all she offered in return was pain and uncertainty.

"I have to go." Breaking away, Claire fought back more tears. "I can't be here anymore. I—I can't."

He let her go, his expression revealing everything in a look meant to reveal nothing. But it was there, in his actions. She wondered if he even realized it.

"Ms. Joyce sent clothes," he said.

She followed his gaze to the foot of the bed, nodded. When Simon finally turned away, she was glad.

Claire tried to stand, but her head spun and her legs felt weak. She settled for sitting on the bed to tug on sweatpants and socks. When she pulled the hospital gown over her head, she wondered if she should have dressed in the bathroom.

What did it matter? She had no pride left to hold on to.

Though she took great pains to clear the clouds from her head, she couldn't shake off the physical effects of the drugs and weaved drunkenly when she tried to stand again. But Simon was there to provide a steadying arm. He didn't offer to take her home. She wasn't going anywhere without him. They both knew it.

She must have slept again during the ride home, but the cold air revived her. She managed the stairs in the building with only his hand on her waist for support.

On the second floor, he stopped her. "You'll stay with me."

With a less fuzzy head, she might have argued. But not now. Now, all she could think of was how she didn't want to be alone.

"Where?"

He motioned his key to the door where a man named Randy Joe lived. Or had. "I sublet this apartment. It seemed more practical than a hotel."

Randy Joe bussed tables and washed dishes at a nearby restaurant, was too fond of vodka and wanted to visit Las Vegas to strike it rich. Knowing Simon, he'd plunked down a chunk of change, and Randy Joe had taken his windfall and the first bus across the border.

"You chased out the most normal guy in the building."

"He'll be back."

Simon had transformed Randy Joe's unique decor of secondhand furniture and glassware collectibles of vodka bottles and cloudy tumblers, into a respectably clean, serviceable abode.

She wondered if he'd leave all the new stuff when he was through with the apartment. If so, Randy Joe was up a few, no matter what happened in Vegas.

She stepped inside, not sure what to make of this new twist, thoughts still too muddled to even begin to wade through how she felt about knowing Simon had not only waited her out, but had done it on the floor below her. "I need caffeine."

"The doctor said you needed to sleep off the effects of the drugs."

More drugs. And here she'd thought she'd moved past this. "You shouldn't care so much, Simon. I don't."

That seemed to surprise him, as if he hadn't realized his feelings were so transparent. But he seemed determined to have his way. "You'll feel better after you sleep."

Claire didn't think so, but she didn't resist when he led her into the bedroom.

Guiding her to the bed, he held the comforter while she slid between the sheets. "You're safe here. Please believe me."

Claire had no right to ask for anything. He'd done so much already, but in that moment, with his promise between them… "Talk to me, Simon. I don't want to be alone in my head."

The mattress sank with his weight, and shifting to her side, she buried her face in the pillow and closed her eyes, telling herself she shouldn't *need*, not from Simon.

But the sound of his silky voice became an anchor. He talked about Safe Harbor, about the acceptance and hope he saw in those who lived there, about how he sometimes forgot to look beyond life's ugliness. How she helped him see past it.

She liked that he'd found something good in her. *Someone* needed to. Before Simon had shown up, she'd lived in survival mode, minutes strung together one by one. She'd felt a sense of accomplishment whenever she slept for more than two hours without awakening in a cold sweat. She'd been so proud when she'd earned enough money for the deposit on her efficiency.

If not for Simon's arrival, she would still be living in the present, enjoying her friends, savoring each and every good day, moving further and further away from her forgotten past.

But Simon had shown up, and revealing the intimacies of her life to such a together man only proved how broken she was. His commanding presence in her life had accomplished what Ms. Verna and the psychiatrists hadn't been able to do in all the time she'd been at Safe Harbor.

Make her face who she'd become.

A joke.

Somewhere deep inside, Claire knew the woman she'd once been would never hide from her life no matter how much it hurt.

She wondered why he'd had this effect on her, remembered what Dr. Davenport had asked about him reminding her of someone from her past. If she'd had someone like Simon in her life, shouldn't she move heaven and earth to find him?

Claire only knew that Simon's voice was an anchor to cling to, a sound that made her wish she was a whole person again.

God, how she wished.

Claire slept. She didn't know how long, but when she awoke the night was black beyond the glow of candles. They were everywhere—on the dresser, night tables, windowsills. Short squat ones on glass plates. Long tapered ones in crystal holders. Small ones in jewel-colored votives.

She stared into the golden haze, calmed by the sight. She liked candles. Claire hadn't known until then, but seeing all the flames and the sparkly bright colors, she knew.

Somehow Simon had known, too.

The warm glow welcomed her, made her release her grasp on sleep. Slipping out of bed, she felt drowsy but stronger while making her way across the linoleum.

She found Simon dozing on the couch, papers scattered on the floor beside him. He looked different when he slept. His face lost the stern edges. His granite jaw looked touchable. Just a man.

It was an odd thought, but she found it strange how she'd never before noticed how lush and silky his lashes were, how she'd never gotten past the iciness of his eyes to notice something so simple and beautiful about him.

He'd changed into sweats, and while he was fully dressed, something about watching him unobserved, caressing a gaze over the powerful lines of his body made each glance intimate.

Despite the furnace at full tilt, the temperature had dropped, so Claire went back to the bedroom to drag the comforter from his bed. She covered him. He inhaled deeply and realigned himself on the couch.

She sat on the floor and pulled a corner around her, wanting to claim this drowsy moment as her own. She could pretend that Simon thought of her as a healthy woman who might care for him. She could imprint this moment upon her heart—she wouldn't trust her faulty memory—and cherish it as hers after he left.

Resting her face in his open palm, Claire closed her eyes, savoring the feel of his pulse beating softly against her cheek.

Maybe it was the change in the rhythm of his breathing or the featherlight touch of fingers stroking her skin that woke her, but when she opened her eyes, she found him watching her.

They didn't speak. Awareness swallowed up any need to intrude on the quiet. He watched her with an expression she'd never seen before, a pleasure that softened his hard features, thawed the iciness from his eyes.

The power of that look held her. She felt safe and protected, the way she'd felt in his car the night they'd met. His fingers trailed along her jaw, an almost absent touch.

A touch that made her want.

She remembered this feeling from some long-ago place, not the details but the feeling as if her next breath held the promise of the future. Claire sat up and let the comforter slide from her shoulders.

"Don't go."

She wasn't sure what to make of that request. There was no light at the end of this tunnel, no place for them to go. Her journey was survival. Simon hadn't shared his. She suspected he didn't share with many. But she felt safe with him here and wanted him to feel safe, too.

Kneeling, she motioned for him to stretch out and get comfortable. She didn't meet his gaze while tucking him in as he'd done for her earlier.

She scooted back, meant to leave him to sleep, but suddenly those strong fingers gripped her wrist and held on.

"What can I do to help you feel better?"

Maybe it was the need in his voice. Maybe it was the aftereffect of the drugs, but when those strong fingers tightened their grip, Claire knew what she wanted, no matter how much she shouldn't.

SIMON SHIFTED to his side so Violet could stretch out beside him. Her body aligned neatly against his in that surprising way like the night they'd danced. Her long legs molded his. Her backside curved snugly in his lap.

He flipped up the comforter, cocooned them in warmth. He hesitated only briefly before slipping his arm around her, holding her loosely, resting his cheek on her head, inhaling deeply of her cool silk hair.

The scent and feel of her hit him hard, made detachment such a struggle. For so long he'd distanced himself, had only allowed himself to be her director, never a man. He'd placed Excelsior between them, and now finally understood his instincts had warned that she would feel exactly the way she felt now.

Like a woman who belonged in his arms.

But Simon didn't want to analyze his feelings. He wanted to comfort Violet. He wanted to lend her strength as she crossed the chasm between her past and her present.

"Do you plan to watch over me every second?" Sleep hadn't dulled her shame. Her voice reflected it in throaty roughness.

"I plan to try."

"That's crazy, Simon."

He wanted to prove that he would be here. He wanted her to believe. Holding her tighter, he asked, "How much do you remember about today?"

One simple question shattered her defense. "I…I don't want to think about it. I can't."

Here it was again—that pendulous swing of emotions. The scales dipping despite her struggles to stay balanced. And as Simon lay with her in the darkness, feeling the warmth of her body so enticingly close, he remembered something else.

She just wanted to feel better.

Her feelings were all she had. All *he* had to bridge this distance between them. He had to trust her feelings. And his.

"I do care, Claire."

"You shouldn't." She twisted around until their gazes collided. Tears silvered her eyes. "I know you're a visitor in my life. I can't care about you. I can't depend on you. I'm not…able. But you feel so right, and I don't know why."

He remembered his first look at the tribunal photo, visual proof she'd suffered. The fierce desperation he'd felt to deny the evidence. He recognized that fierceness in her and wanted to absorb her fear, take away the tears dampening her lashes.

"I'm not a visitor. Let me share my strength."

Simon didn't know what to expect, but the moment stretched between them, filled with expectation, a closeness that carried out on each breath. She exhaled a ragged sigh and lifted her mouth to his, her lips poised so close they almost touched.

"I remember this." She trembled. "I remember feeling good."

"A real memory?"

"No." The word burst warmly against his mouth, enticing. "I don't know who I've made love to, but I know I must have. I know this…*want*."

Simon knew the want, too. But this was about what Violet needed, not what he wanted. He wanted so much.

Yet no matter how many good experiences she'd had, she'd also suffered, and he had no protocol to guide him, no way of knowing if his admissions would comfort her, or stir up some deeply buried nightmare.

All he had was Violet.

She would lead, and he would follow.

"I want to remember something good," she whispered. "Help me remember."

Her soft lips parted in invitation, and the almost touch of her mouth against his answered all his questions, resolved any doubts. Simon gambled his feelings and her future. He demanded that Claire trust him the way Violet had.

Sliding his hand behind her head, he slanted his mouth across those tempting lips, let her sample his want in a prelude to a kiss. His pulse stilled as he waited, the moment provocative as he wondered whether she would accept what he offered, whether he could accept her rejection.

They shared a breath. Then her eyes drifted shut, and she kissed him with a humbling simplicity. Though she called herself Claire, she was Violet, and she trusted him with her fragile emotions as she'd always trusted him with her life.

He drank in the taste of her, the taste of their mingled breaths, and she responded, not tentatively as he'd expected, but by dragging her tongue against his in an erotic move.

Not a woman wary, but a woman who wanted.

Swallowing a groan, he fought to follow her lead when her kisses evoked a heated response he could barely contain, one she wasn't likely to miss.

Her sigh mingled with their kiss as she slipped her cool hands beneath his shirt, smoothing her fingers along his back.

"Help me remember, Simon." She exhaled the words against his lips, explored him with a freedom that suggested she'd waited forever for the privilege.

Her eagerness touched him in places he hadn't allowed himself to feel in so long, places that made him respond as if he was nothing more than a man who wanted a woman.

But Violet wasn't any woman, she was a woman who sacrificed too much for mission objective. He fought not to let instinct claim them. He needed to be rational, to be aware of her responses before his own.

But as they lay together in the darkness of this chilly apartment, their bodies pressed close, he wanted nothing more than to let all the circumstances between them fall away.

"Help me remember," she whispered before deepening their kiss, arching her body, pressing her breasts to his chest, cradling what had fast become a raging erection.

The rational part of him warned how huge the risk was here, but he couldn't stop himself from answering. Not in this moment, not when she wanted only to feel good.

Dragging his hands along her throat, he tipped her head back to drink in the sound of her sigh, speared his tongue inside to taste her impatience.

Their kisses grew urgent. Their hands explored. The moments grew breathless, surreal. She was in his arms, warm and alive and excited, her sleek body wrapped all around him, urging him to touch her, to coax more sighs from her lips, to discover how to fuel her hunger the way she fueled his.

Only hard-edged discipline held him back. Sanity

demanded he prove worthy of her trust. Far too much was at stake for him to lose himself. Not when she'd trusted him.

Threading his fingers into her hair, he forced her head back to trail kisses behind her ear. Tasting. Tempting. Testing. Her responses. His restraint.

His breaths came hard as he worked his mouth over her sweet jaw, was rewarded when she trembled. He lingered over her pulse, found his own response to that quick heartbeat powerful.

Violet. Alive. In his arms. A groan slid from his lips, and he ground against her, unable to stop, awed by how she clung to him, urged him to give in to this fire they made together.

Then she trembled again.

Cherishing the scars below her jaw with his kisses, he reveled in the taste of her skin, in the way her chest rose and fell sharply as he nibbled his way down her throat.

Through the heat of his desire, Simon felt her hands flutter nervously behind his back, her arms loosen their hold. Her body lost its eager litheness, grew taut.

She drew in a series of shuddering breaths.

He didn't need to see her face to know she'd lost the beauty of the moment. He just held her close, not speaking, knowing no words to ease what she'd endured on Excelsior's behalf, no words to dull the pain of not knowing how many people cared for her. Of feeling abandoned.

So he stroked her hair, offered her shelter in his arms, his own desire forgotten beneath a need to comfort her that felt so foreign, yet right.

Time passed, marked by the slowing of her pulse,

the calming of her heartbeat, the relaxing of her body in his arms.

"I'm okay."

Simon lifted his head to meet her gaze. He saw resignation in her eyes, and something else…a melting softness as she watched him.

"Thank you." She reached up to thumb his lower lip.

He'd done nothing worthy of thanks, but he couldn't deny her need in that moment, so he simply shook his head and said, "Thank you."

"For what?"

"For letting me be here for you."

She laughed softly. "I think I'm getting the better end of this deal."

Now it was his turn to smile. "No. You're wrong there. You touch me. I admire your kindness, and your strength."

"I feel strong when you hold me."

He had no idea how deeply her words could reach, but they reached into places that made him want to lie here in her arms and forget the rest of the world. He wanted to be a man without obligation, a man not forced to shut down so much of himself to make such hard choices.

Just a man.

Tipping her head to the side, Violet kissed the corner of his mouth, whispered, "Make love to me."

He searched those jeweled eyes, and the excitement he saw there mirrored his desire without question. Her eagerness suddenly felt like a privilege he hadn't earned.

Slipping her hand between them, she zeroed in on his crotch. He held his breath as her fingers sought the thickness there, made him ache.

All his careful deliberation fell away. That last hesitation, that fear their arousal might trigger violent memories, vanished. Violet. Claire. She was his now, and this moment existed of bold moves and hot pleasure.

"Yes." His voice broke, a rough sound in the darkness.

With a throaty laugh, she pressed her palm knowingly, eliminating all questions about what was happening between them. Wanting. Desire. Hunger.

She wanted him.

It was so simple.

In a quick move he hoisted himself over her. She gasped out a laugh as he rolled off the couch and stood.

Simon stared down at her, almost overwhelmed by the sight she made, by the need gathering his body in a tight ache.

She was lovely in her desire. Pale hair spread out over the couch. Her incredible eyes lifted to his, pleased yet so vulnerable that he felt the potency even more clearly than when she touched him.

He lifted her into his arms.

She took the liberty of exploring his hair with idle fingers, the line of his jaw, the bruise around his eye. She pressed her open mouth to that tender skin. She didn't apologize again, and Simon was glad. He wanted no more hesitation or regret. Right now he was a man holding a very desirable woman.

He was only a man.

Carrying her into the bedroom, he laid her on the bed. He undressed her in the candlelight, unveiled her beautiful body in almost reverent moves, growing dazed with unreality as the flames blurred her sleek curves in a golden haze. She looked dreamlike, all long feminine lines and sensual grace.

She stretched languidly, her body pale against the sheets, a performance meant to entice. "You make me feel beautiful."

"You are." His words weren't elegant, only earnest.

She must have known because she lifted her arms to him in invitation, welcomed him in her embrace.

He'd undressed her in a careful unveiling, but suddenly her hands were everywhere, shoving his shirt up, dragging down his sweats. She explored him as though she didn't want to miss anything, and there was no modesty, only need. He was charmed by her boldness. Aroused by it.

Then they were naked.

She didn't speak. She only draped herself against him as if she wanted to imprint the feel of his body against hers. Perhaps desire had reached her forgotten past. He only knew that her honesty made him want her more than he'd ever wanted.

His hand shook when he swept an open palm down the column of her throat, skimming along in the warmth of her skin, barely touching. He molded the curve of her breast, hovering as he explored the soft fullness. Her nipple gathered. He heard her sharp intake of breath.

She fluttered her hands around his shoulders, pressed openmouthed kisses into his hair, excited, caring gestures that spurred him to greater intimacies.

Lowering his head, he flicked his tongue over a nipple, earning a sigh. Even in the candlelight's glow he could see a blush tinge her skin, physical proof of her desire. For him.

She breathed soft words of encouragement into his

hair, warm bursts that filtered through him, igniting fire through his blood that made him want more.

He drew that tight peak into his mouth, his groin pulsing in time with each slow, wet pull. Her hands molded the curve of his head, held him close. His awareness fine-tuned to the scent and taste of her skin, the sound of her low moan, the feel of her long bare legs entwined with his.

And he knew only how much he wanted her.

Skimming his hand down the smooth expanse of her stomach, he speared his fingers through her silky hair. She arched into his touch eagerly, encouraging him as he dragged kisses down her stomach with heated purpose. He wanted to taste her, to hear her sultry moans fill the quiet as he brought her to pleasure.

Without a word, she sank onto her back, stretching out before him in breathtaking detail. She spread her thighs. Guided by her responses, Simon explored her, but it was his body that burned out of control, and when she dipped her toes underneath his hip to reach all sorts of places that had never been teased to life in quite this way. He ached.

She began a swaying motion to ride his mouth to fulfillment, and he barely clung to his restraint. She speared her hands beneath the pillows. He sank his fingers into her backside and lifted, helping create the friction she needed. She exhaled a series of shuddering gasps then, with her soft thighs trembling against his face, she came apart.

Simon lay there panting, savoring each sweet spasm, trying to control his own urge to work his way back up her body and sink deep inside her wet heat.

She didn't give him a chance.

Violet may have lost her memory, but she was as highly trained as he was. In one unexpectedly energetic move, she twisted out from beneath him, then stretched full length along the bed, and pulled him into her arms. The dreamy impatience on her beautiful face made him smile.

She reached out to brush her fingertips against his mouth. "You should do this more often."

"What?"

She thumbed his lip. "Smile."

Her voice was an echo from the past, a purely Violet sentiment, one he'd heard all too often.

But she didn't give him a chance to dwell on anything but the present as she maneuvered against him, slim curves molding his. Soft breasts pressed against his chest. Hoisting a leg over his, she spread her legs, trapping his erection.

He braced himself against her sexy assault, caught her jaw between his fingers and tipped her mouth up for a kiss.

"You want me," she whispered against his lips.

"I do."

Then she arched her hips, sliding him inside just enough to earn a reply. Tangling his tongue with hers, he tried not to move, fought to let Violet control the moment.

She wrapped herself around him, rocked against him, starting up a sultry teasing motion that stole his breath, that proved his control was only an illusion.

She urged him on with excited gasps that broke against his lips like velvet kisses. She held him tight, met him thrust for thrust, and Simon surrendered even the illusion of control, and lost himself inside her.

## CHAPTER THIRTEEN

CLAIRE DRIFTED toward awareness, reluctant to give up the peaceful feeling of sleep. She savored the warm strength of the man beside her. The intimacy of the hard thigh nestled between hers. The weight of his arm over her hip and the soreness of a cut there, a deep one from the feel of it.

Simon.

She lay there, feeling the luxurious ache between her legs, the tenderness of the skin he'd caressed with skilled, knowing hands, kissed with such utter possession.

She lay wrapped in her lover's arms, as if she was a woman with no cares but how she might awaken him with a kiss, how she might share this drowsy sense of wonder at what she'd found in his arms.

She wasn't that woman. She was the woman who'd bruised this man's face, had needed to be drugged into a stupor before she could find herself again.

Sometime during the night, the comforter reappeared from the living room. Claire didn't remember when. But they'd managed to kick the top sheet into a heap beneath it, and the stark reminder of their abandon made her tremble. Slipping out from beneath his arm, she dragged the sheet off the bed and wrapped it around her.

Moving to the window, she stared at the flickering flame of one of the last enduring candles, felt stunned and unsure.

Life was coming apart at the seams, and she'd vowed not to let that happen. Yet she'd forsaken every shred of judgment and made love to this man.

Why?

That answer, at least, was simple. Simon made her feel good, and she'd grasped the feeling with both hands.

What wasn't so simple to figure was why he was in her life at all. Why now, when she lived minute to minute, when she had so little of any value to offer?

"Claire?"

His voice made her jump, and she turned toward him, mind scrambling for ways to ease her sudden awkwardness.

The sight of him rising naked from bed, the cut lines of his body, every muscle shifting with lean grace, knotted the reply in her throat.

Black hair sprinkled in the hollows and ridges of his chest, arrowed down his trim stomach into a profusion between hard-muscled thighs. He was so beautiful, dark and powerful. The bright morning behind the blinds let her see clearly how beautiful he was.

Coming to stand beside her, he laid a hand on her shoulder, pressed a kiss to the top of her head. "Good morning."

"Simon, I…" She what? Suddenly Claire didn't know.

He circled her, at ease with his nakedness in that uniquely male way. He lifted a strand of hair from her neck, wrapped it around his fingers and brought it to his lips. "Hmm?"

"Last night was just one night, okay? No obligations. Nothing complicated."

"I see." His clear gaze grew smoky around the edges, a look that suggested he saw so much more than she'd meant to reveal.

Closing in, he crowded her against the wall. He stepped on the sheet, and she clutched at it, but he persisted until it gaped open and exposed her.

One night they might excuse as chance. This morning meant making choices she had no business making. She wasn't a normal woman who could get involved in a relationship. She couldn't commit to a tomorrow, let alone a future.

"This isn't complicated, Claire," he said. "I feel close to you. I don't want to lose that."

Lowering his face to hers, Simon used his nose to nudge hers up until he captured her mouth. He met her resistance with the temptation of taste, of touch, of tenderness, of truth. Then there was no denial, no restraint. Not in the face of this man and his desire. Not when he made her feel.

She melted against him, found it so easy to surrender to sensation and pretend they were no more than new lovers in awe of each other.

Claire didn't resist when he kneed apart her thighs. She opened herself to him and sighed.

*1:48 p.m. CET*
*Strpski Grad Republika, -2°C*

IVAN HAD BEEN DEEP in conversation with a Stabilization Force commander when the blinking red light on his telephone unit signaled the call he'd been waiting for. Any other line, he would have disregarded. But this call outranked even the games he must play with these international soldiers who bullied his people into accepting crumbs within the entity borders. Those boundaries separated Strpski Grad Republika—*his* Bosnia— from the weak Federation Bosniaks who let the West lead them by the nose for the protection of their armies.

A pitiful state of affairs that would not be allowed to last forever.

Ivan prided himself on his diplomacy and smiled graciously.

"If you'll forgive me, Commander. I must take this call." He pressed the intercom button. "Ciril, please allow Commander Sells to refresh himself before we leave for our luncheon."

The commander nodded good-naturedly and stood, and in seconds, Ciril arrived to escort their guest away.

Ivan waited until the door closed and reached for the phone. "Hello."

"Christ almighty, what did you get me caught up in here?" the bootlegger demanded. "Your deliveries didn't make it, and they apprehended my carrier."

"You assured me you could make these deliveries. You assured me you had someone capable."

"Way more than capable. But these are some freaking heavy hitters you're dealing with, buddy, and this is way more aggravation than you paid me for. *Way* the crap more."

"Surely with your price scale you could afford a fail-safe," Ivan said coolly. "What happened to the package I wanted returned?" *What about the photograph of the woman?*

"My guess is it was apprehended with the carrier. I haven't talked to him because he's in custody."

Ivan forced himself to relax the sudden tension that forced his grip to tighten on the receiver. "I wanted that package."

"I didn't want my most skilled carrier to get busted."

There was no place to go with this. If the assassin had been apprehended, the bootlegger would have no choice but to bury himself deep enough not to be caught by the American government. No hired man would remain loyal for long when his life was on the line, and while Ivan knew the bootlegger would not have left any obvious trails to his identity, Ivan also knew no man or plan was infallible.

"See what you can do for me, will you?" the bootlegger asked. "Blow some smoke in another direction. The sooner I get settled, the sooner I can get back to work."

Until a week ago, Ivan would have simply placed a call to his Western contact and commanded the man to fan the flames elsewhere. But that avenue was now closed to him.

"I'll keep this telephone line available. Let me see what I can do." Ivan disconnected.

He would have preferred to sever all ties with the man as he had severed the call. The bootlegger had failed, and Ivan would rather risk no further contact. He could easily punch in a code to run an automatic security transfer on the secured lines.

With one click, this number and its signal bouncing through five different countries would simply vanish as if it had never been. A new number would instantly replace it.

A number no one possessed.

But Ivan stared at the phone, debating whether he trusted the bootlegger not to get caught by the *heavy hitters* who'd placed them in such a precarious position. Ivan only had to decide how much risk he wished to take.

*Always safe, never sorry.*

*9:12 a.m. EST*
*Sault. Ste. Marie, -1°C*

"KEEPING VIOLET INSIDE that apartment for two days was some trick," Niky said. "What'd you tell her?"

Simon ignored the question, though he glanced at Niky's shoulder, where the bulging bandage covered the damage from the assassin's bullet. Physical proof he cared about Violet.

*"Doesn't taking a bullet earn points around here?"* Maxim had asked him.

Did Niky deserve points?

Striding inside the audio-visual room above Safe Harbor's school auditorium, Simon shrugged off his coat and stood in front of a wall-size window. From this vantage, he could see Violet on the stage below with several teachers, painting the set for Gabrielle's kindergarten play.

Coordinating this outing and containing the environment hadn't been easy, could only take place after the students and most of the faculty had left for the day.

He'd spent the hours while Violet had slept last night in communication with his perimeter captain and TJ, working on his laptop so he could claim to be writing in case she awoke.

The outcome had been worth the effort. Even from this distance, Violet looked relaxed. Simon wanted to believe their time together had something to do with her good mood.

Switching off the audio, he cut off the chitchat filtering in from below, and faced his team. Niky sat on a soundboard, his feet propped on a chair. Quinn stood beside him.

He turned to Major. "Status."

"Maxim got a name from the assassin—Kurt Turba."

"The bootlegger, from Miami?"

"After the FBI chased him out of South Florida, we pegged him in Panama. He operated there for a few years then nothing for the past nine months. Looked like he shut it down. My guess is he needed money and relocated. St. Louis this time. He gouges his customers when he's inside the States."

"Did we apprehend him?"

Major shook his head. "By the time we got there, his operation was down."

"How long to track him?"

"Don't know. He had an escape hatch. Maxim's on it. But I want you to see what else we found. The sniper wasn't only taking potshots at Violet."

Major withdrew a photo from his briefcase. He handed it to Simon who peered down at an image of Violet, Niky and Gabrielle, moments before Violet had knelt to retrieve a fallen mitten.

"The sniper wanted to ID her *before* the hit," Simon said. "He couldn't have been looking for proof she was dead."

Major nodded. "Neat twist, hmm?"

Simon recalled some details on the bootlegger. This death broker serviced a large network of prominent clients, who kept him well funded.

Well funded enough to put a hit on a deputy commander who'd sought asylum in the West?

Perhaps. Simon couldn't say for sure, but he knew it wouldn't be hard for Kurt Turba to drop out of sight. Maxim would pick up the trail again, but it would take time. Time they didn't have.

"Violet has an enemy with connections," Simon said. "Without the bootlegger, we don't have a place to start looking. We've bought some time until they can arrange another hit, but I've got to get her out of here."

"How?" Major asked.

He glanced down at the stage, where Violet knelt with a paintbrush over a cardboard cutout of a castle. She laughed at some comment a teacher made, and he could practically hear her laughter across the dark expanse of empty auditorium seating.

The sound burned in his memory, along with impressions of the woman she'd become at Safe Harbor. Her determination to make her days useful, to savor each moment as precious from the instant she opened her eyes until she closed them again. The feel of her warm and wanting in his arms. The sound of her sighs in the darkness.

"I wanted to give her the time she needed to remember," he said. "But I have no more time to give her. She's a target and placing others at risk."

"I'm still waiting to hear what you told her to keep her inside that apartment for two days," Niky said. Quinn shot him a quelling look.

"I told her that the shots were fired by friends of those boys she had trouble with outside the cafeteria."

"Gang retaliation?" Quinn asked.

He nodded. Violet would have recognized that a

sniper had marked her, but Claire had accepted what he told her, had trusted him. "It's going to take me a few days to convince her to leave town with me for a writing conference. Until then, I'll keep her contained in the apartment. We can protect her there."

"A writing conference? Isn't that a long shot? Why would she go anywhere with you?" Major drilled him with a razor stare.

Simon held his gaze. The sudden silence ached as team one pulled the pieces together.

"Simon?" As always, Quinn was the voice of reason, but her frown held him accountable.

He'd known his actions would place him on volatile footing, with motive and ethics. He'd crossed a solid line, and now, as he faced his team, detachment failed him again. He didn't want to rationalize the reasons he'd made his choices, didn't want to explain Violet's need, or his own, didn't know if he could make them understand when he didn't himself.

"Tell me you're not sleeping with her." Niky shook his head as if to clear it. "Tell me that's not how you got her to stay with you inside that apartment."

Simon's silence condemned him, and he steeled himself against their stares, unsure what he found more disconcerting—having his judgment questioned or team one viewing him as a man.

"What the hell is wrong with you?" Niky demanded. "She hasn't suffered enough? Why would you mess with her like this?"

"I'm reaching her with the only tools I have." His rationalization fell far short of its mark. "You'll have to trust that."

"You're doing what's best for you." Niky kicked

away the chair and came to his feet, bristling. Quinn contained him with a hand on his forearm. Major took a step closer.

"Don't make this personal, Niky," Simon said.

"This is personal. This is *Violet*."

"Mission objective is to keep her safe and bring her home. I plan to do that."

But team one knew him too well. They wouldn't consider that he might have found something with Violet that changed the rules. They wouldn't give him the benefit of the doubt when they knew he'd sacrifice himself, and Violet, for mission outcome.

Simon had only himself to blame because he'd never given them any reason to believe he might feel like a man, that he wouldn't ruthlessly use Violet to his own ends.

"Simon." Major looked as if he still hadn't accepted this truth. "What are you doing, man?"

"This is beyond dangerous. Violet is emotionally fragile right now." Quinn leaned against the soundboard, looked as if she needed the support to hold her up. Such an uncharacteristic reaction made him wonder if she was sorry she'd ever revealed Violet's confidences.

He couldn't blame her if she was. What had seemed so simple in the dark suddenly twisted with complications in the light.

"I won't risk losing her again." He wondered if any of them understood how deeply he meant that.

He wondered if he did.

"You're way out of line," Niky spat.

"If any of you question my decision, my jet's on standby. Get on it."

They stared at him as if the man they'd known had vanished, and he expected them to head toward the door. A mass exodus because he'd crossed the line. This was team one, handpicked and personally trained by him to be the best. They expected the same from him.

The silence stretched hard.

"You can't keep her hidden away with you indefinitely," Major finally said.

No one took off, but Simon knew they believed he'd betrayed their trust. He had.

"Agreed. But I don't have many choices here. Violet can't stay, and my explanations to convince her to leave are seriously limited. And I have a logistical problem. I can't bring her into Command until I know who wants her dead."

"If you can get her to leave Safe Harbor, she'll be out of her comfort zone," Quinn said, considering. "You might trigger more memories."

He would take her away from caring Ms. Joyce and adoring Gabrielle, replace the people she loved with strangers. He saw no other choice.

*"I know it in my head, but I don't feel it."*

Niky looked disgusted. "This isn't some Jane Doe you're playing with."

Handing back the photo to Major, Simon suddenly could see an image of Niky and Violet together in his memory, one of the countless times he'd monitored their work from Systems Ops. Niky's head bent low over Violet's, his expression thoughtful, hers alive with laughter, their noses almost touching. Simon could remember thinking they'd looked poised to kiss.

Niky had so much more experience caring for Violet, protecting her. "Niky, try to—"

"This is *Violet,* and you're using her—"

Simon grabbed him by the shirt, backed him against the wall. A chair crashed against the door, punctuated the sudden violence. "Do not make this personal."

This was *not* about Violet. This was about protecting her. This was about trust.

But the frustration that had Simon tightening his grip around Niky's throat branded him a liar.

He saw the flash of hurt in Niky's face. Simon released him and stepped away. He watched Niky turn without a word and walk out the door.

Quinn's voice was sharp in the sudden silence. "You realize the path you've chosen is likely to explode in your face and hurt us all."

"I will not lose her again."

CLAIRE OPENED HER EYES and stared into the darkness of Simon's bedroom. A street lamp from outside illuminated the slats of the blinds, but she saw nothing that might have awakened her.

The night felt dreamy, safe, and she could feel his warm body all around her, arm draped possessively across her waist, a knee pinning hers beneath him. Turning her head on the pillow, she found him still asleep, expression content, jaw relaxed. She smiled into the darkness.

Then the scene shifted, a blur of motion and shadow so sharp and sudden that she blinked hard to clear her vision, waited for the moment to become right again.

*Simon dressed in camouflage, glossy dark hair untouched by gray, teeth flashing in a fast grin.*

*A knife blade pressed below her jaw.*

Fear gripped her chest like a vice. Her throat constricted. Her mouth went dry.

Rolling out from beneath him and off the side of the bed, Claire stared into the dark bedroom, not understanding the fractured image when she could see Simon clearly. He exhaled restlessly, sank into the spot where she'd lain as if noticing her gone. The temperature in the room spiked. A clammy sweat filmed her skin. She felt hot and cold at the same time.

She couldn't breathe.

Scrambling to her knees, Claire caught the edge of the dresser, needing to get away, to get control of the shadows creeping around the edges of her vision.

*No, no, no! Not here. Not tonight.*

She shook her head to clear the shadows.

The crucifix caught in her hair. The chain tugged at her neck. Reality receded again. The signal in her head changed as if someone had spun a dial. Static crackled. She couldn't hone in on any one frequency.

One minute she staggered from the bedroom. The next…

*Stripped tree branches formed a lattice above her face. The smell of death and fear grew so potent she curled up in a ball, tried not to touch all the corpses around her.*

*They were all dead, at peace.*

The signal shifted again. She couldn't make sense of what was happening. The static shrieked, unbearable. She could see a man—Mr. Camerisi?

*Strong arms caught her. With hands that trembled, he stroked the hair from her brow. He explored every hollow and line of her face, her neck. His expression collapsed at the discoveries he made.*

*His fingers came away bloodied.*

Claire scrambled blindly through the darkness. The

breath trapped in her chest. Her head swelled until she thought it would explode. But she knew what to do.

She had to escape the nightmares.

SIMON PULLED OPEN the closet door, found Violet wedged into the corner, knees drawn close. She stared at him unseeing, might have screamed if she could have. But he recognized terror in the naked angles of her face, heard it in her stark gasps. She was trapped in the horrors playing out in her head.

He made a move to pull her from the cramped space, but something about the way she curled into herself stopped him, drove him to his knees. He gathered her against him, instead, offering the only comfort he could. His strength.

"Claire."

Her every tight gasp for breath shattered the silence, shattered *him*. Simon couldn't see her demons, couldn't fight them. He could only lock himself tightly around her, try to find that forgotten place inside him that once knew how to comfort.

His fingers tangled in her hair, and he ran his hand along the cool strands, whispered, "It's all right, Claire. It's all right now."

A shudder rocked her, and she began to shake. He dragged her across his lap, and she clung to him, skin clammy, chilled from the cold seeping through the bare floor. Simon willed his body to warm her, ran his hands over her icy arms.

"It's all right. Breathe with me." He struggled to keep his voice calm, to mime a breath. "Come on, just breathe."

She tipped her face back to stare at him, gaze slowly

coming into focus. She sucked in a ragged gulp of air, then another. "Who are you?"

Simon didn't want to react. He should have been in control of his emotions, so she didn't have to deal with them.

The fear etched on her face told him he'd failed.

"Who are you?" Her voice rose on a strangled whisper. "I keep seeing your face, but you're not you, not like now…."

His heart pounded hard. Stroking damp hair from her face, he brushed silent tears from her cheeks, decided how best to reply. "I know you from before."

"Tell me." With her characteristic impatience, she refused to spare herself, no matter how painful. "Why did you hold a knife to my throat?"

He stared at her blankly, watching shock and confusion play across her face until he finally understood. "I trained you."

"You're not a journalist?"

"No."

She frowned, clearly trying to pull the pieces together and unsure whether to believe him. Just as he'd had to rationalize his actions to team one, he would have to present his case to Violet and explain the choices he'd made.

"Who am I?"

Not all the questions had occurred to her yet. They would. She struggled to understand, her raspy breaths giving life to the reality of their bodies tangled naked in the darkness. Her smooth bottom curved neatly into his lap. Her breasts rose and fell against his chest with every breath.

She'd definitely want answers.

"An operative with a United States security agency."

He didn't offer more. He had nothing but instinct to guide him, so he waited for her to take the next step, noticing the cold floor, the cramped closet. Violet pressed close, her body temperature rising, a steady warming that paralleled his.

"I knew you'd recognized me when we met," she finally said. "Why didn't you tell me? Why this deception?"

"I thought it would be…less difficult for you if you remembered yourself."

Her brow furrowed, and he guessed she was pulling together the past and the present, his actions against what she'd lived at Safe Harbor. "I was hurt."

"On a mission."

"The nightmares," she said with such a striking combination of disbelief and resignation that Simon tightened his grip. "I know Mr. Camerisi, too, don't I?"

He nodded.

"Tell me, Simon. I need to know everything."

And in that moment, he understood Ms. Joyce's concern about letting Violet face life, trapped between admiration for her strength and fear the reality might crush her spirit.

She stared at him like a stranger. All the beauty they'd known, all the intimacies of these past few days, retreated so fast. Their nakedness was no longer about exploring each other and pleasure. Their nakedness became exposed skin.

He sensed her growing awkwardness as she disentangled herself from his arms. He could feel the heat of her blush as her nipples raked his chest, as he ran his hands along her thighs to steady her when she stood.

His sense of disbelief grew, too. He couldn't stop her withdrawal, didn't know how. The intimacy they'd discovered together was fading, another casualty of the cause they'd committed their lives to.

# CHAPTER FOURTEEN

VIOLET LIERLY.

She liked the name. Feminine. Lyrical. She'd apparently chosen the alias for the woman she'd become in Simon's agency. But now it was just a beautiful name that might have belonged to someone else. While she'd been exploring a spiritual part of herself with Ms. Verna she'd chosen a new name at Safe Harbor. Claire after a character she'd admired in a book, de Beaupré after a saint who helped the lost find safety.

So many personas. Were any of them real?

Staring out the window, she kept her back to the people congregated inside Simon's apartment. Once she'd known them all, but now they were acquaintances, a friendly literary agent, a doctor she'd felt comfortable with, a caring assistant principal who'd placed himself in danger to protect her.

Team one. They clustered around their leader in a ruthless pack fashion. Physically aggressive people who claimed she'd once been one of them.

Violet stood apart now, considering how Simon had hemmed her in on all sides. She found the sheer scope of his deception staggering. He'd walked into her life and cut off her contact with the outside world as completely as if he'd severed arteries. With Ms. Verna's help, he'd placed people all around her. In her writing. In her therapy. In her volunteer work.

In her bed.

Ironically, it was the thought of Simon as he'd held her that grounded her right now, when she felt herself overwhelmed by these strangers who knew her better than she did herself.

She wouldn't let Simon see her struggle, wouldn't let him know he had that much power over her, so she just listened to him deliver the facts in his rich voice, a steady sound that struck so many chords deep inside her. She fixed her gaze on the fading night sky, and his voice dragged her back every time her thoughts raced away with flashing images, snippets of things she hadn't realized she'd known.

Major always wore expensive hand-tooled boots in crazy colors. When she'd met him in the diner, he'd been wearing red. Today, blue. Once upon a time, she'd found his boots amusing. Now she just wanted to know why, out of all the things she needed to remember, this man's boots topped the list.

Violet had no clue, so she watched the sun rise on the day when she would finally get her answers.

Also ironically, the answer that felt most pressing... Who was she to Simon? Had they had a relationship before, or was everything she'd felt in his arms just another deception?

He hadn't explained that yet, and she didn't think they'd be getting around to it in front of all these people. She'd already guessed dealing with his emotions didn't come easy to him. This man in command was unrecognizable from the man who'd made love to her with breathtaking frequency these past few days.

He told her about their agency. Covert operations. A world she'd remembered in her writing.

He told her about a critical mission into a Serbian detention camp to extract a defector.

He told her about an avalanche that had exposed the team and forced him to lock down his command center.

He detailed the sequence of events from Niky's return to learning she'd been alive, how she'd sent him another defector to replace their original target. He made her sound very noble, like someone she might write about. A political prisoner who'd sacrificed herself for the greater good.

None of what he said felt real.

Not even five months in a detention camp felt real, even though she'd lived nightmares that left no doubt he told her the truth. Nothing felt real right now except for the sounds of the city coming to life beyond the window.

An old-model station wagon cruised by, close enough to hear the knocking of the lifters, the tires churning through slush melted by dirty sand. From somewhere in the rise of broken-down apartment buildings a couple argued. A garbage truck stopped on the nearby street in a grinding hiss of steel and hydraulics.

What felt real was how all the pieces started coming together in her head. She might not remember, but Violet knew enough about Simon's world—*her* world—to understand that she'd placed this man between a rock and a hard place.

"You didn't expect to find me when I met you on the street that night?" she asked.

"No."

Now that she knew what had happened, she understood his surprise, recognized how quickly he'd assumed control of her and the situation. He claimed he thought it would be easier for her to remember, but she didn't know what to believe, not when there was still so much more to this story.

Forcing herself to turn around, she faced him, took in the rigid cut of his jaw, accepted the reality that things were now different between them. "Am I a target?"

He nodded.

Shock would have been normal, she supposed, but she didn't feel surprised. Her nightmares had been so vivid when she'd first arrived at Safe Harbor, urgent, frightening.

Simon hadn't insisted they call the police after the hit-and-run. He'd lied to her about the shots fired on the ice. He'd needed to protect her and the people at Safe Harbor. All those children...*Gabrielle*.

No, she wasn't surprised. His actions made brutal sense. On some level she'd known. And she finally had her answer.

She'd been mission objective.

*This* felt real. Clutching the windowsill, she dug her fingers into chipped wood and peeling paint to ground herself. This was her building. Her world. The one she'd created, had been so proud of not so long ago.

Hanging on to that windowsill, she refused, absolutely *refused* to look away. She would face them all, even though this moment felt like the zenith of her whole pathetic life.

"Ms. Verna suspected all along, didn't she? That's why she tried to keep me inside Safe Harbor."

Simon inclined his head. "You're a highly trained operative. Your specialized skills are noticeable. Until she knew who you were, she wanted you to be safe."

"Who's after me?"

"We don't know." He explained the series of events between catching the sniper and pursuing the death dealer who brokered assassins. "Once we track down this man, we can learn who financed the hit. I've got people working on it. Until then we can only assess the facts. You've got a powerful enemy. The most likely scenario is that you learned something inside the detention camp that someone considers a threat."

Simon barely glanced at Quinn, who'd been sitting on the arm of the couch, but it was enough to get her to pick up where he left off.

"We're hoping you can help us piece together this puzzle," she said. "There's so much we don't understand about what happened to you between Bosnia and Safe Harbor. Without knowing it's almost impossible to determine who's threatening you."

"I've had nightmares and hallucinations. Things I'm suddenly realizing I know. But I don't know what's real and what isn't."

"That's the perfect place to start. We'll work from there and see what we come up with. Feel up to taking a stab now?"

Violet shrugged, trying not to let Quinn's concern rankle. They were all handling her gently, probably afraid she'd melt down before their eyes, and they'd never get their answers.

She let her gaze trail to the bandage beneath Niky's sweater. Was it any wonder the man didn't smile? He'd lost a team in Bosnia and had taken a bullet to protect her.

"Standard procedure fits all field operatives with two imaging devices—a primary and a backup," Quinn said. "You sent one to us with the defecting deputy commander. With your photos, Simon convinced NATO to take action against the detention camps.

"But there was a second one, Violet, the backup. I've reviewed your medical records, and it doesn't appear to have been on you when you arrived at the Austrian safe house. We need to find out what happened to that device."

"Imaging devices? Like cameras?"

"Yes indeed, little lady." Major pushed himself up from the dining room table and strode the few steps into the kitchen. "But not the disposable kind you buy in a pharmacy. High-tech stuff. Every operative is assigned different ones. No duplication on the same mission. One of yours looked like a fingernail, practically translucent and tough—"

"Was one a tooth?"

Major gave a laugh that echoed from the confines of the refrigerator. "Look here, Simon. She's already coming around."

Simon's gaze cut to hers, and she forced herself not to turn away, tried not to look for things that weren't inside those clear eyes. "It was an incisor crown. You touched it with your tongue to capture an image. Do you remember?"

She appreciated the distraction when Major returned. He passed water bottles around, flashed a grin when he handed one to her. She was glad someone felt good right now.

"One device was here, wasn't it?" She held up the index finger of her left hand.

"Sure was," Major said.

"I don't know why I know that, but I do. It's just information inside my head. I had dreams about a tooth." Nightmares, actually. She'd never been able to figure out why a tooth had figured so prominently. "I hid it because it was important. I don't know why."

"Do you remember where?"

Violet let her eyes drift shut. She willed herself to face those nightmares, somehow less threatening now than the pressure she felt from Simon's stare.

*He was bright gold, larger-than-life, as tall as the ceiling, a man holding a cross that should have symbolized hope.*

*There was no hope inside this place.*

"I hid it inside the saint. I remember poking it through his teeth with a stick."

"What saint?" Niky asked, the first time that he'd spoken in so long the sound of his voice startled her. "There weren't any saints inside the detention camp. The army commandeered a private airfield."

She opened her eyes to find him frowning and shrugged.

"Tell us about this saint, Violet," Quinn prompted.

She described the bright gold figure of a man, her memory of having to maneuver onto some sort of ledge to reach his mouth. "There was enough space to get through the gap between his teeth. I remember being surprised by how far I could push the stick inside. I half expected him to start choking and get me caught." She remembered the sense of urgency when she'd awakened in a cold sweat after that nightmare.

Something about that won a reaction from Simon. Suddenly he was smiling. "The saint wasn't inside the detention camp."

"Where was it?" Quinn asked.

He didn't reply. Instead, he spoke into the air. "TJ, find out if the Brijevek hotel I stayed in during the exhumations is still there."

"Hotel." Niky exchanged a narrowed glance with Quinn.

Violet waited, curious. From what they'd told her, she didn't think she'd slipped out from a detention camp for a weekend away.

Simon inclined his head, clearly receiving his report. "The hotel is still there, but there's no Web site to show you your saint. It was a locally owned place. TJ's trying to track down something for visual confirmation. The saint is a statue in the hotel lobby."

"You visited the hotel?" Niky asked her.

"I don't remember."

"She must have," Simon said. "I stayed there for weeks. The statue is exactly as she describes it."

Major frowned. "There's no reason to believe that device will still be there after all this time, Simon. And if anyone happened across the imaging device, they would think it was a lost crown and probably toss it in the trash."

"Agreed, but there is a possibility. The statue is massive, not something mobile."

"Bubblegum." Another memory from a nightmare. "I remember a young girl handing me a big wad of chewed bubblegum. I stuck the tooth inside. That's how I got it to adhere."

Major laughed. "Well, I take that back then. A few years and chewing gum should have cemented it in snug as a bug."

"Why would I have been inside a hotel?" Violet asked.

That question seemed to galvanize them. Four intense people, all sucking up the air inside this dumpy apartment, and they stared at her as if they suddenly didn't know what to say.

Simon's expression tightened, a look with so much simmering beneath the surface that she turned away, staring out the window again to brace herself for what she sensed was coming.

"Sometimes detainees were removed from the camp," he said. "They were brought into the hotel where the officers stayed."

The image of that saint swelled in memory, shiny and bright in a place with no hope. She didn't need to ask why detainees were brought to the officers.

She clung to the water bottle, an anchor, refused to look at any of them, didn't want to face any pity, didn't want to see Simon's expression. "So I know something important about someone. I took pictures with an imaging device and hid it outside the detention camp to keep it safe."

"The pieces fit," Simon said.

"I can't stay at Safe Harbor."

A beat of silence.

"No, you can't." His voice softened, reminding her of the dark in his arms.

"What happens now?"

"We need to decide what to do," Quinn said. "You have options."

Options? She was a threat to the people she cared about. Someone was trying to kill her. She had no memory of why and her only clue was an imaging device half a world away. Everything was changing, and she had to figure out a way to cope. That was her only option right now. Finding some way to handle this.

"We have a few objectives." Simon's voice was still throaty soft, and she clung to the water bottle, just held on. "Obviously the first is keeping you safe. We need to get your imaging device back. If we can determine what's on it, we can determine our next move."

"Then let's go get it," she said.

"Excuse me?"

Here was something else that felt familiar—Simon's tone, as if he'd shoved his words between clenched teeth. Sure enough, when she turned to face him, his jaw looked ready to crack.

"I thought you said we needed to get the imaging device back." She stared into those clear eyes, found genuine shock. "What's the problem?"

"Violet, you're a target."

*Violet.* He'd avoided saying her name. Hearing him say it wasn't as much a surprise, as knowing he hadn't meant to.

"I see. You weren't talking about *me.* I'm supposed to sit around while you take care of everything. Is that it?"

"I don't think you understand the situation over there right now," he said. "You're talking about heading into a region whose infrastructure was totally destroyed. The Dayton Peace Agreement ended the war between Serbia, Bosnia and Croatia and served up territory for each of them. The Serbs headed into Kosovo to fight for more territory they considered rightfully theirs.

"Bosnia is officially called the Federation of Bosnia-Herzegovina, but the land is split between the people. The Bosnian Muslims call themselves Bosniaks and were given fifty-one percent. The Bosnian Serbs call their forty-nine percent Strpski Grad Republika. The only thing keeping peace between them right now is thirty-thousand NATO troops."

She wanted to tell him she didn't need his permission. Pride got in the way. She had no resources, no identification, no money. She hadn't even known her name until he'd told her.

Was this agitation a knee-jerk reaction to feeling bullied? He'd made love to her then had the nerve to stand there issuing orders as if nothing had ever passed between them. She hated that it even mattered.

Glancing around at the others, she asked, "Do I usually let him boss me around like this? It doesn't feel right."

Major laughed. "Simon's hoping, little lady."

Violet spread her hands in entreaty. "I'm sorry, Simon. I don't mean to be difficult, but if we don't find that imaging device, how are you planning to keep me safe? You've had all kinds of people protecting me. Niky still got shot. I might not remember everything, but I'm not stupid. I've been at Safe Harbor a long time, and no one tried to kill me until you showed up." The idea gained speed in her head. "You can't guarantee I'll be any safer inside your command center, can you?"

His expression didn't change. He didn't say or do anything to show how he felt, and that total absence of emotion cued Violet that she'd hit a nerve. She wasn't sure why she knew that, but she did.

"No."

"Simon, you've been operating on the premise that if you tossed enough familiar people Violet's way, she'd start remembering," Niky said. "Wouldn't retrieving the imaging device do the same thing? And you've got to do something with her. She can't stay here or go to Command. Keeping her on the move might be a good option."

If Violet had been choosing who might support her, she wouldn't have guessed this man. But he seemed resolved when he faced Simon, who just looked stressed.

"This is not up for discussion. Heading into Strpski Grad could be walking right into the enemy's grasp."

"No one knows about the imaging device," Major pointed out.

Niky agreed. "And if they don't know we're looking for anything, heading into the hot zone will be about the last thing they'd expect her to do."

"Don't rule it out entirely, yet, Simon," Quinn said. "You were right about infiltrating her life. She's remembering. We want to keep her moving in that direction."

"Tactically, it's a cakewalk," Niky said. "Brijevek isn't far from the Krajina. SFOR's troops are concentrated around the entity borders. You're talking a day max. All we'd need is a decent cover, transportation and permissions."

"We?" Simon arched a dark brow. "*We* agreed a long time ago we wouldn't assign you to that region."

"If Violet goes, I go."

"You have a bullet hole in your shoulder. Technically, you're on medical leave."

"If Violet goes, I go. I have to."

Such a somber declaration, and while she didn't understand what would motivate Niky to such resolve on her behalf, she didn't doubt he meant what he said.

His determination fueled hers. Suddenly everything seemed so simple. She would face these changes. One at a time and head-on. Only when she took charge of her present and faced her past would she get a shot at a future.

"It's my life, Simon. I want it back. Please just think about it." She crossed the room and opened the door.

"Where are you going?"

"To my place. I have to pack. Regardless of what you decide, I can't stay here."

"Violet—"

She slipped into the hallway. She finally had her answers, and now she had to take back what was hers.

Her life.

SIMON STOOD INSIDE the lobby of Safe Harbor's administration building, watching Major and Niky cross the parking lot to the limo.

"Violet's avoiding me," he said to Quinn, who stood with him while Violet said her goodbyes to Ms. Verna and Gabrielle.

"Give her time. Everything she's comfortable with has changed in the past twelve hours. I think she's handling those changes remarkably well."

"Except she won't speak to me alone."

"I'm curious, Simon. How did you expect her to react to your new relationship when she finally remembered your old one?"

"I expected a chance to explain."

Quinn exhaled heavily. "If it helps any, she understands. We talked at length about the situation earlier. She had questions she needed answers for."

"She *thinks* she understands. She doesn't."

"You've accomplished mission objective. What more do you want from her?"

"I care."

Quinn stared up at him, searching for something that made him feel raw and exposed. "If that's honestly how you feel then I'm sorry you chose the route you did. You don't maneuver emotional terrain easily on a good day. You would have had your work cut out for you dealing with that and Violet's condition. Now you've shot yourself in the foot."

"How is she?"

"Resolved. Hurt. She remembers just enough about certain things to misinterpret a lot."

"What can I do to help?"

"Give her space. She'll let you know when she's ready to hear your explanations. Right now her life is all tied around you. While she understands why you made the choices you did, she also knows I revealed her past feelings for you. She thinks you used that information. Her pride is stinging."

He *had* used her feelings for him. But his feelings were about so much more than mission outcome. He hadn't understood, but looking back at his actions, the choices he'd made…he'd been struggling to keep Violet at a distance he could handle.

"Simon, you know as well as I do Violet's a self-reliant woman—she wouldn't be alive today if she weren't. Her amnesia keeps placing her in uncomfortable situations. Be cognizant of that and try not to make her feel any needier than she already does."

"King Arthur, the pilot radioed. Whenever you're ready," TJ said over the audio device. "Just don't wait too long or they'll have to deice again."

He had no more time to give her. Motioning Quinn to join him, he went to get Violet.

She glanced their way as they approached and gave a barely perceptible nod. They arrived to hear her tell her guests, "I guess it's time."

Gabrielle wrapped her arms around Violet's legs and hung on tight. "Don't go, Claire."

Violet stroked the wispy head, tears filling her eyes. "I'll be back. I promise."

"But I won't be special if you're not here."

Violet disentangled herself from those tight arms and knelt so she could meet the child's gaze. Taking both the little hands in hers, she kissed them, gave a moist smile.

"Of course you'll be special." She pressed their hands over Gabrielle's heart and held them there. "You're special in *here.* I knew it when I met you, and you need to promise me you'll remember, too. Whenever you miss me, I want you to think about something special we did together. I'll do the same when I miss you. We had enough fun together to get through a little while apart, don't you think?"

Gabrielle nodded grudgingly.

"What if I bring you a present? Then when I get back it'll be like Christmas."

"Will you bring me sparkly pink shoes?"

Violet lost it then, tears rolling down her cheeks, an anguish so real that she buried her face in the child's hair. Quinn stopped him from going to Violet with a sharp glance, and he stood there helpless as Violet and Gabrielle clung to each other, wondering whether he had ever held anyone so tightly. Had he ever held anyone as if his heart would break to let go?

Ms. Joyce placed her hand on Violet's shoulder and said, "Gabrielle and I will look forward to hearing about your trip."

Violet nodded, face still pressed against that wispy head, but she smiled when she leaned back and kissed Gabrielle's brow. "I'll bring sparkly pink shoes."

The child smiled. Then slipping her hand inside Violet's, she held on while Violet and Ms. Joyce embraced.

"I'm here for you always," Ms. Joyce whispered. "Just call if you need to talk. I will see you soon."

Simon stepped forward, placed a hand on Violet's elbow. She let him lead her away blindly, tears flowing, but when they reached the door, she glanced over her shoulder and blew a kiss.

Quinn exchanged a few words with Ms. Joyce then followed, and they made the drive to the private airfield in silence.

The executive jet had been custom equipped to monitor Systems Ops in flight. Comfortable for when he entertained politicians or dignitaries from allied nations. But Simon had never noticed before how spacious the cabin was until Violet found a seat that isolated her from him. She stared silently out the window.

Moving to the workstation behind the cockpit, Simon made contact with Command while the jet taxied. Slipping on the headset, he waited until Maxim appeared on the display.

"Status?" Simon asked.

Maxim briefed him on their active missions and brought him up to speed on his interrogation. "I've got all I'm going to get out of our sniper. You want me to toss him back across the border? I don't think you can afford to keep him much longer. Your contact from Canadian intelligence already called in a favor, and it's a whopper. I don't think you want to run your tab any higher."

*Quid pro quo.* The intelligence commander had sensed he'd had Simon in a corner and had jumped on his advantage. When the tables had been turned in the past, Simon had demanded as much for favors rendered. "Agreed. Send the sniper back. Now tell me, what's happening with the bootlegger?"

"I've got a lead that's pointing south of the border, but it hasn't panned out yet. Keep your fingers crossed."

Simon nodded. "What about our investigation into the deputy commander's death?"

"Now here's something that'll make your day. Try an anonymous tip from a retired clerk with the DMV."

"Anonymous?"

"Well, he was anonymous until I got a hold of him. Get this…six months after our deputy commander is run down, this guy calls the local precinct to anonymously report that he might have seen the car involved in the hit-and-run. Says he was running late for work one day and almost got hit head-on by a car tear-assing down the street.

"He avoids a collision by pulling onto the sidewalk and watches the car head down a delivery alley. Didn't think much of it until he read in the paper that a man was hit and killed barely a block away. He even had the tag number."

"Why didn't he come forward before?"

"Claimed to be knee-deep in some shit at work with a high-level asshole trying to screw him out of his pension. He was afraid if he came forward this jerk would get a hold of it and nail him for being late. He called in as soon as the ink was dry on his retirement papers."

"Anonymously."

"Afraid of withholding evidence. The guy's old. What can I tell you?"

"Did the police investigate?"

"They put a few hours into it. After six months, they didn't expect much. They did track down the car—stolen, naturally. There was a report and a recovery. Guess where the car was stolen from?"

There was a beat of silence. Simon waited, not in the mood for guessing games.

"Try in the parking garage of la Costa Brava condos in good old Alexandria. Some coincidence, hmm?"

"You know how I feel about coincidences."

"Sure do. So tell me, how many people including you and me knew where we were hiding our star witness?"

The president. Oversight. Someone inside Command might have gotten the information. Had Niky been that man?

"Not enough." Simon sank back in his chair and pressed his fingers to his temples to ease the ache there. This was exactly the connection he hadn't wanted to exist.

He was back to wanting again.

"Good work. At least we've got a time frame."

"I'm thrilled to know our leak has been happening since your investigation in the detention camp."

Simon ignored the sarcasm. Only time would tell how much information had been passed along, and as this situation proved, only if they knew where to look. "Keep digging, and keep me informed. Now what did you come up with on the hotel?"

"Your hotel changed hands after you were there."

"The statue?" he asked.

"We ran tourist threads, property insurance. Zip. We even tried local contractors who'd worked on the property during the past few years. Bigger bust. Economy sucks over there, and all these mom-and-pop shops are opening and closing faster than you can blink. I finally had Teodora pick up the phone, call the hotel and ask a few questions. Your saint's still there."

"Tell her good work. What did you come up with for cover?"

"Well, there's always the old standby of journalist. The positive is mobility. The negative is that you're heading into the heart of Bosnian Serbdom. Those folks are still touchy about how the media portrayed them as the only bad guys during the war. Not optimum."

Simon agreed. "What else?"

"If you want to take advantage of the locale, you've got two ways to go. Religious pilgrims heading to Medjugorie—out-of-the-way, but plausible if you travel south from Croatia. You'll be checking out every saint and church along the way.

"Or there's your garden variety NGO. Aid groups are big in the Balkans right now. With SFOR running the show, though, I'm not sure how much you'd be welcomed in Strpski Grad. You'll probably get a better response than if people think you're a bunch of zealot Christians. Like I said, they're still touchy."

Simon frowned, his patience thin. "Get to the punch line."

"Because I love you, I came up with something to get you close enough to kiss your saint, no questions asked."

"Which is?"

"Disaster contractor, better known as a catastrophe chaser. After wars, natural disasters, famines and plagues, they haul in the big equipment and rebuild the place. There's some seriously good money in it. Who knew?"

Simon tried that on to see how it fit. Contractors were private industry without government affiliations. They'd have mobility to scout the geography. As with the NGOs, they'd be perceived as lending aid rather than prying. "Good. Disaster contractor it is then."

"So you've decided to take Violet back?"

Simon glanced at her across the cabin. Her tears had dried, but she stared out into the gray sky, her expression so solemn, almost unrecognizable from his memory of how she once lit the corridors of Command with sunny smiles and excitement.

*What kind of person gets hanged?*

He hated what survival had done to her, hated that finding her hadn't resolved all the problems. But Quinn was right. He needed to accept that Violet had to find her own way back. He would stand beside her while she did. He would help when she asked. And he would take every opportunity to prove he cared, so she might eventually give him a chance to explain.

Simon exhaled heavily. "I'm taking her back."

"What are you going to do about Niky?"

"Take him. He has expertise in that region and with the detention camp."

Simon wanted Niky where he could see him.

# CHAPTER FIFTEEN

NIKY SCROLLED DOWN the Balkan region map on the desktop system. He mentally traced the gridlines along the route he had once taken into death camp number twelve.

The point symbol and elevation for the snow-topped mountain that came crashing down to expose the team.

The directional arrow the outpost guards followed to march them into the valley with AK-47s to his head and his team's.

The coordinates where a guard threatened to shoot him when he fell—again—because of that damned broken femur.

Where Violet dared the guards in their own Serbo-Croat to shoot her if they didn't like how she helped Niky walk.

He followed the gridline south to Brijevek, the capital of Strpski Grad Republika.

*Ivan Zubac.*

It was Niky against Zubac now. Niky had a bullet hole in his shoulder to prove it. Simon might have missed the sequence of shots from a distance, but Niky had taken the first hit. Had he not noticed the beam of the assassin's sight and lunged for Violet when he did, the shot would have taken out his brain stem. The second shot had been Violet's.

But now Niky had a chance to fix the problem. Simon had authorized the recovery mission, and Niky would get his chance to end the problem of Zubac once and for all. For him and for Violet. Niky's transponder made it impossible to move without Command knowing exactly where he went. The only way he was getting inside Strpski Grad was with Simon's sanction.

Niky knew Zubac spent his days in the ministry building, in a fancy office down the hall from the prime minister. He spent his nights in a suburban villa. Niky knew because he'd made it his job to know about the devil he'd sold his soul to. What he hadn't learned was how well guarded Zubac's haunts were.

He intended to find out.

Turning away from the screen, Niky took in the expensive furnishings of a sprawling ranch-style house in the Maryland countryside. Excelsior maintained safe houses around the world, places where Simon sent his operatives to hole up for debriefing or to entertain dignitaries under his official cover.

This place didn't belong to Excelsior. Simon was trying to keep Violet safe while Niky healed and they prepped for the upcoming mission.

But Violet wasn't safe. Not as long as Zubac was alive. The only thing that made facing Simon any easier was knowing how bad the big guy had screwed up himself. Niky often caught Simon looking at Violet, wondered how he rationalized using her.

Quinn worried about the whole situation and had

been hovering annoyingly, but neither she nor Major was impressed with Simon now, either. And even without a memory, Violet had good instincts. She'd been dodging Simon every chance she got.

It had been a long couple of days.

"We're briefing," Major said, sticking his head through the open office door. "Come on."

Niky abandoned the computer and headed down the hallway to the room that had become hub since their arrival.

A blow-dryer roared from the kitchen where Violet sat, draped in a cape, her white-blond hair trimmed neatly. She looked much more pulled together than she had in Sault Ste. Marie, and it was more than the new clothes and the liquid latex that filled the ridged scars below her jaw—all too noticeable and easy to identify.

She looked more like the Violet he remembered. Brilliant, beautiful Violet. The most cherished person in his life. The woman who'd always been there for him, the way he'd always been there for her—until death camp number twelve.

*"Friendship creates a strong bond between operatives—emotional attachment impairs clarity,"* Simon had always preached, a stance Niky had never questioned.

Maybe he should have.

But Simon had an instinct for his work. Until now, he'd only expected from his operatives what he'd been willing to give. He'd been fair. And he'd done so much for Niky, pulling him up from the downward spiral of his botched-up naval career. Simon had believed in him when no one else had, had given him Excelsior and a reason to believe in himself again.

Violet had believed in him, too.

Niky wanted to believe in himself again.

"Well, here's a blast from the past, eh, George?" He sat on a stool at the bar. "Bet you didn't expect to be dolling up this one when you came to work this morning."

George chuckled, a jovial sound that rumbled from his beer gut like far-off thunder. "You got that right. Best damn news I've gotten all year, and Simon says I have to keep my mouth shut. Can't tell a damn soul."

"Frances, Maxim and TJ know. You can gossip with them."

"Gossip?" he bellowed over the dryer. "I *do not* gossip."

A lie. George lived to gossip. In another life, he would own a salon near the White House, where he'd know more about what was going on with the president than the secret service.

Of course, in this life George reigned as Excelsior's wardrobe director and would probably break Niky's knuckles if he even mentioned the word *salon*. George might do hair, but he didn't *do* hair. That was only one small facet of his skill.

To hear him tell it, he was a god. He created new people, and in less than seven days. No argument there. The guy was brilliant. He'd once transformed Niky into a convincing Asian for a month-long stint in a Chinese Triad. Niky shook his head at the memory. *Asian,* for Christ's sake.

More importantly, Simon trusted him enough to bring him into the fold to prepare Violet for the mission.

The blow-dryer clicked off, and Niky asked, "Do you remember George at all, Violet?"

"No, but I like what he did to my hair."

"Of course you do, sweetheart." George fluffed his fingers through her trimmed hair. "You always said I was a genius."

"I never heard her say that," Niky said.

"Do you mind not pissing on my fantasies? I'm having a good time with this amnesia thing. Someone new to tell my jokes."

Niky winked at Violet. "Do you want me to shoot him so he'll shut up?"

*That* earned a smile, and these sudden glimpses of the Violet he'd known still hit him like a fist. They might have stolen her life, but they couldn't steal the essence of the woman she was.

"All right, people, listen up." Simon strode into the room with Quinn at his heels. He raked his gaze over Violet in a way he had no right to look at her. "Good job, George. We've got our covers. Violet will be Claire Denton from Michigan. Niky, you're Steve Marsalis, her brother. I'm John Denton, her husband."

No doubt Simon had made this announcement to stun them all into speechlessness. Violet eyed him narrowly.

At a sidelong glance from Quinn, Niky bit back a comment. If watching Simon coldheartedly seduce Violet to swing mission outcome was a prelude to what was coming, they were all in for a helluva show.

"We've got Denton and Marshall Construction," Simon said. "Disaster contractors coming off an eighteen-month stint in Romania after an earthquake. We'll be siting the area for potential work. Maxim is laying our covers right now."

Major moved closer, propping himself with an elbow

on the bar. "Quinn will take control. I'll be field-op-in-charge hubbed in Sarajevo. Simon's team leader. Niky, you're team second. Violet, your job will be to remember whatever you can."

"Sarajevo?" Niky asked.

Simon nodded. "Coming through the Krajina into Strpski Grad might be the quickest route, but I'm concerned about our reception if the permissions come from Croatia."

No arguments there. Worldwide the Serbs had been portrayed as the villains in the demise of Yugoslavia, when in fact, they'd only been part of the problem. In this northern region of Bosnia in particular, the Croats had done their fair share of ethnic cleansing.

"I'll pass around your scripts and expect you to be ready for reality check in thirty minutes." Quinn flipped open a folder and moved around the room. "Any questions."

Violet silently accepted the sheath of papers. Whatever else she'd forgotten, she hadn't forgotten this drill.

He glanced at his script.

*Steve Marsalis.*

The name of the man who was about to put an end to this nightmare once and for all.

*11:05 a.m. CET*
*Strpski Grad Republika, 0°C*

VIOLET CLOSED HER EYES against the suffocating panic, the all-too-familiar precursor to flashes from her past. She'd been fighting the feeling ever since they'd left Sarajevo, and thought wildly that she needed to welcome the memories, needed more pieces of the puzzle to make her life whole again.

*She tried to place a face with the voice. What would the man who sounded so cool when he brought so much pain look like? Angular features that were all knife-edged sharp? Distinguished? Definitely middle-aged. But she could see nothing through the mask, could only hear that cruelly resolute voice.*

*"Woman, I will take you apart in pieces until I find it."*

Violet opened her eyes and stared blindly at the thick stands of pine foresting the mountainside. That voice had haunted her dreams. And now she knew what he'd been after.

The panic that made her fight for each breath faded, and she inhaled deeply, rested her head on the window as if trying to sleep. Niky was too busy whipping their Range Rover around these switchback mountain turns to notice her clammy skin.

Simon would have noticed.

But he sat in the back seat, always near, their stamped permissions and fee receipts strewn over the seat as he organized paperwork for their next trip past Strpski Grad militia patrols. He'd been hypervigilant to the details since leaving Sarajevo, an approach that had paid off when their trip through the interentity border had taken less than an hour.

She stared through the window, down dizzying hills that plunged into villages tucked snugly in forested mountain folds. This was the high country, and she'd seen it before. She might not remember what had happened then, but the terrain felt familiar even in the post-war reality. Mile after mile of lush, sun-glazed hills interspersed with startling ruin. Hamlets filled with shattered houses, shelled-out barns. Ethnically pure ghost towns.

"I know why I was kept alive," she finally said.

Niky shifted his gaze from the road, reducing speed as he maneuvered yet another hairpin turn, and Simon's hand suddenly appeared on the seat as he pulled himself up.

"Why?" He leaned into the front enough so she could see the thick fringe of his lashes around those clear eyes.

"I keep hearing a voice. I've heard it before, but I didn't know he wanted the imaging device. Major said the other team members had them. Did you find any when you brought them home?"

"Only the one that came with me," Niky said.

She wondered if the length of time it had taken Simon to bring the team home had anything to do with that. Had the devices deteriorated along with her teammates' bodies? She really didn't want to know the details and chose another question. "What happened to your second one?"

"It's with the chunk of leg I left on a tree trunk when the mountain fell on top of us."

"The device was on your leg?"

He nodded. "It looked like a birthmark."

"We place those devices differently on each operative," Simon explained. "Two areas of the body since we can't anticipate where they'll be needed in a tight situation."

Two areas so they wouldn't be easy to find in the event of capture. That information popped into her head from nowhere.

"Did you record any images?" she asked.

"Posthumous images of my team to confirm their deaths," Niky said grimly. "You, I didn't get. I was dragged out for my turn in the red room before I had a chance."

Simon frowned at him, and Violet knew he didn't like casual mentions of what had happened inside the detention camp. He wanted to protect her, and she should appreciate his efforts. Maybe by the time they found her imaging device, she would.

"You said imaging *device*—singular," Simon said. "Meaning one?"

"Yes."

"And he asked for it specifically?"

She nodded.

"*He,* who? Any idea?"

Violet closed her eyes, willed herself to relax as that haunting voice filtered through her.

*"Woman, I will take you apart in pieces until I find it."*

"He spoke Serbo-Croat." At least that was what it had been called the last time she'd headed into the Balkans. One language. Different dialects. During her briefing on the flight, she'd learned the language had since been politically separated. A few words were still the same in each dialect, but nowadays Serbians spoke Serbian. Croats spoke Croatian. Bosniaks spoke Bosnian.

It was up to her decide which this man had spoken.

She understood the meaning of the words depended on the pitch of the vowels. How the same vowel could have either a rising or falling pitch based on its location in a word.

"He was cultured," she said. "I think education wiped out all but a hint of accent, but when he got angry, I could hear something. He lapsed into…I'm not sure what."

"It'll come when you're ready." Simon used that bedroom soft voice, the one she could feel in the pit of her stomach. Could he possibly know how she reacted to the sound of his voice? Would he even care if he did?

Shaking her head to clear it, Violet concentrated on the words she wanted, words that were right on the tip of her brain. She opened her eyes.

"I know what it was. When he wasn't angry he spoke more Slavic. I think it was an Ekavian dialect, but when he got angry, his speech speeded up. I can hear something else in there, a subdialect maybe…"

*"Woman, I will take you apart in pieces until I find it."*

"When he was angry, he would lapse into those Western European influenced words, like the Croats use. This man consciously switched to Ekavian, so when he got angry he'd lose it. He wasn't Serbian, he was a Bosnian Serb."

"He couldn't have known about your imaging device," Simon said. "Not unless one of the team revealed something."

"There's no way to know," Niky said. "None of my operatives came out of the red room alive. Except for Violet."

Simon frowned. "I don't remember any Bosnian Serbs running that camp. Maybe I'm mistaken. I'll get TJ on it the next time we make contact. We might be able to narrow the playing field."

"Those linguistic skills of yours are pretty neat." Niky smiled at Violet.

She smiled back. Contributing to this expedition made her feel good, as if she belonged in this car with these men.

Or maybe that feeling had more to do with proving herself to Simon. She'd obviously spent a lot of time doing that even before he'd shown up at Safe Harbor.

She kept trying not to think about it. Or him.

THE CEMETERY OCCUPIED a sloping track on the bank of the small river. In spring, hearty wildflowers broke through the winter-hard earth, bright spots of color that signaled the approach of new life. In summer, this slope grew lush with green lawn, fed from the fertile river. Now the bank lay blanketed in white, rendering snow-covered earth with rows of simple headstones barely recognizable. Ivan knew his way.

Four rows back. Seven plots to the east.

Letting his gaze slip to the engraved name on the stone, he braced himself against the stab of pain he knew would come. Each time he saw it felt like the first.

*Nina Zubac, devoted wife and mother.*

Nothing so dramatic as war had taken his woman from him, his life companion. Cancer had ravaged her, and while she'd fought a valiant battle, the disease had won. Though she'd been physically wasted, she had not broken. She died in the same manner she'd lived, surrounded by those she'd loved and with laughter on her lips.

*"I will be united with you again soon enough, my darlings,"* she had said, her voice but an echo of its former strength, yet somehow it swelled through them with hope. *"Live well."*

They had not been given that chance. When they

should have been together, remembering this loving woman and reminding each other of her important life lesson, the war had scattered them like cannon shrapnel. His son had left university to take his place with the Citizen's Army. His daughter had fled besieged Sarajevo with her family to Paris.

But Ivan was grateful Nina had not lived to see their son killed by Croat gunfire as their army drove the Serbs from the Krajina. That would have broken her spirit. He forced his gaze to the headstone beside hers—their beautiful son, who had shared her gift for laughter.

Placing a hand on each of the icy headstones, Ivan bowed his head and prayed.

When his cell phone ringer shattered the peace of this valley, he had no idea how much time had passed. He did know only one line would follow him here, and he regretted bitterly his private battle had intruded upon this peaceful place.

"Were you able to make contact?" he asked.

"Your death-dealing friend came to me without any questions. He trusted you to see him out of harm's way."

"Did I?"

A harsh laugh. "You did. With a bullet in his brain."

"Any problems with disposal?"

"None. He will surface soon, and your enemy will know you have ended the trail to you."

"Excellent. Now what else have you learned?"

"No news you will welcome, I fear."

Ivan stared at the tree with branches so low they almost touched the frozen river. In summer this tree would swell to lush life, so thick with greenery it would be impossible to see through the branches to the river. Now those branches were bare like old fingers, gnarled beneath the weight of snow. "Tell me."

"The botched delivery scared your recipients away."

"Were you able to locate them?"

"It brings me great distress to tell you no. I tracked them into the U.S. capital, but their trail ends there. If you wish I will keep looking. Something is bound to turn up eventually."

"Yes, and when it does, we will act. Until then do not distress yourself unduly. Your news is not unexpected. These people have the resources of the United States government at their command, and it is hard for one man to match, which is why I wanted this threat ended from the start."

"Then you should have called me sooner. You have saved me from persecution. I am indebted with my life. I would not have failed with this job."

Ivan eyed his wife's headstone. "I do not doubt you. But bringing you into the open involves much risk for both of us, and I did not know I had been betrayed until too late."

"What would you have me do?"

"Wait. Since you are out, I would have you enjoy breathing the free air until I discover where these people have hidden. Then you will come and handle things as you should have from the first. Just do not allow yourself to be noticed."

"I will not, but I shall generously hope my holiday is short-lived for your sake."

"You do that, Dragan. With my thanks."

# CHAPTER SIXTEEN

THE TOWN OF BRIJEVEK had changed a lot in the two years since Simon had visited. A traditional Balkan town that had been pinched and packed into a valley, it was now a startling union of immaculate new architecture and ruin.

On the drive through the outskirts, they passed streets that might have been any suburb in the industrialized world, rows of homes that suggested owners spent Saturdays mowing their yards and chatting with neighbors. But mingled with these were homes gutted with blackened roofs, marring the streets like rotted teeth. Homes that had been ethnically scoured.

Army jeeps and Land Cruiser vehicles patrolled the streets, the letters *S-F-O-R* stenciled on their sides. These international soldiers operating under the high representative ensured all participants of the Dayton Peace Agreement abided by the terms.

When Simon had last been here, the train depot had been no more than shelled-out wreckage, all services to neighboring countries suspended indefinitely. Now the depot had been rebuilt, a new construction that stood proudly among the shattered walls that marked so many buildings in the center of town, a jungle of twisting girders and shrapnel-pocked facades.

He tried to gauge the effect of this grim sight on Violet. As Quinn had suggested, he'd been watching closely, looking for signs of stress, any indication of anxiety that she might need help dealing with. He didn't know what she felt. She used her gift for shaping herself to any circumstance to become the professional she'd chosen to be for this trip.

Her attitude toward him remained constant, though. Since the night she'd begun remembering, she'd been remote. Again, he'd taken Quinn's recommendation and hadn't pushed. There would be time later for explanations. After she was safe.

But he found himself chafing against that restriction. He didn't have much hope of convincing her to believe what he felt for her was real. His actions toward her, whether as Violet or Claire, didn't support his cause. When he watched her interact so easily with Niky, Simon understood how little a basis for a relationship they had. All these years, and he'd never been more than the man who dictated her career.

He intended to change that, hoped to prove that mission objective hadn't been his only concern.

They were silent as Niky wheeled the Range Rover into the parking lot. Hotel Brijevek wasn't exactly five star, but it was the town's finest lodging. The facade had been spared much of the Croat shelling from the hills above, an accident of good fortune and smart placement of car tires that had been strung from the roof and windows to absorb the shock of the blasting.

Niky put the car into gear. "Showtime."

Simon got out, and an eerie sense of déjà vu filtered through him. The last time he'd been in Brijevek, he'd been facing the harsh realities of this war. Not a conventional campaign in any sense, but one built upon centuries of religious and ethnic conflict that had simmered until tolerance was short and hatred deep.

He'd become involved in these events, events that had spiraled out of control and cost his people their lives. Whether he'd brought them home dead or alive, he only had to look at Niky and Violet to know both were facing demons.

Violet looked pale, but resolute. Niky stoic, and Simon led them toward the front entrance, feeling the effects of his choices weighting each step.

Niky reached the door first and opened it, grabbing onto Violet when she went to enter. He motioned to Simon, who strode through first, sweeping his gaze the length of the lobby, remarkably unchanged.

A few people milled around the front desk. Two clerks stood behind. Simon sensed nothing awry, no threats lurking in shadows, and only after a scan of the interior did he reach for Violet's hand to lead her inside.

She threaded her fingers through his, her touch making him intensely aware of everything about her.

The way she trembled as they moved through the door, their steps in sync.

How she faltered before coming to a stop and forcing him to do the same.

The bewilderment that veiled her eyes and dipped her mouth in a frown.

Simon followed her gaze, but didn't understand. The saint was there, swelling to the lobby ceiling in a bright sweep of sculpted finery, positioned deliberately to draw the eye, flanked on one side by the reservation desk and the other by a lush display of greenery that cut off the view of the entrance from the reception area beyond.

"Did I get it wrong?" Her grip tightened.

Then Simon realized… The statue's mouth was closed.

Not only was the golden mouth shut, but it was almost completely hidden beneath a sculpted mustache and beard.

Simon's memories surfaced, he recognized other differences. The saint he remembered had held a cross. This one held a book.

He steered her past the statue saying, "No. You didn't get it wrong. This is a different saint."

Following, Niky shot him a questioning glance. Simon assessed the reception area, settled on an alternative plan.

He wanted to know what had happened to their saint.

Gazing down at Violet, he searched her beautiful face. "You holding up?"

She nodded then flashed a bright smile at a woman in a maid uniform who made eye contact while passing.

He directed them toward an empty concierge desk. "Let's ask some questions."

Niky nodded. They strolled toward the desk, rang a bell and waited until a slightly built man appeared, dressed neatly. He greeted them in Serbian then at Simon's prompting switched to French, which he and Niky spoke fluently and was one of the languages that the local business people used to communicate with the internationals.

"Greetings, guests."

Simon explained their interest in the hotel's interior design. "We want to understand any changes that reflect the new architecture, so we can tailor our bids and get work with the reconstruction effort."

Some of the concierge's enthusiasm dimmed, perhaps to learn they weren't guests, but more foreigners here to help. "Rebuilding is good. We are making our buildings strong this time."

"I understand the hotel changed ownership a few years back. Did the new owners renovate?"

"Of course, the old owners were Croats. The new owners are Serbs."

That explained a great deal. "I saw your saint in the lobby. There were religious icons the new owners had to deal with?"

The concierge nodded.

"That's very good to know." Violet shot the man an appreciative look. "We're hoping to impress your government officials, so let me ask who did the work around here. The craftsmanship of that statue is impressive."

The concierge sighed. "Our saint is much of a local legend, a tourist attraction, if you will. People come to Brijevek and they want to see the saint. After the old owners left, the new owners had to take down the old saint. We had no saint for many months, yet people still came and asked, 'Where is the saint?' So our new owners had Belgrade artists make our Saint Sava, and now people come and say, 'Ah, there is the saint.'"

Simon looked at Violet and Niky. "We didn't consider this when we decided to site the area. We'll have to stay on top of these religious distinctions."

Niky nodded and asked the concierge, "So what happened to your old tourist attraction? Did they sell him back to the Croats and turn a profit?"

The concierge smiled. "That would have been smart. But no, the old owners fled. The new owners moved the old saint to a warehouse."

"So he's stored away?" Violet asked.

"No, when the bombs damaged the building, someone stole the saint. The militia said that vandals took him, but many of us who have worked at Hotel Brijevek for many years heard whispers that some old employees spirited him away for pride."

"There are still old employees in the area?"

"Not many. The land between these borders is ours," the concierge said flatly. "Most Croats went north to Zagreb, but for a few stubborn old women. We tried to make them leave, but they hid in their old houses. The internationals told us to leave them alone. They don't have much life left, so we'll soon have our land back."

"I'll bet this mystery about your saint has been good for business, too," Violet said.

The concierge nodded in approval, his gaze lingering on her when she flashed him that high-beam smile.

Their next step was to find out if any of these old women were still alive. "Shouldn't the internationals have forced the old women to respect the agreement?"

"Bah, the internationals." The concierge waved a dismissive hand. "They say they're here to keep the peace, but they only patrol like watchdogs to see if any hatred crimes happen. No one cares if the old women break our treaty."

"You've been helpful. Thanks." Pulling several marks from his wallet, Simon tipped the man.

On their way out, Violet paused at the front desk to ask about the town library, and when they were out of earshot, she asked, "You thinking media?"

Niky nodded. "The library is only a few blocks away. We can leave the car parked here."

This was a rare opportunity for Simon to work in the

field with his operatives. He'd trained team one to be the best, and as they walked through Brijevek's streets, he couldn't help but feel proud of the way both Violet and Niky faced this return to Bosnia. They'd slipped into their roles like the professionals they were, united in the common cause.

Violet might not remember her teammates, but she'd fallen into easy pace at Niky's side. They were operatives who'd clearly worked together often, sharing a silent camaraderie of people who were comfortable together. Simon only wished he felt as if his place was alongside of them instead of halfway across the world monitoring via satellite.

"There it is," Niky said as they turned a corner onto a main street that circled through a historic town square.

After Brijevek's infrastructure had collapsed, the government buildings had been the first to be reconstructed, and parts of this historic square sparkled with newness. The Federation flag snapped in the wind, but with it flew the flag of Strpski Grad Republika, proudly proclaiming its status as a semiautonomous entity and its connection to Serbia in the three horizontal stripes of red, blue and white.

The library had sustained damage, but the original structure still stood, crumbling eaves mingled with sparkling new windows, slightly scarred but proud compared to the newer buildings surrounding it.

The library was permeated with that stillness that was a part of libraries everywhere, and there was no avoiding the librarian who glanced up from a desk that seemed more sentry than customer service.

"You do the talking," Simon whispered to Violet as

they approached. "In Serbian. Don't identify us. Just say we're journalists researching the area if she asks."

Violet nodded, and when they reached the desk, she greeted the woman. His knowledge of Serbian was limited, but he recognized some of the conversation, and in a few moments, they were led back to an archival section crammed with file cabinets. Microfilm. Simon inwardly groaned.

"We'll need to pick a time frame," Violet said, when the librarian moved beyond earshot.

"You were here for the exhumations, Simon," Niky said. "That puts us after Dayton."

"Let's just start with November of '95 and work from there," he said. "We'll reevaluate if we need to."

Niky scowled at the cabinets. "This will take forever. I saw computers. Let me see if I can log on and speed this process along. I know enough Serbian to get the browser to translate the sites into something I recognize. Maybe we'll luck out."

Simon nodded, and Niky took off.

Slipping a hand on Violet's arm, he led her across the archival section, pleased for this unexpected opportunity to have her to himself, to savor the feel of her moving along by his side, to inhale the scent of her hair.

To feel as if he did belong beside her.

NIKY SLIPPED DOWN a public hallway, avoiding the librarian. The few straggler patrons didn't pay him much notice, and those who did watched him walk down the hall toward the bathroom.

But he was looking for egress.

This was an opportunity he damn sure wouldn't miss. He knew the layout of the ministry building next door, and he wished he'd had more time to learn more about the other buildings in the square. Niky only had a skeleton of a plan so far, didn't know what he would be up against or how he could accomplish his own personal mission objective.

A dead Zubac.

Passing the bathrooms, he found what appeared to be a staff lounge with an employee entrance. The door was locked, which meant the library staff would have their own keys.

He noticed a cabinet that looked as if it might hold personal items, but he looked for something to jam the lock. In a utility drawer, he found a roll of tape that fit the bill.

Opening the door, he taped down the mechanism for reentry and headed outside, keeping close to the building so he wouldn't be seen from the windows or by the guard manning what appeared to be an employee parking lot that serviced the rear entrances of several buildings.

*Perfect.*

Protestors had gathered in the square when they'd entered the library, and when Niky worked his way across an alley that ran between the library and the courthouse, he could see that even in the length of time they'd been inside, that crowd had grown considerably.

The impulse to meld into that crowd and keep going hit him hard, but just the thought was a joke. Violet might have left her problems behind with the gift of oblivion, but that was only a vacation. No one walked away from Excelsior. Niky could walk straight to hell. Simon would eventually find him.

Emerging from the alley, he blended in with the

crowd that marched around the square, loud, but contained and controlled. Police patrolled the edges, their presence a warning.

Those police would give him access to the ministry.

Prowling the crowd's perimeter, he became anonymous among the protestors while isolating his target. When Niky found him, he assessed the various ways to apprehend the man yet remain unseen by the masses. Ironically, he made his move beside the library's stone stairway.

"Sir, sir," he ground out in his rudimentary Serbian. "This man needs help."

Flagging the young policeman, he crouched behind the stairwell as if someone had collapsed behind it. The policeman had been trained in the universal creed: to serve and protect. He strode into the alley to offer assistance.

One offensive move. One hard twist of the man's neck. Niky rolled the body into the shadows, temporary shelter from notice. Tugging off the dead man's hat, he took the outer coat and uniform jacket. These he swapped for his own, grateful for his dark slacks that would pass a casual inspection.

Strapping on the utility belt, he checked the alley, waited until police herded some protestors away then hoisted the body over his shoulder and covered the short distance to the parking lot. He rolled the body under a parked car and concealed his own coat behind a bush near the rear entrance. Just over ten minutes after leaving the archive room, he headed to the Ministry.

So far so good.

The grandeur of political stature was remarkably

similar from culture to culture, evident in high ceilings and long corridors. He didn't stop walking and stuck to nodding perfunctorily through the crowded lobby.

Violet might stroll through this place filled with locals and pass as one, but Niky wasn't so talented. The less he had to open his mouth the better.

Inclining his head at the security personnel staffing a desk beside several receptionists, he strolled past as though he had every right in the world to do so.

No one tried to stop him.

The floor plan of this building was etched in memory. Doorways on the east wall then a stairwell leading to the fourth floor. He marked his route for easy egress. He knew an outer reception-style area preceded Zubac's office where an assistant greeted guests.

Niky wasn't sure yet how he would get around the assistant. He didn't want to leave a trail of corpses. The more bodies, the more chances of getting caught before he got out.

He circled one flight of stairs then a second. A woman entered on the third, gave him a bright smile as he grabbed the door for her. He could hear her heels clatter on the steps all the way down to the lobby.

The third and fourth floors housed the offices of the ministers. Sixteen in all, ministries from the more conventional defense, justice and finance to the eclectic culture, development and physical planning. There were also a few unique to the region—namely the ministry of the displaced refugees. A ministry for constructing a solid new nation.

Niky knew the prime minister worked in this building while the president of this semiautonomous entity resided in a secured facility not accessible to the public. Internationals in Strpski Grad, working under the high representative based in Sarajevo, had their own building—a former warehouse—well removed from this historic square.

Niky would be noticeable as soon as he stepped foot onto this floor of offices, so he cracked the door to assess. Offices lined the hall, some doors opened, others closed. He heard voices and spotted Zubac's office easily—one of two doorways flanking the prime minister's office.

Niky pressed the door shut when a young man dressed in the universal style of up-and-coming government underlings swept by, motioning to someone farther down the hall. The man looked grim, but polite as he welcomed his guest. He said something but Niky could only make out the reference to General Zubac.

The newcomer was Strpski Grad militia. Niky recognized the uniform, guessed this high-ranking officer had been called in to support the local police in dispersing the crowd outside.

Withdrawing the service pistol from the utility belt, Niky checked the clip. He hadn't wanted to fire this weapon. Without a silencer, shots would be heard, diminishing his chance of safe egress. He'd have preferred to pistol-whip an assistant and break Zubac's neck. Neat. Quiet. But if this SG militia commander went into that office, Niky might not have a choice.

Suddenly two men stepped into the hallway from another office. Niky recognized the Strpski Grad prime minister.

*Zubac.*

Niky could see the man as he'd been three years

ago, a flashback of the nightmare he'd endured during one of their meetings in person.

In the red room.

But he forced himself to concentrate and the differences came into sharper focus. The almost bruised look around Zubac's deep-set eyes. The craggy lines on stern features. The steely gray hair. The man showed the effects of his political appointment.

Or maybe he showed the pressure of leading a double life— defender of a new nation by day. Devil, murderer and who knew what else by night.

Niky didn't care if these Balkan people blew each other to hell and back again. He didn't care about anything except the men striding through the hallway, talking, leaving Niky struggling to make out what they said.

*"Evacuate the outer offices."*

*"Chemicals to contain the crowds."*

His fingers poised on his weapon. He could make the shot, but he would have to kill the prime minister first to pick off the shorter Zubac.

He would create an international incident by murdering these dignitaries. He would involve the United States in an assassination and thrust Excelsior into a tenuous position with the president and Oversight, who would try to conceal which agency Niky worked for. And all at the cost of his life because he would never get out of this building alive.

A choice he'd faced before.

VIOLET TOOK the microfilm from the projector and wound it into a compressed roll that slid neatly into the canister. She glanced up to find Niky heading into the archive room. He didn't look right, pale and clammy. Something about him seemed frazzled, rushed.

"You okay?" she whispered not to be overheard.

He nodded. "Let's get a move on. Those protestors are going nuts. We've got a riot starting. Word's out that bombers have entered Strpski Grad's airspace."

"Coming here?" she asked.

Simon shook his head. "Belgrade."

As if on cue, an electronic beeping jarred the quiet, followed by a loud and apparently frustrated Serbian curse by the librarian who hurried past the archival section.

Engines rumbled overhead, loud enough to rock the mortar buried as they were in the bowels of this old building.

Jets flying at low altitude.

Violet remembered this sound, and she watched Simon take off toward an emergency door with a grid-reinforced glass pane.

"A bomber with an escort," he confirmed. "It's going to get ugly fast. Come on."

Violet remembered this feeling, too, the rush of urgency as she pocketed the microfilm canister and followed Simon and Niky. The sharp spike of adrenaline as a siren blared as Simon shoved open the emergency door.

Riot, definitely. People jammed the square so tight they overflowed onto the side street. One seemed to shout louder than the next as if the noise of their raised voices might reach the contrails overhead.

Before she realized what was happening, Simon and Niky each had an arm as they burst into the crowd, shielding her with their big bodies. Violet hurried along not to hinder them, fighting for balance when they were jostled by the sheer crush of people, trying not to let panic take hold when every breath filled her nostrils with the scent of growing violence.

Simon and Niky steered her toward the outer edge of the crowd, where they could see that the media had already started gathering. Local police tried to contain the protesting crowds, and Simon had to redirect them twice to avoid a scuffle.

It was no good, though. The blare of a siren shrieked, then a row of police plowed into the crowd like a human battering ram. As people jostled and shoved them from all directions, Niky lost his hold on her.

Simon clung all the tighter, painfully, but she was torn from his grasp as people lost their footing around them.

Blindly Violet latched onto some man's coat to avoid being sucked under and trampled as more helmeted police rammed the crowd. She went under this time and hit the ground hard. Stars burst behind her eyelids. Air exploded from her lungs. Something sharp stabbed into her hip, a piercing pain that shocked her into action.

She clawed at the man pinning her to the ground, her fingers scratching against thick wool in her vain attempts to get free. She didn't know if he was unconscious but that sharp object in her hip was agony….

*The man had once been big. Now a body that should have been thick with muscle was sharply angled. Sweaty. The stench almost overpowered her. He looked so apologetic every time he jostled her, as if he knew how bad he smelled.*

*She smiled. "Don't worry. I smell just as bad."*

Violet blinked and realized the man pinioning her

to the street was a neatly dressed man in a warm coat. That sharp pain in her hip wasn't an ill-placed limb but...

*A sidearm.*

She recognized the policeman's utility belt, even as she snapped out, "Get off," in Serbian. She reached for the gun, slid it from the man's holster in an instinctive move from a forgotten past.

By the time he rolled away, Violet had the weapon concealed beneath her coat, and when Simon reappeared, dragging her to her feet, she slipped it into the waistband in the back of her pants, appreciating the solid feel in the small of her back.

She knew the feeling of being armed.

He shoved her hard in the direction of Niky, who was breaking free of the crowd in an area where a panel van with an antenna and the logo of some news media stamped on the side.

They slammed past several men, sent one staggering into the van with a curse. Then they raced down a side street away from the crowd, only slowing once they were well away.

Niky scowled at the street sign. "We're on the wrong damn side of the building. We've got to circle around that mess to get back to the hotel."

"Lead the way," Simon said while raking that clear gaze over her, assessing her condition. "You okay?"

"I'm fine." She stepped away, suddenly overcome by his nearness, by his matter-of-fact manner, by her own desire to sink into those arms that would hold her close and make her stop shaking. "I'm fine. Thank you."

Some emotion flickered across his face, and she felt contrite. He might not offer what she wanted, but Violet knew he cared. No man would be so loyal to his people without caring. And she was one of them, even though she wanted to be much more.

## CHAPTER SEVENTEEN

IVAN STOPPED back in his office to find Ciril at his desk.
"I saw the commander out. I am joining the prime minister to watch the situation unfold, so hold my calls unless the commander has need of me."

"Yes, General."

"The evacuation is only a precaution against the tear
gas, Ciril. Our men will soon have the crowd under
control."

"I have no doubt, sir."

Satisfied, Ivan strode toward the prime minister's
suite at the end of the hall. He met the woman who
headed the Ministry of Displaced Refugees and held the
door for her to pass.

"General." She inclined her head politely, a welcomed civility as they disagreed much in council ses-
sions.

He smiled. "Minister."

Several others already congregated around the prime
minister's desk, watching the television anchored high
on a wall. The buzz of sound bites had been muted, but
sound was not necessary to understand the scene displayed. Police in combat gear. A crush of people
protesting in the square. Every few seconds the camera would pan to the internationals' vehicles, which

was typical, Ivan thought. SFOR hadn't even gotten close to this riot, let alone help to subdue it. The slanted media still persecuted his people every chance they got.

Prime Minister Zoran Vladanovic descended from a family who settled in the Krajina centuries ago to fight the Ottomans. While he had served only mandatory time in the Citizen's Army, he had good politics. He believed in a stronger Strpski Grad, and if he conceded to the internationals, he made concessions carefully and did not yield on matters of true importance.

Ivan respected the man and greeted him as he entered. The prime minister waved him in impatiently. "They have gotten out of hand again. And I can't honestly fault them this protest. The last time NATO bombed Belgrade they demolished the television stations and cut off a vital connection to our brothers."

In true Western fashion, NATO had issued several warnings for the Serbian television press to stop the propaganda before sending in their bombers. The Belgrade stations had replied to those warnings by accusing NATO of missing a target and bombing a schoolhouse filled with children. A lie, true, but one designed to gain the sympathies of the world.

Ivan did not know if the ploy had worked. Every charge Belgrade aired against NATO was countered with photos of the tens of thousands of Albanian refugees fleeing Kosovo. And the rebellious television stations paid for their boldness when NATO dropped more bombs, hitting their intended target.

The office door opened again, and the finance minister arrived. He greeted his compatriots, and Ivan was about to reply in kind, when an image on the television caught his attention.

The camera panned on a trio who fled the crowd, two men and a woman as they rushed the camera, their faces grim, growing larger and larger. He stared, at first disbelieving—surely he must be mistaken—but Ivan knew this man. *His Western contact.*

Then he noticed the white-haired woman.

She was also changed, but he could see her as she once was, starved and unclean, defiant even after months in number twelve camp, refusing to yield, only glaring with magnificent eyes as he grabbed her hand, placed it over his chest. Suddenly, he could hear his own voice.

*"I have bone where my heart should be."*

Ivan had seen the photos the deputy traitor had provided the tribunal. He had seen this woman hanged. Yet here she was with his Western contact in Strpski Grad.

Outside his office.

VIOLET'S FIRST GLIMPSE of the part of town where the old Croat women still lived didn't come as a shock. She'd become inured to the remnants of this terrible war, not unmoved, just resilient. She'd grown accustomed to seeing devastation coexisting uneasily with hope around every corner.

Here there wasn't much hope.

She'd opened the back window as Niky drove the Range Rover through what had once been neat suburban streets, needing the bitter air on her face to dispel the anxiety that lingered from the scene in the square. Her hip ached. Her hands still shook. She could still smell the stench of unwashed bodies and icy sweat with her breath.

Somewhere in these mountains, she'd once been packed inside a bitterly cold place with too many people. Now she could hear the wind howling down the mountainside, and she wasn't sure if that forlorn sound was in her memory or simply the wind hissing through this suburban graveyard.

None of these homes had windows. Most didn't have walls or roofs, but the few that did had boards over the openings where the windows had once been. A sign, nailed to the lone standing post of what had once been a picket fence, read in Croatian: *Ava's Avengers. Enter with your life in your hands.*

But upon closer inspection there were symbols of hope. Violet recognized how several of the front yards had been staked off into garden plots that might grow vegetables when the ground wasn't frozen, making for an odd patchwork-style landscape. A cat with straggly gray fur shot under a porch when Niky pulled the Range Rover in front of a house with boarded windows. Violet noticed how the path to the porch had been recently shoveled.

Hope in the unlikeliest of places.

"Here we are," Niky said before casting her a sidelong glance. "Is this woman someone you met inside the camp?"

She shrugged. "I saw the name in the library and it felt familiar."

"It's a place to start." The approval in Simon's voice washed through her, refreshed her in places she hadn't realized needed to be refreshed. "If this lead doesn't pan out, we'll move on to the next address on our list. These women lived in the neighborhood, so we should be able to track down someone."

Simon had no sooner stepped out of their vehicle when a spray of automatic gunfire ripped through the quiet afternoon, tearing up the ground barely a foot in front of him. He stopped dead in his tracks as chunks of ice kicked up on his slacks.

"Ava, I presume," Niky said dryly.

Violet bit back a smile, as she realized these boarded windows weren't to keep the cold out at all.

They were gunner's hatches.

A woman as old as Moses pushed open a board beside the front door and aimed an automatic rifle with a full magazine.

"*Zbogom,*" she said in a voice ravaged by too many years of tar and nicotine.

"*Oprostite. Ne,*" Violet called out as she slipped from the back seat, shaking her head when Simon grabbed her arm.

She knew the regional languages were now called by politically correct names, but Croatian was only a version of the same Slav language spoken by all the peoples of this region. The differences were merely a matter of dialect, like the differences between English spoken by Americans and Brits.

She knew those differences.

"We bring no harm." Violet told the woman in Croatian. Raising her hands, she turned in a complete circle, hoping the woman accepted that she meant what she said. "We only want to ask questions about the saint from the Hotel Brijevek. We're not with NATO or the United Nations. We're private citizens, who place our lives in your hands."

The woman only waved the gun, a gesture of defiance. But she didn't shoot. Violet found that encouraging.

"I know the name of the woman who lives here," she said. That got the old lady's attention.

Their gazes clashed across the icy distance. "I don't know you."

Violet could feel Simon's and Niky's stares, knew they were giving her license to handle the old woman, to use her command of the language, but they wouldn't give her long.

Once she would have known what to say to convince this woman of her identity and to win her trust. Now, Violet wished Simon or Niky would step up before she botched things completely. Then she remembered....

Reaching behind her ear, she used her nail to find the edge of the liquid latex George had used to transform her scars. Once she caught it, she peeled away the thin length, watching the woman's eyes widen as she did. She tipped her chin so the woman could see the scars.

"They hanged me inside the detention camp."

The woman squinted through the wrinkled folds of flesh then lowered the weapon. "I do know your face. Are you an angel?"

*"Ne."* No.

Simon and Niky exchanged glances, but Violet took another step forward, encouraged when the woman didn't retrain her gun.

"Can we ask you questions about the saint?"

"You may come." She pointed the gun at Simon and Niky. "They stay."

Violet strode toward the front door, ignoring Simon's muttered curse. Once upon a time, she had probably known how to handle this situation. Now she'd likely have her head blown off by whoever might be inside with the old woman. But it wasn't as if she was unprotected, and the fact that neither Simon nor Niky had come after her was something.

"*Bog,*" she said politely when the door cracked open. *Hello.*

The woman was so bent, she looked like a bump beneath a pile of mismatched shawls and scarves, couldn't possibly have been tall even if she had stood upright. She let Violet enter then latched the door tight with a makeshift bar that slid into metal grooves. Each move a shuffling effort of will.

"Did I know you inside the detention camp?" Violet asked.

The woman eyed her oddly.

"I know your family name, but I don't remember why. How do you know my face?"

"You are the angel in the picture, no?"

"What picture?"

"From the death camp. They showed the picture at the criminal tribunal."

Simon had told her about a photo the defecting deputy commander had taken on his way from the camp. "I've heard about that picture. How did you see it? I didn't know the tribunal evidence was public."

The woman shook her head and a few steely curls slipped from beneath her woolen headscarf. "They tried the monster who butchered my husband and grandson."

"I am sorry," Violet said. "So you were at the trial?"

"I wanted him to tell me where he buried my men."

"Did he?"

"*Ne,*" she spat. "He said he didn't remember, so now I travel into town whenever the internationals come. They bring books filled with pictures of the things they find inside the graves. Belts. Watches. Shoes. Teeth. I look through the books every time, but I have not yet found my men."

Their gazes locked. This dogged woman's eyes doubtful and hopeful at the same time.

"If you're the woman in the picture, you must be an angel." The old woman raised a trembling hand to trace the scars with leathery fingers. "How are you still alive?"

"I don't know. I lost my memory a long time ago. The men outside are trying to help me find it." Violet held her breath, not sure if she had just broken the cardinal rule of covert ops—telling the truth.

To her surprise, and profound relief, tears flooded the old woman's eyes, and she tightened her grip on Violet's chin, forcing her closer so she could press a kiss to one cheek then the other.

*"Hvala,"* she said in a broken voice. *Thank you.*

"For what?"

She gently twisted Violet's face side to side then smiled through her tears. "Come, come. You share my meal, and I will tell you how you know my family name. We are friends now, *da?*"

*"Da." Yes.*

Her name was Natalia, and she'd once had a husband named Pero, who played the *saz* and sang her love songs known as *Sevdalinkes* that were so romantic and sad she wanted to jump in the river and drown after every one.

Apparently tragic love songs were good things around here because Natalia explained how Pero had been training their grandson to sing so he could woo his own beautiful woman when he grew to manhood.

The gardens were Natalia's, too. In the spring she planted vegetables, which she harvested to help feed her neighbors, the only ones left around here, all much older and poorer than she was. Violet gazed at a boarded window where enough wind whistled through to frost a ceramic canister. She had trouble imagining much poorer conditions.

Lunch today consisted of pickled onions and something that looked like beef jerky. Violet declined the offering as she watched the old woman gnaw on a tough strip with what was left of her molars. Instead, she accepted a cloudy tumbler.

"Slivovitz." Natalia raised her own tumbler and downed the liquid in one long swallow.

Violet did the same, nearly choking when the intense plum alcohol roared down with a heat that melted the icy anxiety that had chilled her since the incident in the square.

They sat at a beautifully crafted wooden table that Pero had made to celebrate the birth of their first son. Natalia had a fireplace with no fire and electrical outlets, but apparently no electricity. Violet asked about that.

"The internationals turn the service on," she explained, rolling her eyes. "But the Serbs turn it off again when I have no money to pay the bill. Then the internationals make them turn it back on again. It is a game. I pay the bill when I can. I chop the wood when my old bones let me."

Obviously those old bones hadn't been cooperating lately, and any money she might have come across must have gone for munitions and brandy.

"How many of you are left here now?" Violet asked.

"Only seven. The rest have died."

"Who was Ava?"

That earned a smile. "Ava had the loudest mouth of us all, but she's dead now. This cold is hard on an old woman's bones."

"You have no family left?"

"I do, angel. Thanks to you. You helped my niece and her children escape those demons in the death camp."

That wasn't what Violet had expected. "I don't remember."

"I will tell you then about my niece's friend, Silvija, and what she told me about the angel in the picture."

Violet sipped her second glass of slivovitz while Natalia shared a difficult story about two frightened women who wanted to keep their children from starving and suffering so much that they braved death to escape death. With the angel's help, they were able to seize opportunity when it came.

Their journey was a long and hard one that started in a dairy truck and ended when they reached the frontier and freedom. The cost had been high. Natalia's niece had died of a gunshot wound when a border patrol had tracked them crossing the gray river that now formed the entity border with Croatia. While the children sobbed over their mother's corpse, Silvija had been forced to murder the patrol.

"The angel" they had called the woman who had helped them escape the death camp, and during the tribunal—the only time Natalia had ever left her town in seventy-six years—they listened to the terrible crimes committed on their loved ones. When Silvija had seen the picture, she had collapsed onto the bench crying, "The angel. Godspeed her to His side."

Now Silvija lived a good life in Croatia, raising all five children as a family while working as an assistant curator in a museum.

"This is what she studied at the university, what she loves to do," Natalia said fondly. "She would still be here had the Serbs not murdered her man and tried to starve her children."

Violet remembered nothing of these events, but liked that she'd helped, that something good had come from those terrifying nightmares. She told Natalia as much.

"Then I am glad you visited so I can tell you," she said.

"I'm glad, too, Natalia. I don't have much good in my memory about that time. You've given me a gift. But why don't you go live with Silvija?"

Natalia shrugged, took a bite of an onion, chewed and swallowed. "I am an old woman. Silvija thinks I am a fool, but my neighbors understand. The Serbs take our families, our jobs, our lives. They would burn our homes to build new and forget what they have done to us. We are too stubborn to let them forget. At least until we find our men."

The internationals and the concierge were wrong, Violet thought. If the rest of Ava's Avenger's were anything like this one, they still had plenty of life left.

Natalia patted Violet's hand, poured more brandy. "Now tell me what you want to know about our Saint Josip. Many people try to make me talk, but I shoot at them. *You* I will talk to."

Saint Josip. He'd clearly been a symbol of hope to those who risked everything to spirit him from beneath the Serbs' noses.

Violet gave Natalia a summary of why she needed

to see the saint without admitting that she'd hidden something inside him.

Natalia's creased and wrinkled face collapsed. She grabbed Violet's hands in her own and gripped with unexpected strength. "Oh, dear angel. No good happened during the war inside that hotel. I know. I have friends who worked there. Serb women. Not everyone wanted our land cleansed." She squeezed again for emphasis. "Leave that part of your memory forgotten."

Violet was touched by this woman's concern. "If I get a chance to pick and choose, Natalia, you have my word."

"Would that we all had that choice."

Amen. "We heard you and your friends smuggled the saint away after the warehouse was bombed. Is that true?"

"When the old owners were forced to sell the hotel and flee for their lives, the Serbs buried our Saint Josip in storage. The fools thought people will accept not having a saint. But who cares if the saint is a patron of the Croats? In these terrible times, people *need* a saint more than ever. Even a Serb saint."

She shook her fist in the air. "When cannonade blew up the warehouse, we seized our chance to break in and say, 'Take that, you Serb bastards. You will not steal our saint, too.'"

Violet laughed, amusement pouring through her, warm like the slivovitz.

"See I gift you with smiles, *da?*"

"*Da.* It's been a while. So you really did smuggle Saint Josip away. Good for you. That couldn't have been easy."

"*Ne.* What in life is? But it felt good, I tell you. It

feels good now knowing he is safe. I only hope I live to see him brought into the sun again."

"When will that be?"

"Once this terrible war is over and the internationals go home. He'll be displayed proudly and his story shall be told to all the world as one of hope."

*Displayed?* "Silvija has him."

Natalia winked. "Tucked away like a treasure. That is where we got the idea to steal our saint and hide him with Silvija. But for you, angel, for *you,* I think she will talk. She'll be grateful for a chance to thank you for all their lives."

Violet clasped the old woman's hand. Camaraderie where she hadn't expected to find it.

After another toast to their continued health and peace in the Balkans, Natalia set Violet up with everything they would need to contact Silvija, and they headed outside.

Natalia held the door, and Violet walked through, so aware of Simon and Niky watching her that the world tilted sideways with each step. Simon strode down the walkway toward her, grabbed her arm and steadied her against him.

"Are you hurt?" he asked.

"I'm fine."

His gaze narrowed.

Niky gave a laugh. "You're drunk."

"Slivovitz," Natalia yelled from the door, a word that translated in any language.

Violet only smiled, enjoying Simon's surprise. Even with her thoughts swimming, she enjoyed this rare glimpse of an honest-to-goodness reaction.

"Give me money," she said. "Natalia won't take it,

but I'll leave it anyway. And would you cut some wood for her fireplace? There's an ax around back. Cut a lot. Her bones don't work."

Simon, still looking somewhat speechless, just reached inside his coat for his wallet.

"The old lady won't start shooting, will she?" Niky asked.

*"Ne."* Unable to suppress a laugh as she plucked the bills from Simon's hand, Violet headed back inside, feeling as if she were finally shining.

IVAN STRODE INTO the reception area outside his office with such urgency that the door swung back against the wall and startled his young assistant.

"General, is—"

"Arrange access to the logs of every person who has applied for permission to cross our borders for the past week."

"All the checkpoints, General? Entity and interentity?"

"Yes."

"The evacuation?"

"The situation is nearly contained. A street riot has not affected your office equipment or your ability to work, has it?" Ivan asked, and at the look of contrition on Ciril's face, he wished he had not spoken so sharply.

"No, General. Of course not. Right away."

"Thank you. I shall be in my office waiting."

Ivan tried to distract himself with work, but found concentration impossible. The moments ticked past as an exercise of restraint, so he left his desk, clicked on the television and let the news of the bombing in Belgrade distract his thoughts.

The Bosnian Serbs must stand by and do nothing while NATO rained terror on their brothers in Belgrade. Indeed, they must aid NATO by allowing bombers to fly over their airspace, bound and left helpless as they were by the Dayton Peace Agreement. Concessions and compromise.

Insults and exploitation.

His people had been forced from the Krajina. Yet Muslims, the newly named Bosniaks, had been given fifty-one percent of the remaining region. A tiny advantage, yet one that tipped the scales of power away from Strpski Grad.

Geography was another form of control. Their forty-nine percent, a horseshoe of land that wound around the Federation, was impossible to defend or unite. One more way of telling Bosnian Serbs they could not be trusted.

And yet…had it not been for the American president, Ivan's position as defense minister would have wielded no more power than the Ministry of the Displaced.

While the other European nations would have left Bosnia defenseless and dependant upon SFOR to fight their battles, the American president had stood firm in his belief that all the Federation of Bosnia-Herzegovina could not become autonomous without building their own military.

It had been a start to righting the wrong that had been done them. Now that Ivan was charged with growing his country's military, and he would not allow anyone to stand in his way.

Especially not a coward and a woman who should be dead.

## CHAPTER EIGHTEEN

SIMON CROSSED the parking lot of the Internet café and headed toward the Range Rover. Niky stood outside as he had for the past twenty minutes, the bodyguard protecting his charge.

"She's still out?" Simon asked, although he already knew the answer. He'd selected a computer near the busy doorway to the café specifically so he could watch Niky and Violet through the window while he worked.

"Shouldn't be too much longer," Niky said.

Peering through the back passenger window, Simon found Violet sprawled across the seat, head resting comfortably on the roll of Niky's coat, hair threading across a pale cheek.

"Did you make contact with Major?" Niky asked.

Simon nodded.

"Any problems accessing on that public computer?"

"No. The uplink worked just like TJ said it would. No one should trace the connection."

"Then why don't you look happy?"

"The bootlegger is dead. He floated up in a river in Belize. Standard execution. We were meant to find him."

Niky's gaze trailed into the back seat. He exhaled heavily.

"I confirmed there were no Bosnian Serbs running that detention camp."

They both knew what that meant. The man Violet remembered hadn't been from the Citizen's Army, so they didn't have much to work with now the bootlegger had become a dead end. The Bosnian Serb who'd interrogated her remained a nameless, faceless, potentially deadly threat. Violet had been masked and hadn't seen the man's face. They only had her memory of his voice to lead them.

"Let's go," Simon said, glancing at his watch. "I don't want to tackle the frontier tonight, but we've done all we can here. It's time to move on."

"That's sloppy, Simon. We came over the border to conduct a site inspection. Heading out too fast will invite attention."

"Our permissions are in order. If anyone asks, we'll say we'd sent our equipment ahead to Zagreb, and there was a problem. We've had to cut the trip short."

"It's risky. We should at least spend a night and use the time to look at the people running this town. See who was doing what during the war. We might find something."

Simon shook his head. "Quinn's already got people on it. We don't need to be here. We need to get Violet to the saint for some answers."

He had no idea where a threat might come from, and he couldn't shake the feeling that every moment they stayed only darkened the bull's-eye on her head. Niky might have continued arguing, but Violet awakened.

Yawning drowsily, she blinked against the light, then forced herself up from the seat. He extended his hand, and she took it. For an instant, she looked pleased to see him, a sleepy look he remembered from those nights in Sault Ste. Marie.

The expression faded in degrees, and he could almost mark exactly when she remembered they were no longer in his apartment, no longer lovers, that her life had been threatened and he'd forced her to trade everything she knew for memories of pain and uncertainty.

He held on as if he could keep her from remembering, as if she would still see him as the man he'd been for those few short days, the man who'd made love to her with no other agenda than to bring her pleasure.

"Would you like a few minutes to stretch before we get back on the road?" he asked.

"Thank you." She withdrew her hand, and the moment was over, leaving him with the lingering feel of her skin and the hope she might believe he could be that man.

Niky handed her the coffee. "Forgot you're a lightweight in the drinking department, did you?"

"Couldn't have reminded me?"

"Then you wouldn't have gotten plowed with the old lady. While you feel like shit right now, we have the information we need about our saint. Good work."

She rubbed her temple. "Small price, I suppose."

"Don't you know it. Want acetaminophen? Quinn stocked us."

She nodded, and Niky circled the Range Rover to fish inside his suitcase, leaving Simon standing beside Violet, only a foot away, but miles apart.

Once he'd used Violet and Niky's easy camaraderie to his benefit. He'd counted on their closeness to work situations less convincing operatives couldn't manage. He'd never once questioned the effect of that closeness on them.

Now he understood Niky's continuing struggle to make peace with losing his team. Simon had thought he'd understood, had thought Niky had suffered a survivor guilt similar to his own, had thought him undisciplined for not learning to cope.

But as he watched Violet accept the geltabs and down them in a swallow, he recalled what Quinn had told him at Safe Harbor.

*"You don't maneuver emotional terrain easily on a good day."*

And when Simon remembered the town house with a brass angel on the door, dust-cloth-covered furnishings inside, he knew he'd been the undisciplined one, that his guilt had been similar to Niky's, so much more than survivor's guilt, only denied.

How long would he have continued to ignore his feelings if Violet hadn't been lost?

Too long.

"Let's go," he said, reaching for the front door handle.

Violet lifted her gaze to his. "Would you mind if I sit up front? I won't make it in back for long."

"Of course." Slipping his fingers around her elbow, Simon assisted her into the front seat while she juggled the coffee cup, not an intimate touch, but another connection, a promise to himself, a silent promise to her.

Then stepping aside, he closed the door.

"So where are we heading?" Niky asked.

"North. We'll find a hotel in the next town. I haven't decided where to cross the border yet, but I don't want to spend the night here."

"Bad feeling?" Niky asked.

Simon nodded, ignoring the curious look Violet shot

back. He pulled out the map of the area and settled into the back seat to assess where to make the crossing, distracted himself from so much unsettling self-analysis.

He needed to think, to make sense of this latest twist in their investigation, and the back seat of this Range Rover was as good a place as any.

He made comparisons between two maps—one a map of the main roads through the region, the other a tactical map from SFOR that showed the country lanes and convoy routes that twisted and plunged through the mountains.

Simon's preference was to take the tactical routes. Not only were they less likely to encounter Strpski Grad militia patrols in the less populated areas, but if they did encounter questions about the brevity of their stay, he'd rather provide the answers to SFOR military personnel. A fail-safe.

The problem with the convoy routes was they wound through the mountains and valleys around number twelve detention camp. Both Violet and Niky knew the region intimately. They'd been briefed extensively for travel when the extraction team had attempted to infiltrate the camp. They'd survived an avalanche that had driven them into the camp boundaries, where they had encountered the patrols who'd captured them. They'd both existed inside the camp. They'd both escaped.

Simon knew the route Niky had taken out. With Violet, he only knew where the Global Coalition envoy had found her.

He didn't want to subject either of them to the stress of a return visit.

When Niky shot a glance in the rearview mirror and said, "We got a tail," Simon no longer had a choice.

Peering through the back window, he found a local police cruiser speeding up to overtake them with lights flashing.

"You want me to stop or hit the gas?"

They were still on the outskirts of town. Trying to outrun this cruiser would only invite the entire local police force to join the chase. But as Niky had been traveling the speed limit and obeying the local traffic laws, this situation boded ill.

"Stop. We'll stick with our cover, show them papers and find out what they want."

"And hope like hell luck is on our side today."

Simon could see Violet in profile, looking uneasy, as Niky pulled off the road onto the shoulder, avoiding the entrance to a parking lot that would have made escape difficult in the event they needed to quickly merge again with traffic.

The patrol cruiser pulled in behind them, and Simon could see two policemen. The driver shoved his door wide, while the passenger spoke into a radio before following. And when they approached, flanking the Range Rover with their sidearms raised, Simon knew this was no routine traffic stop.

"Keep your window closed," he told Violet, opening his own.

Niky did the same, asking, "What's the problem, Officer?"

"Hands where I can see them," the swarthy-skinned man instructed in heavily accented English. He and his partner trained their weapons. "All of you."

They did as instructed.

"Permissions."

Simon inclined his head to the seat beside him, and

the policeman standing beside his open window motioned toward the papers with his gun.

"Pass them to me."

He glanced only briefly at the paperwork before nodding to his partner. "Get out of the car. Slowly. Put your hands up."

"What's the trouble?"

"You have information about a war criminal," the policeman said, the gun he trained on Niky steady. "Bastard foreigners."

"Now. Out," the other barked.

Set up. Whoever was after Violet had just put the locals on them, effectively cutting off their movements in Strpski Grad.

In his periphery, Niky looked for instruction, and Simon inclined his head. For an instant, he felt in sync with his team as they reached for their doors, knowing what to do in that silent communication that only came with highly trained people. For once he was a part of them. They might not have worked in the field together before, but he'd trained them both.

They flung the doors wide, forcing the policemen back, and Niky gunned the accelerator. They tore off down the shoulder, dirt and gravel kicking up in their wake, the doors slamming shut with the momentum. Simon heard shots fired but didn't know what they hit because the Range Rover sped out of range.

"What's your next brilliant idea?" Niky asked.

Simon peered out the back window through the haze of dirt to see the two policemen running toward their cruiser, waving on two more patrols, who approached.

"Drive. I'll tell you where to get off the main road."

Dragging out the SFOR tactical map, he scanned for

a route likely to lose the parade forming behind them. Not many choices. The country lanes and convoy routes intersected, shooting out in all directions through the mountains, giving them places to run and hide. The main roads weren't only populated, but the towns had more police that could ambush them with roadblocks.

"Pull off at the next exit. We'll take a convoy route north."

A trip on memory lane. Simon could only hope they blew through this region so fast that neither Violet nor Niky would get much chance to reminisce.

Two cruisers clung to their tail, a third not far behind. Niky maneuvered through the traffic at high speed. As they neared the exit, Simon saw two more cruisers shoot onto the road a half mile ahead.

"Hang on," Niky warned, waiting until the last second to steer onto the off-ramp, forced to brake as the Range Rover skidded hard through the curve.

The cruisers followed.

"Once we get through this suburb, we should be out of the town limits," Simon said. "Traffic will drop off. You should be able to pick up some speed."

"What's the point? This is a two-lane road."

"It's a two-lane convoy route that connects with other two-lane convoy routes that wind through these mountains. If you stay far enough ahead, you'll be able to use the blind curves and the dusk to our advantage."

"Gotcha—"

"Watch out." Violet gasped.

Niky swerved away from a sedan backing out of a driveway, braking hard only when the car's rear end was already well in the street. The near-miss cost precious seconds, and they all fell silent as Niky leaned on the horn as he approached a stop sign at the end of the neighborhood.

He whipped through the intersection without stopping, and as Simon had said the road began to climb. Downshifting to maintain speed, Niky maneuvered easily as the road twisted and the hills reared and plummeted. He turned off the headlights to make the most of the dusk. The forest swelled around them, swallowing up the twinkling lights of Brijevek.

The sirens faded. On these lonely roads, there was no one to warn. Simon only wished the blind spots didn't stop him from seeing how many cruisers had joined the conga line behind them.

"There's a fork ahead. Keep right. See if you can gain speed before you make the turn. If we can get the police to split up we'll be two steps ahead."

The powerful engine screamed beneath the strain of Niky's handling, but he did manage to gain them some distance. The twisting of the road worked in their favor as well as a switchback turn that blocked the cruisers' sight. They'd be forced to split up.

Violet clung to the handhold as Niky veered a hard right. Simon grabbed on as the deep-treaded tires skidded off the road and kicked up rock and dirt on a shoulder that narrowly buffered the steep slope of the mountain edge.

When they emerged out of the bend, there was only one cruiser in the distance.

They chased through the fading light. Violet showed the signs of stress in the way she clung to the handhold as the Range Rover swayed over the road. Niky was silent, pushing the engine to its limit as the terrain grew sharper. He scowled when forced to slow to maneuver—barely—another perilous descent.

"We're playing tag here, Simon," Niky said. "Unless you got any more magic tricks, we're going to keep playing until we run out of gas. I'll have to turn the lights on again soon. I'll get us killed if I can't make out the road."

Violet glanced down the steep mountain slope. "Where are we going? They've probably alerted the authorities to look for us in other towns, too."

"There's another road bisecting this one in a few miles. If you can gain enough distance before you make the turn, we'll stand a fifty-fifty chance of losing them."

That was the best he could offer.

Unfortunately, the terrain wasn't with them this time. No forested curves to blind the sight of these turns. No way to hide on the ribbon of road that twisted down toward a valley.

"Shit," Niky ground out.

In the distance, the headlights of an approaching cruiser shafted through the deepening dusk. Likely the one they'd shaken earlier, Simon guessed.

Instead of heading away from the cruiser, Niky turned toward it, and the instant he did, Simon knew Niky meant to play chicken with barely three feet of gravel shoulder to the edge.

Violet must have noticed, too, because she leaned back, still clinging to the handhold with a white-knuckled grip.

Easing into the middle of the road, Niky took the offensive to force the cruiser to edge to the far shoulder.

The cruiser's headlights swelled in a silent battle of wills. Niky's fingers tightened on the steering wheel. Violet turned her head to the side, closed her eyes.

Wind hissed as the cruiser rushed past, so close

Simon could see the flash of a lighted instrument panel, followed by the sound of gravel kicking up violently as the cruiser hit the shoulder at high speed, the taillights jerking sharply as the driver struggled to control the car.

Simon's heartbeat lurched into a pace along with the Range Rover's racing engine. He inhaled deeply. Niky picked up speed again, making the most of his final moments before the deepening dusk forced him to turn the lights on and slow down to maneuver the hairpin turns.

Niky scowled. "He's only going to turn around and come after us."

"Already has," Simon informed them grimly. "The other one's caught up, too."

"I think we need a new plan."

Something about that seemed to startle Violet, and Simon watched curiously as she leaned forward, straining the seat belt while reaching inside her coat.

Suddenly she held up a 9mm automatic pistol.

"Where did you get that?" Simon asked, surprised.

"A policeman's utility belt. He fell on top of me in the square."

Niky barked a laugh. "Some things never change, Wolfgang, do they? You and those damn sticky fingers."

"Felt like the thing to do." Pulling the clip, she glanced inside. "It's been fired. One bullet left for each car. I can't trust myself to make the shot."

Simon gazed out the window, could just barely make out the tires in the glare of the cruiser's headlights. "Got it."

Violet turned around in her seat and handed him the gun.

"Good thinking," he said.

The smile she flashed him lit the dusk.

Pulling himself through the window, Simon braced against the door for support. Time slowed to a crawl as he sighted the front passenger tire to make the shot, the wind hissing in his ears, the cold almost stinging enough to make his eyes water, half expecting the police to start firing.

He pulled off the shot.

The cruiser jerked a hard right, headlights cutting off into the distance as the driver fell out of the chase.

Within seconds, more headlights appeared as the next cruiser streaked past to replace it. Several shots fired and Simon fell back through the window as one hissed across the roof, puncturing a streaking runnel in it.

"Hang on." Niky wove over the width of the road, missing the shoulder by inches before traveling back, each move timed with smooth precision, each move making them tough to target.

Simon watched the cruiser's headlights swaying behind them. Left to right then right to left with hypnotic precision. He tried to make out the tires, nearly indistinguishable, and for a stunned moment he stared at his limitations, face-to-face with a pride that made it difficult to admit, "I can't guarantee the shot while we're moving. It's too dark."

Violet turned to Niky. "You can, though, can't you? We've done this maneuver before. I remember."

"If we move fast."

"I should have given you the gun sooner," she said.

"The dark's working in our favor." Simon reassured her. "Otherwise their bullets would be hitting us right now."

"Do you remember how to drive?" Niky asked.

"We'll find out."

Niky laughed, grabbing the steering wheel hard and pulling himself forward in the seat. The Range Rover lurched as he temporarily lost his rhythm. "On your mark."

Simon didn't know if instinct or memory took over, but there was no missing how his operatives settled into a groove they'd once known while working together.

Only they didn't feel like operatives right now. Niky felt like a man Violet was comfortable with. A man who'd taken the time to become her friend.

"Three…" Violet flipped the seat belt away and leaped into a crouch on the seat in a fluid move.

"Two…" She reached for the handhold near Niky's head.

"One…" Pulling herself into the wedge of space between Niky and the seat, she positioned herself to make the switch.

"Go."

Niky released the wheel and rolled toward the passenger seat while Violet slid into position, taking control of the vehicle with only a jerky deceleration to mark the move.

The entire maneuver hadn't taken more than ten seconds, had been stunning in speed and simplicity, so much more striking when viewed up close.

Violet immediately wove the length of the road then back again, picking up Niky's rhythm. She nailed the shoulder on the return trip, and the Range Rover bounced hard as the tire scrambled for purchase in the shifting gravel. "Sorry."

"You're doing fine," Simon said.

Niky maneuvered in the seat, hung inside the window until he got the rhythm of her pace then leaned out, aimed and fired.

The second cruiser's headlights lurched in the failing light then disappeared as Violet put the miles between them.

"Excellent work." Simon meant it. His pulse was finally slowing. "I need options to get out of these mountains. Our enemy has the power to send the local police after us on fake charges, so we can expect them to use all their resources. That means helicopters and roadblocks. We're driving a bull's-eye."

The silence fell heavily, interrupted only by the humming of the engine and the unearthly glow of the instrument display.

"You know where we are, don't you?" Niky shot a meaningful gaze toward Violet. "I know this terrain. I've got an idea if you want to chance it."

She turned to him, eyes flashing in the now almost complete darkness. "Don't worry about me."

They couldn't have gotten any closer to number twelve detention camp had they paid for a guided tour, and no matter what Violet said, Simon would worry.

It was all part of being a living, feeling man.

## CHAPTER NINETEEN

MOONLIGHT BARELY SEEPED through the swollen, gray clouds in the night sky, but Violet could see the slender outcropping of rock jutting upward, its silhouette almost regal against the dark forest. She'd seen it before. That rock was a marker. The locals had used it during the war to mark a trail. *She* had used it.

Suddenly she couldn't walk another step. They'd ditched the Range Rover over a cliff and had been walking for hours. Her legs felt boneless, and she reached out to grab Simon's arm, only managed to claw at his thick wool sleeve before sinking to the ground. But he was there, catching her, pulling her to him, supporting her against a fallen tree along the trail where she could sit.

"What's wrong?" He knelt before her, taking her hands in his, staring into her face with those eyes that saw so much.

Niky was suddenly beside her, too, and she forced words past her constricted throat.

"We're walking…the wrong way."

Simon inhaled deeply, a visual reminder for her to do the same. His warm hands tightened their grip, and she forced herself to follow his lead, to keep breathing past the waves of ice spilling through her one after another, altering her senses, making her question whether this dripping-ink night was really before her eyes or in her memory.

"The hamlet," she finally managed. "It's that way. We need to hike to it. Not away."

Niky shook his head. "We're steering clear of the locals."

"That." She pointed to the jutting rock. "The locals call it the signpost. It leads to the town and the well. See how it leans in that direction?"

"What's the well?" Niky asked.

"A way out of the mountains."

Simon's fingers threaded through hers now, his grip solid, warm. "The way you got out?"

Violet only nodded. She'd been seeing the well and feeling that bone-chilling water ever since she'd opened her eyes at Safe Harbor. She hadn't understood what it meant.

Escape.

*She couldn't feel the rough wood anymore. Her fingers had long ago gone numb. The only thing she felt now was tired. She wanted to escape the cold in dreams, but every time she dozed, icy water would douse her. Trickles that ran through runnels in the rock ceiling. A splash shooting through a crevasse like a tiny waterfall. The upsurge of the current as a stream crashed in from somewhere in the mountains.*

*Damn water kept splashing into her face and waking her.*

"Were you in a boat?" Simon asked.

She shook her head, tried to focus on the memory. "I could grab the sides. A raft, I think. It was small. I couldn't stretch out. My elbows kept dragging in the water."

His eyes looked dark in the blackness, his skin just an indistinct blur of pale, but he was solid. There. As he always was. Not perfect—he hadn't found her for so long—but he'd retrieved everything she'd sent back to him, found the clues she'd sent in her stories. He'd found her. Even when she hadn't known herself. He hadn't given up. He would never give up.

And knowing that, along with the feel of his hands tight around hers, anchored her. Pulled her clear of the whirling memories and kept her steered toward the reality of now. Violet wasn't on that icy stream anymore. She was with Simon.

"We can take the stream," she said, not recognizing the ragged whisper of her own voice, honestly not knowing if she could bring herself to travel that path again. But it would bring them safely away from the searching police so much faster than how they traveled now. "The refugees took it to the border. It goes south from here, but if they could get close enough to the frontier, sometimes they could make it the rest of the way."

Niky's hand settled on her shoulder, another gesture meant to reassure. "How did you find out about it?"

"In the camp." Lowering her face, she couldn't bear to see Simon's expression while she remembered.

Tears finally spilled through her lids, splashed onto their joined hands. "They hanged me. I didn't die. People wanted to help. I don't know why."

She could hear voices, so many voices. Worried. Angry. Scared. *Always* scared.

*"The commandant is angry, woman. He threw you in here so we would watch you die and be frightened. But we will help you. Come on, woman. Drink."*

Her tears fell freely now. "They gave me their water.

They shared their secrets and created a diversion to help me escape. They asked me to send someone back to help them."

She was drowning in anguish, choking on her tears, barely able to breathe. But she heard Simon's voice as an anchor, there as he always was, her gravity. He rested his brow against hers and said, "You did."

NIKY UNDERSTOOD the premise. He'd been briefed on the whole groundwater movement thing before he'd ever led his team on the extraction mission into death camp number twelve. Europe's largest subterranean river flowed through Bosnia, emerging in Croatia. Because of all the water-soluble rock, this region was infamous for underground streams, aquifers and caves.

What Niky didn't understand was why he was freezing his ass off in an inflatable raft heading *away* from Brijevek.

Once they crossed the frontier into Croatia—*if* they made it across the frontier into Croatia—any chance of assassinating Zubac would be gone. Niky could never come back to this part of the world without Simon's knowledge. His transponder marked him on a display in Systems Ops night and day.

So what was he supposed to do—follow Simon across the border and let Zubac keep sending assassins until one finally hit them? Niky didn't even consider confessing anymore—he wondered what that said about him.

Leaning his head against the inflatable raft, he could barely make out Violet's face in the dark. This was rough on her. When she'd taken this stream as an escape route from the death camp, the homes in the hamlet hadn't had amenities such as inflatable rafts. While she was still sketchy on the details, it sounded as if she'd fashioned a raft from a panel of someone's wooden fence. Who knew what she'd used to keep it afloat.

He wished he could see her face, but while they'd taken the flashlight from the Range Rover before rolling it over a cliff, they wouldn't use it except in an emergency. In this unearthly blackness, there was no way to know where the ground opened. Light beaming through at the wrong time could betray them.

Turned out the well Violet had remembered was nothing more than a sinkhole that some clever—or desperate—folks had concealed beneath a stone well. Apparently this underground escape route had become part of the local flavor because it was still there, even after all the refugees had been swept behind their appropriate borders.

Niky hoped like hell Zubac hadn't heard of it.

So far everything had gone like a charm, though. They'd finally reached the town after midnight, and the moonless night had worked to their favor. Simon hadn't wanted to play Noah, so they'd broken into storage sheds looking for a boat. With all the water and snow in these mountains, the locals were big into the great outdoors.

They'd come across skiing equipment and had lucked out in the second shed they'd pilfered, finding the raft. The town had long since rolled up its sidewalks, and they hadn't run into any trouble climbing down into the well. It had been off the main street that ran through the town anyway.

The only negative had been inflating the raft, which they couldn't do without climbing in. They'd stood in frigid swift-running water to inflate the damn thing. Now Niky was freezing his ass off, and Violet couldn't stop shivering.

Closing his eyes, Niky tried to come up with something more constructive than recriminations about how he'd failed again with Zubac. He'd been given a second chance. He'd blown it.

Didn't look as though he'd get a third.

"You said we would wind up in a cave, Violet?" He needed to hear something other than the accusations in his head.

"If I remember right, it's a series of caves and springs. I found one that was secluded."

"Hot springs, I hope."

"Mmm-hmm. I'm about done with cold water myself."

He thought he could hear a smile in her voice, and a plan started to form in his head.

Maybe he could manage a third chance, after all.


"THERE'S NO REASON to stay here. I can keep going." Violet surprised herself by sounding so much stronger than she actually felt, soaked to the skin, frozen to the bone and unable to stop shaking. Even the steam rising off the hot spring didn't warm her. "You shouldn't go out alone like this."

"We can't move in the daylight," Niky said. "It'll be easier for one person to scout out what we're up against at the border. We need a plan to get across the frontier. On foot won't work with half the frigging militia after us."

"You can make contact with Major in an emergency," Simon said, an obvious attempt to reassure her.

"Besides, beautiful—" Niky flashed a grin from another lifetime, one that should have been dashing but felt all too bittersweet "—I'll rustle up some slivovitz and cevapcici in town while you're eating soggy protein bars. And I'm going to steal dry clothes. Sounds like the better deal."

"He'll be back in twelve hours."

Violet appreciated Simon's efforts to assuage her worries, but twelve hours stretched out before her like forever. Niky was heading out into danger, and she'd be stuck inside this cave with anguished memories bleeding from every shadow.

She'd be alone with Simon.

"Get some sleep." Niky flashed that grin again. "I'll be fine. I promise."

"Good luck," she whispered, but he'd already disappeared into the shadows.

Violet sank onto a rocky ledge, uncaring of the cold damp seeping through soaked slacks. Though the cave was dark, some trick of the hot spring made the rising steam glow from within, and she stared into that eerie sight, refusing to give into an almost crushing sense of despair.

Was this worry or some remnant of a past memory? Had she known her identity the last time she'd been here? Or had the death camp robbed that before she'd traveled down the stream?

Violet didn't know. She only knew that she felt soul weary and on edge. She could still hear those who'd once helped her escape, mutterings on the fringes of her brain, indistinct and busy, like voices over a party line in the days before satellite connections and conference calls.

But through it she could hear Simon moving around in the darkness. Assessing escape routes, perhaps. Or setting up booby traps to alert them to intruders. Maybe even trying to fashion a camp with no supplies. They had protein bars and flashlights. An emergency field unit to contact Command. Not much, but he'd be taking control of a situation that had gotten out of his grasp.

Even if she hadn't remembered that from the past, she'd seen enough evidence since he'd come back into her life not to doubt what kind of man he was. Capable. Controlling. Caring. He'd used every chance since their arrival in Bosnia to show her that he believed in her abilities, that he cared.

As her acting director or as a man?

"Let me have your coat." His voice filtered through the bubbling quiet, deep and steady, gravity in the humid blackness. "I've found a draft and some light. Maybe we'll get lucky and it'll dry out."

She shrugged out of her coat and would have brought it to him. Only when she turned, she found him already there. They didn't speak, but suddenly she was so aware that they were together, alone.

She'd avoided him since leaving Safe Harbor. The past and the present always collided around him, tangling long-ago desires with nowadays needs. She hadn't wanted to tackle making sense of the way she felt yet. Not while she still only had pieces of a faulty memory to guide her.

But here they were again. Close. He took away her coat, saying nothing, but she could feel his gaze caress her, knew he saw everything despite the darkness.

"Your clothes, too. You need to get warm."

She wasn't surprised and didn't have the strength to argue. He turned as she undressed, waited until she'd slipped into the steamy water before carrying her things away.

The hot water seeping through her skin came as another memory from long ago. There was a ledge nearby...the sand shifted beneath her feet as she sought out that place and curled up, rested her face on her arm and let the heat ease her trembling.

She must have dozed because she awakened to a soft splash and knew Simon had gotten into the pool. She had no right to deny him their only source of warmth, but knowing he was naked, so close... She remembered each hard line of his body, knew what his skin would feel like slick with wet.

And that she could still want him now, even after knowing the truth of the way things were between them... The feelings she'd had for him had been so much a part of who she'd been, but they were feelings he'd never returned.

He prowled the edges of the pool, familiarizing himself with their environs, the master of all he surveyed. Something about that made her feel like smiling.

She watched quietly as he swam toward the middle where the pool grew deep. He moved with long clean strokes, clearly enjoying the freedom to move after so many days spent in planes, cars and in a raft.

And when he finally came to stand beside her, she was grateful for the water that covered her nudity, although she could see him from the waist up, his hard chest and broad, broad shoulders so tantalizing in the darkness.

"Are you still remembering?" he asked.

She only nodded.

"I want to help."

"Why? Because you feel guilty." She might not remember the past, but she remembered that before she'd lost her memory, sitting naked next to him would not have been possible. "You did what you had to do. I'm okay with that."

"I don't feel guilty. But I do realize my feelings for you were never clear. I distanced myself because I didn't understand how I felt. I do now. I'll prove that, but until we're back and you're safe, don't shut me out. Let me help however I can."

She remembered this feeling from the night they'd first made love. She'd been poised over her whole life, knowing she shouldn't get involved with him, but jumping feetfirst into something she couldn't handle because she couldn't resist.

She still couldn't resist and, with a sigh, she jumped again.

"Make me forget, Simon."

His arm came around her with whipcord strength, pulling her to her knees and locking her against him. Her breasts crushed against his chest, and she was spread against him thigh to thigh, her stomach cradling his growing erection.

He speared his fingers into her hair, arched her head back until she was forced to look into his face. Those clear eyes cut through the dark, a trick so unique to him. She trembled.

There was no past, no present, only desire, and the answering awareness in the pit of her stomach, the melting softness between her thighs.

"Make me forget."

His mouth came down on hers hard, feeding a forbidden ache from a lifetime ago, yet satisfying a need she'd only known in his arms. If Violet believed nothing else right now, she believed their bodies remembered each other and were grateful.

He made love to her mouth with his kiss, stealing her breath, returning it only when she was gasping and eager and unable to keep her hands off him.

She touched him freely, savoring the strength of his hands, the hard heat of his need. This moment was theirs, and she didn't want to hear anything but the rumbling deep in his throat when he sank his fingers into her bottom and rode that tight ridge of skin against her.

No voices from the past. No warnings about the future.

She only wanted to hear Simon, who was so honest in his passion. She hadn't understood how significant that was at Safe Harbor, but she recognized it now. Not a man to ever lose control, he gave so freely when he touched her....

Rocking her hips from side to side, she cradled his erection, reveling in the tension that gathered his muscles in reply. Sinking her fingers into his tight butt, she pulled him impossibly closer, drank the next growl from his lips, tasted the sound of his desire.

He raked a hand up her back, his palm skimming along her moist skin with an urgency, a possessiveness, to touch her everywhere. Threading his fingers into her hair, he guided her head back, broke away from their kiss to trail his mouth along her jaw, behind her ear, down her throat.

He nibbled the soft skin at her pulse, dragged his

parted lips down her chest, caught her nipple between his teeth, a carefully restrained move that made her breath stall and her sex pulse. He sucked that tip inside in a hot, wet pull.

She sighed, feeling the jolt of his touch as a scalding wave that crashed through her. He laved his attention on one greedy peak then the other, until she twined her fingers through his hair to hang on.

Then he continued his exploration, sinking down before her to cherish her skin with his mouth, her stomach…she winced when he found her bruised skin where the policeman's gun had dug into her hip.

He tipped his head back, the whites of his eyes flashing, his voice accusing. "You said you were fine."

"I am."

No bruise could possibly detract from the sight of his dark head poised so erotically over her pale skin. Once upon a time he had been her fantasy, and even if the details had blurred and dimmed, instinct remembered. No faulty memory could take away her pleasure in the moment, her eagerness to feel his next hot touch, her thrill with the freedom to touch him.

He only lowered his mouth to the bruised skin in a phantom kiss that made her tremble.

Then he stood. Catching her in his arms, he maneuvered her around until he sat on the ledge with her in his lap. For a breathless moment they just sat there, the steam from the spring coiling around them, slicking their skin in hot mist.

He rested his cheek on the top of her head. His arms were tight as he held her, such an unexpectedly tender embrace. She felt surrounded by him, hard muscle and sleek skin, her world narrowing to the feel of her cheek against his shoulder, her face pressed into the curve of his neck, her nostrils filled with the scent of his skin.

His pulse throbbed steadily. His heartbeat thudded dully. Tangible reminders that he was real, that he wanted her. She found the intimacy of being held by this man overwhelming.

Pulling free, she came to her knees and straddled him, needing pleasure as a distraction, needing control to tame the moment where past and present united.

This was Simon, and for this precious moment he was hers to touch, not under the guise of a new lover, but as the man she had wanted forever.

This memory was hers to make.

Slipping her hand between them, she stroked his velvet length. He inhaled sharply, and his hot flesh jumped in her hand. Spreading her thighs, she dragged the thick head through her folds, sighed as he glided easily in her body's moisture.

Dragging his hands up her ribs, he thumbed the sensitive undersides of her breasts, lowering his face to tease one aching peak while he caught the other between a thumb and forefinger. He squeezed, and she arched against him, wanting him to touch her everywhere.

The way she would touch him. Easing him inside her just barely, she gasped as her body stretched to accommodate him. His muscles coiled tight. She dragged him along the sensitive knot of nerves endings that made her sex pulse in aching need.

His body vibrated beneath hers, and she couldn't resist the urge to sink down on top of him, feel him swell inside her, watch pleasure sharpen his features as he reared back to gaze into her face.

Raking his fingers down her waist, he settled those

strong hands on her hips and held her immobile while he pressed inside, nudging so deep, his groin riding against that sensitive place that poured fire through her.

And for an instant, the expression on his face was one she knew she'd dreamed of, a look where he poised on the edge of control, of losing himself in her. Then there was no more teasing, no more savoring, no more restraint. Their bodies remembered this need, and they began to move.

She rode him with long, hard strokes. He rose up to meet each with such force that he thrust the breath from her lungs, made her gasp out tiny sounds that mirrored the mounting pleasure.

"Oh, Violet."

The sound of his need throbbed through her, and when he threaded a hand around her neck and pulled her against him, thrusting, always thrusting, she caught her name as it tumbled from his lips again.

And she forgot everything but the feel of him inside her, the taste of his mouth on hers as he lost control and ground out his pleasure, dragged her to the edge with him, making her forget everything but the magic they made together.

IVAN STARED at the telephone, the explanation of number twelve camp's former commandant ringing in his ears. He had left this former Serbian general sitting in the United States capital, enjoying the free air after more than two years of existing underground to escape persecution as a war criminal. "You are telling me the American woman was dead when you had her cut from the noose?"

"Of course she was dead, Ivan. You saw the photo

that bastard traitor gave the tribunal. I had them throw her body in with the detainees to show them what to expect if they gave my guards any more trouble."

"Did you make sure she came back out again, Dragan?"

"Of course I did."

"How long?"

There was a beat of hesitation. "A week. Maybe more. I don't remember. Long enough to stink."

"What did you do with her corpse?"

"Burned her in a pit. Like you ordered."

Dragan Mlakovic's fear smelled riper than the American woman's corpse ever had. Ivan could smell it across an ocean.

"I ask you again, my friend," Dragan said. "Why do you question me about this woman now? Does her death have something to do with these people who escaped you? Tell me. I will help however I can. You know that."

No. Ivan no longer knew. While he had gained much by befriending this man before the Dayton Peace Agreement had ended his part in the war, Ivan had also risked much to harbor him, and others like him, in safety now that the war crimes tribunal sought retribution for genocide.

He expected more than lies for his efforts.

"All right, Dragan. I shall bring you home."

"I will help. Give me that chance. And of course, breathing pure mountain air will refresh my soul."

"Make ready then." Ivan disconnected the line and stared at the telephone. He would not allow his work to be jeopardized by the actions of others. He had worked too long and hard. While his government let the internationals punish them for their Serbian blood, he would plan and build for the day the internationals withdrew. Then Strpski Grad Republika could rise to independence.

Until then, he must continue playing this game and safeguarding his advances. Reaching for the intercom, he depressed a button.

A woman immediately replied, "Yes, General."

"Ask the prime minister when would be convenient for him to hear an update on our investigation."

Ivan had only just gathered together the recently faxed reports from the local police when the intercom beeped. "The prime minister will see you now, General."

After a short walk down the hall, Ivan found the prime minister standing at his window, hands clasped behind his back.

He did not turn around but said, "Come, Ivan, sit. Tell me what you have learned."

Ivan did as requested and relayed the details of the commander's investigation. He explained how the suspects' vehicle had been found in the ravine, how the militia had tracked their earlier movements from Sarajevo to Brijevek.

He would have preferred not to mention the library. Placing the suspects anywhere near the square during the riot could potentially raise questions about the mystery death of the policeman Ivan would rather not answer.

He had no answers. His trail of the suspects led to a dead end because of a stolen canister of microfilm. The librarian could not tell him what the suspects had been researching, so he had no way to track where they'd gone from the library.

But they had been seen on a local network, and while he'd had his commander confiscate the footage, news could easily leak. Explaining the omission to the prime minister would be more awkward later than explaining the connection now.

The prime minister finally turned around. "They were here? In our square?"

"In the library. My commander has questioned the librarian and staff personally. It appears the suspects were inside during the time of our unfortunate policeman's death and did not leave until the sirens had been sounded. They escaped through an emergency exit to avoid lockdown. We are investigating."

Ivan did not believe his Western contact could be so close with no purpose.

"Any lead on how they're traveling now?"

"Several reports of ransacked storage sheds, but nothing of any relevance stolen. I believe they would be foolish to move again until nightfall."

The prime minister's gaze settled on him with weight. "And you believe the information these people have is worth using resources from four municipalities?"

"My secret police report that these people have information about the whereabouts of General Dragan Mlakovic."

The stare grew thoughtful. "If you apprehend these suspects, do you believe you will apprehend General Mlakovic? Handing a war criminal to the tribunal now would go a long way toward goodwill with the international community. Recent events with our Belgrade brothers have cast us in dim light."

Ivan understood the often-difficult path this man walked in his position as a diplomat and a warrior and felt proud that at least something useful would come of these disturbing events. "I believe the information I have received is correct, and I have every confidence I can deliver General Mlakovic into custody."

SIMON WATCHED as Violet sat shivering on the rock ledge outside of the pool. Through the day, their clothing had dried enough to be damp and uncomfortable. The urge to go to her became physical. He wanted to wrap her in his arms, warm her, hold her. Just hold her.

But Violet had done exactly what he'd asked. She'd let him help. They'd made love then slept in each other's arms. Upon awakening, she'd slipped away and forced them back into familiar roles. Two professionals awaiting a teammate's return. Two people with so much distance between them.

She was comfortable here. He wasn't. The closeness they'd shared slipped through his grasp, and he didn't want to let go. He wanted to reassure her, and by reassuring her, himself. He needed some small hope that they would work out in the end.

He wouldn't push, though. He would only respect her wishes, and wait until she gave him another chance. He owed her that. Her time frame. She deserved to be in control. He would wait. It was so simple but the waiting…the restraint… He found both more difficult than he'd ever found detachment, found that feeling required far more discipline than he'd ever imagined.

"Niky's late, Simon. Do you think he ran into trouble?"

Glancing at the glowing display of his watch, he noted the time. "He's only an hour behind. Maybe he misjudged the time he'd need to get back. Or he might have had to hide until a patrol passed. We don't know how tight the net is out there. They'll assume we'll make for the border."

"Could he have gotten lost? This is a huge series of caves. There must be other entrances."

He could think of so many ways to reassure her, to distract her from the anxiety that made her frown into the darkness. "He'll have noted landmarks. We don't need to worry yet."

Simon wished he believed his own reassurances, but he had a bad feeling. Despite what he'd told Violet earlier, he would have preferred not to let Niky out alone. Unfortunately, he hadn't had a choice. They'd needed reconnaissance and couldn't travel unnoticed together. Violet hadn't been up to continuing no matter what she said, and he wouldn't take his eyes off her. So by default, Niky got the job.

Yet he couldn't deny that underlying all those rational reasons were some intensely personal ones. Simon wanted to be alone with her. He'd wanted to bridge the distance between them in the only way he knew how. And he had. For a while, at least.

Now her silence echoed in the cave. Making love again seemed to have strengthened her ability to distance herself, and diminished his. This raw ache made it so hard to stand here.

Simon tried to compartmentalize his feelings as the time passed, tried to have faith in Niky, but he found himself pacing instead, wondering if he'd made a mistake by sending Niky.

Wondering how badly he'd damaged his chances with Violet.

He'd already had so many chances. *Years* of chances. And rather than face his feelings, he'd buried them so completely he hadn't even known they were there. Until he stood watching her on that ledge with her arms around her legs, her chin on her knees, so remote that their intimacy in the pool might have never happened.

His ability to deny his emotions amazed him.

Just as his desire for Violet amazed him.

He wanted so much from her that his need became physical, so he went to sit beside her, hoping she wouldn't deny him when he *needed.* Tipping her head back, she gazed into his face. He wondered what she saw there, whether she recognized his need, not a weakness in that moment, but a strength.

He could finally admit what it was to want, to understand that to send his people to face death meant sharing their pain, not detaching from it.

To acknowledge he was only a man.

Violet slipped her arms around him, laid her cheek against his shoulder and held him. Just held him.

# CHAPTER TWENTY

THE SECURITY AROUND the ministry building had been too tight for Niky to attempt infiltration again. Instead, after a bus trip back into Brijevek in his new cover of an old Serb man, he'd bought a pair of binoculars and spent his day casing the security around Zubac's villa.

Perimeter cameras. A guard that swept the gate every quarter hour. Sentries at twelve-hour shift changes.

Piece of cake.

He had a lock on the monitoring station, too. The only thing he couldn't pinpoint was how many dogs were inside the kennel, so he'd made visits to a butcher and pharmacy for supplies, knowing he might have to use dosed meat just to get over the gate and inside the grounds.

Then he sat in the shadows, and he waited.

Niky intended to be back at the cave before dawn. He had a four-hour time buffer before Simon would change the plan, so as long as he returned by then, he would simply claim he'd had to hide from the border patrol.

Niky glanced at his watch then leveled his gaze across the street. The guard should be making a sweep anytime now...sure enough, he appeared beneath the glow of the street lamp, a bit of a swagger in his step, patrolling the interior of Zubac's gate with all the pride of those who guarded the Tomb of the Unknown Soldier back home. Niky wondered what he got paid for that kind of loyalty. Was it worth his life?

Niky had no weapon, for all the good one had done him in the ministry building. Today, he had something better—the luxury of time. To case the place. To think his plan through.

To anticipate the freedom that was almost his.

*And Violet's.*

Zubac would be on red alert. He'd called out his local posse of secret militia, and Niky wondered who'd spilled the beans—had it been the old woman with the assault rifle? He didn't think so. The librarian most likely.

Zubac hadn't arrived home until well after seven, and Niky had been gauging the activity inside the house ever since. Lights flicked on and off. Kitchen. Bedroom. Bathroom. Office. Zubac had been there ever since.

Niky would make his move soon—before Zubac packed it up for the night and the guards battened down the house. Under normal circumstances, Niky could have bypassed any security system, but he flew solo tonight, no Command at his back.

It was just him and his prey.

*Zubac.*

Long past time.

When the light finally went out in the office window, Niky made his move. The guard had continued his perimeter walk to the back of the property. The moon had slipped behind dense clouds as though luck kissed his cheek.

He needed six minutes to cross the grounds, allowing himself time to hunker down at intervals to avoid the sweeps of the surveillance cameras.

His pockets were filled with enough meat to divert and stop hungry dogs long enough to get those six minutes. He would keep some meat to ensure egress.

Emerging from his cover in the landscaping of an upscale town house, he crossed the street avoiding the pools of light spilling from the street lamps.

Zubac's property was surrounded by a ten-foot-high iron fence. Decorative with scrollwork. Functional with iron spear points on the top of each picket. Masonry gateposts broke up the ironwork at six-foot intervals.

Niky sheltered himself against the brick, waited. If any dogs were close by, they'd smell him.

Nothing.

Wedging his foot between pickets, he hung on to the capstone and hoisted himself up, leaped over the vicious spear points and dropped to the ground.

He was in.

Targeting the two nearest surveillance cameras, he crouched in the shadows and waited for that ten-second window when he could pass between them without detection. He could almost hear TJ in memory.

*"Move to the first mark."*

Racing to a stand of trees, Niky rolled under a decorative bench, marked the next pass of those surveillance cameras.

*"Move to the second mark."*

Four marks to cross the lawn, and he made them all without encountering any dogs. He could only guess they hadn't been let out for the night yet.

And another peck from Lady Luck.

He would enter the villa through a door that led into the kitchen from a delivery entrance at the back of the property.

Once inside, he would have to rely on his memory of the floor plan. Anyone he met would be dealt with fast and quiet. If an alarm sounded, he'd be trapped.

Concealing himself in the well of darkness beside the door, he peered through the glass panes to find the kitchen, lit only by a night-light above the stove, empty.

He thrust his hand inside his pocket, where chunks of raw meat seeped juice into the lining, and punched through a small glass pane at the top with no more than a muffled thump. He stood and slid his arm inside the hole, and with a utility knife he'd purchased earlier, he fitted the blade into the transom where he guessed a monitoring sensor had been hardwired through the lintel. He disconnected the sensor, unlocked the door.

No siren blared.

From the kitchen, Niky would use a service stairwell to access the upper story. He paused inside to listen for sounds of movement. Luck held, and he moved through the dark hallway to the stairwell without encountering anyone, his memory of the villa's floor plan serving him well.

The second-floor hallway was vacant, but Niky could hear the muffled sound of footsteps echoing from the staircase at the front of the house.

Two sets of footsteps.

Zubac's security guard? He'd find out soon enough.

Slipping silently inside a nearby doorway, he took in the small lamp that cast a glow beside the bed, a water bottle that had been placed on the night table along with medication.

Zubac's bedroom.

Niky was struck by how normal the scene looked, nothing more than the routine trappings of an older man, not a devil.

But he knew better.

Wedging himself into the shadows between a massive armoire and the wall, a place where he could cover the doorway and claim the element of surprise.

Freedom was almost his. He could feel it.

Footsteps sounded on the carpet outside the door. Fingers flexing on the hilt of the knife, he poised to strike.

The door opened.

Two dogs appeared in the flood of light from the hall, immediately went rigid, ears back against their skulls.

They began to growl.

Niky had meat inside his pockets to divert and stop the dogs, but dosed meat wouldn't divert the two men who appeared in the doorway, leveling guns to cover both sides of the room.

Zubac and a uniformed guard.

Niky stood concealed in the shadows of the armoire, but it didn't matter whether or not the men could see him.

The dogs knew exactly where he was.

With low growls, they lunged. Two hundred pounds of solid muscle suddenly collided into him. With the knife, he fought off the attack of snapping razor teeth, but above the throaty growls of agitated attack dogs, Niky heard the familiar voice say, "My compliments to the American government. You're proving as tough to kill as the woman."

THE RUSHING GRAY RIVER at the border town of Maglador formed the entity border between Strpski Grad and the Krajina, or the frontier as the locals referred to it. At first glance, Violet thought this town looked much like the others she'd seen.

The wreckage of war mingled with the newly rebuilt, damaged facades fitted with new glass windows that sparkled. The most stunning example of this contrast was the new bridge that had been built beside the shelled ruins of the old.

But there were differences, too. Not so much had been rebuilt here in Maglador as in Brijevek. This town wasn't the capital and Maglador obviously didn't lack fortification.

From their vantage point on a country lane that wound down from the mountain into town, she counted twenty-two SG Militia and SFOR vehicles.

"I hope this place always looks like this, and they're not waiting for us," she whispered to Simon, so as not to be heard by the boy driving the cart.

Simon didn't reply, just peered toward the mess below, looking grim.

Crossing the entity border into Croatia looked as if it might take an act of war, and Violet questioned whether their cover as two Serb farmers visiting the town would protect them. She'd rather not wind up in any of the military vehicles that infested the streets like roaches. They stood a much better chance with the Internationals who patrolled the streets in the white Land Cruisers.

If Niky was going to run into trouble, Violet thought this seemed a likely place. Wherever he was, she hoped his luck held as theirs had been holding today.

Before dawn they'd left the cave and headed into a hamlet, where they'd lucked on to a Red Cross relief truck with two exhausted relief workers. Neither had awakened when they'd helped themselves to clothing.

Her headscarf covered most of her face, and while there was no disguising Simon's size, his two-day stubble and wide-brimmed hat effectively covered the cut lines of his handsome face.

A ride in a cart had been another stroke of luck. A farm boy on his way to market day had, by his own admission, been thinking more about his girl than the icy road. He let the cart slip off the steep lane.

He'd been in a bit of a bind when they'd come across him with a wheel stuck in a rut. He couldn't free the cart alone, and if he unharnessed his mule to go for help, someone might come along and liberate his cart. He'd been dead positive that if he showed up home without the cart and grain for the pigs, his father would kill him.

It had taken Violet in front of the mule with the reins, chattering a steady stream of Serbian to get the stubborn animal to move, and both Simon and the boy pushing from behind to get the cart back on the road. The boy had been so grateful for their help that he'd offered them a ride into town.

His name was Dusko, and his farm wasn't far from the hamlet where they'd earlier encountered the relief workers.

When they pulled into the line of traffic to pass through the gates into town, Violet cued Simon that she would sit up front as damage control. He nodded, and she clambered into the bench seat, trying not to get tangled in the long coat she wore.

Dusko couldn't have been more than sixteen, but he was a handsome boy with dark hair and eyes and an easy smile. "Your husband doesn't say much."

"No. He is slow-witted with his tongue but very strong with the ox."

"Girls have to make choices," Dusko said sagely. "That's what my girl says."

Violet smiled. She didn't know how much Simon understood of their exchange because he'd wisely tucked his head on his arm and looked like a sleepy farmhand. "Your girl is wise. And pretty, too, I'll bet."

"She is beautiful." The words came out on an impassioned sigh, and Violet couldn't help but be reminded of Natalia and her husband who had sung love songs. "She has bubbly laughter and shiny hair and such soft curves."

"You are wise, too, Dusko, to place your girl's laughter before her soft curves."

He nodded. "My mother agrees. She is wise."

"I'm sure she wants to see her son happy."

"Then she should let me take a job in town during the nights. I want to marry my girl, but she won't marry me unless I can take her on a wedding trip to the sea."

They were forced to silence while approaching the town gate. International guards talked to the people trying to gain entry, a mélange of small cars, carts and pedestrians carrying baskets. They searched the cars, checked paperwork and grilled the pedestrians, while the SG Militia, intimidating in their uniforms, randomly asked to see permissions.

An international guard approached their cart, asking for paperwork.

"Bah, foreigners." Dusko pointed to the back of the

cart. "We need no permissions. We come to buy grain for the pigs."

"All of you?" he asked.

"They come to town with me."

"To market," she added with an equal amount of disdain.

"We are looking for foreigners," the international guard said. "Seen any strangers around your farms?"

"Only the pigs," Dusko said, and Violet heard no humor in his voice.

She only shook her head.

One of the SG Militia officers approached, eyeing the proceedings with interest, and Violet hoped she and Simon hadn't just dragged an unsuspecting Dusko into trouble.

"What about him?" He pointed to Simon.

"He is my husband. Wake up, sunshine," she called back to Simon, her heart racing as the swarthy-skinned man eyed Simon coldly. "He is hungry and too grumpy, so we let him sleep."

Simon sat up and rubbed his eyes. *"Sta ima? Kafa?"*

*"Ne, ne kafa."* She motioned to the officers and gave an exasperated huff, heart pounding as a mini power struggle waged between the two officers across the cart.

The Serbian officer was the one to wave them through. She suspected he didn't want to give the International a chance.

"Are you hungry, Dusko?" she asked when they were out of earshot.

He gave her a plaintive sigh with his nod, and she bit back a smile. No surprise here.

"Can we take you to breakfast to thank you for the ride."

Dusko happily agreed, taking them to one of the local *Aschinicas* that served a traditional menu. It wasn't long before they were sipping hot coffee and eating freshly cooked eggs and ham and sweet, sticky bread. Just getting some real food into her stomach made Violet feel better.

It wasn't hard getting Dusko to talk. Between bites, he filled them in on all the news in the town.

This was the first he'd heard about a search for foreigners.

Yes, there were more patrols than usual.

Simon eyed Dusko over his coffee cup, and she wondered how much he understood of the exchange, and what he'd find more interesting—that the gate was guarded so closely or that the patrol had made their search for the foreigners public.

After the meal, they left the busy café and walked Dusko back to his cart.

"Give me some money," she told Simon.

He arched a dark brow curiously but whipped out his trusty roll without comment.

She helped herself to several bills. "I don't think you brought enough."

"Not to travel with you," he shot back in respectable Serbian.

She swallowed back the urge to laugh, and turning to Dusko, asked, "Can you keep a secret?"

The young man nodded gravely.

Slipping the bills into his hand, she gave a squeeze. "Hide this away and don't tell anyone where you got it. Give your girl a nice wedding trip."

Dusko whooped excitedly and crushed her in a hug that almost lifted her off her feet. "God go with you."

"You, too, Dusko." She followed Simon into the crowd.

They passed through the market where stalls displayed wares from clothing to grains. And food. Not much by way of fresh vegetables, but lots of meat. Even a booth filled with bright-colored clothing and trinkets.

To her surprise, Simon tightened his grip on her hand and led her inside.

"You promised Gabrielle," he said in Serbian.

She met his gaze, felt the warmth she saw in his clear gaze filter through her like a promise. Despite their worries about Niky, their fears they would be recognized by every SG Militia and International guard who walked past, Simon had remembered something so important to her.

She was suddenly aware of the strength of his fingers locked tight around hers, and she lifted his hand to her mouth, pressed a kiss to his warm skin. And to her pleasure, the stern faded from his mouth in a prelude to a smile.

To the people in the market, they would look like two lovers shopping, people just enjoying time together. The easy touch of his hand on hers, the simplicity of shopping for a child's gift made her feel exactly like a woman enjoying a few stolen moments with a special man.

Suddenly, he pulled her to a stop and leaned close. "Shoes," he said in Serbian, and she followed his gaze to a child-size pair of beaded shoes.

He motioned to a rack beside a table with shelves of costume shoes, covered in sparkling sequins and bright foil and feathers. His fingers lingered on hers before they finally trailed away, and she searched for a pair in Gabrielle's size.

"Do you have this size in pink?" She handed the shoes to the woman sitting with a cash box.

The woman clambered off her stool and shuffled to a table, sweeping aside a cloth to look below. As Violet waited, she could almost feel Gabrielle's little foot in her hand, the angle of perfectly shaped toes, the arch of her instep, the sturdy curve of her heel.

With a bored look, the woman produced a pink pair.

Violet didn't have to ask Simon for his wallet. He handed it over without comment, and she bargained with the woman and settled on an agreeable price.

Stuffing the shoes into her bag, she could feel Simon's gaze caress her, an intimate look that made her respond with a warm pull, a ripple over the memories of sensations she'd felt in his arms during their time in the pool.

It was a moment that stepped them out of time with the danger and hustle of the market. A moment that connected them with a closeness that felt so distinctive, so *right*.

And then a group of young girls descended on the stall, chattering as they perused the tables and racks.

Reality intruded, and the moment was broken.

Simon wanted to check out the bus depot and train station. They found both heavily guarded, and inside the train station, a crowd of people clustered around a blaring television beside the arrival and departure boards. She didn't recognize the man on the screen, only that his uniform labeled him a high-ranking officer in the SG Militia. Text flashed below his image— General Ivan Zubac, Minister of Defense, Strpski Grad Republika.

Then she heard the voice… Violet stared up at the television, at that unknown face.

"General Zubac," the announcer was saying. "You've captured one of the suspects and have instructed the police to consider this man's companions armed and dangerous."

"For their safety, our citizens should not approach the suspects. They should contact the authorities immediately."

The voice was calm now, a voice that played well to the media. But she recognized the training behind the speech, the emphasis on the words.

*"Woman, I will take you apart in pieces until I find it."*

She reached for Simon's hand again, this time her grip biting, urgent. She tried to drag him away from the crowd to tell him, but he stood rooted to the spot. She followed his gaze back to the television screen to see a grainy photo of a man's face from a live video feed.

*Niky.*

SIMON TURNED to shield the wind from the palm-size field unit. Even with the earbud, he found it difficult to hear Major, whose face appeared on the small display.

Learning the identity of General Zubac confirmed Simon's decision to remain in deep cover while traveling through Strpski Grad, but he had to reevaluate that decision now. As much as he didn't want to risk a remote satellite uplink with Major—especially knowing their enemy's resources—he had no choice.

Without information he couldn't formulate the next step in their plan. One television broadcast and the memory of a voice had turned a recovery mission for an imaging device into a search and rescue to retrieve a captured operative.

"Casanova never made it to Maglador," Major said. "Delinquent marked him heading south to Brijevek while you and Wolfgang were holed up inside that cave."

Simon frowned into the display, recognized his own surprise mirrored in Major's expression. Brijevek? Had Niky been apprehended so quickly and taken back to the capital?

"How long after we separated?"

"Looks like as soon as he came down the mountain. He hit the valley then made his way south."

Simon's thoughts raced with possibilities. Like Violet, had Niky had some contact inside the detention camp that would have let him ID Zubac if he chanced upon a broadcast or a picture?

Or let Zubac ID him?

If Niky had learned their enemy's identity, he would also have understood the scope of the man's resources and influence. Not only did Zubac have the SG Militia and police forces in sixty-three municipalities at his disposal, but he had his own secret police made up of highly trained SG Militia officers. The net he'd woven around them proved he would use those resources.

So if Niky had recognized the man, why would he head back into his stronghold?

To end a threat against Violet?

Another bitter wind whipped snow from the ground to sting his bare cheeks and freeze his lungs. He stared out at the terrain where crinkled gray sky clashed against craggy white peaks with a bleakness that reflected his growing doubts.

At the core of this situation was Niky. Always Niky. Had he been so pressured to safeguard Violet because he'd failed once that he would try to neutralize a threat against her?

Or to neutralize a threat against himself?

Had Niky known who they were up against all along?

"The media released Casanova's location as the federal prison outside of Brijevek," he said. "Have Delinquent confirm."

Major nodded then moved out of range of the display. Simon could see the interior of the hotel room where they'd left him in Sarajevo, considered whether he would need to bring him into the hot zone with transportation to get them all out now that mission objective had changed.

He couldn't answer that question until he locked on Niky.

Another bitter wind blasted the mountaintop, such a strong gust that he saw Violet lie low against their stolen snowmobile to break the wind behind the screen. He couldn't move easily without snowshoes and didn't want to risk his uplink by moving, so he motioned to get her attention.

When she signaled him thumbs-up, he inhaled deeply, barely noticing the brutal cold that singed his lungs.

"Here we go, King Arthur," Major said. "Delinquent's got a lock on Casanova, but he's nowhere near Brijevek. We've got another municipality entirely. Ten miles due east."

"Send the coordinates."

Major nodded. "What do you think this is all about?"

"A diversion to protect his suspect, maybe."

"Or maybe it's a trap. If Zubac wanted to protect his suspect, he'd secure him inside a facility with live video feeds, barbed wire and armed guards."

"Perhaps he's overconfident that his net is tight. He doesn't know we can get a lock on Casanova. I came to this mountain so we lessened the risk of him picking up this signal without knowing our exact location."

"You lessened the risk, but it's still not within acceptable parameters. If he's looking, he'll find you."

But Simon's options were limited. The best plan he could come up with meant trusting Violet to be the operative he'd trained her to be so they could exfiltrate their teammate.

"Have Delinquent download a map of the grid where Casanova's being held," Simon said. "And a floor plan, too, if he can map it quickly. Have Counselor organize a team to secure the saint statue. I'll transfer the coordinates."

"Secure? Sure you don't want them to acquire the target?"

Simon glanced at Violet sprawled over the snowmobile, considered. "No. Protection only. Wolfgang and I will accomplish original objective before our return."

He could see Major's skepticism, but Simon remained resolute. He might not operate comfortably on emotional levels. He might have blinded himself to them in the past, but he understood that retrieving the imaging device was a link to Violet's past that she needed to handle.

He would give her that chance.

Transferring the coordinates through a system scrambler, he waited until receiving confirmation before sending another set. "I'm bringing you in, Cowboy. Secure an all-terrain vehicle and meet us at these coordinates in twelve hours."

"Done. Anything else?"

"Wish us luck."

The connection severed, and Simon's tension eased. With Zubac's ministry resources, establishing an uplink on this mountaintop was like waving a flashlight in the dark.

Simon hoped Zubac wasn't looking.

Tucking his field unit inside a pocket, Simon made his way to the snowmobile and explained the situation to Violet.

She frowned. "It's too easy. Smells like a trap."

"Then we outmaneuver him." Simon reached up to smooth the crease between her brows, amazed at how one simple touch could erase all his doubts. "We will not leave our operative behind."

# CHAPTER TWENTY-ONE

NIKY AWOKE TO DARKNESS. His body ached back to life so hard that he wished it hadn't. He'd been resisting for hours now, maybe even days. Staring into blackness, disoriented, he tried to pull together the pieces. A gagging dryness in his throat. A tender throbbing in his brain. Open wounds that burned like hell. Cuts from teeth.

*Dogs.*

Goddamn it.

He tried to move, found his arms and legs bound. The spasm through his shoulder blades was a gift of the handcuffs forcing his arms behind his back at this weird angle. His mouth was out of commission thanks to a rag and tape, so he dragged in a steadying breath, grew dizzy trying to suck in enough air through his nostrils.

He waited for the dizziness to pass before lifting his face and turning his head. The pain stabbing down his spinal cord made him glad for the gag that muffled his groan.

His eyes adjusted to the darkness.

A cell.

If his hands were free, he would have broken his own freaking neck. The thought came with a wild hysteria that made adrenaline surge and awareness gratefully recede.

He must have passed out again because when he opened his eyes, the room seemed brighter. A light had been turned on outside the cell, glowed through a small window in the door.

How long had he been out this time? How long since he'd missed his meeting with Simon and Violet?

Jesus. He'd blown it. Simon would give him time to deal with whatever problem had come up and make the meet. He might have given him most of the night. Then he'd track Niky down.

What would Zubac do?

The bastard would play games, just as he had when he'd sold Niky his freedom at the unwitting cost of Violet's life. What games, though? Surprise. No great stretch here, either—that's why Niky was still alive to savor his failure.

He was bait.

Simon wouldn't only walk into this trap; he'd drag Violet with him. He'd never leave an operative behind. Especially when he would want answers about why Niky wound up back in Brijevek.

Unfortunately, Simon wasn't playing on the home team. He didn't have a clue who was yanking his chain.

Zubac knew who he was looking for.

The burden of leaving his teammates vulnerable tormented Niky as he drifted in and out of consciousness, unsure how much time passed whenever he opened his eyes.

Time enough to feel the weight of his failure. Why couldn't he remember any of the good he'd done? He'd been on team one for over a decade and all he could remember was losing his team and dragging Simon and Violet into this sick mess.

Time enough so Niky grew used to the light-head-edness that accompanied what felt like a significant blood loss.

Time enough so that when the cell door finally swung open the light pouring through temporarily blinded him.

He could only lean his head against his knees and try to draw some decent air, so lack of oxygen and blood didn't take him out again before he figured out what the hell was going on.

A body tumbled into the room and hit the floor with force. A figure he could barely make out appeared in the doorway. He blinked hard.

*Simon.*

Shit.

Kicking out, Niky's bound feet caught the body on the floor, knocking him sideways. Niky tumbled off the pallet, right into the path of an oncoming Simon. Every joint shrieked in pain as he hit the floor, but he managed to get away as Simon came down on top of what turned out to be a dazed cop.

It only took a few powerful and well-aimed blows to subdue the cop. Then Simon liberated the man's service weapon and keys, and unlocked Niky's shackles.

"Let's go."

Niky couldn't even stand. And where the hell was Violet? Catching the edge of the tape, he ripped it from his face, practically tearing off skin in the process. He spit out the rag, felt cuts on his face start to bleed again. More blood loss. Great. "Jesus, you walked right into a trap."

"Later," Simon said, grabbing him by the collar and yanking him to his feet.

"You should have left me—"

"Later."

Niky couldn't walk, and Simon slung an arm under his and helped get him to the door. They'd no sooner stepped out into the hall when Niky saw Violet.

And another cop coming up behind her.

"Wolfgang," he shouted, but she'd already known the cop was there. Spinning, she took the guy's legs out from under him.

They went down in a heap. Simon left Niky grasping the wall for purchase and cursing his stupid weakness. Simon hadn't covered the distance to help Violet before she leveled her gun at the cop's head.

But it was Simon who fired, blowing open the cop's temple so Violet wouldn't have to.

"Let's go," Simon said.

"This is a setup," Niky said, willing his legs into motion, clutching the edge of a desk. "He was counting on you to come after me."

"I guessed that much." Simon slid back the clip to check the ammunition. "What I don't know is if I can trust you to help us get out of here."

God...Niky squeezed his eyes shut for a staggering instant, a knee-jerk reaction to hide from the question in Simon's face that struck him like a physical blow.

But there was no hiding. So many years of trust passed between them in that instant, of friendship, of respect, of unconditional loyalty.

"Yes." Niky never meant anything more in his life.

Simon nodded, and they advanced together back-to-back and made their way down the hallway, Violet and Simon pivoting their positions and Niky wishing like hell he had a gun. From the expression on Violet's face, he must look as bad as he felt.

The place turned out to be a provincial police holding facility, a local jail that would run a small staff on the busiest of days. And they hadn't met a soul yet. Not good.

Niky said, "He plans to execute us and make it look like we were trying to escape."

Whoever ran this local facility was obviously on Zubac's payroll, and none of them would be alive to contradict him.

Simon nodded. "He'll make his move outside."

Sure enough, as they approached an exit doorway, an armed guard dropped down from the ceiling, forcing them to break formation. The exit door swung wide, and all hell broke loose.

THE GUARD HADN'T fallen on Violet by chance. He'd timed his move to separate her from Simon and Niky, and she didn't resist when he told her to drop the weapon. The beefy arm he squeezed around her throat and the gun he pressed to her temple took away her choices.

Even without a memory, Violet knew she was leverage.

So she dropped the gun in the hallway, heard it clatter against the linoleum. She met Simon's gaze and saw nothing in his eyes. Not awareness of the men who trained automatic weapons on all of them. Not surprise that she'd been taken. Nothing but a cool professionalism that reassured her she'd always trusted her life to this man for a reason. Her heart, too.

Simon would come for her. As long as he was alive,

he'd come after her. And it was that knowing that fed her courage as her assailant dragged her back through a door.

Not an exit.

Struggling to breathe, she tried to keep from stumbling while being half dragged, half carried down a flight of stairs. She clung to that image of Simon, fighting off panic, determined to face this situation with the same professionalism.

The terrain changed. Bare bulbs lit the stairwell at spaced intervals. Generic plaster walls yielded to raw concrete. The stairs descended down, down, down, to open into a tunnel, or series of tunnels from what she could see.

At some time she'd been briefed on how underground military installations made of thick layers of reinforced concrete were one of Yugoslavia's specialties. Her memory served up how the Yugoslavs had built many for clients around the globe, including Saddam Hussein and Hitler. She remembered hearing how the Berlin Bunker would have been lost inside the one that had been scooped out of the Belgrade hillside for Yugoslavia's former president.

She wondered what this bunker was for. Small municipality not far from the capital. Convenient location. Probably hiding war criminals from the U.N. Tribunal on their way underground. Or maybe something as mundane as interrogating suspects.

Violet forced her eyes on the details, she forced herself to be the operative Simon expected her to be. She counted three doorways before they stopped in front of a fourth.

A quick knock. The door opened. That beefy arm

loosened its grip and she was thrust into the room, stumbled to her knees, gasped for air. When the dizziness faded, she stared up into the face of the man from the television.

"Thank you, Milan," Zubac said.

The voice that had haunted her nightmares.

Although he'd covered his savagery with a veneer of civilization, she heard his threats in her memory. The guard came up behind her. Twisting a hand into her hair, he forced her head back and rested the barrel of the gun against her skull.

"Ratko's dead, General. Shot," he said.

Zubac fixed those deep eyes on her and shook his head. "Always full of surprises you are."

She could have said the same. The steel against her skull cautioned restraint, though. It wasn't his amused disdain that she remembered as much as the feeling it evoked in her. A challenge to show him he couldn't intimidate her, even though she was on her knees at his feet.

"We can do this easy or hard," Zubac said in that haunting voice. "I want answers. Why have you returned? What are you after? You die fast or you die slow and messy. Choose."

She glared.

"I expected you to resist," he said mildly.

"Then I wonder why you bothered risking yourself by dragging me here."

"No risk. I must end your search and turn your corpses over to my government. We frown upon those who profit from harboring war criminals."

"A lie and you know it."

He inclined his head in dignified concession. "I

wanted to see you for myself. See that you lived when
you had everyone convinced you were dead."

"Your war is over. Your country is rebuilding—"

A smile played around the edges of his mouth. "Tell
me what you are looking for. Why did you steal the microfilm from the library? What is on it?"

Violet had sent one imaging device back with the defecting deputy commander. Simon had told her all the
images on it had been submitted to the war crimes tribunal. Zubac would have known that, which meant he
had no idea what they were looking for. He didn't know
she'd had a second imaging device.

"Answer the general's question." The guard yanked
her head back so sharply she cried out.

She swallowed hard, the angle of her head making
each breath lodge a hard knot in her throat.

"If you don't answer my questions, woman, then
you are wasting my time." Zubac nodded to his guard.
"Give her more motivation to talk, Milan."

"Yes, General." He dragged her head back so far that
tears sprang to her eyes then he trailed the cool gun barrel beneath her jaw, tracing the scars. "You like pain, I see."

WHEN MAJOR SHOWED UP, rapid-fire shots rang out and
the four local policemen who'd been guarding the doorways while Simon and Niky fought with several of
their comrades, collapsed to the floor. Simon pushed
himself to his knees, watched Major step over one as
the shots faded into ringing silence.

"Throw that lock," Major said. "The general's private
stock of militia is on the way. I bought you two minutes
max." He shot a gaze at Niky. "What in holy hell got
you?"

"Dogs."

"Where's Violet?"

Simon was already pulling out the transceiver to make contact with Command. He stabbed in the earbud and said, "Give me a lock on my low-frequency signifier."

"What the hell's going on, King Arthur?" TJ shot back. "I've only got one signal on you. I can't get a lock on your second signal. I know you're not in two places."

"It's Wolfgang. Run a trace and tell me where you lost the signal."

"East before it descended under the building. Then it disappeared. Looks like subterranean tunnels."

"Wolfgang's isolated. Get me to that tunnel."

Coordinates flashed on the display followed by a map of the grid and a clearly marked route.

Niky helped himself to one of the dead men's sidearms, and Major said, "The militia will be all over that signal."

"Then get ready to defend yourselves," he said.

"You've got a guard on the other side," TJ warned. "He's armed."

Nodding to Major, Simon motioned Niky behind him then kicked open the door. Simon lunged to the side as Major dived through at knee height.

Two shots rang out in sharp succession, but impacted the wall at the far end of the hall. The policeman went down with Major on top of him. Simon and Niky moved through the doorway.

"Take the stairwell. You're clear for the first flight, but I can't help you after that."

But time ran out. A woman's scream echoed.
*Violet.*

NIKY HEARD THE SCREAM reverberate off the concrete walls, echoed in his memory from a mountaintop where they'd once lain in a pit together. Simon jumped into the fight with Major. That left Niky to save her.

He didn't know where he was going, for Christ's sake, down into a tunnel because there wasn't anyplace else to go.

Then he heard her again, louder this time.

Behind door number four.

Leveling the gun, he shoved the door wide.

For the space of a heartbeat he stood there, his brain registering the sight. Violet slammed up against the wall by a man Niky recognized as one of Zubac's security guards. But it was the sight of Zubac that shocked Niky into motion.

He fired.

The bullet struck Zubac's side, driving him to his knees. Violet struck out at the guard who held her and broke away, giving Niky a clear shot.

He fired again. Blood blossomed on the guard's forehead and that one crumbled to the ground, dead.

But Zubac, still on his knees, already had a gun trained on Violet. Niky squeezed off another shot…out of bullets. He lunged toward Violet.

Niky met Zubac's gaze as he crashed into her, saw those cold eyes register satisfaction as he squeezed the trigger.

The shot impacted Niky's chest like a fist. He knew he should feel pain, but he felt nothing but familiar satisfaction. A feeling that he'd reached the finish line. A pride that he'd done the job, had upheld Excelsior's ideal, had protected his country, had lived up to the expectations of the man who'd always believed in him.

Suddenly, the door crashed open, and that man was there. *Simon.* Another shot fired.

Almost before Niky's sluggish thoughts registered what was happening, Zubac's face registered surprise. He fell forward.

Dead. *Finally* dead.

"Niky," Violet called his name as if from a distance. Wrapping her arms around him, she eased him to the floor. He felt more pressure on his chest, heard her fear. "Niky."

He managed to bring her face into focus. Eyes wide, mouth parted around his name, she looked so stunned and so beautiful that his heart lodged in his throat. Sweat poured off him. His muscles burned.

"I didn't know you were alive." He forced each word out, found his confession so easy he couldn't remember why he'd been afraid for so long. "I didn't know."

"I know." Tears squeezed through her lashes, slid down her cheeks, making her look so beautiful, so alive. "I know."

SIMON KNELT BESIDE NIKY, used his shirt to apply pressure, to staunch the blood flow. Violet watched him, tears glittering in the dim light, and she held on to Niky while Simon administered emergency first aid.

The point of impact was right above Niky's heart. Simon had no way of knowing what trajectory the bullet had taken, what tissues it encountered, whether bone fragments had splintered.

"Come on, Niky," he said. "NATO's getting us out. Major's meeting them upstairs. Medics are on the way."

Niky's mouth worked, the effort painful to watch, stabbing Simon with the sharp edge of his helplessness. "I couldn't give him Excelsior. You understand."

He met Niky's gaze, recognized the regret flashing in his dark eyes. "I understand."

It was the only comfort Simon had to offer. So inadequate by comparison to the sacrifices Niky had made, to this suffering, a reassurance he should have spoken three years ago.

"I'm sorry," Niky whispered.

Then his eyes closed. He exhaled a last breath that sounded calm in the stark quiet.

Simon began CPR. Since joining Excelsior, he hadn't lost sight of the ideal. He destroyed terrorist factions, diverted threats, kept people safe. He made sacrifices. He made hard choices. He believed in his cause. His people believed.

But as he tried to keep Niky alive, a man who'd been a trusted friend, a man who'd obviously been drowning beneath the weight of terrible secrets, Simon no longer knew if the ideal had been worth the price.

## CHAPTER TWENTY-TWO

THEIR TRIP INTO CROATIA had been delayed for several days while Violet and Major holed up inside a hotel and Simon worked with the Strpski Grad prime minister and the high representative to begin a highly classified intergovernmental investigation to unravel how deeply Niky and Zubac had been involved.

Major kept Violet briefed on how both governments and NATO had begun efforts to track the men's movements, and the prime minister and high representative debated how best to present Zubac's death.

Ironically, the version they gave the public was close to what Zubac had intended to present the world—his search for the suspects had led to the apprehension of a war criminal.

Simple, but in many ways the truth.

Violet understood the need to present Zubac's death in this way. Zubac was a highly visible defense minister, and Strpski Grad was a semiautonomous entity in a new nation. The people needed a government they could believe in, not more remnants of the war that had ravaged their way of life—especially with the situation in Kosovo still so volatile.

She only wished death in the line of duty didn't sound so noble. Especially when all indications suggested that Zubac had been responsible for smuggling the war criminal from Bosnia in the first place.

Now the prime minister was forced to investigate whether Zubac had helped smuggle out other fugitives and uncover why Zubac had kept people in his debt all around the globe. Simon believed the scope of the man's spy ring meant he'd been building a private army. Time would prove or discount his theory. In the meantime, like the prime minister, he was left to search for answers about Niky.

What he'd learned already made Violet's heart ache. Niky had bought his freedom from number twelve detention camp from Zubac, but that debt had meant dividing his loyalties. Yet he hadn't betrayed Excelsior. That had ultimately been what was important to him, and she tried to find comfort there. He'd given his life for hers, ended Zubac's threat and freed himself.

He had been noble, and Violet embraced the anguish she felt, didn't hide from her bittersweet memories, wanted to take back the ones she'd lost and hold them tight.

When they finally put Strpski Grad behind them and crossed into Croatia, she was anxious to accomplish mission objective, impatient to go home.

She watched Simon emerge from the museum entrance. Even from this distance, she could make out his tight expression, the tense set of his shoulders, the heaviness of a mood that seemed to glare beneath a bright winter sun.

She must have seen him like this a hundred times before, that expression set in steel as he faced whatever crisis the day served up, the grim determination as he made split-second choices that carried such far-reaching consequences.

Violet wondered if she'd ever really understood the weight he carried, the sacrifices he'd made, how much he cared and how very much caring cost him. She didn't think she had. Otherwise, seeing him now, so strong beneath the weight of the past days' events, wouldn't feel so overwhelming, so humbling.

He strode down the museum stairs toward them, ready to deal with another step along this journey to bring her home, and in this moment, Simon felt more real to her than he ever had, now or in her memories of life before Safe Harbor.

Major swung out of the driver's side and circled the rental car to get her door. She stepped out in time to greet Simon.

"The assistant curator will take us in now," he said.

Natalia had already contacted her late niece's friend, so Silvija had known to expect their visit. Still Simon had insisted on talking with the woman first. He said he wanted to assess the situation, a precaution. But Violet guessed he'd really wanted to explain the circumstances, to warn Silvija that Violet might not remember her.

She appreciated the effort. She didn't have energy left for surprises right now, only enough to deal with the possible disappointment of not finding the imaging device. The past few days had yielded enough shocks and sorrows.

Simon held the door, and she inclined her head as they passed through to be greeted by a trim woman wearing a business suit, who looked equal parts excited and uncertain as she waited for them to approach.

"You're Natalia's friend?" Violet asked.

"Yes."

Violet didn't remember her, but that didn't seem to matter. With an enthusiasm that reminded her of Natalia living life in the frozen tundra of her house, Silvija extended her arms, grabbed Violet and placed a kiss on each cheek. Then she finally lost her battle with restraint and hugged her tight.

"We called you the angel," she whispered. "Thank you for all you have done."

Violet might not remember this woman, but the warmth she felt in her embrace seemed familiar. "I'm glad you're okay."

It sounded so inadequate in the face of the woman's gratitude, but it was enough to make Silvija break away with a laugh. "Come, come. I'll take you to our storage as you asked, but I want you to see them now. Even if you don't remember, I want you to know who they are."

She whipped out a small plastic album from her jacket pocket, and while she led them through the sizable museum, she showed Violet photo after photo of her family.

Antun was her oldest at eleven and Margareta the baby at five. Her middle boy, Luka, loved soccer. Natalia's niece had two beautiful girls with shiny dark hair and bright eyes.

"Aleksandrina is so smart," Silvija said. "She is just like her mama that way and will grow up to be someone very important. Little Gavrijela loves to dance and ice-skate and sing all day."

*Gavrijela.* Gabriella.

Violet smiled at a school photo of the child, who

looked as if she'd had to be reined into her seat for the sitting. Her shiny hair escaped its careful clips. Her eyes twinkled with a lighthearted joy the photo had managed to capture.

"They're beautiful," she said, thinking of the sparkly pink shoes she had tucked away in her luggage. "I know a little girl named Gabrielle, and she loves to ice-skate, too."

"I hope she fills your life with as much love and laughter as all my sweet turnips do."

Violet nodded. "She has."

Then they were descending a staircase into the museum's storage facility.

"I ordered Saint Josip unpacked from his crate," Silvija said. "I hope that was right. He is so big I was afraid it would take many men and a long time to do the job."

"Yes, thank you," Simon said.

They turned a corner and there he was.

Like a golden sun, her saint loomed up from the boxes and crates that stuffed this gloomy facility. He held a cross, and his mouth was parted.

"He is huge," Violet said. "However did Natalia and her friends manage to get him to you?"

Silvija laughed. "Those crazy old ladies. They bullied some street boys into raiding the bombed warehouse and loading Saint Josip onto a truck. Those poor boys. They were too afraid of Ava's Avengers to say no, and too afraid of the paramilitaries to admit what they'd done.

"Natalia and Ava drove him right through the sentries while cannonades were still raining over the city. They tricked everyone into thinking that Saint Josip was a land mine they'd found on their farm. No one wanted to touch him. The sentries told them, 'Go, go, old ladies.

You drive faster and get out of here.' Have you ever seen a land mine *this* big?"

Even Simon smiled.

"Well, let's see if this big boy has anything for us," Major said. "Mind if I take a look?"

Silvija shook her head and made a move toward a ladder that had obviously been used to break down the sides of the crate.

Simon motioned her back and dragged the ladder to the front of the saint. He held it steady while Major climbed to the top then paused and withdrew a utility knife from his pocket. Inserting the blade inside the saint's mouth, Major fished around a bit.

Violet's breath caught and held when he appeared to find something. Exerting a little force, he popped a small pink glob into his hand.

He held it up for examination. "Delinquent will have fun with this."

She exhaled heavily, aware that Silvija watched them all curiously. The woman didn't ask questions, though, and the whole process seemed so anticlimactic in the face of all they'd lost to get here that Violet's heart ached with slow, hollow beats.

Four of them had flown to Sarajevo, but only three would return together. Niky's body had already made the trip. But they'd accomplished mission objective, and Violet hoped he'd have been pleased.

She didn't know what they would find on that imaging device, but Simon had finally brought all his people home. She'd collected another piece of herself. As she stared up at the saint that had haunted so many of her nightmares, she inclined her head in silent thanks at his keeping her secret safe.

She was ready to return home and face her losses and finish the journey back to herself.

She wanted her life back.

Simon thanked Silvija, who insisted on escorting them upstairs, where they said their goodbyes.

She slipped her business card into Violet's hand. "I would like for you to write me, so I may tell you about the children. I want them always to remember your kindness, so they'll grow to be kind, too."

This time Violet gave her a hug. "I will."

"I wish you good health and much happiness, angel." Silvija smiled as she waved them off.

Major pushed open the door and held it. The sunlight of this unusually bright winter day flooded the lobby. Violet slipped her hand inside Simon's, felt his fingers close around hers, solid and real, and she walked through that door at his side. She was going home.

*Five months later*
*Excelsior Command, 84°F*

SIMON STARED DOWN at his daily status report from the Center. He had four operatives on-site right now, two for training, one for a difficult debriefing after a hostage situation in Iraq and Violet. She'd been in residence for five months. A month for each of the months she'd spent in number twelve detention camp. The irony hadn't escaped him.

He'd been briefed on her condition with daily evaluations detailing her progress in clinical terminology that told him so much and so little. Five months of waiting and wondering and wanting to help, yet having no choice but to respect that she'd chosen to face this alone. He found himself wanting physical contact and yearning to hear the sound of her voice.

She never picked up the phone.

More than once Quinn assured him that this behavior was natural, considering the extent of her trauma. Much of her memory had returned, and she needed to direct her energy toward dealing with the past. Natural, maybe, but difficult all the same. Simon hadn't wanted her to make that journey alone.

How much he wanted to be with her came as a source of constant surprise. With that thought in mind, he closed the file from the Center, and decided to get out of his office.

"I'll be monitoring in Systems Ops," he told Frances, who tipped her head away from the telephone receiver, covered the mouthpiece and said, "Get out of here and don't come back until your conference call with the head of SIS."

"Three o'clock?"

She nodded.

Systems Ops pulsed and hummed with energy. Operatives monitored several missions on the display screens around the room. Simon shook off his restlessness in the maze of activity.

"What's happening in Iraq?" he asked.

TJ flipped up his headset, inclined his head toward the computer monitor. "Team three just moved to the second mark."

Simon glanced at the level two operative who'd assumed the role of control for this mission. When the man confirmed with a nod then fixed his gaze back onto the monitor, Simon moved to the next station, where a surveillance mission had just been upgraded in priority.

He monitored for a while then sat in on the debriefing of a team leader from the Ukrainian mission.

Business as usual.

Niky's death had been felt clear through Command much in the same way Violet's had been. A wound Simon didn't think would begin to heal until Violet returned and the investigation into Niky's involvement with Zubac finally ended.

Which wouldn't happen anytime soon.

A basic sketch of events had come together. A satellite call made on a transport from Palestine. Information dealing. Assassination attempts in Strpski Grad. Niky appeared to be Zubac's man in the West, someone with the skill and resources to carry out Zubac's dirty work in an area of the world where he'd had limited connections.

Niky had been the one to reveal the defected deputy commander's whereabouts after the trial, enabling Zubac to send in an assassin.

Simon had also tracked Zubac's movements. An assassin in Sault Ste. Marie. The bootlegger's disappearance from St. Louis. The emergence of a war criminal in Central America. The bootlegger execution. Zubac had helped Dragan Mlakovic flee Eastern Europe and hidden him somewhere only to bring him back again when he'd needed another pawn.

Simon managed to keep Niky's involvement confined among the inner political circles and out of the media. A tough maneuver given the data they'd recovered from Violet's imaging device.

While she'd been inside Hotel Brijevek, she'd captured several images of General Zubac meeting with a man identified as a heavy-hitting Russian arms dealer.

If Zubac had ties to this man, there was little doubt he'd been involved in an arms purchase.

Of what? Heat-seeking ground-to-air missiles? Nuclear technology? Biological warfare agents? The images had been taken over two years ago. How much had Zubac purchased, and where had he been stockpiling arms or developing technology?

Excelsior had been monitoring the sale of everything coming out of the former Soviet Union for several years now, but Simon estimated that for every one crackdown, two deals involving weapons or technology happened. It was simply impossible for one agency, or one country for that matter, to police the globe.

Simon had proved Niky's involvement was limited, but this had stressed relations with the Strpski Grad prime minister, who'd begun to suspect he wasn't dealing with a generic branch of the National Security Agency. That situation had yet to resolve, but Simon was committed to seeing it through.

He owed it to Niky to uncover how far Zubac's power extended and put an end to it.

An insistent beeping dragged Simon from his thoughts.

"Now what is going on here?" TJ slid his chair toward hub one, where he redirected a Command surveillance monitor.

"What's up?" Simon joined him.

"Unexpected company." TJ motioned to a signal floating across the screen through the interior corridors of Command.

Only a handful of people were monitored by this particular protocol, and Simon's pulse jumped into gear. "Who?"

"Wolfgang."

Simon watched, his whole body on standstill as that tiny red signal floated across the screen toward Systems Ops.

She appeared in the doorway with little fanfare, as if three-and-a-half years hadn't passed since she'd left. Her pale yellow tunic ensemble emphasized her fair hair and the healthy color in her skin. Her eyes sparkled.

If Simon hadn't known better, he might have thought she was returning from a mission, impatient to be debriefed, bristling to get on with whatever life held in store for her next.

She smiled easily and headed toward him.

Pausing beside TJ, who stared at her openmouthed, she leaned over and kissed his cheek. "Blink your eyes around here and perfectly good boys grow into really handsome men."

Her hair swung across her shoulders, and Simon noticed that she'd cut it, though it still angled under her jaw to cover the scars. She wore the amethyst pin he'd bought for her second birthday away, which meant she'd visited her town house.

Then she gazed up at him with those incredible eyes. "Simon."

"Welcome back, Violet."

"Nice to be back."

All he could think about was holding her, such an unexpectedly primitive urge that he almost laughed. Almost.

He had to act quickly to distract her from the rounds of welcomes that would be forthcoming. Taking her hand, he ignored the curious gazes as he led her out the door and hurried her down the hall. He gave her enough time to hug a startled Frances before ushering her inside his office and closing the door.

"How are you?" he asked, the question sounding unbelievably absurd when she was finally standing in front of him.

That urge to wrap his arms around her hit hard again, but he stood there, paralyzed by an unfamiliar indecision as he waited for her to take the lead.

She leaned against his desk, a smile playing around her lips. "Clean bill of health, *finally.* Enough of my memory is back so I can deal with whatever else crops up. *If* it does. I may never remember everything."

Simon considered that a blessing.

She gave a casual shrug. "But it's time to move on. I'm ready to have my life back."

"What are your plans?"

"Oh, I've got some great plans. And everything seems to be falling right into place. You might be interested to know that I've gone into a new line of work."

He recognized the sound of her excitement, an eagerness and impatience to get on with life that made him grateful she'd found that part of herself again.

"Really? Tell me about it."

Rummaging through a small purple purse, she withdrew an enameled case and extracted a business card.

*Violet Lierly. Linguistics Consultant.*

"I've gone into the consulting business."

"I see. And who are you consulting?"

"Well." She inhaled breathlessly, smiled. "Global Coalition for one. I've got a freelance position out of international headquarters, and I'm hoping to pick up another client today."

There'd never been a question that she'd go back into

the field, but knowing she wanted to continue her affiliation with Excelsior made some place deep inside him sigh in relief. "So if I act fast, you'll let me keep you on the payroll?"

"*If* you act fast. I know how particular you acting directors are about letting your people go. I figured I'd give you a fair shot at my time."

"Two clients? Doesn't sound like much of a business. Will that be enough to keep you busy?"

"We're talking two very demanding clients. Besides, I have another commitment I haven't mentioned yet. Suffice to say I won't be able to work all the time anymore."

"What commitment?"

"Her name's Gabrielle, and she's a beautiful little girl who's packing as we speak to come live with me here in D.C."

In his memory, he could hear the sound of Violet's laughter as she twirled on the ice with the child she'd grown so fond of, and that sound was what he needed to bridge the final distance, to dare to believe she would really be okay. "Sounds like you have everything worked out."

Shaking her head, she met his gaze with an expression that mirrored everything he felt inside. "Almost. Gabrielle and I want a man to share our lives with."

"I see. You have someone in mind?"

"We do. He just needs a little convincing."

Simon covered the distance between them then, finally giving in to the need to touch her, to feel her warm against him. Spearing his hand around her neck, he tipped her face up, and those incredible eyes sparkled with an awareness that breathed life into so many long-dead places inside him.

"No, Violet, he doesn't."

*Everything you love about romance...*
***and more!***

*Please turn the page for Signature Select™*
*Bonus Features.*

BONUS
FEATURES
INSIDE

4    Deleted Scene from *In the Cold*

16   Behind the Scenes: Excelsior

23   Sneak Peek by Jeanie London

## Deleted Scene
## from IN THE COLD

*When Violet learns that Simon is a reporter in town to interview her, she asks to read his article. In my first draft of the story, I played out this thread. I really liked that Simon would have to face his feelings for Violet by writing about them. I wanted Violet to understand the effect she was having on him, to increase her conflict.*

*In this thread, Violet learns that Simon rented the apartment below hers much sooner than in my revised version, so I had some time to develop their relationship and move some action into Simon's place. I cut this scene after deciding to tighten my story timeline.—JL*

"COME TO MY PLACE," Simon told Violet as he steered her off the stairs at the second floor. "I finished my outline and plan to write the first draft of my article tonight. You can take a look before I send it off for editorial comment tomorrow."

"I need to get some work done."

"Use my computer. I'll work on my laptop."

"You're sure you don't mind?"

"I'm sure." Swinging the door to his apartment wide, he flipped on the light and stepped aside to let her enter.

She brushed past, her slender body tightly contained, trying not to touch him. But the top of her head almost brushed his chin, and he could smell the crisp winter air in her hair.

Then she moved past. The moment was over.

Violet headed straight for his computer, booted the system then went into the kitchen to put his espresso machine to use.

"Would you like a cup?" she asked.

"Please."

Tonight he'd welcome the caffeine. He needed to concentrate and work, which would be impossible if he sat close to Violet, so he set up his laptop at the dining room table.

A great deal of Simon's work involved writing. Keeping up his cover as the Special Liaison required public political involvement that meant documenting reports, communiqués and the like, all of which did nothing to prepare him for the endeavor at hand.

Sure, he could draft a coherent report, but could he write an article that embodied all he'd learned about the woman who called herself Claire?

Major had acquired the full-length fiction manuscript from a credentialed but struggling writer that Simon had been passing off as his own. He could have farmed out this job. He'd thought about it, but he didn't trust Violet's feelings with another.

She would see this article as his opinion of her, and that burden sat heavily on his shoulders. He had to make her understand how he felt when he wasn't even sure himself.

So following her example, Simon infused himself with caffeine. He accepted a second cup after finally deciding on his slant. As he sipped the rich brew and stared at the laptop screen, he searched for the words to convey his admiration for Violet's strength and her courage.

But as he chronicled her life at Safe Harbor and reflected on how she affected those around her, Simon realized it was more than her strength and courage that had touched him so deeply—it was how much she cared.

Violet had agreed to this interview to benefit Safe Harbor, even though exposing her situation bothered her. She worked hard not to worry Ms. Joyce and the other people she cared about. She gave of herself so freely to the children.

And she cared about him, too. Across three years and a memory loss, she'd let love light her way through the darkness to trust him when she trusted so few.

So how did he, a man who'd ignored his own feelings for so long, deal with the gift she'd given him?

Simon wrote, trying to convey a message he hoped she would understand.

He wrote, discovering answers to questions he'd never dared ask.

He had no idea how much time passed, but he was so absorbed that Violet startled him when she said, "You don't look too happy, Simon. Am I giving your writing muscles a workout?"

Not in the way she meant. "I'm done with my draft. Would you like to read it?"

Swiveling the chair away from the computer, she fixed him with a stoic stare, and he knew then that she was as hesitant to read what he'd written as he was to let her.

Neither of them had a choice.

Leaving his laptop open to his article, Simon got up from the table and headed into the kitchen. He washed his coffee mug then dismantled the espresso machine, cleaned the filter basket and wiped the countertop. The chores could have waited, but he found the activity occupied his hands and distracted him.

Violet read *him* in this article. Before number twelve detention camp, she would have understood the singularity of this event but the woman he'd come to know as Claire wouldn't. She believed this was nothing more than a job to him. Writing this article was so much more.

*She* was so much more.

When Simon heard the chair slide across the floor, he set the mug in the cabinet with absurd precision, flipped the cup upside down and angled the handle exactly like the others.

He could hear her approach, her soft breaths, and found the sounds strangely reassuring in the quiet.

"Simon." She touched his shoulder lightly.

He turned to her. Tears clung to her dark lashes. Her mouth tucked in at the corners in a soft half smile. He studied her expression, every inhalation, every tremor a clue. Her jewel-colored eyes mirrored the vulnerability he felt inside.

Raising up on tiptoe, she pressed a kiss to the side of his mouth, lingered with her lips barely grazing his skin. A tear rolled down her cheek.

The need to comfort her lashed at him from nowhere. Simon wanted to thread his fingers into her hair, slant his mouth across hers and absorb her pain, absorb *her*. Yet the power of this unleashed emotion wasn't what Violet needed. He didn't trust himself with her. He wondered if he ever had.

Then she slipped away, and he let her go, feeling the lingering warmth of her kiss, now only a memory. She headed toward the door and grabbed her coat.

"You're leaving?" he asked, the urgency in his voice surprising him.

She thrust her arm into a sleeve, didn't meet his gaze. "Just going outside to smoke."

It took him a moment to realize she intended to sit outside on the fire escape. "You can smoke in here."

"Thanks, but I need the air."

Unlocking the window, she thrust it upward. A blast of cold wind streamed through the room as she swung her legs over the sill and disappeared. She shut him in and soon the glow of flame illuminated the glass, a beacon that guided him through the unfamiliar onslaught of his emotions.

Simon grabbed his coat and followed her. The comical act of wedging his considerable bulk through the window broke the awkward silence. Laughing, Violet clamped a cigar between her teeth, clutched his hand to assist him as he maneuvered in the narrow space to draw the window down.

"If I'd have known you smoked cigars, I'd have mentioned it in my article."

"Your article is fine the way it is."

"I'm relieved you think so."

"Relieved?"

"Relieved." The word ground over his tongue, one of those unfamiliar feeling words that had rusted inside him long ago.

Drawing his collar around his neck, he leaned against the railing. They faced each other across the distance, silent.

He broke first. "I don't suppose you have another of those with you?"

"As a matter of fact, the band brought me back a whole box from Ybor City." She procured one from her pocket along with a matchbox. "I don't have a clip."

"No problem." He bit off the end.

The red tip of her cigar flared in the darkness as she drew deeply, her cheeks hollowing before she exhaled. He lit his own, savoring the taste of the smooth Cuban tobacco. He blew out a cloud that was part smoke, part cold vapor, and he enjoyed sharing a ritual that bound them in a fragrant haze.

"You were very kind in your article," she said.

"I wrote how I feel. Journalism, the truth and all that."

A stray dog's bark shattered the late-night quiet, drew his gaze to the street below. The darkness that crowded around the sickly wash of light from a street lamp seemed to symbolize the shadows crowding Violet's world. A cramped efficiency on a street in a poor neighborhood. A memory that protected her from all she was and all she'd endured.

He didn't know what to say.

Violet did, though. "I'm glad we met."

"I am, too. I've enjoyed spending time with you."

A car drove along the street below, churning through the slush. He followed her gaze past the rusted iron railings to see red taillights gleam. Bringing the cigar to her lips again, she drew deeply, and he waited, amazed how they could sit among so many windows, so many potentially prying eyes, and feel as if they were all alone in the world.

"You remind me of someone, Simon. Someone I want to find."

"You're going to start looking?"

"An all-out search is beyond me right now, but I've been rethinking my options, giving some thought to a new game plan."

Suddenly he thought about bringing her home. They'd stand together on her portico, beneath the brass gaze of that quirky seraph. He'd fit the key in the lock and make everything right again. "Claire, I'm curious. What do you see happening with your friends from Safe Harbor?"

She didn't answer, drew deeply on the cigar until the tip glowed red.

"My article's already written," he said. "This one's for me."

"I'd answer honestly even if you hadn't already written your article. I'm just not sure what you're asking."

"What happens when you leave Safe Harbor? Will you have a difficult time saying goodbye to the friends you've made here?"

"I don't plan to say goodbye. I might not remember the life I left behind, but I do know what I've found here. I won't give that up. No matter where I go, I'll still have my friends."

"You care so much." He understood that now.

"I've been blessed with some very special people in my life."

"Like Gabrielle?"

She nodded. "Not long after I came to Safe Harbor, the doctor brought her in to visit me. Neither of us could talk. My jaw was wired shut. Gabrielle simply wouldn't."

"Why?"

"The doctor said it was her way of controlling her environment, a defense against the things she'd had to deal with. One day she was a normal little girl with parents who loved her, and the next, she was the only survivor of a car bombing. It wiped out half her street along with everyone she knew. A protest against French parliament."

Simon tried to imagine the little girl bound by silence, the tragedy of her past tempered only by the clipped tone Violet used to relay the facts.

He remembered countless briefings when Violet had masked her emotions behind that tone. She'd detached from the emotional woman she was, to be who he demanded her to be. A level-one operative who placed the global good above everything else.

Violet cared so much, *too* much, he'd always believed because it interfered with her work. Only now that big heart of hers didn't seem nearly the flaw it once had.

"We hit it off," Violet continued. "Gabrielle would draw pictures to decorate my room and sing these little songs. No words, just the sweetest sounds in that lilting little voice. The first time I ever heard her speak was when I tried to talk."

A smile tipped her lips, a hint of white teeth in the darkness. "It was pretty bad. *I* couldn't even understand what I was trying to say. Here I'd had all these surgeries to fix my jaw, and I still couldn't talk. She said, 'Don't cry, Claire.'"

Simon wished he could share her fondness for the memory, but he only felt a terrible irony at how far Violet had traveled to become the woman she'd always been, the caring woman he and Excelsior would never allow her to be.

"Gabrielle has a lot of love to give," he finally said, nudging Violet's hip with his foot until she looked up at him. Their gazes bound them in the darkness. He wanted her to know that he understood things so much clearer now, willed her to understand even across the distance of her memory. "You have a lot of love to give back."

"I've been lucky."

"Have you, Claire? You don't remember your name or where you came from or who might be looking for you. Do you think that's fair?"

"It's not about fair. If you think life is all dark and ugly, it will be. But if you look for the good stuff..." She paused, that gentle smile widening. Strands of silken hair lifted up on the wind, and with her heart-shaped face pale above her black wool collar, she reminded him of an angel.

"I couldn't see it when I first came to Safe Harbor but I can now. Well, most of the time, anyway. Ms. Verna and Gabrielle and all the other wonderful people there have helped me. I just have to keep my eyes open."

She tamped out the cigar. Its heat hissed against the cold railing. Sparks sprinkled down toward the street.

Simon watched her, considering what she'd said, the conviction in her words. He couldn't help but feel as if the student was teaching the teacher. Or trying to. Violet obviously possessed a wisdom he was incapable of grasping.

BONUS FEATURE

Behind the Scenes:
# EXCELSIOR

## MISSION DOSSIER: CLASSIFIED

### Death Camp Number 12
### Mission: Extinction

[16] Operation Chokepoint:

*Mission:* Extract a defecting military
commander from active
duty in a Serbian detention
camp for political asylum
and testimony to the NATO
Secretary General and the
North Atlantic Council
about atrocities being
committed inside the
"death camps."

*Target:* Defecting Serbian military
commander Ivo Dzevat

*Location:* Number twelve detention
camp; north of Brijevek,
Bosnia

*Terrain:* Dinaric Alpine ranges;
extension of the Swiss Alps.

Mission Command:

- Control: *Davenport*

- Field op-in-charge: *Hickman*

- Team Leader: *Camerisi*

- Team Second: *Lierly*

- Operatives: *Compton, Reiger,
Parella*

Mission Outcome: *Failed*

# The Excelsior Agency
## Classified

**Excelsior**, *ek·sel' si ·ór* [Latin.] Higher, upward.

**The Excelsior Agency**: a Black Ops intelligence agency that reports directly to the president and an oversight committee. The men and women recruited into Excelsior are the elite of United States national security. Under command of the acting director, these highly skilled operatives move through the international community as shadows against any global threat.

**Their mission**: to protect and defend our nation *at all costs.*

**Their promise**: to carry out mission objective *without a trace.*

**Acting Director:**
**Simon Brandauer**—code name: *King Arthur*

As acting director of this Black Ops intelligence agency, Simon is a man who keeps his finger on the pulse of world politics, a brilliant strategist who dispatches operatives into any emerging crisis or international incident that threatens the United States or her allies. During his tenure, Simon has lost only one team—during an extraction mission into number twelve detention camp. While the president calls this record exemplary, Simon considers this loss much more than a statistical inevitability; he considers it a personal failure.

## Acting Director's Command Staff:

**Frances Raffa**—code name: *Ma'am*
Frances acts as the liaison between Excelsior Command and the White House while overseeing administrative details whenever Simon enters the field under his official cover as Special Liaison to the National Security Council. She has kept Command administration running smoothly for over forty years. Her late husband, a former tech director, was Simon's mentor. Frances holds top-level security clearance.

**Maxim Snow**—code name: *Soldier*
Maxim met Simon early in his U.S. Marine Corps career when both officers attended Amphibious Warfare School (AWS) at Quantico. They paired up on a military operation, and their skill in amphibious assault and ability to carry out mission objective under extreme conditions earned them the nickname "Dream Team." Maxim accepted Simon's appointment to be second-in-command and acts on Simon's behalf whenever the acting director goes into the field.

**Tavares Jenkins "TJ"**—code name: *Delinquent*

TJ is a computer genius who, as a teen, wrote a video game program with a subroutine teaching other gifted young hackers to breach law-enforcement software. Sentenced to a juvenile detention center, TJ jumped at Simon's offer of a high-tech education within the confines of the agency. He couldn't resist the chance to play with Excelsior Command's computer and satellite network. For the past seven years, TJ has devoted his talents to the benefit of Excelsior.

## Team One:

**Violet Lierly**—code name: *Wolfgang*
Operative number: 51693

Reared all over the globe by her anthropologist parents, Violet not only honed her linguistic skills but developed a gift for adapting herself into any culture. Simon recruited her to fill a linguistic position on his Command staff, but when he discovered her gift for fieldwork during training, he placed her on his personal team. Violet held the command of team second during the doomed extraction mission, but through a surprising twist of events and her own specialized skills, she survived execution and lived to carry out mission objective.

**Nikos Camerisi**—code name: *Casanova*
Operative number: 60390

As a young naval officer, Niky earned a reputation for aggressive flying skills and brilliance at tactical field command. His talent for thinking outside the box helped him succeed in impossible situations but ran him afoul of his commanding officers. Simon recruited him into Excelsior, where, as team leader of the doomed extraction mission, Niky couldn't save his operatives from execution. He escaped from death camp number twelve to return home with a renewed sense of purpose and a terrible secret.

**Quinn Davenport**—code name: *Counselor*
Operative number: 70998

Dr. Quinn Davenport, a psychophysiology researcher from a prestigious northeastern university, came to Excelsior by way of the Center—a government facility that ministers the psychological needs of highly classified agencies. When Simon learned about her proposed experiments in psychological conditioning and manipulation, he offered her the clearance necessary to conduct her testing and a place on his team. As control during the doomed extraction mission, Quinn monitored the situation from inside System Ops.

**Major Hickman**—code name: *Cowboy*
Operative number: 20796

A youth spent on a midwestern ranch left Major enough time to indulge a fascination with military history and develop a love of adventure. While running his family's ranch, he worked toward obtaining various degrees from several online universities. His treatises on military strategy caught Simon's attention. Major's skill for assessing intel and profiling missions earned his place as Excelsior's master strategist. He was field op-in-charge of the doomed extraction mission, running operations from just outside the hot zone in Zagreb, Croatia.

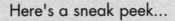

Here's a sneak peek...

# *Going, Going, Gone*

by
Jeanie London

BONUS FEATURE

## CHAPTER 1

LIFE MIGHT NOT HAVE DEALT Bree Addison a royal flush in wealth or circumstance, but it had dealt her enough high cards to play toward a winning hand. Intelligence. Good looks. Ambition. Lately, she'd been playing every one.

And while she had walked home tonight after her shift at Toujacques—New Orleans' premier casino— Bree had known she was on the verge of pulling an ace from the deck.

But life had also dealt her stellar instincts.

She had an internal alarm system that could sense trouble from across Lake Ponchartrain. Whenever she paid attention, she never regretted it.

The trick was paying attention.

When she realized the same car had been following her for the past two blocks, Bree couldn't ignore the alarm shrieking inside her head. Her brisk and carefree stride suddenly vanished, along with the moon that slipped behind a cloud. The street fell into shadow along the lengthy stretch between street lamps, and she caught a heel in the uneven sidewalk, and stumbled.

Grabbing the hem of her cocktail dress, she managed to catch herself and regain her balance before going down, but the effort left her pulse spiking painfully hard.

The car drove along barely in her periphery, but she wondered how she could have missed it. How long had she been waltzing down these streets, so filled with good fortune at being named one of the two women under consideration for the promotion to Toujacques' head VIP hostess job that she'd missed a car on her tail?

26     Bree didn't know, and she didn't like not knowing. It meant she'd been ignoring her instincts, *never* a smart thing in the best of circumstances. 3:00 a.m. in New Orleans' French Quarter wasn't the best of circumstances.

Glancing around at the familiar surroundings that seemed strangely unfamiliar in the dark, she gauged the distance to the entrance of the court where she lived, relieved to see she was nearly to the brick wall separating Court du Chaud from the rest of the French Quarter. If she could just make it around the corner and down the block to the alley….

Did she want that driver to see where she lived?

Taking a calculated risk, Bree stopped suddenly and leaned over as if to adjust the strap on her sandal. Beneath the fall of her long hair, she peered at the car—a generic sedan, probably a rental. It kept moving toward her, achingly slow.

Tires ground over a street clammy with late-night dew, a spongy sound that grew steadily louder. Chrome glinted as the sedan inched beneath a streetlight, and Bree recognized her opportunity. She straightened while lifting her gaze across the windshield…

And staggered as if she'd been punched.

For one startling second her heart seemed to stall in midbeat and she stood suddenly paralyzed, her face shielded by her hair, purse dangling from her shoulder. The February chill that had invigorated her earlier now prickled through her coat in icy needles.

*Jude.*

He'd always been a striking man. The ruthless beauty of his face still held the power to make her stare stupidly, as if she couldn't quite believe he was real. No man who looked this way could possibly be real.

His long black hair was pulled back, a look that emphasized the flawlessly carved lines of his face, his unusual eyes.

Up close those gray eyes would glint crystalline from beneath thickly fringed lashes. His eyes could play award-winning performances to any crowd.

Bree knew that firsthand because she'd been an audience he'd played to. Once upon a time, he'd played her *big*.

With every instinct shrieking to run and hide, she forced herself to suck in a breath that went down so hard, she choked. By a sheer effort of will, she forced herself to step in the wash of light from a street lamp, becoming a bull's-eye in her gold-spangled cocktail dress, a vulnerable target in four-inch heels that made running impossible.

What was *he* doing here?

She wasn't waiting around to find out.

Bullying herself into moving as if she hadn't a care in the world, she walked the same way she had since leaving work. Unconcerned. She fought the urge to turn and see what he was up to. Taking her eyes off this man was never smart. But she couldn't let him know he'd been made.

She wouldn't tip her hand. Not to *him*.

Not ever again.

He obviously knew where she worked, but she didn't have to lead him to her front door—if he didn't already know where she lived.

*Lose him.*

That was the only thing to do. But she couldn't outrun his car in her overpriced strappy sandals....

With her pulse hammering loud in her ears, Bree eased her way toward the trunk of a live oak and slipped into its shadow. Hiking her hem high to conceal it beneath her coat, she edged along the dew-slick brick of the courtyard wall.

He was almost past her before his taillights sparked red. He braked and, for a split second, she could see him leaning over the steering wheel, a would-be casual pose. Bree knew this man too well. He was scanning every inch of the street.

Looking for her.

His car inched forward, and she dared to breathe, hoping, *praying* he'd just keep on going. But Bree knew firsthand Jude was nothing if not determined.

The brake lights flashed again. He was turning around.

She stood frozen, knowing his headlights would expose her. If he saw her crouched in the shadows, he'd know he'd been made.

This little game of cat and mouse would end.

What he'd do then was anyone's guess. Once, Bree had thought she'd known what this man was capable of.

She'd been wrong.

Why he was back in town was another mystery. The last she'd heard there was still an outstanding warrant for his arrest. But it figured he'd come back when she finally had the world by the tail, on the very night she'd learned all her hard work was paying off and she might actually realize her ambition.

Hadn't he always had impeccable timing? Making

his move on her when she'd been too young and stupid to see through him had been a skillful manipulation.

Jude had already wasted as much of her time as she would let him waste. He wouldn't get another second.

One fast glance around the street convinced Bree there was nowhere to run. Even without the street lamps flashing all over her cocktail dress, her formal-length hem and four-inch heels made her easy prey. He could be out of his car and on her before she screamed long enough to get anyone's attention.

So Bree did the only thing she could do.

She lunged for the lowest branch. Catching the limb, she winced as the spiny bark bit into her palms, but forced herself to hang on and swing her legs high to build momentum.

She tried to catch the branch with her foot, but her narrow dress left no room to maneuver. Luckily the seam gave at the last possible instant, and she managed to hook a knee over the limb and scramble on.

"Argh," she ground out as prickly twigs and rough bark scratched nasty trails along her skin.

She could repair the seam of her fancy dress, but this was the end of a brand-new pair of seventeen-dollar panty hose.

Damn that Jude anyway.

With irritation fueling her efforts, she reached for an overhead branch and pulled herself upright.

She clung to the branches for balance, her heels providing surprising leverage. The slope of the insteps caught the branch snugly, and she was able to gain enough footing to reach the top of the wall.

The sedan's tires ground, engine belts whining in protest as Jude negotiated a tight turn. The headlights swung around, slicing through the darkness, aiming for her. Gritting her teeth, Bree hoisted herself onto the wall, glancing around desperately for something to hang on to as she lowered herself into the courtyard below.

Light shone through the French doors of the town house, casting the landscape into blackness despite the solar lights along the hedges. She didn't recognize the town house she was invading, had no idea which of her neighbors might be awake at such a late hour.

Whoever he or she was, this neighbor obviously kept the landscaping tidy and the branches neatly trimmed. *Not* good for her. When the headlights sliced directly below her, there was no place for Bree to hide, nothing for her to do but tackle the twelve-foot drop.

With the wild thought that she should have known better than to walk home tonight, she let go of the branch and fell with a nauseating plunge until…

*Something* cushioned her fall at the very last second before she landed in the shrubbery with a noisy crash.

*"Damn!"*

Though she didn't come down as hard as expected,

every bone in her body rattled when she hit the ground. She felt an icy wave pour through her and fought to free her arms from the tangle of twisted coat. Another seam split, and branches took out what was left of her hose.

It took a second to catch her breath, another to shake off her daze, but Bree didn't move until assessing the damage. All things considered, she'd have expected that drop to be a lot worse. She had no idea what had broken her fall—did her coat catch on a branch and slow her descent?

She didn't get a chance to find out.

By the time she realized she'd survived, despite some stinging scratches and a bruised hip that would wind up the color of a bayou sunrise, a shadow sliced across the light illuminating the courtyard.

Great. Just great. Someone was coming.

She had no clue which of her neighbors would find her, but seriously hoped she hadn't stumbled into Madame Alain's courtyard. That lonely little old lady would sound the alarm until every resident would come to witness the carnage.

She might even call the police before realizing who was crouching in her azaleas. Then there'd be sirens and, worse still, *explanations.*

Any explanation involving Jude was likely to land Bree in the back seat of a police cruiser, and if she landed in lockup tonight, she'd have no choice but to call her twin sister to spring her, which would mean even more explanations about this man who'd unexpectedly shown up in her life again.

Even worse, if work got wind of the man who'd been part of her unfortunate past, Bree wouldn't stand a chance in hell of beating out Lana for that promotion....

Think, *think!*

The light pouring through the French doors should work to her benefit rather than the neighbor's, so if there was any way to slither unseen from the bushes and make a break for the gate... Rational thought stopped the instant her neighbor appeared in full view of the doors, and Bree realized whose courtyard this was.

Josie Russell's.

Under normal circumstances, Bree would have asked Josie to harbor her until Jude had moved on. Unfortunately, tonight was decidedly *ab*normal.

Last weekend, Bree had attended Josie's wedding, and now the new Mrs. Max LeClerc honeymooned with her new hubby somewhere in the South Pacific.

The occupant currently residing in Josie's town house could be none other than the new bride's brother, who'd traveled in from California for the wedding.

He wouldn't have a clue who she was.

Josie had mentioned him, of course, but Bree

couldn't even remember his name. She'd noticed him at the wedding, though. Not only had he stood as the groom's best man, but she didn't think any woman alive could help noticing such an attractive man.

But while Josie's brother might be *really* easy on the eyes, he was also one of those rich and powerful men like the high rollers she worked for as a VIP hostess at Toujacques, which meant he probably wouldn't have a lot of sympathy for her trying to give her bad-news ex the slip.

*If* he even believed her.

He'd probably take one look at her torn dress and shredded hose and figure she'd run afoul of a particularly nasty john.

Boy, did she know this guy's type.

Well, in all fairness, Bree didn't actually know if Josie's brother liked to gamble, but Mr. Rich and Powerful had worn his custom tux—it probably cost more than the down payment on her town house—like a second skin. Even without the expensive suit, his attitude had flashed like a neon sign.

*I'm way beyond bored with my high-powered lifestyle, expensive toys and all those rich-bitch women throwing themselves at my feet.*

He'd obviously heard the noise from her fall, and with the same arrogant self-assurance that had impressed her across a banquet hall, he strode to those

34

French doors to find out what was happening in his sister's backyard....

Bree blinked. Again.

Mr. Rich and Powerful wasn't wearing an expensive tux tonight. He'd obviously taken a shower because he wore nothing but a towel covering his seriously toned, tanned and dripping wet skin.

Adrenaline had already been working a number on Bree. Now her heart started throbbing again. Her pulse rushed too fast. Her tongue stuck to the roof of her mouth, and she could only stare as he reached the doors and raised an arm to the lintel—to flip a lock presumably—gifting her with the sight of shifting neck muscles, gathering biceps and rippling abs. The towel slipped enough to reveal a lean hip and smooth skin angling down toward the telltale bulge of the goodies he kept hidden beneath plush cotton.

Honestly, the man was entitled to parade around in the wee hours dressed in anything he chose. Bree couldn't blame *him* because she found herself in his bushes.

She could, however, blame him for flipping off the light. Not only had he ended the show that was diverting her from her aches and pains, but he'd left her with a problem. She'd been staring into the light and was now totally blind.

Had he already called the police?

When the door creaked open, Bree decided to play it safe.

"Mr. Josie's Brother from California," she called out. "I surrender. I'm not here to rob the place. I just sort of...*dropped* by for an unexpected visit."

Her voice echoed eerily through the darkness. Blinking furiously to adjust her sight, she crouched in the shrubs like a sitting duck, unable to hear a thing above the sound of the wind rustling through the branches of an overhead tree and her own aching pulse.

And just when she could finally differentiate the outline of the hedge behind the strings of solar lights, Bree found herself blinded yet again by a wickedly bright flashlight.

36

Suddenly the man himself appeared, and she hadn't even heard him coming.

"You're one of the twins who lives in number one."

"Guilty."

He lowered the beam from her face, and she could make out lots of bare skin and chiseled features. Even half-blinded, she could see the man was more striking up close than he'd been from far away.

"So what did I do to deserve a visit from such an illustrious person at this time of night?" he asked.

"Illustrious? What did I do?"

"You found the captain's treasure."

And here Bree thought she'd made an honest impression. "Actually, my sister found the treasure."

"Still part of an illustrious family."

Bree inclined her head. No lie there. "Bree Addison, illustrious descendant of the pirate captain Gabriel Dampier."

He shifted the light over the gold spangles littering the ground, and grabbed her hand with a strong grip. "Lucas Russell. Number sixteen. You weren't kidding when you said 'dropped by.'"

"Unfortunately."

He chuckled, and the throaty deep sound rippled silkily through her.

*Surprise, surprise.* Adrenaline was doing all sorts of screwy things to her tonight, because under normal circumstances, Bree wouldn't have given this guy a reaction no matter how attractive he was. Not a man who was a carbon copy of those she catered to at work. No way.

With Lucas Russell's solid grip providing leverage, she cautiously extricated herself from the shrubs. She swallowed back a groan when every muscle in her body throbbed in protest and spangles showered the ground around her.

She tried not to think about how she must look with foliage in her hair, in her clothes and in her shoes.

All things considered… For chancing upon a poisonous snake tonight, Bree had fared remarkably well. No broken bones. One very handsome savior whether she was interested or not.

Things were looking up.

Lucas helped extricate her from the tangle of her coat and steadied her against him, bringing her up close and personal to a *whole bunch* of naked man. Adrenaline worked a little more magic, distracting her from her aches and pains to notice shoulders so broad she couldn't see around them.

He towered above her, and she wasn't exactly short. But even more striking was the strength she felt in the hand he kept locked around hers, the warmth of his 38 bare skin. After all the shocks she'd gotten tonight— both good and bad—Bree shouldn't have had any energy left to react to this man.

But she was reacting.

Especially when he swept his gaze over her. The darkness hid the color of his eyes, but he was clearly inspecting her for damage. She must have looked as bad as she felt because his brows knitted in a frown.

Lucas, however, looked as good as he felt. At this close vantage, his face was all cut lines and chiseled angles. He was handsome in a very aggressive, male way.

She should have been immune. Damn adrenaline.

"You're bleeding." The flashlight beam sliced down her leg.

One glance at the carnage of tattered hose stained

with blood, and she groaned. "So I am. Guess I'll say thanks and be on my way. It was a pleasure."

She moved to extricate herself from him, but Lucas didn't let go. "Come inside. Let's take a look at your leg."

"I appreciate the offer, but there's no need. Just a few scratches. I'll live."

"I'm trained in emergency first aid."

"Really? Josie told me you were the king of a software empire. Do your employees hurt themselves working the keyboard and the mouse?"

"I write *law-enforcement* software," he said dryly. "So I spend a lot of time consulting with various national agencies and participating in civilian training."

Great. Just great. Jude was back in town and she'd run for cover inside the backyard of a man with *law-enforcement* connections.

Why had she thought she'd been dealt a decent hand tonight again?

She tried to assess the threat.... Any man who rescued a lady from treacherous shrubbery wearing only that skimpy towel couldn't be all bad, could he?

"Can you walk or shall I carry you?" he asked.

Yummy or not, Lucas Russell was determined to get his way. It was in his dry, almost amused tone, in the grip that assured her he had no intention of letting go.

No surprises here. "Really, this isn't necessary."

"It is. I'm not dressed to walk you home."

"I'd argue. The neighbor ladies would love watching you parade through the court in your towel."

He arched a dark eyebrow, and under any other circumstances, Bree might have laughed at his surprise.

Not tonight.

Like it or not, without knowing why Jude had followed her, she wasn't all that eager to head home just yet herself. About the last thing she wanted was to run into him on her doorstep. Not in her present condition. And especially not in the dark.

Bree didn't have too many options right now, and stalling seemed like a good one. She decided not to look this gift horse in the mouth. If Lucas wanted to play the knight in skimpy towel, then she'd oblige him.

"Well, then, thank you." Tipping her gaze to stare into his face, she found herself almost startled again by his sheer maleness. He'd been handsome from across a banquet hall, but up close... "I appreciate the help."

He only inclined his head in that regal way of the wealthy, as if it was both his privilege and duty to help those in need. Ever the gentleman, he didn't mention the golden trail of spangles she left in her wake to mark a trail for the squirrels.

He didn't release her hand while leading her across the yard. She almost smiled at how he managed to look large and in charge while walking through damp grass half-naked and barefoot.

It was in the DNA. Had to be.

He held the door as she slipped inside then motioned her to a breakfast nook separating the dining room from the kitchen.

"Have a seat while I hunt down Josie's first-aid kit."

Bree did as he asked, appreciating a chance to admire the back half of him as he strode from the room.

Everything about this man was attractive, she decided, exhaling a sigh that had nothing to do with her bumps and bruises. She wasn't hurt, not really, just achy and sore from the fall, and jittery from too many adrenaline rushes.

As she and her sister had only moved into the court last year, Bree didn't know Josie all that well. They both worked a lot. Bree was at Toujacques' beck and call both day and night, so get-togethers generally happened at meetings for the homeowners' association and Krewe du Chaud or brush-bys for coffee in Café Eros, the bistro that stood at the entrance of the alley between their courtyard and the French Quarter where her sister worked.

But Bree liked Josie and wished her well in married life. Many of the court's residents seemed to be getting on with their futures lately. Even Tally had gotten engaged to Christien and bought the Blue Note. Claire and Randy from a couple of other houses had hooked up. Then there was Perry and Jack. And after learning about her shot at the head hostess job tonight, Bree had thought she'd been moving on with hers, too.

Until her past had followed her home.

"Found it," Lucas said when he returned from upstairs.

He'd thrown on sweatpants, and she couldn't help but wonder if she'd have been so affected by this man if she hadn't met him when he'd been half-naked in the dark.

Guess she'd never know the answer to that one, but somehow doubted it.

Up close Lucas had the same sable-colored hair as his sister, and bright green eyes. The combination tempered his chiseled features a bit, which was a good thing because that strong face and drop-dead gorgeous body combined made him almost *too* male. *If* such a thing were possible. She hadn't thought so until meeting this man.

She couldn't help but wonder if he wielded his striking looks like a weapon—the way her bad-news ex did. For some reason she expected more from Josie's brother. Perhaps because Josie was so decent, and by default her brother should be, too.

Setting the first-aid kit on the table, Lucas sank to his knees in front of her. He hesitated with his hands poised over her ankle as he asked, "Do you mind?"

42

"Have at it." She lifted aside her destroyed dress to give him a bird's-eye view of the carnage.

Both knees were a mess. Scratches streaked her skin, and blood had congealed on the torn edges of her hose. One particularly nasty branch had carved a crevasse up her thigh.

Lucas frowned and stood again, giving her a tour of that magnificent chest. He grabbed the first-aid kit and said, "Come with me."

"Where are we going?"

"To the sink for soap and water."

No argument there. Despite the miracle that she hadn't broken her neck with that fall, she'd definitely come out on the bad end of her tussle with the dirt and mulch in Josie's flower bed. She followed him into the kitchen.

He flipped on a light, deposited the kit on the counter and ran the water. "Take off your stockings."

"We only met ten minutes ago."

*That* got a reaction. A half grin tipped the corner of his mouth. "We need to clean those cuts. Trust me."

"Another lesson learned in civilian law-enforcement training?"

"From my mother."

"That doesn't surprise me. I'm sure she tended lots of boo-boos while you were growing up."

The half grin morphed into a full-fledged smile, a smile that softened his features and brightened his eyes and won a reaction low in her belly. A crazy sort of swooping feeling that shouldn't have overridden her aches and pains, but did.

"I'd be lying if I said no." His gaze traveled a suggestive trail from her face down. "Now lose the stockings."

"I'll bet you say that to all the girls." She made a little *humph* sound and couldn't resist giving him a show while slithering her hose out from underneath her dress.

She could feel his gaze on her when she bent over to unfasten her sandals and wondered if he noticed the way her neckline drooped, if he watched her cleavage plump forward. Did he think she was taunting him, or flirting?

She wasn't entirely sure which it was herself.

But there was something about this man that made Bree want a reaction. Probably nothing more than a need to flex her control muscles after the shock of seeing Jude again.

*That* thought sobered her up fast.

Jude wouldn't be back in town without a reason. If she was right and there was still a warrant out for his arrest, that reason must have something to do with her. Otherwise he wouldn't have let her know he was back.

But when she remembered Lucas's words upon

finding her in his shrubs—*You found the captain's treasure*—she guessed what the reason might be.

Tally's illustrious treasure hunt had brought a rat out of the woodwork.

And not only a rat, Bree thought when Lucas grabbed her. His strong hands circled her waist, and he lifted her up to a seat on the counter.

But a knight in a skimpy towel.

Without preamble, he brushed aside her torn dress and got to business. She braced back on her arms, feeling a bit breathless as he cleansed her skin with soapy gauze.

"That feel okay?" he asked.

"I'll live."

"So, why'd you drop by tonight?"

Questions were inevitable, but she had to give Lucas credit for not starting the interrogation the minute he found her.

"I noticed someone following me while I was walking home from work. It was late, and I'm not exactly dressed to defend myself. I decided to beat a hasty retreat."

He peered at her from beneath the silky fringe of thick lashes. "So you scaled a wall in a formal gown and high heels? I'm impressed. What kind of work do you do?"

That was another question she'd expected, and Bree wondered what type of work he thought she did.

Evening formal wear. 3:00 a.m. Dark street. *Hmm*.

Bree also wondered why she cared. "I work at Tou-jacques. I'm a VIP hostess."

"Do you always walk home from work?"

"Not when it's so late. I usually take a cab."

"But not tonight."

"Not tonight." She knew he was waiting for some further explanation, but that was her personal business. Her brother's car had broken down so he'd taken her Jeep, and since she lived so close to work... She wasn't about to volunteer that information to appease Lucas.

He didn't push. Not immediately, anyway, which she thought demonstrated some restraint.

46    Tossing the filthy gauze into the trash, he lathered a new batch with soap under running water before starting work on her other knee.

"Did someone threaten you?" he asked.

"Didn't give him a chance. Didn't want to lead him to my front door, either, so here I am."

Bree expected a lecture on the perils of walking through the French Quarter alone at night. Men like Lucas were invariably throwbacks of the feudal days when the rich and powerful protected the weak and defenseless.

Lucas surprised her, though. Instead of a warning, Bree got strong hands on her thighs.

It was a casual touch—if any stranger's touch in such an intimate place could really be casual. Perfunctory might be a better description. The thing was…those long fingers didn't *feel* perfunctory.

Even though he only tended her cut, she felt his touch everywhere. Heat melted through her, and she was so very aware of her parted thighs. Probably because she didn't wear panties beneath her panty hose, which put this man's strong hands in very close proximity to some oh-so-bare private places.

"So, are you enjoying your stay in New Orleans?" she asked to distract herself from the feel of his hands and to end the topic of why she'd dropped in for a visit.

"I always enjoy coming home."

"Josie told me she bought this house from your parents after they retired to Florida. So you were reared here?"

"Court du Chaud home grown."

"Is that why you're hanging around after Josie and Max left on their honeymoon? Are you visiting friends?"

He inclined his head. "One of the reasons. My parents stayed to visit after the wedding, too. I wanted to see them off. And Josie has me doing some work around here."

Mr. King of a Software Empire? Not manual labor, surely. "What sort of work?"

"Cleaning out the attic. My mom's a pack rat. She stored memorabilia for years and left it all when she moved. Josie's afraid the fire marshal will condemn the place. Now that she and Max are married, they're making some decisions about living arrangements, and she wants to make sure I get everything I want in case they decide to sell the house."

"Couldn't live without your baseball trophies, hmm?"

"Or the sculpture of Cupid I made Mom in third grade."

"It's still around?"

"Give or take a few limbs."

"I can see why you'd want to save it."

"Absolutely. Some superglue and I've got the perfect Mother's Day gift."

48

Bree smiled, unsure why she found the image of him as a young boy making sculptures for his mother so surprising. But somehow, such a caring gesture seemed to fit this strong man who cared for her injuries.

"So tell me, are you the twin I've heard singing?" After tossing the gauze into the trash, Lucas fished through the first-aid kit.

"Fraid I'm going to disappoint you again. My sister's the singer in the family."

"Just you and her?"

"Got a musically inclined brother, too. I'm the untalented one of our illustrious bunch. No treasure hunts. No musical talent. The younger twin, wouldn't you know? Something to do with the gene pool, I'm guessing. Watered things down a bit."

Glancing up from his task, he dragged his bright gaze over her in a lazy caress. "Untalented?"

She gave an equally lazy shrug. "Sad, but true. There's always one in every bunch."

"Scaling a tree in this dress and those shoes? Have you thought about stunt work?"

She laughed, and for some reason, she found that as unexpected as a younger version of him sculpting presents for his mom.

She must be off her stride after all the night's shocks. Otherwise she would *not* be reacting to this man. She had much more self-control. But Lucas made her laugh, and notice him.

He surprised her.

Such as when he patted the antiseptic wipe against her thigh then blew gently on the cut to soothe away the sting.

"Still okay?" He exhaled another warm burst.

"Mmm-hmm." The antiseptic burned, quite a lot in fact, but the caress of his breath and her awareness of his mouth near her skin overrode any other sensation.

Gazing into Lucas's handsome face, she saw the tiny frown between his brows and the tight line of his jaw. He didn't want to hurt her. She could feel concern in his touch, in the warm burst of breath against her skin.

Bree made her career catering to overindulged rich men who lived life for new challenges. She recognized Lucas as one. No mistake.

But there was something else there, too.

And she was surprised. Not so much because Lucas Russell had chosen to play the knight in skimpy towel tonight—what self-respecting macho guy wouldn't rescue a damsel in distress, after all?—but at how glad she was that he had.

...NOT THE END...

50

*Look for Jeanie's next Blaze novel, in stores February 2006.*

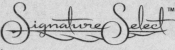

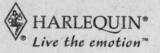

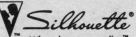

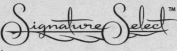

SHOWCASE

The first book in the
Roselynde Chronicles from...

Beloved author

# ROBERTA GELLIS

**ROSELYNDE**

With a foreword by bestselling historical romance
author Margaret Moore

**One passion that
created a dynasty...**

Lady Alinor Devaux,
the mistress of Roselynde,
had a fierce reputation for
protecting what's hers. So
when Sir Simon Lemagne
is assigned as warden
of Roselynde, Alinor is
determined to make his life
miserable. Only, the seasoned
knight isn't quite what
Alinor expects.

**Plus, exclusive
bonus features inside!**

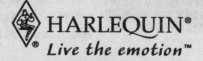